THE DREAM SEEKER

JAZZ MAN IN THE POCKET

MICHAEL J. SULLIVAN

Publish Authority

This book is a work of fiction. Names, characters, places, and incidents are products of the author's imagination or are used fictitiously. Any resemblance to actual events or locales or persons, living or dead, are entirely coincidental.

Copyright © 2022 by Michael J. Sullivan

The Dream Seeker

ISBN: 978-1-954000-35-3 (paperback)
ISBN: 978-1-954000-36-0 (eBook)

All rights reserved. No part of this book may be reproduced or used in any manner without written permission of the publisher except for the use of questions in a book review. For information, address: Publish Authority, 300 Colonial Center Parkway, Suite 100, Roswell, GA 30076-4892

Editor: Nancy Laning
Cover design lead: Raeghan Rebstock

Published by Publish Authority
Newport Beach, CA & Roswell, GA USA
PublishAuthority.com

Printed in the United States of America

This book is dedicated to my wife of twenty-two years, Ginny Sullivan.

In October of 2020, she suffered a debilitating stroke leaving her paralyzed on her right side. After a week in the hospital in Sonora, California, she was transferred to a rehabilitation hospital in Modesto, California, where she spent the next four weeks. Due to Covid-19 protocols, I could see her through the window of her hospital room. I could only communicate with her when she was able to activate her cell phone with her non-dominant hand. It was agonizing watching her struggle at that task, to say the least. That time was a living hell for her, for me, and for our family. After four weeks, she was finally released to come home. Unable to walk, even move her right leg or right arm, and with speech impairment, she began the long road to recovery. She started seeing a physical therapist three days a week. The other days I do follow-up physical therapy in our home. It had been over a year since my wife came home.

Each day I wake up and wonder if today is the day that my dream comes true, that my lovely wife will walk again and that I can hold her in my arms and dance with her one more time.

INTRODUCTION

He had lost everything that had constituted his being. If he had been inclined to believe in such things, and certainly he was not, Dylan Steward would say that his very soul had been ripped from his body and left to drift in some alternate universe. Trauma, especially the intensely psychological variety, has a way of tearing away the very essence of a person, reducing them to a vapid remainder of their former selves. He had suffered just that sort of ordeal once before when his best friend died in Steward's arms in a rice paddy outside some nameless village in Vietnam. The completely unexpected and, in his view, unnecessary demise of his wife of 10 years threw Steward into that same deep abyss of isolation. The shock of his wife's rapid departure was painful enough, but the fact that it was obviously the result of medical malfeasance absolutely ran him asunder.

Willow had been everything Steward was not. In addition to a special beauty that simply radiated from within her, his wife was the kindest, most positive person he had ever met. Even on their trip to the doctor for what was supposed to be a simple procedure, Willow reminded her husband that she had prepared several meals for him and had picked up his laundry from the local cleaners. Never a thought about herself—that was Willow.

As he saw it, all Dylan had left was his job as a reporter. Even that profession, which he had loved and pursued for so many years, now seemed vacant and pointless to him. This carried over to the work itself and had not gone unnoticed by his editors. His unceremonious dismissal loomed closer than he could ever imagine. Yet not everyone was so ready to dismiss this former asset to the paper. The paper's feature editor, the popular if aged stalwart of the firm, one Jimmy Donahue, had a special assignment in mind for the struggling writer. Little did either know what an impact it would have on both their lives, changing them irrevocably forever.

PART ONE

The pursuit of dreams provides the light
on the darkest of days and the hope for the
bleakest of tomorrows.

MICHAEL J. SULLIVAN

CHAPTER 1

Damon Willard, Managing Editor of the *Los Angeles Times*, had just about lost all patience with his feature editor, James Donahue. Evolution had come to the newspaper in the form of Otis Chandler, son of the paper's founder, Norman Chandler. Otis Chandler moved the *L.A. Times* from a second-rate southern California paper to one with worldwide offices and a reputation for hiring only the best-educated and most experienced journalists from newspapers nationwide. James (Jimmy) Donahue was more akin to some prehistoric relic from the La Brea Tar Pits.

James Donahue was born on August 7, 1920. He started at the old *Los Angeles Daily Times* as a copy boy in 1935 when he was 15 years old. The newsroom was different back then. A dozen or more reporters wearing Fedora hats and half-smoked Camel cigarette dangling between their lips would pound out their stories on their Underwood manual typewriters. When they were finished, they would hold up their copy in the air and holler, "Copy Boy."

Along with two other copyboys, Jimmy's job was to run as fast as he could to the demanding reporter, grab his copy, and weave his way to the feature editor's office—through aisles crowded with reporters and secretaries trying to make the day's deadline. It was now 1975, and Jimmy Donahue was sixty-five years old. Norman Chandler, or "The Old Man," as he was affectionately referred to by the others on the staff, had promoted Jimmy to the position of assignment editor before turning over control of the paper to his son, Otis, in 1960. Though not an impressive title on the paper's letterhead, the assignment city desk editor wielded enormous influence within the paper. It was his job to decide which reporter would take the lead on which story. It was an assignment the younger Chandler would have never made, considering Donahue's lack of formal education.

Donahue could have retired years ago, but then where would he go? What would he do? Jimmy had never married. The *Times* was his life. He had lived and breathed the new business for over fifty years, from the deafening sound of the printing presses to the smell of fresh ink as the dailies rolled on the line, to the rush of adrenaline as a front-page story was about to break. Without it, Jimmy Donahue had no life. His latest confrontation with his boss, Damon Willard, the Editor-In-Chief, was the handwriting on the wall that Jimmy Donahue's tenure with the *L.A. Times* was short-lived.

STATUS MEANT everything to Damon Willard. From his master's degree from Northwestern to his Ph.D. from the University of Missouri, which hung on his office wall, to his large corner office with its massive oval oak conference table, everything was dedicated to his aggrandizing ego as the true power at the *L.A. Times*. Not lost on anyone entering his office were the numerous pictures of Willard with the rich and famous of the southern California political and entertainment landscape. Centered on his wall of fame, as the staff referred to it behind his back, was the 1972 Pulitzer Prize for Journalist of the Year. His selection had more to do with the pressure exerted by Otis Chandler on Columbia University, who presents the award annually, than any talent Damon Willard may have had. Willard was politically astute, and he used that Machiavellian power to rid himself of subordinates he felt were a threat to his position. He had come to see Jimmy Donahue as such a threat.

Willard knew that titles were not the only indicator of the powerful and influential. Within any organization, there were individuals who bore tremendous weight with their peers. Their opinions were sought out privately, behind closed doors, when it was hard for some to distinguish the forest from the trees. James Donahue was that person. Over the past year, he had introduced several changes to the paper, from rearrangement of responsibilities among his editorial staff, office reassignments, a radical shift in the political emphasis of the paper, and control over the decision to hire new staff. Every innovation Willard tried to introduce was met with, "Have you run that by Donahue?" or "What does Donahue think about that?" If Willard did not, every one of his editor staff knew that Jimmy Donahue had an instinct for the newspaper business, and a wise man would have at least listened to his opinion. But then, no one thought of Damon Willard as wise. Well-educated, yes, but wise, not a chance. His last move was the proverbial straw that broke the camel's back.

The sixth-floor corner office of Damon Willard had two stunning yet contrasting views of Los Angeles. One overlooked the crossing of business Highway 101 and US 101. The sight of thousands of vehicles inching slowly through bumper-to-bumper traffic toward their destination reminded Willard of worker ants mindlessly following each other through a maze of pathways doing the mundane work demanded by the queen ant. The other window offered a majestic panoramic view of greater downtown Los Angeles. Willard instinctively chose the latter. It fed his Napoleonic ego as the managing editor of one of the nation's most influential newspapers, at least in his mind.

At the end of his weekly staff meeting, Willard abruptly stood up from his massive mahogany desk with inlaid gold trim and walked to his favorite view. He stood silent for a moment as his editorial staff wondered what pronouncement he was about to make. Monty Johnson, sports editor, was the longest-serving member of the editorial staff of the *Times*. His ruddy complexion and hoarse voice were a testament to the rabid sports enthusiast. He wore his perennial blue and gold polo shirt embroidered with Notre Dame, an anathema in a town owned by USC. Johnson could have cared less about what was about to come out of Willard's mouth as he was still suffering from the humiliating defeat of his vaunted Irish by the Anthony Davis-led USC Trojans, 24-55. He was now more concerned with the mounting rumors emanating from the Los Angeles Dodgers camp that one of their star outfielders was gay. Sylvia Markham, an avowed feminist who covered Europe, was enthralled with the rise of Margaret Thatcher in the English Parliament. Markham's silver hair, which she considered a sign of wisdom, not age, was smartly coiffed, resembling that of a department store mannequin. The professorial-looking Harvey Goldman, dressed in an expensive tweed coat, with rumpled hair and thick black horn-rimmed glasses, covered politics and policies on the national level. He was consumed with the national fallout of the convictions of H.R. Halderman, John Ehrlichman, and John Mitchell of Watergate crimes, not to mention the pardon of President Richard M. Nixon by Gerald Ford. Martin Milner, the minion among them, focused his attention on Willard. Like some flamboyant pandering sycophant in King Louie V's court, Martin Milner focused on what Willard was about to say. The recent controversial expansive action of the Environmental Protection Agency was the farthest thing from his mind. Finally, Willard spoke, but not to them. He spoke through the tinted glass window to some imaginary audience on the other side.

"I'm changing the hiring procedure for new journalists. James

Donahue will no longer oversee that process as of the first of the year. I will be making that decision."

His words were expressed forcefully, even defiantly. He preferred to use the term journalist as opposed to reporter, which was too plebeian for a man of his education. Suddenly the atmosphere in the room became like a funeral parlor. The silence was overbearing. After a pause that bristled with mounting emotion, a voice spoke.

"Have you talked to Jimmy about that?" asked Markham, a longtime loyalist of the pugnacious Donahue and one not afraid to challenge the exultant Willard.

It was a question the others had all asked themselves silently. Willard turned slowly to face his questioner. He pulled decisively at the bottom of his striped vest, then adjusted the gold cufflinks on his Brioni white silk shirt, making sure those present saw his carefully manicured fingers adorned with two expensive gold rings. He brought his fingers slowly across his brow, being careful not to disturb his crafted pompadour hairstyle. Staring at Markham with ice-cold eyes, he responded, "As the managing editor, Donahue answers to me, not the other way around. Need I remind you of that?"

To a person, those present thought, *This is going to be a colossal mistake!*

CHAPTER 2

He still operated out of the same threadbare and smallish office he had occupied for decades. A large and badly scarred oak desk dominated what space there was in the room. Copy was strewn about its ancient surface, hiding the coffee stains underneath. Although the janitorial staff thoroughly cleaned this office every evening, it always bore an untidy appearance. Jimmy Donahue stood up and walked to the window behind his cluttered desk. He inhaled deeply on the last remaining bit of his beloved Arturo Fuente cigar before crushing it in a large glass ashtray on his desk. Then, running his thumbs under the black suspenders attached to a pair of gray trousers, he let them snap back against his chest. He had tired gray eyes, the result of decades of editing the work of so many reporters that he had lost count. Over the years, his waistline had expanded exponentially thanks to his daily fare of a pastrami on rye and a side of kosher slaw from Saltzman's Deli, conveniently located next to Lenny's Barbershop. His naturally brown hair had long ago turned white, a feature about which he was not particularly happy. In keeping with memories from the past of his bosses, Jimmy kept it neatly trimmed, thanks to his weekly Monday morning visit to Lenny's

Barbershop, three blocks from the Times Building. Lenny was an invaluable source of information as his shop was frequented by politicians from city hall and police brass from near LAPD Headquarters. Next to Lenny's was Lefty's, a throwback to the whiskey bars of the 40s. Soft lighting, music from the Big Band Era, and call liquor only; just the kind of place for old-timers to gather and swap tales of the old days.

He stretched and arched backward, hoping to get some relief from an arthritic back. Then he leaned forward, placing his hands on the windowsill. Jimmy loved the view of the interlacing highways below. He peered intently at the gridlock of commuter traffic taking place before his eyes. What untold stories must be in each vehicle that linked together in that mass of slow-moving humanity below him? He grinned to himself and turned around to view his office, maybe for the last time if the rumors were true.

No degrees, awards, or photographs with the famous or infamous adorned the walls of his office. Donahue preferred to gaze upon snapshots sent him by reporters he had mentored, receiving awards and recognition for their work. All signed, "Thank you, Jimmy!" This was his legacy, and he was damned proud of it. His moment of reflection was interrupted by the voice of Sylvia Markham. She called through his ever-open door.

"Have you got a moment, Jimmy?"

Jimmy knew this was not truly a question. Donahue liked Markham. Maybe not her extremely short, cropped hair, but certainly her legs and rapier-like wit.

"Anytime for you," he smiled. "Have a seat?"

The gentle sarcasm of his canned answer was not lost on her.

Sylvia grinned. "Which one? There's such a variety," she responded with a flippant chuckle.

Purposefully, Donahue kept scant furniture in his office. It was a place for work, not socialization. Against the far wall was a long nondescript table, cluttered with the major newspapers from a dozen cities as well as those independent rogue papers like the *San*

Francisco Free Press and the *Berkeley Barb*. He pulled out a well-worn black leather chair whose wooden arms were scratched and faded.

As she sat down, she leaned forward with the eagerness of someone wanting to share a deep secret. Each time she sat in this relic, she had to stifle a fear that it possessed hidden microbes waiting to assault her. She spoke as a comrade, sincerity flashing in her eyes.

"Damon's got it in for you, Jimmy. He's decided to…"

"I know. He's taking over the hiring of new reporters, or should I say journalists," interrupted Donahue as he scanned the tabletop for one of his treasured cigars. He seemed unfazed by the news.

"So much for secrets," sulked Markham. She was relieved that Donahue knew but a bit disappointed that she was not the first to tell him.

Donahue smiled. "Damon and I shared the same barber as well as a fondness for kosher food. Need I say more?"

"He was not happy when I asked if he had given you the courtesy of speaking with you before making the announcement at the staff meeting. You know he is not going to stop with that. He's determined to get rid of you, Jimmy," Sylvia added. She spoke the last time with sincere gravity. Her voice dropped off at the end.

With a concerned look on his face, Jimmy answered, "Be careful, Sylvia, or you'll find yourself in the same situation."

Sylvia sat back in her chair, keenly aware of Damon Willard's propensity for revenge.

"I think not, Jimmy. Skeletons are hard to keep hidden, even for a man in Damon Willard's position." As she stood up, Sylvia smiled and added, "To be forewarned is to be forearmed, my friend."

With Markham's departure, Donahue immediately went to his stack of newspapers. He knew exactly what he was looking for as he hastily rummaged through the periodicals and was relieved when he found an old copy from an independent paper in northern California. He had purposely saved it because of an article written by a reporter on the Pentagon Papers. Even for a underground paper, it was remarkably logical and analytical in its approach to what had been, at the time, a huge government scandal. He had scribbled the reporter's name in red pencil across the top. Jimmy Donahue would have one last chance to add his type of reporter to the *Times* staff. This reporter could write, and that was all Donahue cared about. Jimmy quickly dialed the telephone number he had gotten off the editorial page. After several rings, it went to voicemail. Donahue listened impatiently until he reached the extension he wanted. More elevator music. Frustrated, he swore, "Dammit, kid, pick up the phone!"

THE AFTERNOON FOG had begun its creepily slow ascent up Divisadero toward Nob Hill. Dylan Steward turned up the collar of his Navy pea coat, tightened down his wool watch cap over his flowing brown hair, and started the 11-block walk home. Two blocks up Fell, then right on Masonic. Five more blocks then a left on Haight. Four blocks more and home, a second-story two-bedroom apartment with a view of Buena Vista Park. Even in his depressed state of mind, he liked the walk. Not only did it save on gas, but it also saved him the frustration of trying to find a parking spot anywhere near his home.

Once he crossed Fell, the smells and sounds of old San Francisco began to permeate the air. A symphony of sounds abounded from various street musicians exhibiting their creativity on guitars and violins. An occasional soft muted brass instrument added another layer of intriguing melodies. He could close his eyes and still find his way home by following the aromas of a half dozen or more small ethnic shops and markets. Aldo's Bakery, home of the best sourdough bread in the city, and then a right turn onto

Masonic. He dared not forget to bring home a loaf of Aldo's freshest for dinner. From there, he would traverse Asia and Europe. First, Ma Ling's Chinese Market, where Peking Ducks warmed on racks along with sweet and sour ribs. Chicken halves hung near a huge Mongolian grill where a stoop-shouldered elder with a braided mustache skillfully manipulated long wooden chopsticks across the grill top laden adroitly mixing strips of beef, vegetables, and chow Mein noodles. On the corner of Masonic and Haight was Leonetti's, a third-generation Italian market with the finest Italian meats, fish, poultry, and selected cheeses. Long sticks of salami with white powdery wrapping hung in a display window. Half of a long butcher case displayed large sections of prosciutto, smoked turkey, beef pepperoni, bologna, roast beef, and black forest ham. The other half consisted of Leonetti's imported cheeses; Swiss, provolone, parmesan, mozzarella, feta, ricotta, and bleu. He paused to enjoy the sweet aroma wafting out the open door of the market; then, he crossed over to Haight. Four more blocks, and he would be home.

CHAPTER 3

The old blue Victorian had a ground-level two-bedroom bottom apartment with a stunning view of Buena Vista Park. She was curled up on a secondhand sofa, an Afghan engulfing her diminutive frame and sipping a cup of organic Chaga tea. Her shoulder-length auburn hair hung straight, unencumbered by any fashion style. Willow stared out the living room window, enthralled as the late afternoon fog gradually began to enshroud the last of the visitors enjoying Buena Vista Park, like a stage curtain that slowly descends, hiding its performers from view. It had been a particularly grueling day at the pre-school, and Willow could feel the beginnings of a migraine developing. She hoped her husband would be willing to make dinner for the two of them and closed her eyes, resting her head against the back of the sofa. Willow thought about how much she loved him. He was tall and good-looking, with grown-out brown hair and brown eyes. His dry, witty sense of humor expressed in a soft, almost monotone voice forced her to listen closely when he spoke. He was thoughtful, nearly doting when anticipating her wants and needs. But when that man took out his guitar and began playing soft, gentle jazz riffs that would put Wes Montgomery to shame, Willow's heart dwelled in his. She was equally taken with his artistry with words. Willow often thought his skills were wasted working for the diminutive *San Francisco Free Press*. He wrote from his heart, drawing from real-life experiences and not some ethereal constructs taught in journalism school. In her mind, his genius needed a broader audience. Her tea had cooled, and she was about to get up and make herself a fresh brew when she saw him cross the avenue. She waited.

Dylan stopped to get the afternoon mail from the mailbox, an assortment of solicitations from charities dealing with childhood diseases, no doubt for his wife. Was there any organization that women would not give to, he thought? He eagerly grabbed the latest issues of Zigzag and Crawdaddy, his favorite jazz magazines. Being periodical minimalists when it came to subscriptions—a self-created diagnosis Willow made for those addicted to the countless magazines and publications all dedicated to promoting the right way to think, to eat, to dress—Dylan proceeded to the front door with his meager load.

"I'm home," he announced as he twisted the antique brass doorknob on the stained-glass front door. He made his way to the small living room, dropping his coat across an antique rocking chair. The mail found a home on a lampstand next to the sofa, along with his keys and an assortment of items from his pants pockets. He made his way to the small couch and snuggled next to his wife.

"How's my love?" he asked, gently turning her head with his hand so their lips could meet. If her radiant hazel eyes were not enough to arouse his maleness, the sensuous movement of her tongue as their lip parted certainly did. The undersized sofa would not accommodate the activity that immediately seized control of his brain. However, the bottle of DHE on the lampstand next to his wife quickly dampened his lustful desire. Must be a migraine coming on, he thought. Short on being able to pronounce the drug's name, Dihydroergotamine Mesylate, he referred to it simply as DHE.

"One of those headaches again?" he inquired sympathetically.

Willow's job as a third-grade teacher was incredibly rewarding and yet, at the same time, emotionally exhausting, a condition that fertilized the probability of migraines.

She smiled faintly, then shook her head. *Liar,* he thought. She brought her cup of tea to her lips, then lowered it. Intuitively, he asked, "Cold?"

Willow moved her feet to the floor. He stopped her.

"You sit. I'll get it."

As she resumed her position on the sofa, she called out, "Did you remember to get the French bread?"

"Of course, and a bottle of Mateus Rose," he answered.

His wife was a native San Franciscan, and she loved their 40's style apartment, from the arched doorways to the tiled counters in the kitchen. Adding more charm were the leaded glass doors on the kitchen cabinets. A white enamel three-burner gas stove, matching refrigerator, and a small butcher's block belonging to the apartment owners, left no room for a dining table. Thanks to Willow's ingenuity, two discarded old wooden crates from a wine shop near her pre-school with a 1/12" plank served that purpose. Neither cared for television as a diversion from the day's events. They preferred conversation, though Willow would gladly sacrifice that to hear Dylan play his guitar. In place of a television set was a three-speed vintage turntable with two small speakers and a stack of Dylan's jazz albums stacked neatly atop a homemade shelf made of sanded cedar. The previous tenant had used the smaller of the two bedrooms to store his artwork. Soon after they moved in, Dylan's collection of guitars adorned one wall. Against the other wall was an old narrow door which laid across two milk crates turned on-end. The door was his work area, and the milk crates served as bookcases.

Willow smiled to herself. Not that she was particularly fond of that brand of wine, but she liked to use the red clay bottle as a flower holder. His patient wait for the tea kettle to sound its alarm was interrupted by a knock on the door. A glance at her watch and Willow knew Mrs. Podesta, the landlord, was making one of her frequent visits around dinner time.

"Come in, Mrs. Podesta," Willow answered to the heavy-handed knock.

Before she could close the door behind her, the heavenly aroma of Mrs. Podesta's homemade lasagna engulfed their small living room. She deftly balanced a hot casserole dish wrapped in a thick towel on one hand.

"I don't mean to interrupt, but I thought you two would like some homemade lasagna. It was one of Tommy's favorites," she said with moistened eyes, referring to her son who had been killed in Vietnam.

"Please have a seat, Mrs. Podesta. Dylan's getting me some hot tea," replied Willow, as she stood up to take the hot dish from her guest. Willow placed it on the crate-like table in front of her.

Dylan took the steaming tea kettle off the stove and poured its contents slowly into Willow's cup, along with a fresh tea bag. He paused momentarily at the mention of his best friend's name. Few memories of their time together with the 1st Cav in Vietnam were pleasant; mostly abject terror of the wanton bloodshed and waste of human life they experienced among friends and foe. Despite all that, Dylan could not help but smile as he remembered the times Tommy would open an MRE (Meals Ready to Eat) and grimace, "What I wouldn't give for some of my mom's homemade lasagna." He poured himself a small glass of homemade wine from an odd-shaped green bottle wrapped with twine Mr. Podesta brewed in the basement before making his way into the living room.

"Mrs. Podesta, you shouldn't have," Dylan said. His disclaimer of her act of kindness did not fool Willow, who knew anything with meat and red sauce sent her husband into a food orgasm.

"Dylan, how many times have I told you to call me Rosa or Mamma? And nonsense, I take care of you just like I took care of…"

Her words choked to a stop as the memories of a son never to be seen again, never to be hugged again, overwhelmed her. Realizing she was losing her composure, Rosa politely said, "I better get back to my Frank. I don't like to leave him for too long."

"Of course. I understand, and thank you again, Rosa," Willow replied.

Frank Podesta occupied his days running the family market three blocks down on Haight. He was nowhere near the man who used to greet his customers with a boisterous, "Great day, isn't it," or "I've got your order ready, and I threw in an extra bottle of olive oil, fresh from Lascala Farms." Thankfully, his day began at 4:30 a.m., the less time for the nightmares of his son's death to shatter what little sleep the old man would have. After a cup of coffee, Frank would walk the short distance to his market, where he would open for the predawn deliveries from wholesalers. Once opened to the public, he would busy himself stocking shelves and arranging the perishable inventory in the cold locker to ensure it would go out next. Around 11 a.m., he would return home for a small lunch, usually a slice of French bread, some sliced cheese, and a glass of homemade wine, which he made in the cellar. After a short nap, he would return to the store and stay until closing, around 6 p.m.

After his discharge at Ft. Lewis in Washington, Dylan Steward had flown to San Francisco to see his best friend's parents. He wanted to thank them personally for the care packages they had sent their son and which he generously shared with Dylan. If they wanted, he was prepared to tell them the nature of Tommy's death, a subject for which Sergeant Dylan Steward had paid a horrible price. Having no family of his own, Steward took advantage of Podesta's offer to stay in the small apartment that had been Tommy's place. One week led to two weeks, and in time, Dylan considered it his home, especially after landing a position at the *San Francisco Free Press*, a job for which he was woefully unqualified. He had answered an ad asking for Vietnam veterans interested in being interviewed about their war experiences. Somehow, they were impressed with what he had to say and offered him a position to write about those veterans' experiences.

"Here's your tea, sweetheart," Steward said as he paused to lean over the hot lasagna to inhale the magnificent combination of herbs, sweet Italian sausage, and sauce before handing Willow her hot brew. In silence, the two enjoyed their beverages. The tea had a curative effect on Willow's emerging headache. The surprising smoothness of Mr. Podesta's homemade vino added a welcome sense of separation from a somewhat aggravating day at work.

"How were the kids today?" He knew any question about the pre-school charges would bring a smile to his wife's face. He was not disappointed. Willow took a last sip of Chaga then set her cup on the crate top. She turned to face Dylan; her arms pulled her knees close to her.

"You would not believe them, honey," her blue eyes widened with excitement. "We were talking about dreams, you know, what they wanted to be when they grew up. My God, Dylan, they were all over the landscape. It was like trying to herd cats, getting them to wait patiently for their turn before shouting out their answers."

Her enthusiasm was contagious.

"So, what did the little ones see in their futures?" Dylan asked with a smile.

"Everything from being a doctor to a fireman, to a professional baseball player!" replied Willow, whose face was now aglow with her answer.

That last dream, becoming a professional baseball player, quickly dampened Dylan's spirits. His friend, Tommy, had a dream, too; he was going to be the first in his family to graduate from college, and then he was going to coach high school baseball. That was his real passion, his dream. Uncharacteristically, Dylan emptied the contents of his glass of wine. He leaned back on the sofa and stared up at the ceiling. His eyes froze, never blinking. Then he spoke as if no one was there. "Well, dreams are just that, dreams. The reality of life has a way of ruining dreams."

The morose tone in his voice startled Willow, who immediately sat upright. She took his hand in hers. Almost pleading for understanding, she said, "Dylan, you have to have dreams. Everyone has to have dreams; that's part of life."

Not convinced of his wife's rather Pollyanna view of life, Dylan had a more pessimistic view. "And if life crushes them, then what?"

This was not an unfamiliar theme between the two. Willow seized life and lived it to the fullest type of personality. Her husband, the more pragmatic one, was unlikely to take the road less traveled. Willow's prophetic response would lay dormant in his heart for some time. She placed her hands on his face. There was no way he could avoid her piercing blue eyes. Her words were meant to smooth his fatalism.

"Dreams are part of living, and pursuing your dreams fuels life. Would you really want to live life any other way?"

He saw her words as a generalization for others, certainly not intended to apply to him personally. He responded accordingly.

"No, I wouldn't, sweetheart."

CHAPTER 4

Murray Silverman, the Editor of the *San Francisco Free Press*, was no stranger to political conflicts. He had championed gay rights, opposed the Vietnam war, and openly supported Margot St. James when she founded COYOTE (Call off your tired old ethics) to call for the decriminalization of prostitution. Silverman embraced all that represented San Francisco in the 70s; the counterculture of the Haight-Ashbury, the rising opposition to the military establishment, and the war in Vietnam. He also recognized the irony of San Francisco as the epicenter of musical diversity and entertainment. Everything from the famous jazz venues like The Keystone Korner, the Boarding House, and the Hungry I, to the gaudy Carol Doda and the trashy strip clubs on Broadway, made North Beach a must-see destination for tourists. The old adrenaline rush from championing those causes and exposing the dichotomy of the San Francisco scene long before the exalted Herb Caen of the Chronicle surged anew in his soul. *My God, he had better have all his ducks in a row before this story hits the press*, Silverman thought as he slowly read the outline submitted to him. The fallout from publishing this story was precisely what refueled the passion that fed the old newspaper man's soul.

Steward was finishing up his final draft when the phone rang on his desk.

"Steward," he answered with the phone cradled against his shoulder, his fingers typing the last line of his story. He recognized the voice of Silverman.

"Steward, I need to see you."

"On my way."

There was no need to have a protracted dialogue on the phone. The purpose of Silverman's call in the first place was to have that conversation in the privacy of his office. Steward pulled the last sheet out of his IBM electric typewriter, placed it on top of the other pages, gave them a neat tap on his desk, and then headed through the large open area known as the reporter's room to Silverman's office. He leaned through the opened door.

"Yes, sir."

It was a formality drilled into him in the service to use the term 'sir' when addressing a superior, but one that Silverman shunned. He preferred a first name basis. His office mirrored the aged and badly in need of repair three-story building that housed the *San Francisco Free Press* on the first two floors. Some glass windows still retained frosted glass with faded or missing black letters in Bodoni font. Others had been relabeled with the letters SFFP. It was cheaper than paying the glazer to spell out *San Francisco Free Press*. The original granite stone façade had long lost its sparkle and now resembled a dull, foggy brown. The ledge under the third-floor windows had become home to a plague of San Francisco's cursed pigeons whose excrements now decorated the exterior walls all the way to the ground.

Silverman's office was hardly ostentatious though his title as editor might have dictated otherwise. By choice, the walls chronicled his forty-five years in the newspaper business. From the 30s to the 70s, it was all there for anyone to see. They were what drove

Murray Silverman to fight to make the world a better place: Pictures of food lines and FDR speaking into a radio microphone, Al Capone being led down the courthouse steps in Chicago after being found guilty of income tax evasion, the bombing of Pearl Harbor and the Blitz of London by the German Luftwaffe, the landing at Inchon by MacArthur, an autographed edition of Catcher in the Rye by J.D. Salinger, horrific combat pictures of Vietnam, the Democratic Convention in Chicago, and Jack Kennedy's assassination in Dallas.

Without Goodwill Industries, God only knows what Silverman's office would look like. He had an extra-long, old, and faded leather couch, marked with stains of an unknown variety. It sometimes served as a bed when Murray had one of his infamous late-night battles with Jack Daniels. His dark mahogany desk, another relic from Goodwill, was representative of his erratic work pattern. Opened folders, whose contents spilled over onto each other, a large hand-blown glass ashtray filled with half-smoke Pall Mall cigarettes from the failed efforts of the chain-smoking Silverman to quit the disgusting habit. A large rectangular Tiffany lamp anchored the right side of a disorganized mess covering the desktop. The entire left side of his office was occupied by a dozen high back wooden chairs awkwardly spaced around a usually attractive eight-foot-long dark cherry wood table procured from a friend at the Presidio. Several paper coffee cups, some crumpled up sheets of yellow notepad paper, and remains from his last meeting, cluttered the otherwise appealing piece of furniture.

"Have a seat, Steward."

Steward could not resist the overwhelming desire to reply, "Yes, Chief." Murray Silverman was the body double for Perry White, editor of the *Daily Planet*, a large metropolitan daily newspaper that employed the iconic Clark Kent—otherwise known as "Superman," to a generation of fifties television fans. Murray was short and overweight, with silver-white hair and that same raspy, frustrated voice when he called you. Steward pulled a chair from the table, moving a half-filled coffee cup and an ashtray to the side. Silverman took a seat next to him. He dropped Steward's outline in front of him.

"You realize what you've got here?"

Anticipating a scolding, Dylan replied defensively, "It's only an outline."

A wide smile formed on Silverman's face. "An outline of hell! Alleging the Archbishop of San Francisco is complicit in the vote fraud allegations by a candidate for mayor of San Francisco is not an outline! It is genius in the making."

The sense of relief that overcame Steward was short-lived.

"If you can prove it, and we publish it, this will make you persona non grata in San Francisco."

Dylan gave pause to Silverman's words. He liked the old man, even respected him, and the thought of bringing down the wrath of God and the political almighty of the San Francisco politico did not bode well with Steward. He sat forward in his chair; his eyes focused on reading Silverman's reaction.

"What about you, boss?"

Silverman let out an uproarious howl, not unlike his caricature, Perry White.

"Oh no, kid. This is the kind of stuff that makes running a newspaper, even a rag like the Free Press, worthwhile. Again, can you prove it?"

For the next hour, Dylan Steward laid out his story. This first part was not new to Silverman. John Barbagelata, a wealthy developer and a Republican candidate, had waged a nasty campaign against George Moscone in the race for mayor of San Francisco. He had alleged that Jim Jones, the leader of the People's Temple, a radical religious group headquartered in San Francisco, had bused in hundreds of people from Marin County to vote for Moscone, using the names of dead San Franciscans. The Moscone campaign vigorously denied all the allegations.

"That much I already know, Dylan," sighed Silverman, hoping

for the hidden bombshell in Steward's narrative.

"Did you know this?" Steward asked. "Every single bus originated from Catholic parishes in Marin County, a dozen in all. They met at the churches, picked up the so-called voters, then dropped them off at the People's Temple on Geary St. From there, they were taken to polling places across the city. Coincidence, I do not think so," scoffed Steward."

"It's a dot, Dylan, a single dot," replied a skeptical Silverman, who desperately wanted to hear more.

Silverman's challenge gave rise to a more defiant and insistent Steward.

"Okay, tell me when you have enough dots. One, the drivers were paid in cash. According to my source, Mr. Money Bags was driving a white van with a Southgate Properties sign on the sides. Southgate Properties is a real estate development company owned by one Edward O'Toole, a cousin of none other than Archbishop John Joseph McGucker of San Francisco. Two, Southgate Properties has purchased four of the five plots of landboarding Geary, Steiner, and Fillmore Aves. It is a matter of public record that the archbishop is looking for land to rebuild Saint Mary's Cathedral after it burned down last year. Guess who owns the last plot of land on Geary St.? Jim Jones and the People's Temple. If Jones were to be convicted of voter fraud, he could face up to five years in prison for each count as well as millions of dollars in fines. Who benefits if the Peoples Temple goes bankrupt? Got enough dots?"

Murray Silverman knew full well that the mere appearance of impropriety could be as compelling as finding a "smoking gun." In addition, the many programs the Temple ran to help the homeless and drug addicts, including residential homes for the elderly and a ranch for developmentally disabled children, had support with the liberal citizenry of San Francisco. All that aside, Bishop McGucker had no friend in Murray Silverman after ignoring multiple requests to be interviewed concerning the church's position on birth control and abortion. Of course, Herb Caen, the self-anointed, self-appointed crown prince of San Francisco, had no problem getting access to McGucker. That was about to change.

"Give me your finished story," Murray said to the anxious Steward, "and I'll look it over."

"Does that mean you'll print it?" asked Steward.

With an obvious certainty, Murray answered, "I don't review what I'm not going to print."

CHAPTER 5

He stood before the archbishop's residence at Alamo Square, admiring the turn of the century architecture. Twin white granite columns stood on either side of a grandiose archway. Five dormers accented the top level. The branches of a giant oak cast a shadow over the two-tiered stone steps leading to the entrance. The opulence of the structure seems at odds with the church's mission—to serve the poor. Silverman could have called for an audience with His Eminence, but he knew he would be put off with any number of liturgical excuses. Better to get a "no" from the bishop's administrative aide in person once Silverman showed him the article, if the prelate's underling dared. He turned the large black wrought iron handle and entered the oval foyer. He was greeted by an ornately decorated room with a twenty-foot ceiling. On the left wall was a large portrait of Pope Paul VI. Two towering white candles on golden bases sat on both sides of the portrait. A ruby red rope hung between two gold standards. In front of it, a kneeler. On the opposite wall was a portrait of Archbishop McGucker, smaller in size than that of the Pope but with its own wrought iron rack of votive candles and a coin box in which the faithful could pay to light one of thirty candles. Straight ahead was another large set of double doors. To one side was a large mahogany desk with a brass nameplate that read, "Administrative Assistant ". An immaculate green felt desk pad with leather edging neatly displayed an open day planner, a gold pencil and pen set, and two small pictures at the corners of the pope and the archbishop. The priest sitting at the desk stood up as Silverman approached, a well-worn leather valise under his arm.

"Good day, my name is Father Stephen. How may I help you?"

He was rather young for such a position, Silverman thought. No gray hair, a sign of maturity and experience that would have been nice for the faithful to see. Even in his traditional black pants, black coat, and white collar, the priest looked trim and well built. His brown hair was neatly shaped, not a hair out of place, too neat for Silverman's liking. He had focused brown eyes and a firm grip. Probably a good poker player, guessed Silverman.

"Yes, Father, my name is Silverman, Murray Silverman. I am from the *San Francisco Free Press*. I was wondering if I might have a few moments with the archbishop. It won't be long, I assure you."

Without even looking at his day planner, the priest answered, "I'm sorry, but Bishop McGucker is not taking visitors today." With that, the bishop's sentry took his seat and resumed reviewing his day planner for the day's activities.

Silverman knew his visit would become a reality, but first, he wanted to toy with the arrogant priest before him. He smiled and, in a most condescending way, replied.

"Oh, come now, Father Stephen. I'm sure a man of your influence could find me a few minutes with the archbishop?"

The priest laid his pen on his desk and politely but with a defined sense of "what part of no don't you understand" answered, "As I already stated, the archbishop is not taking visitors today."

The smugness was almost too much for Silverman to contain.

"You know, Father Stephen, you look like a learned man, someone who likes to read, am I right?"

Exasperated with what he considered an inane question, Father Stephen put his pen down and replied sarcastically, "Yes, Mr. Silverman, I like to read. Why?"

Silverman opened his valise and took out a multiple-page document. He handed it to him and said, "Take a few minutes to browse through this, wouldn't you? Then we'll see about that meeting with the archbishop."

Clearly annoyed, the aide shut his day planner with sufficient force to express his displeasure for Silverman's insistence. He had not read more than two pages when he abruptly stood up and, without a word, left immediately through the large oaken door behind him. From the priest's sudden departure, he assumed the priest would return forthwith with a response. Such was not the case. Silverman was left to cool his heels for almost an hour before the priest returned.

"Nice read, wasn't it, Father?"

The priest saw no humor in Silverman's sarcastic retort, and his own response offered even less wit.

"His Eminence has made available time for you to see him on Thursday at 2 p.m. The delay is necessary so the diocese's attorneys can be present."

In a most dismissive manner, Father Stephen handed Silverman his document and took a seat at his desk without so much as looking up.

Taking his leave, Silverman turned and walked away. No problem with a three-day delay, he thought. I have time to check out a few details myself. But it would be a problem, as Murray Silverman would soon discover.

IT WAS LATE the following afternoon, and Silverman was still savoring the anticipation over the opportunity to expose the election fraud in the mayoral race. It was short-lived. Nathan Strauss, the paper's owner, appeared out of nowhere, and from his furrowed brow and pursed lips, he was not there to deliver good news. Strauss had sunk every bit of his inheritance into setting up the *San Francisco Free Press*. From the presses to the office equipment and furniture to the long-term lease on the building, Nathan Strauss had risked everything he owned to make the SFFP a success. All that was about to end.

"Nathan, this is a pleasant surprise, I hope," said Silverman.

Strauss had trouble looking Silverman in the eye. He sat on the edge of the oak table with his arms folded. His hands clinched a large manila envelope. His feet tapped nervously on the floor. His eyes darted left then right like a man looking for an escape route. He looked every bit of a seventy-year-old dream chaser.

"I received these today," Nathan said as he pulled two multi-page documents from the envelope. "One is a notice from the Sedgwick Law Firm to sue me personally for libel and defamation of character if I allow some story about the archbishop and election fraud to be printed. The second is a notice from the landlord saying that he has sold the building and is giving me two weeks to vacate the premises for the new owners. Of course, there is a substantial payment for voiding the lease agreement, including buying the presses and office equipment."

Strauss's chest heaved as his breathing became labored. His eyes moistened. His throat constricted, making his words come out raspy and hesitant.

"Murray, finding another location to lease in the city is virtually impossible, and the legal fees will bankrupt me."

"But if you win, Nathan?" replied Silverman, who was hoping there was a shred of fight left in the old man.

"And what chance do you really think I stand against the most powerful legal firm in the city and the Roman Catholic Church!"

Silverman knew the sound of a beaten man, a man he loved and respected. He had no intention of prolonging his friend's agony.

"Nathan, I understand. I really do."

THE WALK home was not a pleasure stroll for Dylan Steward. The news of the paper's demise hit him hard, not only because his uncovering of the election scandal had been squashed but because of his friendship with Murray Silverman and a host of other counterculture personalities on staff. Their electric enthusiasm for working at the independent newspaper was contagious. There was also the challenge of finding a new job. He savored every sound and smell on his way home as he considered how to break the news to his wife. He tempered that task with Silverman's last words to him when discussing his future. "Follow your dreams."

She wondered if something was awry when her husband rounded the corner as she approached their home from the opposite direction. He usually would not be home for an hour or so after her. For Willow Steward, reading her husband was easy. The man wore his heart on his sleeve. A quickly disappearing grin replaced his typically broad smile. Though quiet by nature, when dealing with unpleasantries, quiet became withdrawn. As they met at the steps, she greeted him with a kiss and, "Why home so early?" They walked up the five steps hand in hand to the front door before he answered.

"The short version is that the paper has been sold, and I got a two-week severance check from Murray."

There were times when Willow wished her husband's explanation was as descriptive as his writing, and this was certainly such an occasion.

"How about the long version?" she asked as she opened the door with its rickety brass doorknob. Dylan went straight to his workroom without so much as a word. He returned to the living room with his antique Martin guitar. Taking a seat on the sofa, he began playing. The dissonant sounds of his combination of major and minor chords offset with their diminished and suspended counterparts were ghostly sounding with a premonition of sadness. When finished, he hugged the body of his Martin and stared at the floor for what seemed to Willow, like an eternity. Finally, he revealed the reason for his morose attitude.

"I guess the story I was working on about election fraud in the mayor's race was too hot for Murray to publish. With the implication that the Catholic Church appeared to have a hand in it, he paid a courtesy visit to the archbishop. The archbishop's aide set a meeting for the end of the week. Before that could happen, the paper's owner, Nathan Strauss, got a notice from the biggest law firm in the city that if the story went to print, they were going to sue Strauss for everything he had. On top of that, the next day, Strauss received a letter from the landlord that he had sold the building, and Strauss had two weeks to vacate. He paid Strauss a lot of money for breaking the lease." He looked up at Willow with the eyes of a lost dog looking at a stranger for help. "No story, no paper, no job."

It was not the loss of his job that bothered Willow the most. It was knowing that he felt like he had failed her, which was the farthest thing from her mind. He had a real talent for writing, for expressing the sphere of human emotions in a way that anesthetized the reader from the grim realities of daily life. She took the guitar from his hands and laid it against the end of the couch. Then she placed her hands on his face, forcing him to look directly into her eyes.

"Listen to me, Dylan Steward. You are a talented writer, and somewhere out there, someone needs a writer like you, someone who can make words leap off the page and grab at their hearts."

Her tall husband sank back against the couch and allowed his Pollyannaish wife to hold his head against her breast. Willow looked upward, past the ceiling, past the roof, to that higher being. The lifeblood of her heart prayed.

"Dear God, please do not let him languish in depression. I know you have a plan for him. Show us what it is."

With an assertiveness that surprised him, Willow took her arm from around her husband and announced, "I think we need to celebrate with a little of Mr. Podesta's finest!"

"Celebrate what?" replied the disconsolate Dylan.

"The future, silly," beamed Willow as she sprang from the couch and headed to the kitchen. She returned shortly with two small mason jars filled three-quarters full of Podesta's latest cellar creation. They clinked the former jelly containers and let the flavor of Podesta's red flow slowly over their taste buds.

To usher in her toast with something more pragmatic than hope, Willow said, "You may want to check that envelope on the table. Your name is on it. It fell out of your jacket pocket a couple of days ago. I left it on the table for you, but somehow things you need to attend to disappear from your sight when you're around."

"Very funny. I get to things, just not as fast you would like," he replied, with an adolescent sticking out of his tongue in defiance.

Setting his jar on the table, Steward picked up the envelope. He immediately recognized his boss's handwriting. He opened the envelope and took a folded piece of red notepaper.

"What's it say?" asked Willow, who curiously leaned over to read it.

"It says to call some guy. Murray gave me his name and number."

"Do you know him?" asked Willow, who was practically atop him trying to see the note.

"No," replied Dylan, as he held his phone farther away to his left to toy with her curiosity.

Willow leaned away from her husband and picked up the telephone from its cradle on the end table.

"You're about to. What's the number?" she asked.

She punched in the number that Dylan read to her, then

handed him the phone. It rang several times before a male voice answered, "*L.A. Times*, Donahue."

Steward stumbled over his words as he realized he had precious little information to initiate a conversation.

"Mr. Donahue, my name is Dylan Steward. My editor, Murray Silverman of the *San Francisco Free Press*, gave me your name and number with instructions to call you. To be honest, Mr. Donahue, I have no idea why."

The chuckle in the man's voice eased Steward's apprehension.

"Well, I do. I've read your article on the Pentagon Papers sometime back. I will be conducting interviews for a reporter's position at the *L.A. Times*. Murray and I are old friends. When I contacted him about you, he told me of the pending sale of the *Free Press* and said that I'd be a fool if I didn't interview you. Not wanting to fulfill Murray's prediction, I've scheduled you for next Monday at 11 a.m. Can you make it?"

In disbelief at his good fortune, Dylan placed his hand over the receiver and whispered to his wife, "You won't believe this!" Then he replied to the man, "Yes, sir. I'll be there."

CHAPTER 6

Steward neatly folded his corduroy coat and placed it in the overhead bin atop his small faded and cracked brown leather valise—a souvenir Willow had picked up at a secondhand store to make him look more professional at his interview. Then he scrunched his six-foot-two frame into the seemingly petite size seat on the Southwest flight from SFO to LAX. Completely ignoring the instructions that came over the plane PA's system about oxygen masks, emergency exits, and flotation devices, he closed his eyes and contemplated on the bizarre phone call from two days ago. A man he had never heard of, named James Donahue, had called to see if Dylan was interested in interviewing for a position as a reporter on the *Los Angeles Times*. The man claimed to have read an article Steward had written on the Pentagon Papers and was impressed with his analytical approach to the futuristic implications of such revelations. The mere offer seemed to confirm to Willow that her husband was about to be rewarded for his reporting skills. Steward was more skeptical. The chance that some editor from the *L.A. Times* would have read a story in a small independent newspaper with a readership consisting of counterculture personalities who considered attacking the establishment a moral imperative seemed improbable, if not impossible. There had to be more to it. More than legitimate interest in the position, curiosity motivated Steward to spend part of his severance package to buy a round trip ticket to meet the stranger.

The brightest of the mid-morning sun, combined with a clear blue sky, amplified the beauty of the San Francisco Bay area. The Golden Gate Bridge, Alcatraz Island, and the Embarcadero Center with its Fisherman's Wharf served to outline the gigantic structures of the inner city: The Transamerica Building, the Chevron Tower, the Wells Fargo Building, and the Bank of America building. The contrast to the smoggy downtown Los Angeles basin was not lost on Steward as his flight circled LAX for landing. The hurried rush of his fellow passengers to retrieve their luggage from the overhead bins near their seats and then crowd the aisle to be the first off the plane, as though it was an emergency landing, amused the placid Steward. With the aisle beginning to empty, Steward stood up, got his coat and valise from the overhead storage bin, and proceeded down the aisle, thanking the flight attendants who stood at the plane's door. He had barely stepped into the concourse when he was suddenly overcome with emotion, remembering the last time he departed a plane.

It was at Sea-Tac International Airport on June 12th, 1970, and he had returned from Vietnam. Paralyzed with that memory, he quickly found an empty seat before his legs gave way. The back of the plane had been loaded with troops returning from Vietnam. When the wheels of the Boeing 747 touched down, there was a deafening roar from some of the returning vets who screamed out with unabashed joy. Others sat silent, tears running down their faces, haunted by the images of friends who had not survived the carnage in countless villages surrounded by filthy rice paddies and jungle forests home to the Viet Cong. Steward had been one of the silent. Images flicked on and off in his brain, Tommy Podesta's smile then the shell hole filled with muddy water in which Steward screamed for life to return to Tommy's body. He was kneeling next to Tommy, holding Tommy's intestines from oozing out between his fingers as his hands pressed against the gaping hole in Tommy's ruptured stomach. The coolness of the air flowing through the concourse did little to alleviate the sweat forming on Steward's face. For a moment, he thought he was going to vomit. Once composed, Steward stood up and continued his way down the concourse through a mass of people. Some preferred to use the escalator and avoid the long walk to the luggage claim area. Others wove hurriedly in and out of those not moving fast enough to suit them. He wondered what destination warranted such haste; the arms of awaiting loved ones, a tranquil home after a long tiring plane ride, or a celebration over a successful business deal.

He made his way to the exit doors and outside to the sidewalk, where a line of taxi cabs awaited their next fare. Steward headed to the closest one. The driver sat with a pencil in hand and busied himself with a folded newspaper. Must be a crossword fanatic, Steward thought.

Glancing at the piece of paper he had taken out of his pocket, Steward asked the cabby, "Can you get me to 213 South Spring St, downtown L.A.?"

Without looking up from his puzzle, the cabby replied, "The Times Building, sure get in." He tilted his L.A. Dodger hat back on his head and rubbed his forehead. "Son-of-a-bitch! One last one." Puzzlement and irritation lined the stubby bearded face of the slightly overweight baseball fan.

Steward opened the backseat door and slid into a stale aired yellow cab. The faded and cracked brown leather upholstery had been the recipient of countless spilled liquids, and the floor had a few crumpled napkins missed by the cabbie at his last cleaning. As Steward closed the door, the cabby again expressed his frustration with the paper's crossword.

"Dammit! I almost got the whole thing," angrily tossing the puzzle on the seat next to him. Feeling sorry for the man who was obviously annoyed at his lack of puzzle guile, Steward asked, "What's the clue?"

As he turned on the ignition of the cab, the cabby replied, "an eight-letter word for military intelligence, third letter y, last letter n."

Adjusting his seat belt, Steward offered up the answer. "Oxymoron."

The driver quickly retrieved his puzzle from the seat and took the nib of a pencil from behind his ear. After filling in the answer, the supremely satisfied cabby grinned out loud, "Well, I'll be damned!"

Steward found himself feeling amused, not at the cabby's mirth but at the cleverness of the puzzle's creator. Without so much as a glance over his shoulder, the cabby quickly pulled out into traffic. Well familiar with the maze of exits and their accompanying overhead green signs, an undaunted cabby asked, "So what takes you to the Times?"

Steward planted his feet firmly against the cab's floor as the driver moved across multiple freeway lanes to get to the right freeway and ultimately the right exit, using his horn to create an opening in the lanes of swift-moving traffic.

"I've got a job interview at 11," replied Steward, growing more anxious with every maneuver of the driver.

"No problem," replied the determined driver as he swerved into the next lane. "We're twenty minutes away, at most."

Noticing the cab's license on the visor above the driver, Steward comically pleaded, "I'd like to get there alive, Henry."

Taking no offense, Henry answered, "Yeah, newcomers have a hard time with L.A. traffic."

True to his word, at 10:50 a.m., Henry's cab pulled to the curb in front of the Los Angeles Times Building at 213 S. Spring St. He put his right arm over the back of his seat and said, "Twenty-five bucks, even." Feeling generous for his safe arrival, Steward took a twenty and a ten from his wallet and said, "Keep the change, Henry."

With a smile that displayed some needed dental work, Henry replied, "Good luck with the interview."

"Thanks, Henry," said Steward, grateful for the wish of success from a total stranger. With that, Dylan Steward headed toward the large revolving set of glass doors and an interview that would change his life forever.

UPON ENTERING THE FOYER, Dylan Steward was greeted with a line of elevators, above which were photographs of the Owner, managing editor, and assistant editors. A kiosk offering an array of blended coffees, teas, pastries, fruits, and premade sandwiches was on his left. To his right, an elderly black man ran a magazine and newspaper stand. He stood with stooped shoulders, and when he walked, he did so with a slight limp. Steward paused to watch as the man seemed to know everyone by their first name and reading preference. With a periodical in hand, he greeted his customers.

"Great day, Mr. So and so. How is your son doing these days?" or "How is that lovely wife of yours? Here's the latest for you" A hand crippled with arthritis graciously accepted their money and the announcement, "Keep the change, Willis."

Steward wondered if his customers knew anything about the man with a knack for names and relationships. Staring at the photographs above the elevators, Steward hoped to see the face of the man who had called him. The voice of the old black man called out.

"I knows most everyone who works here, son. Who you lookin' for?"

Steward smiled at the man's kindness. "I have an appointment with James Donahue at 11 a.m."

Willis motioned for Steward to come closer. When he did, Willis glanced quickly to his left and his right to see if anyone was within earshot. Though assured no one could hear him, he still spoke softly, "Jimmy's office is on the third floor. When you get off the elevator, turn left, three doors down on the left." Then with the twinkle of his eye, Willis added. "If you are here for a job, don't bullshit the man. Not much old Jimmy ain't already seen or heard. You just be yourself." Again, a twinkle and then," Good luck."

Reaching out to shake his hand, Steward said, "Thanks, Willis. I appreciate that."

Steward's brief encounter with the sage old man ended as Steward headed to the line of elevators. In the background, he heard Willis's voice. "Hey, Mr. Gordon. I heard your son's agoin' to USC next year. Maybe win the Heisman?"

Old Willis took on the imagery of a fine wine, aged to perfection.

Following Willis' direction, Steward got off on the third floor, turned left, and walked down to the third door. The nameplate read, "James Donahue." He knocked firmly three times. He expected to hear the voice of a female receptionist or secretary. Instead, he heard a gruff voice call out, "Come in."

Steward was greeted by the distinctive aroma of cigar smoke. He stifled the urge to cough. Biting down on his treasured Arturo Fuente cigar, Donahue grimaced as he rolled down the sleeves of his white shirt and acknowledged his visitor.

"You're early," Donahue snapped at the surprised Steward.

"Early is on time, and on time is late, the way I was taught," retorted Steward, in a confident tone.

Donahue smiled as he finished rolling up his other sleeve. "Now that sounds like a Murray Silverman protégée. Have a seat, Steward."

Confused over the unexpected familiarity with his old boss, Dylan pulled a black chair from a cluttered corner table and sat down.

"Did you bring your resume and the articles we spoke about?"

Steward tapped his aged leather valise. "Do you want to see them now, Mr. Donahue?"

"I don't want to see them at all, but I guarantee someone will," Donahue replied, still maintaining a gruff demeanor. He walked over to a coat rack in the corner closest to the door, grabbed a black coat, and put it on. Then he loosely tightened his navy-blue tie.

"The interview is down the hall. You are three of three. Follow behind me and do not say a word. Take a seat in one of the chairs in the hallway. When you are called in, remember, you are not interviewing for me; you are interviewing for the other two at the table, understand?"

No, he did not understand, but there was something about the confidence Donahue exuded that put Steward at ease. He followed Donahue out the door of his office and down a long wide hallway. On either side were copies of historic front-page headlines from over fifty years of *Los Angeles Times* history. Steward looked ahead and saw several uncomfortable-looking wooden chairs against the wall to his left. Two people were already seated; a nattily dressed man, wearing black horn-rimmed glasses and holding an expensive-looking leather briefcase, and a woman, wearing a smartly fitted business suit which exposed an appropriate amount of leg and a suitable display of bosom. Steward politely nodded to the two as he took his seat. The woman returned a polite smile. The man took a judgmental look at Steward's corduroy sport coat, khaki trousers, blue shirt, and red tie. He then turned away as though he had seen some form of inferior human life.

Dylan avoided the looming pressure of his interview by

focusing on his wife. He had fallen in love with her the moment they met in the 70s outside a Fleetwood Mac concert at the Fillmore. True to the style of the day—for someone in San Francisco at the Fillmore—she wore a yellow bandanna that held her shoulder-length auburn hair in place. She had on a sleeveless sheepskin vest over a tie-dyed t-shirt, flower printed bell-bottom jeans, and leather sandals. Through the celebratory fog of the crowd, her angelic smile and pearly white teeth served as a beacon to the wandering Steward. He wooed her away from her friends with an offer to ride the trolley car to Ghirardelli Square and Irish Coffee at the Buena Vista. By the time the bartender shouted, "Last Call," Dylan Steward knew he had met his soul mate. His inner soul was at peace for the first time in years. So engrossed was he in that memory, he failed to notice the man next to him had been called into the office for his interview.

"In another place?" asked the woman sitting one chair away. Her tone was sincere but not flirtatious.

Embarrassed by his zoning out at such a crucial time, Steward sheepishly replied, "Thinking about my wife." It seemed a plausible explanation.

"My name is Edith Cranston. My friends call me Edie."

Though a competitor for a position on the *Times*, Cranston was anything but standoffish, she made their introduction pleasant, not threatening. Steward appreciated that.

"Dylan Steward. My friends call me Dylan."

Not wanting to pry further, Cranston said, "Well, Dylan Steward, good luck!"

She glanced upward at an angle as if trying to remember not to forget some vital bit of information for her interview. In a few minutes, the door opened, and the first interviewee came out. He headed straight down the hallway to the elevators, not a word or gesture to the other two. After several tense minutes, the door opened again, and Donahue stepped out.

"Ms. Cranston, won't you please come in."

As she stood up, Steward felt compelled to return her previous gesture of kindness.

"Edith." She turned at the sound of her name. Steward gave her a thumbs up and smiled.

CHAPTER 7

Alone in the hallway, Steward's mind drifted from thoughts of his wife to speculating about the oddity of the note from his old boss, Murray Silverman. Did Murray know this James Donahue, and if so, how? Countless reporters must send their resumes to the *Los Angeles Times*, hoping for an interview, yet he had received an unsolicited handwritten note from the assignment editor to call him. Why? His imagination ran wild with possibilities. His mental meanderings had eaten up the time since Cranston had entered the interview room. Steward was startled when the door opened, and Edith Cranston stepped out into the hallway, followed by Donahue.

"Thank you, Ms. Cranston, for your time. You won't be left hanging; a decision will be made by the end of the week." Donahue smiled and shook the young woman's hand. He waited until she was nearer the elevator when he turned to Steward and said, "You're up, kid." Steward stood up and followed Donahue into the room.

"Dylan Steward, please meet Sylvia Markham, Assistant editor covering European affairs, and Mr. Martin Milner, Assistant editor covering national business and economics."

Politely, yet with a tone of confidence, Steward replied, "Ms. Markham, Mr. Milner, the pleasure is mine."

Donahue began the process. "Dylan, this is a somewhat unconventional interview. Each one on the panel has their own lists of questions, and we will begin with Mr. Milner."

With that, Dylan Steward sat to meet friend or foe, and it did not take long to determine who was which. Martin Milner flipped slowly through Steward's resume as if something were missing. Taking off his black horn-rimmed glasses, he leaned back in his chair and said, "Mr. Steward, I don't seem to be able to find your collegiate background. Could you tell us what your major was and what college you attended?"

There was a smugness in Milner's tone that immediately irritated Steward, and judging from the sideways look on Donahue's face, he was not pleased with the question, either. Steward decided to make his response short and succinct.

"I attended San Francisco City College for three semesters with a major in music education."

Milner stared in the direction of Donahue, who was seated to his right. The disdain on his face was obvious, like some overprotective father who deemed his daughter's suitor unsuitable for a family of their station in life. Though the three were strangers to Steward, he had no problem recognizing the acrimony between the two men. Milner turned his attention back to Steward.

"Mr. Steward, pardon my bluntness, but I hardly think three semesters at a junior college with classes in music education qualifies you for a position as a journalist on one of the most prestigious newspapers in the world."

Steward steadied himself before responding.

"I certainly understand your concern Mr. Milner; perhaps this will assuage your fears about my qualifications. Regarding my major in music education, the ability to discern a major chord from that same chord in its minor, suspended, or diminished form is like a journalist being able to separate truth from partly true and fact from embellishment. That, I am sure you will agree, is an essential quality in a good journalist, even a great journalist."

Donahue stifled his laughter. Markham looked down at the table, hoping to hide the smile forming on her face. Milner discovered too late that the young man across the table from him did not suffer fools well. Steward continued his evisceration of the elitist Milner.

"As for only completing three semesters, I underwent a conflict of conscience, something of a moral dilemma, a calling from a higher authority, you might say. Should I set aside my own personal desires and opinions for those in higher positions, or should I succumb to my own selfish desires? I chose the former. Another quality of a good journalist, don't you think?"

Milner should have ended his questioning lest he expose more of the inner fool. Wise he was not. Twice he had allowed Steward to outwit him. He was determined not to let it happen again.

"And what exactly was this higher calling?" he asked, with sarcastic certainty he had put Steward in checkmate.

With all due politeness and deference to Milner's position on the panel, Steward replied, "The United States Government, sir. They requested that I help defend the constitution of the United States against enemies both foreign and domestic by serving in the United States military. I answered that call, sir, and was drafted into the Army where I served two years in Vietnam with the 1st Air Cavalry, earning two Purple Hearts and the Distinguished Service Cross."

Having been bested for the third time, Milner sat back in the chair and deferred further questions to Markham and Donahue. Markham had taken quite a fancy to Steward's article on the Pentagon Papers submitted with his resume, as well as a series of articles on the lack of women in traditionally male-dominated professions. Of like mind on both issues, she took several minutes discussing the implications of exposing government lies and breaching the chauvinistic bastilles of American industry.

"Thank you, Mr. Steward, that was enlightening, to say the least."

Donahue had but one question. It was a favorite he asked at every interview.

"Dylan, have you ever had a dispute with an editor over the content of an article you submitted, and if so, how did you resolve it?"

Steward was taken back a bit. His entire reporting career had been with the SFFP. His editor, Murray Silverman, had been more a teacher, an encourager, even a bit of a provocateur. Still, Silverman never challenged him to forsake his ethics for the sake of publication.

"I would have to answer no to that question, Mr. Donahue. Murray Silverman of the *San Francisco Free Press* was not that kind of an editor. He was only interested in the truth as it was written."

Two of the three interviewers seemed pleased with the answer Steward gave. Not so Martin Milner, who foolishly attempted to find fault with him for the third time. He made no attempt to hide his disdain for the interviewee or hide his own sense of superiority.

"Seriously, Mr. Steward? In what," he said, glancing down at Steward's resume, "four years with even an insignificant publication like the Free Press, never once did you argue with your editor on the publication of an article?"

The tone of his question shocked Markham and Donahue both. So much so, Markham could not help but rebuke her colleague.

"Martin, there is no need to be insulting. All of us have worked our way up from somewhere."

Jimmy Donahue was far more personal in his admonishment. "For some, that somewhere might have been their bloodline where the climb is not so steep." Milner seethed at the disparaging implication that he earned his position due to his being the son of a multimillionaire.

Now firmly enraged at his questioner, Dylan Steward stated more than firmly, "No, Mr. Milner, never once!"

Milner dropped his pen on the table. "Frankly, Mr. Steward, I find it impossible to believe that you have never even once written a piece when you were not challenged by your superior as to its veracity, and if that is true, I do not think you are a very good journalist!"

At that moment, Steward lost sight of the end goal, a position as a reporter for the *Los Angeles Times*. If Martin Miler wanted an example of writer/editor conflict, then he would give him one, consequences be damned.

"You might be right about that, Mr. Milner. I was challenged once about a report I had written. I was ordered to change the wording, and I did have words with my superior."

Being supremely confident he had finally put the impudent upstart in his place, Milner smirked. "Please explain to the panel, won't you?"

Completely ignoring the others on the panel, Steward leaned forward and spoke directly to Milner. His eyes burned with an intensity that forced Milner to lean back in his chair.

"It was June 1969, outside a small village near Kahn Sanh in Vietnam. I had submitted my after-action report to my captain. I wrote that my lieutenant had panicked and thrown a hand grenade that landed next to my buddy. The blast ripped his stomach open, and he died in my arms, blood pouring through my hands as I tried to hold his intestines in place. I was told by my captain to delete any reference to the lieutenant as it would ruin his career in the Army and tarnish the good reputation of a West Point graduate. I told the captain if he changed one single word of my report, he would eat a grenade, and I would pull the pin. Conflict resolved."

Milner wilted under Steward's satanic stare, the stare of one who had been to hell and back. Steward held firm until Donahue put an end to Milner's agony.

"Mr. Steward, there will be no more questions. Thank you for your time." Donahue scribbled something on a piece of paper and folded it. Steward stood up and again, with politeness and aplomb, said, "Thank you all for this opportunity." Donahue followed Steward outside into the hallway and handed him a note, saying, "Show this to Willis in the lobby." Donahue turned and returned to the interview room.

The atmosphere in the room was like walking into a freezer. Martin Milner sat with his arms folded, staring at the tabletop. Sylvia Markham had moved her chair a noticeable distance from Milner as if he were contagious with some exotic disease. Neither said a word. Donahue went to his chair and gathered up his papers. He looked to the two to his left.

"Sylvia, Martin, thank you for your participation."

"Why" snapped Milner. "This was always your unilateral decision and, thank God, your last," referring to Willard's decision to take over the hiring of journalists after the first of the year.

Markham smiled at Donahue. "Then make it a good one, Jimmy, and hire this kid."

CHAPTER 8

Once out of the elevator, Steward headed directly to the newsstand per Donahue's instructions. The elderly black man was stooped over, struggling to lift a heavy cardboard box onto a rolling cart. An artificial leg made the task even more difficult.

"Let me give you a hand, Willis," said Steward, as he moved to the man's side to relieve him of a task that demanded far more than he could do.

Once the box was positioned on the cart, Steward handed Willis the note from Donahue. Willis chuckled as he read the note

"Jimmy wants you to meet him at Lefty's. Looks to me like he's gonna spring for a round or two."

Steward appeared somewhat confused, a look which Willis quickly recognized.

"Lefty's is a whiskey bar two blocks down Spring Street and right to Carter. It's next to Lenny's barbershop."

Steward looked at his watch. It read 12:30 p.m. I've got time before my return flight at 4:30 p.m.

Extending his hand to Willis, Steward said, "Thanks for your help."

With a broad grin that displayed stained and crooked teeth, the aged black man replied. "It's my pleasure, Mr. Steward. When you get that job, you let old Willis know what ya like to read, and I'll have it here for you."

"I'll do just that," replied Steward with his own smile. He headed out of the building for his unexpected meeting with Donahue. It was only a short walk but still enough time for the midday smog to cause his eyes to sting. He hastened his pace until he saw a neon sign that read, "Lefty's."

When he entered through a black leather door with a small diamond-shaped window, Dylan Steward stepped back in time. Along both walls were several small circular booths upholstered with rich ruby red leather. A small black table covered by a white tablecloth with a round brass lamp provided a minimum of light. *The better to guard the identity of its patrons*, Dylan thought to himself. *How lucky can we get*? thought Steward. The walls were adorned with autographed pictures of Hollywood's famous from the forties and fifties. Music from the Big Band Era softened the sound of his shoes as he crossed a black and white tile floor to the bar. Steward marveled at the unique carving on the face of the dark mahogany bar. It caught the attention of the bartender.

"The panel to your left is the flag-raising on Iwo Jima, the center panel is the landing on D-Day, and the third panel is the crowd in *Times Square* on VE-Day."

"Where did that inspiration come from?" Steward asked, continuing to stare in amazement.

"The original owner, Lefty, had three sons. The eldest, John, was killed on Iwo Jima. The middle son, Robert, died on the landing at Normandy. It was his idea as a tribute to his sons."

Approaching the bar, Steward asked, "What about the third son?"

"That would be me, Laurance, or Lefty, after my father."

Laurance, or Lefty as he chose to be called, had silver hair combed straight back. His skin was a shiny white, probably from years under the artificial lights shining down from above the bar. He wore a white apron secured tightly around his waist, a matching white shirt, with a red bow tie.

Steward took a seat on one of the black leather bar stools.

"What brings you here?" said Lefty, as he polished the bar in front of Steward with a white towel in one hand and placed a white cocktail napkin in front of him with the other hand.

I'm supposed to meet James Donahue here. I just finished an interview with him at The Times.

Lefty leaned against the back of the bar. Two glass shelves ran the length of the bar, each shelf neatly lined with expensive liquor, liqueurs, and other exotic mixtures used for making any concoction requested by a customer. The mirror behind the shelves reflected a small but noticeable bald spot in Lefty's carefully coiffed hair. He folded his arms and said with a wide grin, "Jimmy is a dinosaur, a throwback to the days of real newspapermen. His word is his bond."

At the mention of his name, the bar door opened, and in walked Donahue.

Lefty called out, "Jimmy, your friend is already here. You're late." A robust laugh came out of the bartender.

Unruffled by Lefty's feigned sarcasm, Donahue replied, "I'll take the usual and give the kid whatever he wants."

Upon returning from the men's room, Jimmy found two crystal tumblers with several ice cubes in them and a bottle of Maker's Mark sitting in front of Steward.

"The kid said he'd have whatever you're drinking," Lefty explained.

Donahue pulled up a stool next to Steward. He took the bottle of his favorite bourbon, removed the cork, and slowly filled both glasses three-quarters full. He lifted his glass and held it out to Steward. Being allowed to pour your favorite was a privilege Lefty afforded only his oldest and closest customers.

"Here's to you and your new job."

Surprised at the news, Dylan lifted his glass, clinked it to Donahue, then replied, "I would never have thought that, considering how Milner questioned me."

After taking a healthy sip of his beverage, Donahue relished the smoothness of the Mark before replying, "He's an elitist asshole who was born with a silver spoon in his mouth but forget him for the time being. You were the one I wanted, and that's all that counts."

Dylan smiled and slowly nursed his own drink before asking, "Back in your office, you made mention of Murray Silverman, like you knew him. Care to explain?"

Donahue set his drink on the bar and turned in Dylan's direction.

"Murray and I were in the same squad on Iwo Jima with the 1st Battalion, 5th Marines. We became like brothers, sharing everything. We both loved the newspaper industry. He used to laugh when I told him I dreamed of going back to the *Times* and working in the newsroom. Hell, I had been there since I was a teenager. He would kid me, 'why not be the editor?'"

I told him I wanted to be where the blood and ink flowed. He dreamed someday of owning his own newspaper. He said there was more to the news than the vanilla stories most papers printed. That was his passion. We kept in touch over the years. That's how I heard about you."

"Sounds like both of you got your dreams," Dylan replied, slowly turning his glass on the bar's surface. His eyes focused on his drink as his mind was immersed in envy.

All his years at the *Times* had taught Donahue how to read people. He could tell by a shoulder shrug, a sideways glance, or a furrowed brow when there was an untold story. His intuition told him to dig deeper.

"What did you like best about working for Murray?"

"He wasn't afraid to let me dig into things. He would say there are always two stories, the one people want you to know and the one people do not want anyone to know. Murray let me work the latter."

Donahue smiled, knowing that there were more layers to Dylan Steward than what was revealed at Lefty's bar. Under his tutelage, Jimmy Donahue would help Dylan Steward discover more of himself. Jimmy emptied his glass then reached for the bottle of Maker's Mark. He poured himself another drink, then turning to Steward, he said, "I want you here in a month, ready to work on the stories people don't want anyone to know, ok?"

A sense of excitement came over Dylan. He was getting a chance to do what he loved, and he was more than grateful to Jimmy Donahue.

"Mr. Donahue, I won't disappoint you."

"If you follow your dreams, you won't. See you in a month."

THE CONCOURSE at LAX was crowded with new arrivals moving hastily toward predetermined destinations. For some, there was a sense of excitement on their faces. New dreams awaited them. New frontiers stood before them. Those departing moved at a more deliberate pace. Some moved like zombies, barely taking their eyes off the floor, their minds meandering through some sort of mental forest. Their eyes had a disturbing absence of awareness as though those near them were non-existent beings, all moving together yet in complete isolation. Had their dreams been shattered? Were they traveling back with stories of defeat and rejection in the place known as the city of dreams? This flow of contradicting humanity was not Steward's primary focus. Standing in front of a pay phone, his hand ruffled anxiously through the loose coinage in his pocket. He wanted to let his wife know the results of his interview and the panorama of possibilities that lay before them, a vista of new and exciting places, interesting new people, and experiences. It was just the sort of adventure that Willow

Steward would embrace. For Dylan Steward, it was an opportunity to hone his craft as a reporter on one of the most prestigious newspapers in the country. As Murray Silverman told him, the story some people do not want to be printed is what most people want to read.

He fed every bit of change he had into the modern rendition of Alexander Graham Bell's creation that would connect him to his wife. The dial tone echoed in his ear while he glanced at his wristwatch, mentally measuring the time of his call to make sure he did not miss his flight back to San Francisco. The dial tone continued until two things were apparent to Steward. One, his wife was not home, and two, if he waited any longer, he would miss his flight. He would have to wait until he got home to spring the news on his wife. Their lives were about to change in ways neither could have ever imagined. As it would turn out, Dylan Steward was not the only one with news to deliver.

By 9 a.m., the neighborhood free clinic was normally crowded with the area's poor and underprivileged seeking medical help. Murray Silverman, owner of the *San Francisco Free Press*, was in no position to provide medical insurance for his employees, leaving the clinic the only source of medical care for Willow and Dylan Steward. Willow had called ahead to schedule an appointment with Doctor Henderson, the OBGYN who volunteered at the clinic once a week. Willow desperately wanted to see the doctor before saying anything to her husband. Fortunately, her appointment was the same day as her husband's interview with James Donahue. That morning she kissed him goodbye and watched him head out the door of their apartment to a waiting taxi. Once the cab departed, Willow gathered up her knitted gray sweater with a matching wool cap and gloves and started the six-block walk to the clinic. She arrived there just as the doors opened. She had said nothing to her husband about a potential pregnancy. When her normal cycle returned after missing one, she was glad she had not raised any false hopes for either one. However, the severe cramps and heavy bleeding resulting from her next menstrual cycle caused her grave concern.

Through grants and donations, the University of California Medical Center had renovated an old two-story office building near Haight and Castro into a free health clinic. The University used the facility as both a training center for its interns and a location for the more philanthropic of the medical community in San Francisco to offer their services. There was no dearth of specialists from pediatrics, geriatrics, internists, and general practitioners willing to provide their services to the city's underprivileged and low-income residents. The interior of the clinic reflected the neighborhood and the population it served. The furniture was old and dated. The walls had been repainted, but no amount of paint could completely hide the erosion of decades of use by previous tenants. The janitorial staff did all they could to hide the stains from mysterious liquids, scuff marks, and cracks in the ancient black and white tile floor.

Willow sat alone outside the second-story office of Doctor Linda Henderson, holding a folder with her personal information, which she had received from the receptionist when she checked in. She reflected on her life and why her visit weighed so heavily on her soul. Willow had been raised by bohemian parents, Mitchell, and Marie Corsetti, who ran a coffee/poetry shop in old North Beach called the "It Club." There was no more significance to the name than the fact that it was the cheapest neon sign her parents could afford. Beyond being non-conformists, Mitchell and Marie often allowed their only child to be in the club when Jack Kerouac, Allen Ginsberg, and William S. Burroughs did readings. Above all,

Mitchell and Marie wanted their daughter to grow up free from the organizational constraints of traditional religions. They were more aligned with the non-violent philosophies of Gandhi, Buddha, and the Beatitudes espoused by Jesus Christ. Through the turbulent 60s and early 70s, with the anti-Vietnam demonstrations and the rising civil rights movement tearing the nation apart, Willow was appalled by the phrases, "America, love it or leave it," or "My country, right or wrong." She wanted a better, kinder world, where acts of love and acceptance would replace bigotry and violence. That was what drew her to become a teacher. It was her opportunity to influence young minds to the endless possibilities that lay before them. She wanted to encourage acts of thoughtfulness, not retribution, and see the world not for what it is but for what it could be. Her third grade classroom was the fertile ground to produce just such results.

Providing a sense of organization to a class of twenty-seven third graders was akin to herding cats. Willow had been influenced by the writings of Marie Montessori. She was able to see small cooperative interactions amidst a sea of confusion and chaos to the untrained observer and reinforce those instances for everyone to hear. Those inevitable instances of discontent and dispute among her minions were addressed with equal aplomb. Kneeling in front of the combatants with her arms around their shoulders, Willow would remind them that making good decisions left people happy, and making poor decisions left people sad.

"Are you happy right now?"

Small heads would shake. Tightening her arms a bit around them, Willow would say: "I know both of you are capable of making good decisions, aren't you? And you two are friends, aren't you?"

Amidst the blubbering and tears, heads would nod.

"So, tell me, what was this spat about?"

Whatever had caused the tiff had vaporized in the warmth and tenderness of Willow's arms and soft voice. Small shoulders shrugged. Handing each young warrior a tissue from the small apron she wore, Willow would ask, "So, can we be friends again?"

Former foes became friends without really understanding the dynamics of the situation or strange feelings in their stomachs like a huge disaster had passed by them.

CHAPTER 9

Linda Henderson was a noted specialist in pediatric medicine at the UC Medical Center in San Francisco. Having studied abroad in England and France, where medicine was socialized, she was appalled that her own country was unconcerned about the millions who had no health care. Without the existence of the free clinic and others like it, the underserved population who graced its door would crowd emergency rooms in local hospitals. The free clinic was Henderson's passion. Short in stature, with shoulder-length blonde hair, Henderson was often mistaken for anything but the noted pediatrician she was. Her soft voice was often taken as a sign of weakness in her male-dominated profession. But woe to him who spoke condescendingly to her or disrespected her opinions. Opening her door to the waiting room brought Willow out of her self-induced daydream.

"Mrs. Willow Steward?" asked Henderson, as she glanced at her call sheet of appointments for the day. Her smile illuminated the poorly lit hallway. In a way, she enjoyed this portion of the personal touch. There certainly were no funds to provide a nurse receptionist at the clinic.

The absence of the conventional white coat with a stethoscope hanging out of a side pocket combined with the doctor's complete lack of pretentiousness caused Willow to reply in a questioning tone, "Doctor Henderson?"

It was a reaction to which Henderson was accustomed. Linda Henderson was anything but conventional. She rejected the more traditional doctor's attire for a long-sleeved blouse, tan cotton slacks, and black Birkenstock shoes. Henderson took a seat in the empty chair next to Willow. This sudden intrusion into her personal space startled Willow. Sensing the apprehension she had caused, Dr. Henderson smiled and said, "I much prefer Linda," leaving any reciprocity of informality up to Willow. Henderson's attempt at familiarity eased the startled young woman to the point where Steward replied, "Call me Willow; Mrs. sounds too possessive for my liking." Henderson chuckled at Steward's feminist sense of liberation from traditional titles.

"Then let's go into my office, Willow, and see what brings you here, shall we?"

Feeling more like kindred spirits than the strangers they were, Willow willingly followed Henderson into the doctor's office. By necessity to maximize space in the clinic, Henderson's office was a combination office/examination room. Other volunteer doctors used the area, so there was a minimum of personal items. Against one wall, she had a small wooden desk with a matching swivel chair. There were medical reference books on a shelf behind the desk. On the opposite side of the office was an examination table. Next to it were two cabinets for storage of medical supplies. Henderson directed Willow to one of two soft and well-worn brown leather upholstered chairs near her desk. As Willow glanced around the room, she commented, "It's a bit cramped, isn't it?"

"Space is at a premium," knowing that was an understatement, Henderson chuckled.

It was then that Willow noticed a framed 5x8 photograph on the corner of Henderson's desk. It was of a tall man, sitting on a stool with a guitar leaning against his leg. She focused on the man in the picture, sure that she had seen him before. Seeing the prolonged gaze, Henderson said, "That's my husband, Lawrence." The statement was understated but tinged with warmth.

"That's your husband?" Willow said with the excitement of someone having just recognized some sort of celebrity. "You're married to L.P. Henderson! I do not believe it. I cannot tell you how many times my husband and I have listened to him play at Ghirardelli Square or Buena Vista. My dad used to rave about seeing him perform at the Hungry i. My god, he is a legend in the city."

The exuberant praise from Steward about her husband made Henderson's heart swell with pride. Though renowned in her own right, Linda loved being known as the wife of a well-known local musical legend.

"I'll be sure to pass along your words to him," acknowledged a smiling Henderson. "Now, shall we talk about why you're here?"

Turning her attention back to Henderson, Willow started with her missing period and the unusual amount of bleeding that had occurred. Henderson made a mental note of the heavy vaginal discharge. It was of concern to her.

"When I had my second period, I was pretty sure I was not pregnant, but the bleeding did bother me."

"You were right to worry," responded Henderson.

A concerned look came over the doctor's face as she was about to pose a sensitive but necessary question. As a pediatric specialist, Linda Henderson was keenly aware of the controversy surrounding women's productive rights. She was also a devout Christian which often put her at odds with that issue. She took a deep breath before continuing.

"Willow, some young women who come to the clinic find themselves with an unwanted pregnancy, and they're looking for a… how do I say this delicately, a way out of their predicament."

Instantly realizing what the doctor was suggesting, Willow decried the implication.

"My god, no! I am not here to get an abortion. Nothing in the world would make me happier than to have a child. It's something I've dreamed about all my life."

Willow had surprised even herself with the passion in her words. Henderson had never had children of her own, and thus she relished in the young woman's anticipated joy of prospective motherhood. Willow's words also relieved the doctor of her own moral predicament.

Pleased with her affirmation, Henderson acclaimed, "Then let's get some details, shall we?"

Taking the file that Steward held in her hand, Henderson laid it open on her lap and began with the usual questions a doctor asked; age, telephone number, address, and the dates of the missed periods as accurately as Willow could remember.

"And your husband's name?" asked Henderson.

A beaming smile spread across Steward's face.

"Dylan, Dylan Steward, and he had an interview today at the *L.A. Times* for a reporter's position," she announced excitedly.

"It sounds like there could be a move in your future," smiled Henderson as she jotted down Dylan's name.

"Yes," said her exuberant patient. "He's interviewing for a position on the staff of the *Los Angeles Times*, and that will mean new adventures, new experiences, new everything."

Henderson noted the young woman's pride in speaking of her husband, "Is he as excited as you about being a father?"

A sheepish grin formed on Willow's face. "I haven't said anything to him about missing my periods. I wanted to be sure first."

"Have a seat on the examination table. I'll need to get your blood pressure and a few other vitals."

With the required information entered in the file, Henderson walked over to her desk and pressed a button on the intercom resting there.

"Can you send Helen in to draw some blood, please?"

"Right away," answered Ethel, a volunteer who handled the front desk.

"Is that to see if I'm pregnant?" asked Willow.

The doctor dropped her previous air of non-formality and adopted a more professional tone. The angular nature of her face and the measured way she spoke lent credibility to every word.

"No, from your description of heavy vaginal bleeding, I want to rule out something called placenta previa. It is a condition where the placenta partially or completely obstructs the uterus. It can make a full-term pregnancy difficult and potentially endanger the health of the child and mother."

"Is that something to be concerned about?" asked a now anxious Steward.

Hoping to ease the apparent anxiety in her patient's voice, Henderson said, "For most pregnant women, there is no problem when placenta previa exists. In about 10 percent of the cases where placenta previa is present, pregnant women face possible complications, but as I said, it only affects about 10 percent of pregnant women."

The nurse arrived to take Willow's blood sample, preventing her from asking more questions. Once the blood was drawn, Henderson instructed the nurse to have a flow cytometry done. She immediately noticed a look of puzzlement on Willow's face.

"Don't worry; it's a fancy name for a blood test to determine any irregularities in your blood. It will take about a week or two to get the results back from the lab. I can call you when they come in, or you can stop by the clinic."

Pulling her sleeve down after the blood had been drawn, Willow quickly replied, "Oh, don't bother calling. I do not want to alarm Dylan unnecessarily. He has enough on his mind with the interview and probably moving to LA. I'll come back in a couple of weeks."

Henderson then walked over to her desk and retrieved a medium-size black valise from behind it. She set it on the desktop, opened it, and withdrew several small plastic cylinders from the top tray of the valise. When she turned around to face Willow, she saw a perplexed look on her patient's face.

"Why don't you have a seat at the table?"

Warily, Willow stepped off the examination table and walked to the table. Linda Henderson had dealt with hundreds of women who thought they were pregnant. There were overwhelming fears and questions that awaited each woman as they waited to find out if they were pregnant or not and the complications such a condition would present. Some were not able to deal with the emotional and mental stress. She hoped she would be able to alleviate such an experience of the young woman in her office, though it meant revealing Henderson's manipulation of the Med-center's medical protocol. It was a chance Henderson was willing to take.

"With all the uncertainties in your life right now, your husband's possible new job, relocating to Los Angeles, getting settled in a new home, you do not need to be worrying about a missed period and whether you are pregnant or not. I want to empower you to discover that and share that with your husband without having to find a new doctor and then wait for some lab results to arrive."

Henderson laid the plastic cylinder on the table. Still professional in tone, the doctor now adopted a reassuring aspect to her presentation.

"Warner-Chilcott is one of the largest drug manufacturers in the country. They have developed a home pregnancy kit for women. It is in the final stages of approval by the FDA. They have allowed Warner-Chilcott to make the product available to certain medical schools before it hits the open market for use in their research programs. UC

Med-Center is one of them. This product will revolutionize the ability of women to determine if they are pregnant without clogging the medical testing process. The simplicity of this unit is amazing. All you do is take the strip from inside the cylinder and urinate on it. If it turns blue, you are pregnant. If the solution remains clear, you are not pregnant. I am going to give you two units. Use them sparingly."

Willow Steward was no stranger to carefully crafted language, as her husband often used her to edit his articles before submitting them to his editor. As Henderson put it, these units were made available to women in certain medical schools' research programs, which bothered her. She was not in any such program, nor did she want any special privilege not made available to other women who used the clinic's services.

"Doctor Henderson, I am not in any research program that I know of, and I am really uncomfortable with getting special favors."

Willow's voice was soft yet determined when she uttered her complaint. With the utmost confidence that what she was doing was beyond reproach, and to assuage Steward's fear of conscience, Henderson replied, "Willow, in no way do I want you to feel conflicted with what I am doing. As far as being in a specific research program, you are not. However, I have informed my superiors that I do use certain generic data that does not jeopardize patient confidentiality, from my work here at the clinic in analyzing statistical data as to the variations in the level of care provided to patients in different geographic sections of the city. So, in a broad sense, you are involved in medical research. As far as receiving special favors, I am not giving you anything that I would not make available to any of my patients here at the clinic in a similar situation."

The doctor had returned to her professional manner. Not entirely convinced by Henderson's logic which in some respects appeared to be self-serving, Willow reluctantly accepted the products. It would at least give her immediate answers to the question of being pregnant and thereby eliminate one or more trips to a doctor in what would be an already hectic transition to LA for her husband's anticipated new job.

"If I ever get a positive result, do you want me to contact you, I mean for your research?"

Smiling at what she thought was a tacit understanding of the rule twisting that had taken place, the doctor threw her head back and stated her response in a near comic manner, "Absolutely!"

Carefully placing the cylinders in the pocket of her gray shawl, Willow thanked the doctor. She glanced down at the thin wristwatch with the simple leather band. She had owned it even before she knew her husband. This simple item had marked so many important events in her life. Its tiny hands signaled it was time to perhaps share a most important bit of news with her husband. Willow commented, "Dylan's return flight lands in less than half an hour. I had better be on my way. Thank you again, Doctor."

CHAPTER 10

Dylan Steward spent the entire flight home working through the mental maze of what would need to be done within the next few weeks—find a place to live, arrange transportation of their belongings, transfer their bank account, try to find a new teaching job for Willow—and that just scratched the surface. Steward would need a whole new wardrobe. His collection of faded jeans, madras shirts, and casual tennis shoes would quickly identify him as one ill-suited for the prestigious position he had just received. As his 1955 white Citroen sedan with over 190,000 miles groaned its way through the later afternoon traffic along US 101 north across to the 287 and down toward Haight, Steward knew a replacement car was also in their future. The once vivid paint on the car was now powdery and flaked off at the touch of a hand. This reflected the lack of attention to such details as waxing a car. However, even he had noticed the ever-growing areas where the paint was completely absent, as much the product of a sea air environment as anything. Trying to cover all his bases, he speculated that Willow might need a car of her own if she should land a teaching job.

As he turned onto Haight, Steward could not believe his eyes.

The first miracle of the day was having Jimmy Donahue tell him he had gotten the job. The second miracle was finding an empty parking spot only two blocks from home. Street parking was at a premium in most San Francisco neighborhoods. Suddenly amid a line of dated vehicles—a multi-colored VW bus, its sister vehicle a VW bug, several other older model cars—the parking "gods" had blessed him with an open spot two blocks from his home. Ignoring the yellow light, he raced through the intersection to secure the vacant space. The thought of needing a new car was reaffirmed as the engine in the old Citroen hissed and pinged when he turned off the ignition. The Podestas kept their vehicle parked in their small driveway, leaving Dylan and his wife to fend for themselves. His long legs gobbled up the distance to their home in no time at all; then, he bounded up the steps to the front door. As he opened the front door, he was met by the aroma of some mysterious Italian delicacy emanating from the kitchen. No doubt, Mrs. Podesta had made dinner for them again. He noticed Willow's gray shawl on the floor next to the sofa. Her cap lay on the coffee table. *Odd*, he thought, as his wife was usually very particular about routinely using the hall tree for such items. Willow was not in the living room. Perhaps she was napping, the result of another exhausting migraine.

He called out from the living room, "Honey, I'm home."

From the hallway bathroom, he heard her respond, "I'll be right out, sweetheart," with a tone of trepidation in her voice.

WILLOW STEWARD GAZED into the mirror above the bathroom sink. Was this a dream come true or a nightmare in the making. At the sound of her husband's voice, she buried the angst that had panged in her heart. She wet her hands and dabbed the tears in the corner of her eyes. As she hurried down the short hallway from the bathroom to the living room, she thought only of the other news she wanted to share with her husband. From the glow on her face and the electrified tone in her voice, Dylan knew good news was imminent.

"Have I got something to tell you!" she practically screamed.

Twirling her around, her feet dangling in the air, he announced his own surprise, "Well, so do I."

They were both electrified from the adrenaline-induced moment, but for different reasons. After letting her feet hit the floor and regaining a sense of equilibrium, Dylan slowed things down. Gazing into his wife's loving eyes with his own, he quietly said, "You go first, my love."

Before releasing her arms from around his neck, Willow gave him a slight nibble on his ear. She leaned back and said, "No, honey. You go first." Her round face was wrinkled in a manner that implied a determination that her husband had long learned to honor.

Settling down on their small couch whose springs squeaked in protest, Dylan said, "Do you think you'd like to learn how to surf?"

Another screech from his wife caused Dylan's eardrums to ache.

"I knew it! The moment I got home, I knew it!"

All pretense of seriousness abandoned; she expressed her joy as would a child. Puzzled at his wife's sudden gift of ESP, Steward gave her a sideways glance as if she were being interrogated by a policeman, "And how exactly did you know that?"

Willow leaned to the end table next to the couch and picked up a small notepad. She quickly moved it to her folded knees and, with an adolescent like outburst of glee, announced, "I no sooner got home than the phone rang. It was Jimmy Donahue from the *L.A. Times*. Anyway…" she paused to curtail her excitement and catch her breath, "He gave me the name of a man who might be able to help us find a place to live temporarily, and a woman's name who Mr. Donahue said might be able to help me find a teaching job. Here are the names. I could not believe how helpful he was, Dylan. This is going to be the adventure of a lifetime!"

Dylan took the notepad from his wife. He looked intently at the names she had written down, Larry Corrigan and Edith Cranston. The puzzled look on his face caused Willow to ask, "Do you know either of them?"

"I've never heard of Larry Corrigan. Edith Cranston is somewhat familiar. I just cannot put my finger on where I heard it. But if they'll wind up helping us find a place to live and maybe a job for you, that will eliminate a couple of issues in my mind."

It had been some time since Dylan had seen his wife so full of wonderment and cheer. Some greeted each day hoping to get through it, like factory line workers facing eight hours of repetitive, robotic movements. Willow Steward was the antithesis of such an outlook. She had an undefeatable spirit of optimism that led her to embrace the unknown with the excitement of a child in Disneyland for the first time. Her imagination had no boundaries. It lit the darkness of the unknown with shining and sparkling possibilities. Her husband was a bit more methodical and analytical in his life vision. Preparation and planning lessened the chance of failure and disappointment, yet he had to admit that her demeanor was a joy to behold.

Always the one to counter her husband's focus on problems, Willow sounded more than a bit exasperated. Infusing her sense of optimism into his thought process was always a challenge for her as one who saw a silver lining in every cloud in the sky.

"Honestly, Dylan, try looking at things from my perspective for once. Do you feel better when you focus on some list of issues, meaning problems, or when you think about the wonderful opportunities that lay before you?"

The excitement of his new job quickly began to fade as he felt peppered with another of Willow's life messages. Sounding a bit frustrated at playing a student to Willow, the teacher, he begrudgingly responded, "Obviously the latter."

Willow was not about to surrender the advantage she had with her husband's admission. With enough assertiveness to sound encouraging yet not pushy, she said, "Then let's call them and see what issues they can help us with."

As Dylan reached for the phone, his propensity to avoid uncertainty reared its ugly head.

"Honey, what if they've already left work?"

Now more determined than ever to force her husband to see uncertainty in a more positive light, Willow placed her hands on his cheeks and said with her usual characteristic optimism, "What makes you think these are their work numbers? Maybe they are their home phone numbers."

Finding himself unable to develop a defensible response, Dylan resigned himself to the obvious.

"Give me the phone."

As Dylan began dialing the first number, Willow announced joyously, "I'll get us a glass of wine and check on dinner."

As she bounded toward the kitchen, she heard her husband say, "Mr. Corrigan, my name is Dylan Steward. I was given your number by Jimmy Donahue of the *Times*. He said you might be able to help me and my wife find a place to live in LA. I've just been hired for a job with *The Times*, and we'll be moving down there soon."

Willow had yet to pour the second glass of wine when she heard her husband say excitedly, "Sure, the bartender at Lefty's. I remember you."

There were a few minutes of silence before her husband erupted, "You've got to be kidding me. I can't tell you what this means to us, Mr. Corrigan!"

Another pause and then, "Yes, I understand, Mr. Corrigan. Larry, it is. Wait till I tell my wife! Thank you again, Larry."

Unlike her husband, who doubted any divine presence in the world, Willow looked upward and whispered, "Thank you, God."

She had just set the tray of ravioli casserole on the stove top to cool. The bubbling red sauce and golden-brown cheese topping needed to rest for a minute or two.

"Honey, you won't believe what this Corrigan guy had to say!"

See, I told you so, she thought to herself. "I'll be right there," she called out. With two glasses of wine in hand, Willow headed to the living room, where she found her husband pacing back and forth. The excitement and anticipation of what he had to tell her had sent him into a severe attack of attention deficit disorder. Setting their wine on their plank coffee table, Willow said, "Ok, share!"

Funny, he thought, as he looked around the apartment, I had forgotten how small this place is. Normally sedate, with his emotions always under control, Dylan could hardly contain himself. He began to shiver a bit and stutter a bit.

"Mr. Corrigan, I mean Larry," remembering the admonishment he had received on the phone, "owns the bar where I met Mr. Donahue after my interview. Anyway, he owns a two-bedroom bungalow with a small office space in a place called Venice Beach. It is only a couple of blocks off the beach. You, I mean we, could even learn to surf. Larry said it is kind of an artist's hangout too. It has shops, markets, street vendors, everything you ever dreamed of, and has lots of musician hangouts!"

In addition to pleasing her husband, the description he painted made it look like paradise on earth to Willow. She wondered if the other name would yield the same wild euphoria.

"And what about the other name? What was it, Edith Cranston?"

His adrenaline rush had blocked Dylan's ability to process Willow's meaning.

"Oh yeah, her. I remember where I heard her name. She interviewed for the position I got at the *Times*. We exchanged names before she went in for her interview."

Unable to chide him for his mental lapse, Willow gently said, "Honey, I mean, what did she have to say when you called?"

"Damn!" Dylan responded, realizing he had only done half of what Willow had instructed him, "I'll call right now."

With Willow sitting at his side, he dialed the number for Cranston. After several rings, Dylan said, "Yes, is this Edith Cranston?"

The smile on his face told Willow he had reached the right person.

"Ms. Cranston, this is Dylan Steward. Jimmy Donahue of the *L.A.Times* gave me your name. I was recently hired as a reporter there, and Mr. Donahue thought you might be able to help my wife find a teaching job."

Dylan listened for barely more than a minute and then said, "Well, yes, as a matter-of-fact, she is. She's sitting next to me as we speak."

Dylan listened and then said to Willow, "She wants to talk with you," handing her the phone. The phone was the typical analog unit of the period. It was a generic beige color.

It was now Willow's turn to control her own anxiety. It is not easy to practice what you preach. Willow Steward was determined that whatever this stranger had to say, it would be positive, even a positive uncertainty if there were such a phrase. Her manner was, as always, warm and engaging.

"This is Willow Steward," Willow said. As she cradled the phone against her shoulder, she reached out and squeezed Dylan's hand.

The rest of the conversation consisted of Willow responding yes, yes, yes, and yes. With each affirmation, the excitement in her voice rose, her eyes seemed to widen, and the smile on her face spread ear to ear until she exploded, "Oh my god. Edith, I do not know how to thank you. I just cannot believe this. I just cannot! Of course, I will send you copies of my degree and credentials tomorrow, and I can have letters of recommendation sent to you as well if needed. Thank you again, and yes, I look forward to meeting you as well."

Willow let the phone slip from her hand, letting the coiled cord absorb the shock of contact with the floor. She put her arms around Dylan, pulling him close to her, so close he could feel her breath on his face. Willow was always sincere, but even more so as she gushed, "I love you, Dylan Steward."

It was classic Willow Steward. Affirm to others all the goodness you can before basking in your own happiness. Having satisfied her belief that others come before self, Willow let her inhibitions go to the wayside. In a voice loud enough to alarm the Podesta's in the unit above them, Willow screamed, "I have a job, Dylan. I've got a job!"

This time it was Dylan's turn to get clarification.

"Could you connect the dots for me?" he asked.

After taking a healthy sip of her wine, enough to make her cough, Willow explained.

"Edith Cranston teaches English at Venice High School. Her brother, Joe, is the principal at Broadway Elementary School. It is one of the oldest elementary schools in the district. A lot of its students come from underprivileged families."

"Could we get to the job, please!" said Dylan, who was totally uninterested in any relationship between the caller and the school principal or any school demographics.

Startled back to reality, Willow replied, "Oh yeah, the job. A third grade teacher at Broadway is taking a year off for maternity leave, and they are looking for a long-term substitute. The best news is that according to Edith, her husband does not think the teacher is coming back, so the position will most likely turn out to be permanent, but I still have to interview."

"So we still don't know for sure it will be permanent, do we?" asked Dylan.

From the look in her eyes, he knew instantly he had digressed back to his old ways. Before she could say anything, he quickly added, "Then permanent it will be, sweetheart."

CHAPTER 11

Jimmy Donahue strolled into the lobby of the Times Building promptly at 6 a.m. and headed directly to the magazine/newspaper stand run by Willis Carpenter.

"Good morning, Willis," greeted Donahue.

"Good morning to you, Mr. Donahue," smiled Willis as he handed Donahue his copy of the *New York Daily Times*. The noted columnist for that paper, Jimmy Breslin, had been a long-time favorite of Donahue's who deemed Breslin's perception of political and societal hypocrisy to be near genius.

The formality of Willis's greeting offended Donahue, considering the decades they had known each other. Donahue considered Willis more than just some human vending machine to do business with each day. He genuinely thought of the man as a friend. Donahue replied, "Hell Willis, after all these years, you can't call me Jimmy?"

Coming from a generation where a first-name basis by a black man to a white man would have been considered a death penalty offense by some in his native south, Willis smiled and whispered, "Old habits die hard, Jimmy."

Taking the copy of the *Daily Times* from Willis, Donahue

handed him a ten-dollar bill and replied, "Some should have died long ago, my friend."

Donahue recognized a large canvas tote bag by the corner of the small counter from which Willis conducted business.

"Another painting?" asked Donahue.

Willis smiled. "It keeps me busy when I'm home. You know that old saying, *Idle hands are the devil's workshop?*"

The two men laughed at the often-quoted phrase from Proverbs 16, verse 27.

"How did you ever get interested in painting anyway, Willis?"

Jimmy Donahue was one of the few human beings who knew of Carpenter's passion for painting. In his heart, Donahue knew there was a fascinating story behind the black man's talent. Willis spoke rather furtively.

"The time in that Paris hospital at the end of the war changed a lot of things for me, Jimmy."

Donahue stared into the black man's eyes. Willis stared back. The memories of both men caused a redness to spread through the whites of their eyes.

"It did for a lot of us, my friend. May I see it?" asked Donahue, referring to the painting in the canvas bag.

Willis glanced around the lobby, hoping to avoid the curious eyes of people arriving to work. He motioned Donahue to come forward, then turned his back to shield his work from others. His artificial right leg locked as he picked up the tote bag and withdrew a rectangular canvas frame. His long fingers with enlarged knuckles struggled to hold onto the canvas. A bit of scoliosis prevented Willis from standing erect. He held it at waist level, again to avoid prying eyes. Old milky-colored eyes searched Donahue's face for a reaction. Donahue let out an audible gasp. It took a moment for him to respond.

"My god, Willis," was all he could muster.

The picture displayed a lightning bolt splitting the canvas in half. The light illuminated part of the canvas on each side. The far-left half of the canvas showed the sun slowly rising over the horizon, slaves in a sea of blooming cotton plants worked their way down the rows, their backs stooped from dragging long bags of the man's white product. An overseer on horseback behind them monitored their progress with a bullwhip in hand. The evil on his face was fully reflected in the painting. Closer to the lightning bolt, a small boy was on his hands and knees looking to the heavens, tears rolling down his cheeks, etching trails through the red dust covering his face. His eyes were pleading that this would not be his destiny. On the other side of the lightning bolt, a black woman with her son in hand walked down a city sidewalk. The boy looked back over his shoulder at a drinking fountain they had just passed with a sign on it reading, "Whites Only." Bewilderment in his eyes, he watched a white man bend over to take a drink from the spigot

"Makes you wonder if Dylan was right when he sang "The Times They Are A-Changin'," sighed Donahue, with a deep sense of submission that the answer to his rhetorical question was, "not much."

Willis Carpenter had his own profound answer to Donahue's philosophical statement.

"The times don't change by themselves, Jimmy."

With a shoulder shrug of resignation, Donahue nodded. Then he noticed the initials in the lower right-hand corner of the painting. He smiled to himself, thinking, *That's Willis.*

"You have a good day, my friend," Donahue said as he turned and headed to the elevator.

"You too," spoke Willis affectionately.

In his office once again, Donahue laid his copy of the *New York Daily Press* on top of a notepad on his desk. He shuffled through the paper to find Breslin's column. When he saw it, he uncapped the cup of coffee he had purchased at the food and drink kiosk in the lobby. He took a sip of his coffee, ordered black with no cream, and settled into Breslin's latest journalistic gem. After thoroughly enjoying the political witticism of his favorite columnist, Donahue put the paper aside. He glanced at his watch, a thirty-year-old A-II military special gifted to him by a GI friend returning from WWII. Good, plenty of time before he had to meet them, but first his morning coffee and a date with Breslin.

D­YLAN AND W­ILLOW had spent the previous night at a Motel 6 just off the 405 freeway in downtown Los Angeles and then met Corrigan at his place of employment, Lefty's, the next day. For Willow, walking inside the archaic saloon (a term Corrigan preferred to bar) was like stepping back in time. Willow was a true aficionado of the classic 40s and 50s movies like "The Maltese Falcon," "Murder She Wrote," and "Philip Marlow." She could visualize Robert Mitchum sitting at one of the dark booths, a burning cigarette dangling from his lips, its smoke spiraling upward as he stared into the eyes of a sumptuous redhead sitting across from him. Or maybe Humphrey Bogart gazing into a whiskey bottle, trying to burn the memory of a lost love from his inebriated mind. Corrigan had planned for their visit by having the night bartender come in early. He remembered Dylan from his visit with Jimmy Donahue.

"Nice to see you again, kid," Corrigan called out from a booth where he was sitting when the two entered his establishment. "Have a seat."

"Mr. Corrigan, I'd like you to meet my wife, Willow. Honey, Mr. Corrigan is a friend of Jimmy Donahue, my new boss."

Always the gentleman, Corrigan slid out of the booth to shake Willow's hand. Glad to be out of his work attire of a starched white shirt and red bowtie, Corrigan sported a more casual V-neck argyle sweater, gray slacks, and matching loafers.

"Has anyone ever told you that you resemble a blonde version of Cher?" Corny or not, the line had the intended effect.

Willow blushed at the comparison to half of the duo Sonny and Cher. Dressed in soft leather boots, jeans, and a light tan vest worn over a flowered long-sleeved blouse, at five foot two, Willow was indeed a shorter version of the sultry diva.

"That's so sweet, Mr. Corrigan, but I'm no Cher," responded the modest recipient of Corrigan's praise. "But thank you anyway." Embarrassed or not, she still enjoyed the comparison.

"How much time did Jimmy give you before you have to report to work?"

"A month," replied Dylan, "which is about how long my severance package from my old job will last."

A slight sigh indicated he hoped that it would be sufficient time to complete their relocation.

"Then let's get started," responded an eager Corrigan. As he stood up, he comically said to Willow, "Mr. Corrigan was my father, Willow. Out of some misplaced sense of propriety, my mother christened me Laurence, but I'm Larry to my friends."

Willow responded with a smile and a nod.

"My car is out back," said Corrigan, as he led Dylan and his wife out the back entrance of the saloon to the parking area in the back. The sight of a new Cadillac Coupe Deville took Dylan's breath away.

"I've never seen one of these up close," he said with awe and wonderment.

Corrigan laughed. "One of the things I did not inherit from my father was a sense of thrift when it came to vehicles. It seems appropriate for a man of my station in life."

He continued to chuckle about his self-deprecating and facetious remark.

Dylan mused at Corrigan's obvious attempt to glamorize the position of bartender. With Dylan in the passenger seat and Willow in the back seat snuggling into the softest tuck and roll upholstery she had ever felt, Corrigan headed to the 110 south and then onto the 10 West. He covered roughly seventeen miles in about thirty minutes thanks to a 478 cubic inch V-8 engine and no fear of the California Highway Patrol. The first of Dylan's several issues, a more palatable term than problems, disappeared completely when Larry Corrigan drove up to the front of the beach bungalow in Venice Beach. Corrigan could hear Willow sigh as he pulled up in front of the Spanish-style bungalow on Echo Street, about three blocks from the ocean.

"It is absolutely beautiful," she said as she hurriedly exited the Caddy.

The property manager had been meticulous in maintaining the front and back yard. A trail of stepping-stones meandered from the sidewalk across a lush green lawn that had been neatly trimmed from around the stones. A red tile roof, two arched windows with wooden grids, ledges consisting of red bricks, and a rough-hewn door of dark oak with large wrought iron hinges put one in the mood of old Spanish California. Two red clay flowerpots hung from a thick wooden cross beam that spanned a surprisingly large patio in the front of the house. It was all Willow could do to keep herself from rushing past Corrigan and into what appeared to be the house of her dreams. Seeing the gleam in her eyes, Corrigan said, "Wait till you see the inside, and the backyard has a few surprises of its own."

When he opened the door, Willow could not contain herself. She let go of Dylan's hand and marched straight into her dream. And dream it was! The doorways were typical Spanish-Mediterranean; arched instead of square as in conventional American homes. They had been finished off with small tile squares around their entire dimensions. The walls were cream-colored texture, European hardwood floors ran throughout the house. There was a small open-hearth fireplace against one wall. At one end of the hearth was a brass tub filled with pieces of oak. There was a set of fireplace tools with a brass handled broom, a wrought iron poker, and a small shovel at the other end. Willow turned around slowly, envisioning where their furniture would fit. Corrigan gave the young woman sufficient time to savor the moment, then said, "Let me show you the kitchen, Willow," succumbing to his traditional sense of a woman's role in a home. Willow was anything but traditional when it came to the role of a man and a woman in the domicile. Without sounding offended or overly sensitive to Corrigan's outdated views of men and women, Willow said, "Dylan, come see the place where you'll work your magic." Smiling at Corrigan, Willow added, "Dylan's a great cook."

His last tenant, an artist, had been meticulous in keeping the entire house pristine, especially the kitchen. The white enamel four-burner gas stove was spotless. When Willow opened the oven door, she found even the broiler pan looked new. The counter tops consisted of small-flowered tiles. No amount of cleaning could hide some of the chipped tiles or the discolored grout, but that only added to the charm for Willow. The aqua green Sears refrigerator had been defrosted and thoroughly cleaned. The dining area was small but adequate for their needs. A wine rack made from a piece of driftwood on the wall added to the charm for Willow. A small wrought iron flower stand occupied the corner of the dining area.

Grinning with the obvious pleasure that the tour was bringing, Corrigan asked, "Would you like to see the backyard?"

"You go, Dylan. I want to see the rest of the house."

The adventurous Willow headed down a narrow hallway while Corrigan and Dylan went through the French doors leading to the backyard. The first room she came to was the bathroom to her left. Willow was enamored with its art deco style. The sea-green bathtub had a matching pedestal sink with a glass door medicine cabinet hung above the sink. Hand towels hung on rings to the left of the sink. Opposite the sink was the steam heater and a towel rack above it. Next to the steam heater was a small antique three-drawer stand, ideal for extra towels and a roll of toilet paper or two. Opposite the bathroom was the master bedroom. It took Willow's breath away. Dark wood beams across the ceiling accented the Spanish-style architecture. An arched door made of wood similar to the ceiling beams led to an unusually large closet. Plenty of room for all our clothes, Willow thought. Thin white cotton drapes were pulled back over French doors that opened onto the backyard. Yes, our bed will fit fine, she mused as she turned slowly to see every nuance of the room. Willow went back to the hallway to inspect the second bedroom adjacent to the bathroom. She let her imagination run wild when she entered. Against one wall was an arched desk area outlined with red brick, perfect for a work area for her or Dylan. This room was every bit as large as their room, convincing Willow there was plenty of space for Dylan's collection of guitars. Willow leaned back against the wall and visualized what her dream come true would look like; a crib with a carousel hanging over it, a rocking chair next to it, and a toy box filled with all the joys a child would want. This was a vision she would keep to herself for the time being.

Standing on the small patio off the dining area, Dylan thought, *He was not kidding about the backyard.* The lot was somewhat narrow but long. There were two small fruit trees at the back of the yard, one lime and one orange. Against the wall of the garage, someone had constructed a brick barbeque with an arched hood over the pit. The la touché finale, though, was an old wooden hot tub. Someone had ingeniously taken a fifty-five-gallon steel drum and welded a circular metal plate eighteen inches from the bottom. This made the top two-thirds a leak-proof water tank. The bottom one-third held a flat iron grate for burning wood. A section of two-inch PVC pipe took the heated water from the bottom of the water section into a small electric pump. Near the top of the water tank, a section of PVC pipe returned the water into the heating tank. A long yellow extension cord was neatly rolled up next to the pump. It took no time at all for Dylan to spot the electrical outlet at the edge of the patio as the power source. Dylan envisioned an evening sky full of stars, a bottle of wine, and two naked bodies enjoying any number of aquatic positions of love. His exotic daydream was interrupted by the voice of his wife. She gushed with excitement and anticipation of making this their new home.

"Oh, Dylan! This place is perfect! I know just where our bedroom furniture will go! The second bedroom is perfect for your music room and an office if need be."

Almost immediately, Willow found herself lost in the fantasy of motherhood. There was not much for Corrigan to do. He tried to bring the couple back to earth with the mundane.

"When do the movers arrive with your stuff?"

"Allied Movers is holding our stuff at their storage lot in Glendale. They said to give them a call when we found a place."

"Then let's not waste any more time. Glendale is about twenty-five miles away. Give them a call. Here are the keys to the house. Drop off a check for the first month's rent at my place in a couple of days," said Corrigan. He was seemingly as pleased as the young couple.

"But what about a deposit?" asked Dylan, back to his careful, analytical demeanor.

"Already taken care of," smiled Corrigan without revealing the mysterious benefactor.

"Before you go, Larry, can you tell me how far we are from Broadway Elementary School?" Dylan asked.

The question brought Willow out of her dream state, and feeling the need to explain; she said, "Oh, I'm seeing someone there about a possible teaching job, and with one car between us, it would be great if it were within walking distance of this house."

The young woman's infectious spirit had taken hold of Corrigan. Quick to read people, he found himself captivated by her optimism and humility, and liking nothing better than to answer her question; he said, "If five blocks due east aren't too far, you two will do just fine with one car."

To himself, Dylan thought, how lucky can we get? On the other hand, Willow was not so inclined to contain her feelings. She literally jumped into Corrigan's arms, shouting with glee, "Thank you,

Larry! Thank you so much!" as if he were personally responsible for locating the school so close to their home.

"No thanks necessary, Willow," replied Corrigan, who was now blushing over Willow's unexpected display of affection. His hardened exterior had quietly melted away.

Corrigan departed, leaving his newest tenants to dream of the home to be. Neither one realized the tribulations that lay before them. Not Dylan, whose emergence as the latest addition to the *Los Angeles Times* would jeopardize his position there as well as Jimmy Donahue's. Nor Willow, whose pursuit of her dream would jeopardize her life.

CHAPTER 12

Willow awoke in her motel room bed, completely energized by the previous day's events. She was interviewing for a possible new job, and Dylan would be orchestrating the movers as to what goes where in their new home. With their clothes already packed in their Citron, Dylan went to the manager's office to settle their bill.

Foregoing her usual bohemian attire, Willow decided to dress a bit more conventionally for her interview. Her black and white 3" heels added a few inches to her 5'2" height. She wore a pair of green slacks with a wide black belt. A white blouse with a slightly raised collar capped off what she thought would be a professional yet stylish appearance. What was that expression, she thought, as she turned slowly in front of the mirror in their one-bedroom motel room, "You never get a second chance to make a first impression."

The cool mid-morning breeze wafting off the ocean was the perfect complement to the warmth of the rising sun to the east. Willow insisted Dylan let her walk from their home so she could see for herself the effects of a five-block walk in three-inch heels.

She was prepared for the worst, carrying her favorite pair of Birkenstock sandals in her large woven shoulder bag.

Dylan sat in an Adirondack chair on the front patio. Its sun-bleached blue paint was badly chipped. A well-worn seat pad protected Steward from numerous splinters pointed in the direction of his posterior. He sipped his coffee, a parting gift from the Motel 6 lobby. Willow came out of the front door. Standing in front of her husband, she turned slowly, seeking a reaction to her attire for the interview.

"Well, what do you think?" she said, her hands on her hips and her head tilted slowly side to side.

Sensing he had better respond to her posturing with the appropriate compliment, he gushed, "I think you'll knock them dead." Dylan smiled as he stood up to give his wife a good luck kiss and hug.

Never one to take anything for granted, Dylan said, "Have you thought about what kind of questions they'll ask? You know, scenarios about how you'd handle this situation or that situation?"

His arms were folded across his chest as if he were interrogating someone for information. His eyes strained with the anticipation of someone expecting precise, detailed answers. Willow seemed surprised, even shocked, by Dylan's bluntness. Her feelings were a bit hurt. Did he not have faith in her? His tone and body language would not dissuade her. The forever optimist gave him a mocking sneer.

"Really? I've taught third grade for five years. Unless this school has some form of alien seven-year-old, I've seen just about every behavior or situation you can name. And I know a teachable moment when I see one."

Her exasperation at his question left him feeling more than a bit embarrassed. Attempting to regain her favor, Dylan said, "Never doubted it for a moment, sweetheart." The penitent tone in his voice made her smile.

"I've got to be going. Good luck with the movers."

With that, Willow Steward turned on her heels and began her five-block walk to her new school. It was there she found the love of her life, children. Dylan sat back down in his dilapidated chair. The movers were not due for about half an hour. With Willow gone, his mind returned to a sweet soft jazz riff his brain was arranging. His fingers drummed slowly on his knee as his brain worked through diminished 7th passing tones with a chromatic bass line to build a rising melodic tension. Steward had always thought of music more as an avocation than something to pursue full time. Even the encouragement to do something more with his ability from the guys in the small jazz ensemble he played with in San Francisco went unheeded. What he could not deny was the rush of adrenaline when his fingers moved effortlessly through a difficult and challenging chord progression. Reading sheet music was unnecessary when something in your soul told you to play that passing chord or hold that solo for one more count. Yes, he had a talent for writing, and he enjoyed it, but nothing filled his heart and soul with a sense of completeness like music. For any other human being, his passion for music would be called a dream. His wife recognized it. Every time he played, she saw that ethereal gaze in his eyes. Music took him to a surreal place immune from the pains and struggles of everyday life. Dylan Steward could not bring himself to call his passion a dream. After all, what good did dreaming do his friend Tommy whose death in Vietnam ended any chance of his dreams coming true, or Nathan Strauss, who could not find the strength to fight to maintain his dream of owning his own newspaper. To dream required Dylan Steward to embrace the uncertain, and that was a requirement he kept at arm's length.

On the other hand, Willow Steward was a different kind of animal. She was drawn to the uncertain by the potential of what it could be. The "bird in the hand" could never quell her curiosity about "the two in the bush." She was mesmerized by any discussion or topic that started with the interrogative, "What if…."

She was two blocks away when she caught sight of Broadway

Elementary School. She shielded her eyes from the rising sun to get a clearer vision of the main building. The long rectangular building with a red tile roof and white stucco walls reflected the influence of the early Spanish settlers in California. Red hummingbird sage plants filled in the space at the base of the walls. A well-maintained lawn that ran the length of the building was split in the middle by faded gray steps leading up to matching gray double doors. Up both sides of the entrance doors and across the top were large, flowered tiles. Her pace quickened when she heard the rapture of children's voices emanating from behind the main building. No doubt there was a large playground with swing sets, a basketball court or two, and an expansive area for games of tag, races, or whatever imaginative activities the creative minds of young children could conjure up.

Willow stepped inside the entrance doors and was met by a smallish man with a bald head trimmed with silver hair and thick black-framed glasses. He wore a corduroy sports coat over a long-sleeved white shirt and a blue tie with a fish embroidered on it. His smile was infectious.

"You must be Willow Steward," he said, extending his hand to Willow. "My name is Joe Skaff. I'm the principal. It is my pleasure to welcome you to our school."

Extending her hand to meet his, Willow was gracious in her reply. "Thank you, Mr. Skaff. I'm excited to be here."

Noticing the embroidered symbol on his tie, she added, "I love your tie. That stitching is amazing."

Humble to a fault, Skaff leaned forward to speak softly, "The separation of church and state in public schools requires the most subtle expression of my faith. I sincerely hope I have not offended you."

"Certainly not, Mr. Skaff. After all, the reason for the heavens is a place for that higher authority, don't you think?" She answered with a smile,

Skaff felt relieved. He often found it difficult not to proselytize others. However, that urge had been permanently stifled when Skaff took a summer course in school law to complete his Master's in Education. The two US Supreme Courts cases, Wisconsin v. Yoder and Sherbert v. Verner, made any comments about one's faith something teachers and administrators should avoid at all cost, lest they become the next test case before the highest court in the land.

"Well then, let me show you around."

Skaff took Willow into the school office to introduce her to the school secretary, Lois Tipton. Tipton had retired following the death of her husband, Kent Tipton. In time, she found the calling to return to her former profession as an elementary school teacher too strong to avoid, with one exception. Long days, grading papers, and developing lesson plans no longer held the allure it had in the past. But being around children and fellow teachers burned as bright as ever in her heart. When the previous school secretary retired, Lois applied for the position, and Skaff jumped at the opportunity to bring the experienced educator back. School secretary was an ex officio teacher, enforcer of rules, and consoler of frightened, scared children, and thus Lois Tipton was the perfect match.

"Lois, I'd like you to meet Willow Steward. She's here about the vacant third grade position behind Sherry Adam's pregnancy leave."

The tall Tipton towered over the diminutive Steward.

"Welcome to Broadway, Willow. I am sure you'll love it here," beamed the secretary as she extended her hand to Steward.

"Well, I still have the interview to get through," replied a bashful and prospective young teacher.

"Yeah, the interview!" laughed Tipton, much to the chagrin of Skaff.

"Shall we continue with the tour?" urged Skaff before his secretary revealed more not-so-well-kept secrets.

Skaff began describing each classroom, the teacher, and grade level as they walked down the long hallway. Willow was particularly pleased when Skaff described the freedom that allowed each teacher to modify the state-mandated curriculum to their student's needs. Occasionally, Willow had questions of her own. Could they supplement the mandated curriculum with materials of their own choosing? Could they modify the presentation of material to maximize a student's strongest modality? As they continued their tour, the clamor from some classrooms was like music to Willow's ears. An active class was a sign of learning taking place for Steward. She heard the teacher's voice giving instructions about the activity at hand or reading from some book from other classrooms. She visualized herself in their place. They had no sooner reached the end of the hallway when a loud bell echoed.

"Recess time," responded Skaff. "Let's get out of the way," he added as he guided Steward next to a hallway fountain.

Like a school of fish making their way upstream, children crowded the hallway as they headed out the double doors leading to the playground behind the building. The excitement in the air over the opportunity to pick sides in some game or to engage with friends outside the peering eyes of their classroom teacher caused many to move at a rapid and unsafe pace, causing Skaff to call out a warning.

"Save the running for outside!" Skaff said firmly.

It was obviously a warning the children had heard before, as the flow of raucous children slowed immediately.

"It doesn't take much," he said, smiling at Willow, who in turn smiled back.

After finishing their tour of the building, Skaff took Willow to his office. Willow chuckled to herself when she saw the sign painted on his office door. It read, "Principal Joe," no last name. She loved the informality. It was the smallest office for a principal Willow had ever seen; one large desk of unknown vintage, and a long conference table with chairs at various angles, indicating to Willow a meeting had recently ended. In adherence to district protocol, one wall held pictures of the state secretary of education, the district superintendent, and nine other elementary school principals. Behind his desk, a four-foot-high bookcase ran the length of the room. On it, several photographs were displayed. One caught Willow's attention. It was Skaff in a yellow and gold cap and gown next to a woman, both holding up their degrees. Several others showed Joe, his wife Terri, and their four children over special family trips. Skaff quickly gathered several files left on the table from an early meeting.

"The paperwork never ends, Willow," he sighed in mock frustration. "Please, have a seat."

Placing the files back on top of the bookcase behind his desk, Skaff picked up another file from his desktop and returned to the table. The anxious teacher prospect nervously awaited him. Opening the file, he said in a rather matter-of-fact tone, "Any new job has tons of documentation to go with it, Willow. This package contains the district's mission statement, a directory of personnel from the superintendent down to the bus drivers, the all-important medical plan, and lastly, the district's pay scale. There are forms for you to fill out for medical coverage, taxes, and contact information. I don't want to rush you, but your assignment starts next Monday, and I'd like to have these back before you start."

Stunned at the presentation of this material with the implication that the job was hers, Willow nervously asked, "Mr. Skaff, I thought I was here to interview for the position?"

Smiling, Skaff replied, "You already have, my dear. What do you think I was doing when I took you on that tour? I watched your reactions. I listened to your questions. I had to decide if you would be a good fit with our faculty and our children. I have made that decision."

Still in amazement at what had happened before her eyes, Willow mumbled, "But Mr. Skaff…"

Skaff held up his hand, gesturing for her to pause a moment. He stood up and retrieved the photograph of himself and a woman with their gold and green caps. Placing it on the table, he pointed to the woman and said, "This is Margaret O'Brien—Maggie to her friends—when we received our master's degrees at the University of San Francisco."

If Willow was confused before, she was dumbfounded now. Maggie O'Brien had been Willow's principal at Buena Vista Elementary School back in San Francisco. Confused words stumbled out of her mouth.

"I had no idea you knew Maggie. She never said a thing to me about knowing you. I guess I just don't understand, Mr. Skaff."

Sliding the folder to her, Skaff responded, "First, Willow, I prefer to be called Joe. Secondly, when I reviewed your resume from my sister, I immediately called my old classmate. She told me I'd be crazy if I didn't hire you on the spot. Crazy I do not want to be," he smiled. "So you start a week from next Monday if that's alright with you."

Unable to contain her excitement, Willow jumped to her feet and practically screamed, "Oh my god, yes, Mr. Skaff!" Seeing a twinkle of disappointment in his eyes, Willow quickly added, "I mean Joe, Oh, my god yes, yes, I can!"

Skaff leaned back in his chair and waved to her to leave. Willow grabbed the file in front of her and rushed out of Skaff's office and past the secretary's desk. Momentarily forgetting her manners, Willow quickly turned around and gushed with excitement, "See you in a week, Mrs. Tipton."

She was gone and out the door before Tipton could respond. Skaff appeared in the doorway and looked at his secretary.

"I think I found a gem!" he said.

"So do I," Tipton smiled.

CHAPTER 13

Dylan Steward had not seen his wife so happy in a long time. Upon her arrival home from her interview, she rambled on and on about her new principal and the school. Even the movers were amused as Willow had to be constantly interrupted with questions about where this piece of furniture went or what box went in what room. Her enthusiasm was not abated one bit, even when Dylan reminded her there were dozens of boxes left to be unpacked. "We've got plenty of time for that," she replied and then continued with her zeal full of expectations of the future. Dylan could only hope that his first day on the job would be met with the same level of gusto.

By late in the afternoon, the adrenaline rush from the day's activities had left the two exhausted. Major pieces of furniture were in place. Willow had managed to unpack the boxes marked kitchen. Dylan had reassembled their queen-size bed and arranged his collection of guitars and amps in the spare bedroom haphazardly. They somehow succeeded in getting their clothes into the small closet and personal clothing into his armoire and her dresser before collapsing on the bed.

Ceiling fans in the bedroom, living room, and kitchen provided the only air movement throughout the house to lower the infamous southern California heat. Opened windows allowed the breeze coming off the nearby ocean to cool the house. However, coming from San Francisco, any temperature approaching eighty practically brought on heatstroke for the newly transplanted San Francisco natives.

"Are we done?" asked a fatigued Dylan as he stared at the whirling four-blade fan hanging from the bedroom ceiling.

"No, silly," replied Willow, whose effervescence fought off the aching muscles in her back and arms. "I've got linen boxes to sort through, pictures and knickknacks to sort through, plus the spare bedroom."

"Can that wait till tomorrow, please!" sighed Dylan, mocking complete physical exhaustion.

"Only if you take me out to dinner," cooed Willow.

She got no argument from Dylan, who had about as much interest in shaping the interior of the house as he did a visit to the dentist. Dylan searched through a box marked shoes hoping to find his favorite huarache sandals. Willow grabbed her woven shoulder bag, slipped into her Birkenstocks, and waited for Dylan at the front door. There was little said as the two-headed the short distance to Venice Boulevard. Willow was enamored with the quaint pastel hues of the fifties-style stucco houses. They reminded her of pictures she had seen of the homes on the island of Burano, near Venice, Italy. Dylan seemed captivated by the aromas of ethnic foods coming from multiple street vendors offering their culinary creations to any passersby. His ears quickly picked up the melodies of an array of street musicians. Guitarists played their own creations or popular cover songs of the day; their cases open hoping for monetary rewards from their listeners. Frowning violinists, who were determined to bring a touch of sophistication to the tourist venue, presented more classical works. An occasional bluegrass group wailed songs of Appalachian history. Dylan paused longest when they came upon some solitary jazz instrumentalist, on a guitar or alto sax, who seemed lost in the works of Charlie Parker or J.J. Johnson. Their heads swayed back and forth according to the beat. Their shoulders shrugged upwards when their fingers stretched into the tenth and twelfth frets, searching for that magical note. One such musician caused Dylan and Willow to stand through several songs. Inside an arched entrance to a small café named Pogo's Togo, he sat on a small stool, staring down at a piece of sheet music on a portable stand. A gold chain hung around his neck along with a black sling supporting a Conn-Selmer alto sax. He wore a solid black t-shirt with a tan fedora. His eyes looked tired. His pale face was partially hidden by long shoulder-length hair. The tones from his sax were as sweet as Dylan had ever heard. Eventually, he looked up from his stool. His eyes reflected his frustration for having misplayed the last part of the bridge of "Just Friend" by Charlie Parker. It mattered little to Steward, who knew how difficult that piece was to play. He and Willow both clapped their approval. His head nodded up and down, signifying his appreciation for the man's talent. He smiled broadly and said, "You're in the pocket, man!"

Unaccustomed to hearing a phrase rarely spoken from the passing tourist crowd, the man smiled and asked, "Do you play?"

"A little, on a Gibson L5, not an alto," replied the modest Steward.

Not one to let her husband underscore his talent, Willow blurted out, "He plays a lot, and he's very good if I do say so myself!"

The street musician smiled at the compliment paid to the man. A frown returned to the man's face as he folded the piece of sheet music and put it in a black satchel next to the base of the stool.

"That ending bridge is a bitch!" he muttered.

Steward knew exactly what the man meant. It had taken him months to trust his intuition when he got to that part and a little research to confirm his intuition was correct. The sheet music called for a series of quarter notes at the end. But Dylan's inner self told him quarter notes rushed the ending. It played much better by ending with three-quarter note triplets. It was only after listening to Parker's recording of the song over and over did he realize that Parker himself had ignored what was printed on the sheet music and played three-quarters instead.

"Try playing that last series with three-quarter notes. It elongates the smoothness."

The man looked surprised that a total stranger would have that type of musical insight. And who would have thought to question how the great Charlie Parker played the piece in the first place? Intrigued by the stranger's insight, the man said, "Every Monday night, a small group of us gather here to jam. It's nothing formal. You jump in when you feel it, know what I mean? By the way, I'm Lenny."

"He's Dylan, and I'm his wife, Willow," replied a proud wife and biggest fan of her husband's musical talent.

Steward smiled. Truth be told, Dylan Steward craved those times when he played with his friends in the city. He loved his job at the Free Press, but playing jazz took love to a different level. They even opened for groups like Stan Getz, Miles Davis, and Dizzy Gillespie at local jazz venues a few times. The satisfaction he found in music, particularly jazz, was more, much more than playing the printed note. For Dylan Steward, music was a way to connect his heart with a sound, his feelings with chords. Every emotion that plagued the human soul could be expressed with the interpretation of the infinite combinations of notes, chords, and timing.

"Maybe," smiled Dylan. "I'm starting a new job Monday, and we just moved into a new house today, so spare time will be a premium for a while, but thanks for the offer."

Again, Willow was not about to let her husband miss an opportunity to do what he really loved. Her assertiveness bordered on adamance. "We'll make the time, Dylan."

"She has spoken," Dylan said, inwardly happy that she had made the decision for him.

———

THE TRANSITION from San Francisco to Los Angeles was the first major move in Dylan and Willow Steward's life. As it turned out, the young couple would need every bit of time allotted to them by Dylan's boss, Jimmy Donahue, and Willow's principal, Joe Skaff, to get completely settled in. If Dylan thought the finishing touches to moving in would be swift, he was wrong. Every picture that needed to be hung, of which there were many, required multiple moves, each one met with "No, not there," "Maybe a little to your left," or "Let's try the other wall," until finally the perfect spot was found. The living room furniture was no different. Despite his best efforts to have the movers place their sofa, a small settee couch, end tables, television and stereo cabinets, and their small dining table and chairs in the exact location Willow had indicated, every single item met the same fate of hanging pictures and knickknacks. The couch had to be positioned "just so" to catch the setting sun. Where the TV was placed depended on how the couch was positioned. This quandary of positional asphyxia continued for days until Dylan, nearing choking on his words, announced, "That's it. I'm not moving another piece of furniture!"

Despite the previous tenant's efforts to leave the house clean and in good order, she clearly was not versed in minor electrical and plumbing problems. Each day revealed a new light socket that did not work, or another mystery leak under a bathroom sink, the kitchen sink, or the connection to the washing machine. The complete lack of an integrated electrical panel only added to Dylan's work. Thanks to his father, a jack of all trades, who forced a reluctant son to watch and learn as he went about his work as a general contractor, Dylan was well prepared for the problems at hand. He became such a regular customer at the local Two Guys

Hardware and Keenan Plumbing Supply that he was soon on a first-name basis with the employees.

Willow had discovered, as had Dylan, that there were numerous minor flaws in the home that soon began to grate on her. The curtain rod above the living room window appeared to be level, that is, until Willow hung a new set of curtains. The end on the left was slightly longer than that on the right. At first, Willow told herself it didn't matter; an inch or so out of kilter was no big deal. Within days, that inch or so seemed to grow longer and longer in Willow's mind until she could no longer tolerate it. Adding to the problem was the end brackets at the top had been painted over, meaning installing a new horizontal rod would require the trim to be repainted. Her angst only grew when she discovered none of the curtain rods in the two bedrooms hung level, meaning more tedious painting was needed. The two bathrooms presented their own unique problems. One morning while applying her makeup, Willow noticed in the reflection that there was a subtle difference in the paint surrounding the radiate heater and what could be seen through the slats of the heater. Upon closer examination, she discovered that the previous tenant had elected not to repaint that portion of the wall behind the heater. 'At first, choosing to ignore the variance in color soon became a must-change task for Willow.

After days of what seemed to be an endless list of irritating fix-it items to attend to, all the while being Willow's man-Friday with her lists of do-overs, Dylan Steward was more than ready to start his new job. As their lists of things to fix dwindled, they took time one afternoon to shop for new clothes for Dylan.

After a stop at Gottschalks, J.C Penny's, and Thom McAn Shoes, Dylan arrived home with three new pairs of shoes, four sport coats, half a dozen shirts, slacks, and ties. All were carefully selected by Willow to give her husband the maximum number of combinations to wear. Arriving home later than expected, thanks to their unfamiliarity with the tangle of LA freeways, Willow conducted a fashion 101 class for her husband.

Dylan Steward was, by nature, a man of little sophistication when it came to clothing. He quickly deferred to Willow's judgment as she carefully hung his new purchases in the closet, explaining the compatibility of what coat went with what shirts, ties, and slacks. However, he paid little attention to his wife's dissertation on fashion. Turning around to face her husband, who was stretched out on their bed and feeling supremely confident in her choice selections, Willow held her arms open and said, "There, what do you think, Mr. Dylan Steward, reporter for the *Los Angeles Times*?"

The only thing Dylan heard was the growling in his stomach. Willow had insisted on getting all their shopping done without the benefit of stopping for lunch. It was as if she was on some mission to finish and be home before dark.

"I think you're wonderful," moaned Dylan amid more stomach growling. "Is there any chance we could get some dinner? I'm starving!"

Yes, there is my love, and I know just the place, she thought. Willow's ulterior motive was soon revealed.

"How about we go to Pogo's Café? You remember that place where we met that musician? We could even bring your guitar along in case you wanted to get in a session or two after we eat, of course."

Driven more by his appetite than a desire to play with strangers, Dylan acquiesced to his wife's selection even if it meant bringing his precious Gibson along.

CHAPTER 14

Disappointment swept over Willow as she and Dylan finished their walk along the sidewalk, arriving at their appointed destination, Pogo's Café. The building was typical of commercial establishments constructed in the 1940s. Dual front windows, each trimmed in wood that had seen points of countless colors layered on its surfaces, were now in some stage of peeling—even the original wood now peaked through. The smallish door was as much glass as wood and suffered from the same fate as the trim—not actually red, green, or gray but somehow an amalgam of all these and perhaps others. It was the barely transparent window of the door that sourced the couple's disappointment. In it hung a dilapidated sign that declared: "Closed Mondays."

"I was sure that guy said there was a jam session here on Mondays," she groaned.

His mounting desire for food aside, Dylan shared his wife's feelings. Initially hesitant to join in the Monday night gathering of fellow musicians, Dylan found himself warming to the notion of playing with others again. He set his guitar case down on the sidewalk. The hard shell case was somewhat cumbersome to carry for any lengthy distance.

"Musicians can be unpredictable sorts, honey. Who knows what happened for the change? There'll be other Mondays," he said, trying to boost his own spirits. Dylan turned his head left, then right, hoping to salvage the rest of the evening by finding someplace to satisfy their mutual hunger. As he turned to look across Venice Boulevard for more options, a man crossed the boulevard in the middle of the street and headed straight to Pogo's front door. He was carrying a case that Dylan suspected was a clarinet case. The stranger knocked three times on the glass door. When the door opened, Dylan immediately recognized the man who had been playing in front of the café and had invited him to come to the Monday evening sessions.

"Pete, good to see you!" said the man Dylan recognized as Lenny. "Come on in. We've been waiting." His face reflected the obvious pleasure he felt when one of his fellow musicians arrived.

Lenny stepped out to hold the door open for his guest when he saw Dylan and Willow standing on the sidewalk.

"Hey, you made it!" he greeted them enthusiastically.

A bit confused, Dylan said, "From the closed sign, I thought we had the wrong night."

Lenny smiled and chuckled a bit, "No mistake. We're closed to the public unless you're here to jam. Come on in and meet the fellows."

There was nothing fancy about Pogo's Café. A Venice Beach landmark for over forty years, famous for its Greek cuisine, it appeared much like it did when Alexander Pogo, a Greek immigrant, started the tiny sandwich shop in the forties. Lacking any formal education, but a genius when it came to marketing his food, Pogo bought the wine store next to his shop. He tore out the wall and added a meat counter and an open-hearth brick oven with rotating spits over a bed of coals. He wisely kept the wall decorations of wine racks of various types edged with clusters of purple and green plastic grapes. A single display case held a collection of antique wine openers, suitable for such an enterprise. There were any number of different wine glasses from stemmed glasses for white wines, smaller bowl glasses for red, and flutes for fans of Prosecco. Picnic baskets with small glasses, a wine holder, and a cheese board were the idea of Pogo's wife, Elena. In his original shop, Pogo added tables and chairs and a small stage where local artists performed on weekends. Pogo kept an old upright piano and several Peavey amps for the electrified instruments to accommodate the roving musicians who came to play. His wife also wanted to market t-shirts and hats silkscreened with Pogo's logo. The founding couple kept the secret of its meaning for years until their son, Lenny, finally revealed it to friends. Initially catering to people wanting to take their food with them, Pogo decided to call his place "Pogo's 2Go." The price for the hats and shirts dropped with its abbreviated caption.

"Fellas, meet our newest guests. Introduce yourselves while I get them something to eat," said Lenny. Turning to Dylan and Willow, Lenny asked, "Lamb kabobs, gyro with lamb or beef, or a Falafel? Get your own beverage from the cooler. Salad is optional. It's in the cooler as well. Oh, yeah, we don't stand on formality here if you haven't figured that out," grinned Lenny.

"Gyro lamb for me," replied Dylan, who was now captivated by the aroma from the lamb roast rotating on a spit over a bed of gray coals on the nearby hearth.

Willow did not share her husband's enthusiasm for the food presented. Having recovered from a queasy stomach that morning, she wanted to avoid anything too spicy.

"Could I just have a small salad, Lenny, and a bottle of water?" asked Willow.

"I'm not used to such a lightweight eater," laughed Lenny. "These guys normally eat me out of house and home. For you, though, I'll get it myself."

Groans over the preferential treatment afforded the only

woman present caused Lenny to rebuke his friends. Adopting a false manner and tone of righteous indignation, he declared, "She's a lady in case none of you noticed."

While Lenny tended to Willow's request, introductions began one by one with brevity the keynote.

"Phil Grogan, tenor sax."

"Eddy Isles, alto sax,"

"Geo Evans, bass guitar, the old-fashioned way, stand up."

"Stu Jackson, they call me 'the soul man' on drums."

Dylan thought it was an apt name for the only African American in the group.

"Bobby Hines, I like the Les Paul myself," noting Dylan's Gibson guitar case.

"Richie Gomes, a Fender man all the way."

Lastly, "John Flint, I tickle the ivories. Call me Kimber."

The familiarity was a sign Steward had been accepted as one of them, at least by the piano player.

"I'm Dylan Steward. I collect guitars. I like my Gibson, but my Guild X and Benedetto Manhattan sound good too, and I can play a little drum if necessary."

Anxious to hear what the newcomer could do, Lenny set a small cobb salad and a bottle of water in front of Willow and said, "Then let's get started, guys. Eddy, you start. Join in, guys, when you're ready."

What Dylan Steward was about to experience would reignite a long-suppressed dream. The fact that this vision had been carelessly but efficiently buried in his consciousness only made its realization that much more compelling.

———

TYPICAL OF MEN his age who carried an uncomfortable amount of extra poundage, the slump-shouldered silver-haired Flint made his way awkwardly up one step to the stage. He pulled a large black covering off an antique Starr upright piano. Its original mahogany finish still glistened from years of careful maintenance by Pogo and Lenny. Flint adjusted a small wooden bench to position himself mid-center. Whether to practice or show off, he began a run of arpeggios up and down the length of the piano. When he was finished, his fingers instinctively checked the top three buttons of his white shirt to ensure they were open, then turned to the group and said, "Sweet sound, Lenny." Jackson adjusted the stool behind a vintage Gretsch drum set. Not to be outdone by Flint, he twirled his drumsticks and did his own arpeggio with his snare, base, rack, and floor tom. Isles adjusted himself on a stool, his alto sax hanging around his neck. Standing next to Jackson, Evans ran his fingers across his base strings producing a slow, soft beat. On the opposite side of the small stage from Flint, Hines and Gomes sat on individual stools, their guitars held at the ready.

Flint began a soft introduction to "Lover Man" by Sonny Stitt. With perfect timing, the sweetest, smoothest sound emanated from Isles' alto sax. With the slightest glance from Isles, Jackson followed with the alluring rhythm of his upright bass, swinging slowly side to side. Eight measures into the song, Hines and Gomes joined in, their guitars providing the final ingredient to the jazz classic. Dylan marveled at the skill level of each man. They seemed to intuitively know when to underplay their instruments during another player's solo riffs, and no one seemed offended when someone extended their own riff with an extra improvised rendition. Smiles and nods greeted such creative interpretations. Flint hung his head over the keys, focusing on aged fingers as they made their way across the keys. Evans had a unique sway to his bass as he pulled it closer, then pushed it away as the beat increased or ebbed back to normal. Hines and Gomes would stare at their fingers intently, practically wishing them to reach the farthest fret or race up and down the neck with miraculous dexterity when playing complex chord progressions. Stu Jackson worked his drums with precision, knowing at the exact moment when to play a hard beat or a more subtle pulsating percussion.

Dylan was not certain that out-of-body experiences existed, but if there were such a thing, this was it! The combination of sounds transported him to some strange land where his senses grew more acute. His brain resounded with the sounds of notes before they were even played. He envisioned his fingers creating chord formations and progressions never played before. Willow looked at her husband and knew this was the venue to fulfill his dreams, even if he would not acknowledge it. Making that happen would, unfortunately, come at a severe cost. As the song ended, Flint called out to Dylan, "Come up and join in." What he had just witnessed put something of a crimp in his confidence despite his experience playing with friends back in San Francisco. Perhaps it was playing with strangers that had this effect on him. Recognizing what it was, a bit of stage fright, Lenny offered a supporting invitation.

"Dylan, we're all friends here, some just newer than others."

Dylan smiled though not wholly convinced. Willow brought him to his senses, she of eternal faith.

"Sweetheart, be yourself; that's all that matters. The rest will follow."

With those words, Dylan walked over to his guitar case at the edge of the stage, opened it, picked up his Gibson, and took a seat on the remaining stool. The group waited as Dylan took but a moment to tune his guitar. Satisfied he had the proper settings on his tuning knobs, he looked at Isles.

"What are we playing?"

"How about Come Rain or Come Shine?"

Dylan's stage fright eased as the Wes Montgomery classic was one of his favorites. Once again, Flint led off with a piano intro along with the smooth brushstrokes of the drum brush sticks of Jackson sliding over his snare drum. Dylan positioned his hand just above the body of his Gibson, closed his eyes, and let his ears tell him when to begin. His fingers moved effortlessly to the unforgettable Montgomery creation. At one point, Flint looked back over his shoulder, half-expecting to see Wes Montgomery playing. Hines and Gomes looked at Steward. Their eyes gave the Steward the unmistakable musician's reflection of approval. Steward's rendition was that perfect. When the song ended, Isles looked at Steward and said, "That wasn't your first time playing that, was it?"

Humble to a fault, Steward smiled meekly and replied, "I practice a lot, Eddy." Lenny returned the smile, knowing that level of skill took much more than practice alone to come to fruition.

Sitting next to Willow, Lenny had decided to let the others take center stage. He was enthralled by Steward's handling of the Montgomery classic. He leaned over to Willow and said, "Your husband plays a sweet guitar." Willow managed an appreciative smile before her upset stomach returned. She chose not to dwell on its likely cause, preferring instead to blame the chicken salad Lenny had given her. On stage, Eddy Isles switched from his alto sax to tenor sax. He decided to test the newcomer.

"Guys, let's do a little Lester?" He purposely did not mention the song title, hoping to see the depth of Dylan's knowledge of jazz history.

Isles began the introduction to "She's Funny That Way."

Almost immediately, Dylan's hand moved to the tenth fret to accompany Isles an octave higher. The entire song consisted of the two going back and forth in a musical competition to see who would miss the first note or chord change. To Isles' complete and pleasant surprise, Dylan matched him note for note, chord for chord. At the end, Isles touched his right hand index finger to his forehead as an acknowledgment of Dylan's skill.

From that moment on, whether the group played such classics as Charlie Christian's "Flying Home" or "Star Dust," Grant Green's "Idle Moments" or Charlie Parker's "My Old Flame," Dylan Steward found himself among equals who loved to play jazz and to allow their fellow musician opportunities to push their creative talents to higher and higher levels. He was in a mental state where mind and heart were in unison. His mind envisioned the musical possibilities, and his heart embraced the pursuit. After almost two hours of sheer musical nirvana, Flint was the first to announce his time was up. Stroking his silver goatee, he said, "Fellows, these fingers are done for the night."

"Yeah, me too," responded Jackson. "I promised the wife I'd be home by 10."

As instruments were packed away in the cases, each man went over to Dylan and expressed appreciation for playing with him. It was Eddy Isles who surprised Dylan and everyone else on stage.

"Dylan, I'm looking to put together a jazz ensemble with Stu and Geo. I've got an agent who's working on getting us bookings at some jazz festivals as well as some gigs at local jazz clubs. I've seen enough tonight to know you've got the talent to go places. Here's my telephone number. If you're even interested, give me a call."

The announcement shocked everyone. A few years back, Isles had quit playing professionally; too much time away from the family and too little time to spend on his ranchette in Baldwin Hills. With the death of his wife over a year ago and his own child, a married daughter, moving to Seattle with her husband, the ranchette held little allure for the lonely widower.

Willow held her excitement at bay. Yes, she was starting a new job, one that she loved, and her husband was starting a new future as a reporter with the *L.A. Times*, but if he chose to follow his passion, Willow was all in. Dylan sat stunned. He saw his future working at the *Times*. They had just settled into a new home, and then there was Willow's career to consider. It all seems so improbable. Playing professionally the music he loved seemed an impossibility, yet here was an offer to pursue that very love.

"Eddy, that's more than flattering, but the move to LA and a new job is about all the changes I can handle right now."

Isle smiled. "Dylan, the offer's there when the time is right."

Pogo's was a weekly destination for Dylan and Willow for the next several months. The draw of playing music again with fellow musicians unrestrained by the structure of written notes was an addiction Steward could not get enough of.

Willow wondered if her husband would ever understand. She loved her career as a teacher. What she loved more would be the opportunity to have children of her own. For that, she would sacrifice any career. She knew how much her husband loved music. It was a cauldron of passion beneath a façade of choosing certainty and stability. Her heart yearned for the day when he would be able to pursue his passion. Fate has a way of making dreams come true, but in ways unimagined or expected in that limited intellect that is the human brain.

CHAPTER 15

Willow Steward made a nearly seamless transition to her new teaching position at Broadway Elementary School. After all, the children were still children. Her classroom was still a classroom. She was exactly where she wanted to be. There were no more mountains to scale nor seas to cross. Yet Willow Steward could not completely deceive herself that one last event would complete her perfect world. Dylan Steward would travel a much different road as he moved into the arena of professional journalism. Those who worked at the *San Francisco Free Press* were less concerned about by-lines and notoriety and more about the moral fabric of the story. Dylan was ill-prepared for the battle of superegos and competitive savagery that existed among the elite and those who pretended to be, working at the *Los Angeles Times*.

WILLOW HAD TAKEN to selecting Dylan's attire for work as her husband had no eye for fashion. Casual but not too casual, professional, but not over the top. She was pleased with her selection, tan slacks, a long-sleeved white shirt, a blue striped tie, and a blue blazer. She found herself irritated that her husband found it necessary to rise at six am. By her reckoning, the drive to the Times Building was about 17 miles and not much more than a forty-five-minute drive. With a reporting time of nine a.m., this earlier than necessary start of the day bordered on obsessiveness to her. For Dylan Steward, it was the perfect failsafe plan to account for traffic and getting lost on unfamiliar highways. As he straightened his tie in the bathroom mirror, Dylan went over in his mind those who were on his interview panel. He liked Sylvia Markham, the assistant editor covering European affairs. Her short, cropped silver hair, angular face line with its prominent chin, broad forehead, and strong jawline led Steward to surmise Markham's choice of companions was outside traditional heterosexual guidelines. Having lived in San Francisco for years, that distinction was of little importance to Steward. Martin Milner presented a different expectation. Impeccably dressed in a three-piece suit, perfectly manicured hair, and with an air of royal superiority, Milner represented everything Dylan Steward despised. He was a man devoted to promoting class distinction—an elitist striving to put even more distance between himself and those of perceived lower standing. Social status meant everything to Martin Milner. It defined his persona. The call from the kitchen hastened his final touches to his appearance and terminated his daydream.

"Unless you want a cold coffee with your cold breakfast, you'd better get in here, now!" came the command from the general in the kitchen. Attired in her red silk pajamas, which broke mid-thigh, Willow was tempting fate for a man she had just ordered to the kitchen table. She had no sooner put his plate with eggs, buttered toast, and three sausages on the table when Dylan appeared in the kitchen. The sight of his wife in the alluring sleep attire had Steward rethinking the need to leave as early as he had thought. Though his primal instinct told him, "Carpe Diem," his rational brain told him to abstain. Driven to stay on script, he pulled Willow into his arms, kissed her, then cooed in her ear, "You're too good to me."

Tantalized by his soft breath, Willow whispered back, "You have no idea."

Her sultry response only added to the anxiety of the day to come and the night that awaited him. As he sat down at the kitchen table, Steward asked, "Aren't you eating?"

"No. I think I'll settle for coffee. I'm not that hungry," replied Willow as she took a seat next to her husband.

There was no need to provide a more detailed answer, at least not until she had something more definitive to tell him. Willow forced herself to concentrate on Dylan.

"I'm glad you had enough time to get so much done to the house before starting the new job."

Glancing at the clock on the wall, Dylan realized chit-chat with his wife would have to be kept to a minimum. He quickly finished the last of his eggs, then gulped down what was left of his coffee. Smiling at his wife, he said, "If you can avoid finding anything more to fix, repaint or rearrange for a while, maybe we can begin to enjoy our humble abode."

With mock indignation, Willow retorted, "Then you'd better get off to your new job, or I'll see what else I can find to keep you busy."

"That's my signal to go," replied Dylan, realizing a challenge had been cast his way, one he was not about to pick it up.

As he stood up, Willow said, "Don't forget the satchel that Murray gave you."

The gift had been a real source of pride for Dylan. The dark brown leather satchel was engraved with gold letters that read "S.F.P" for the *San Francisco Free Press*. Murray had presented it to Dylan on his last day at the Press. His words were, "Don't forget your roots." Steward kissed his wife goodbye as she wished him well, then picked up his satchel and headed out the door.

There was no way Dylan Steward could have predicted how the events of this first day would play out.

As he pulled up to the parking lot barricade, the attendant leaned out of his booth and announced, "Permit parking only." Steward had purposely left early, but the time it would take to find street parking would soon eat into the buffer. After circling the Times Building in a several block radius, he finally found an open spot three blocks away. He fed the meter with every bit of change he had, grabbed his personalized satchel, and sprinted to his destination. Ignoring every red light and crossing in mid-block where he could, Steward finally rushed through the double doors and into the foyer at eight forty-five am. He stepped to the side and took a moment to compose himself before entering the elevator. Steward was startled when he heard his name called out. "Good morning, Mr. Steward. How's your day goin'?" He looked in the direction of the voice and saw Willis Carpenter standing behind his magazine stand, a broad smile on his aged face. Steward did not want to be late, but he could not ignore the pleasantry expressed by the elderly black man. He walked over to the newsstand.

"First day on the job, Willis," smiled an anxious Steward.

Pleased that the near-stranger recalled his name, Willis responded warmly, "What's your favorite readin'?"

"Since *Avant-Garde* stopped publishing a few years ago, do you carry *The Progressive*?" inquired Steward.

Willis reached for a copy of the magazine rarely requested by those working at the conservative *Times*.

"Damn shame Ginzburg couldn't make a go of the Garde, but The Progressive ain't bad either."

Willis Carpenter was a complex individual. Though completely lacking any formal education and presenting the façade of a simpleton incapable of any kind of intellectual discussion or pursuit. Carpenter was indeed a thoughtful and perceptive individual. He was well acquainted with the publications he sold. He prided himself on surprising his customers with his knowledge of their histories and pertinent articles in the magazine of their choice.

"Check out the story by Howard Morland. Kinda scary," smirked Carpenter.

Folding his magazine under his arm, Steward replied, "I will. What do I owe you?"

"First one's on me," smiled Willis.

Steward grinned appreciatively, then turned to head to the elevators. Exiting the elevator on the third floor, Steward followed the directory heading to City Desk Editor, J. Donahue. Rm 301. He had been so focused on meeting Jimmy Donahue on the day of his interview he had paid little attention to the maze-like design of cubicles for the nearly twenty-five reporters working under Donahue. He walked the narrow aisle down the side of the room, completely ignored by those at their desks. The cacophony of countless electric typewriters pounding the words to its user's story and telephone conversations pleading for information from some anonymous source so a deadline could be met created a restlessness in Steward to begin his job. The heading on the door read, "J. Donahue, City Desk Editor." Steward knocked. A familiar raspy voice called out, "Come in."

Donahue was facing a partially opened window, his right hand waving rapidly back and forth, trying to rid the room of the smoke from a freshly lit cigar. Steward waited until Donahue turned around before speaking.

"Mr. Donahue, thank you again for the opportunity to work here."

Jimmy Donahue was known to have a big heart and an equally abrasive exterior.

"Hold the thank you until you've been here a while, Dylan, then we'll talk about who thanks who!"

Donahue knocked the remaining ash off his cigar then placed it inside the top right drawer of his desk. He pushed the intercom button on his phone set and bellowed, "Martha!"

Donahue's secretary, Martha Irons, was considered a sacred cow by those who knew her. Irons had been Donahue's secretary for twenty-plus years and his most trusted confidant on staff, next to Sylvia Markham. Though not in her job description and way above her pay grade, Irons was not averse to putting any reporters in their place should their arrogance or conceit reflect negatively on her boss. Woe to the person whose criticism of her reached Donahue's ears.

If Dylan Steward was expecting a Mother Teresa-type persona, he was sorely mistaken. Martha Irons entered the office and slammed the door shut. The air turned icy cold. Approaching sixty, Irons made no attempt to color her gray hair kept in a beehive style. She was of average height, but the intensity of her steel-blue eyes made her appear much taller to her adversaries. Her charcoal shirt and buttoned jacket only served to add to her authoritarian demeanor.

"Screaming my name is not the way to get my attention, at least the kind of attention you want. So keep that Irish temper of yours in check when you call me." There was no need to acknowledge his dressing down by his secretary. A wise Donahue moved on.

"Martha Irons, meet Dylan Steward, our newest addition."

"Mr. Steward, let me welcome you to the *Los Angeles Times*."

Her mellow greeting was in stark comparison to the Wicked Witch of the West performance he had just witnessed.

"Thank you, Mrs. Irons. I'm looking forward to working here and with you," replied Steward.

The addition of 'and with you' was Steward's way to acknowledge the woman's status in the hierarchy of the staff and the true power behind the throne.

"Martha, I've got my staff meeting. Afterward, would you mind taking Dylan down to accounting, human resources, and IT;

the typical stuff, payroll information, our political correctness policies, and the bane of my existence, those damn new computers?"

Irons was amused at the old-fashioned Donahue's reaction to the onslaught of changes in the workplace.

"Certainly." A smile now replaced the pursed-lip, clenched-jaw frown that had formed on the woman's face.

Donahue picked up a notepad from his desk, walked to his office door, opened it, and said, "Shall we?" His overly polite request was appreciated by Irons, even if it was a bit theatrical. Once in the outer room, Steward noticed the last few remaining staff hurriedly grabbing coffee cups and paper pads and heading out the door. No doubt they were hoping not to be late for their staff meeting. Donahue, followed by Irons and then Steward, made their way out to the main hallway. Pictures of past editors and Hollywood celebrities adorned both walls. At the end of the hallway, they came to a pair of double doors with the words CONFERENCE ROOM painted in black letters on them. Donahue's momentary display of chivalry when the trio exited his office became a thing of the past as he opened one of the doors and went directly inside, leaving Irons to hold the heavy wooden door open for herself and Steward. Instinctively Steward reached out to take the door from Irons. Apologizing for Donahue, Steward spoke softly, "I was raised differently. Ladies first." As he did, she managed a whispered warning to the new hire.

"I call this the lion's den. Keep your mouth shut and your eyes open. You'll see what I mean."

The minute they entered the conference room, the sidebar conversations ended. All eyes seemed to focus on Steward. He could tell they were sizing him up. Some looked directly at Steward. Subtle nods of acknowledgment appeared. Some seemed to examine his clothing. Others appeared completely uninterested in whoever the stranger was. He had to be the new hire the gossip mill had been talking about. The large room occupied the corner of the third floor of the Los Angeles Times Building. The outer walls of glass looked out over the city of Los Angeles. The inside wall displayed scenes from history that had been given front-page coverage by the *Times*. Steward managed a few seconds to gaze at some of the photographs; the Dodger's first game at Chavez Ravine, the Zoot Suits riots in 1943, and a wedding picture of Marilyn Monroe and Joe DiMaggio. A gigantic cherry wood table, easily twenty-five feet in length and six feet across, occupied most of the floor space. Matching cherry wood chairs with plush black upholstery were occupied by the staff. At the midpoint of the table were three empty chairs. Donahue took one, Irons another, leaving Steward no choice but to sit next to them.

"Alright, folks, let's get started," announced Donahue. There were perfunctory announcements from the managing editor, Damon Willard, regarding policy changes, staff reassignments, etc. Irons passed out copies of the aforementioned changes. There were audible groans when Donahue gave out the schedule for mandatory training by human resources on the treatment of women in the workplace, not that Donahue was any kind of crusader on this issue, coming from a generation where the woman's place was generally accepted to be in the home. What he did detest was any public display of disagreement or dissent when he gave directions that had been passed down to him. The rise of the Feminist Movement led by Gloria Steinem made the *Times* anxious to avoid any confrontation whatsoever with the crusading Steinem.

"That's enough people! Liability in a civil lawsuit is the question here, not your personal opinion. You got a problem with that; take it up with HR."

Wanting to get back on schedule, Donahue began his regular routine. Steward sat amazed as the man went around the table and, with encyclopedic like memory, addressed each person on their current assignment. Were there any problems that needed his intervention? Were there deadlines that needed to be extended, and if so, why? Few offered any concerns, knowing Donahue was playing to a corporate format. What he preferred was an old-fashioned one-on-one conversation. With his roundtable questioning at an end, he made his announcement about Steward.

"The stranger here is Dylan Steward, our newest staff member. I brought him on board from San Francisco."

"From the *Chronicle*?" interrupted Julian Fleming, addressing his question more to Donahue than Steward.

"No…" before Donahue could answer, Conrad Knight interrupted, *"The Oakland Tribune?"*

Irons gave Steward a slight tilt of her head as if to say, "See what I mean."

Steward took control. "Actually, I worked on the *San Francisco Free Press* for nearly ten years."

"Is there even a paper called the *Free Press*?" questioned Fleming as he looked up and down the table at his peer, displaying an incredulous look of disdain.

Joining in, the sycophant Knight said, "It can't be much of a paper if it's free!" If there was such a thing as a textbook example of a sneer, this was it.

Steward responded with his own smirk at his questioner, then replied.

"Yes, there is a *San Francisco Free Press*, and free is a reference to the minds of its readers, free from the prejudice and bias of midstream American consciousness. The mere fact that it is a three-time winner of the Arthur Rowes Award for independent journalism and a five-time winner of the National Newspaper Award for independent newspapers speaks to its legitimacy as a journalistic publication."

Eviscerated by Steward's retort and embarrassed by their lack of information regarding the *San Francisco Free Press*, Fleming and Conrad sank deep into their chairs. Still, they could not avoid the glares of condemnation from their fellow reporters—round one to Steward.

Donahue looked at Irons and said, "I don't think we're needed here anymore." Irons nodded, and the two got up and left the group to meet their newest colleague.

Steward's confrontation with his two colleagues would not end here.

Ironically, it would be Julian Fleming who would give Dylan Steward the story of his life and justify Donahue's decision to hire him in the first place.

CHAPTER 16

His rather public gutting of the two more experienced reports at Donahue's introductory staff meeting left a bitter taste in Steward's mouth. If the interrogative questions posed to him by Martin Milner at his interview weren't insulting enough, he had to endure the belittling remarks of Julian Fleming and Conrad Knight at the staff meeting. He had hoped for a more harmonic reception. He was sadly mistaken if he expected his first encounter with these miscreants would soften their future interactions. Steward's complete orientation to employment at the *L.A. Times* would take the better part of three days. The most intriguing for Steward was the four-hour session with an attorney who carefully went over half a dozen forms in which Steward was to relinquish all copyrights, independent use, or personal gain from any article published in the *Times*. Had he really signed on to be nothing more than a slave to the literary plantation bosses at the newspaper?

On the morning of the fourth day, Steward arrived at work carrying his trusted portable Olivetti Electric typewriter. It had been his long-time work partner at the Free Press, and Steward saw no need to abandon it because of his new position. Upon entering the large City Desk room, Steward's work area was clearly identified by a multi-colored balloon with printing that read, "Welcome." This was notably the work of more congenial co-workers. Standing there in the aisle were two people whose faces he recognized from the Monday meeting. With refreshing smiles and earnestness in their voices, they greeted him.

"I'm Geoffery Roberts. Call me G.O," said the man who Steward judged to be in his late thirties. He wore thick horned rimmed glasses, and his hair was in need of a trim. The sleeves to his white shirt were rolled up to his elbows. From a loose tie and opened collar, Steward judged him as more of a plebian type of worker than a front runner.

"I'm Elizabeth Alunda. Call me Liz. I'm in the cubicle in front of you. Welcome to the *Times*."

Steward formed an immediate positive impression based on the woman's attire. Her tightly coiled Afro had traces of copper highlights. A pencil protruded through the tightly bound tresses. She wore platform shoes—though her five-foot-five frame hardly needed enhancement. Her flared tan slacks and multi-colored dashikis completed her ethnically inspired attire.

Relieved to at last have found some kindred spirits, Steward replied, "Dylan Steward, and it's nice to meet some real people."

"Don't let Fleming and Conrad define everyone who works here, Dylan," responded Alunda with an air of mild defiance in her voice.

Collective judgments and sweeping generalizations were traits Steward abhorred in others. Inwardly he was bothered that he had fallen briefly into that same mold. By way of atonement, he replied, "I'll remember that."

"Those monthly meetings are normally rather boring. Assignment meetings are something else," joked G.O, in a failed attempt to lighten the air.

"How so?" asked Steward. Not completely familiar with these two, he was reserved in his remarks.

Roberts nodded to Alunda to explain.

"There isn't anyone in LA that Jimmy D. doesn't know—radio people, news people, politicians, the Hollywood famous, and some underworld figures if you believe some of the gossip. Anyway, he hears every bit of gossip before it becomes gossip. You know tips about who did what, where certain skeletons can be found, and what causes someone who wants to be championed without being identified as an advocate. He'll gather us together and pass out new assignments based on that information and his intuition. Listen to him, Dylan. Jimmy D. is a genius for smelling a story when no one else does."

"And Frick and Frack?" Steward asked, hoping to learn more about his two antagonists at the earlier meeting. Not desiring an open confrontation with Fleming and Conrad, he still thought it would be good to know what to expect from them.

"This much I'll tell you. The rest you'll have to learn on your own. Fleming thinks $300 suits make the man, and a Master's in Journalism from Stanford entitles him to sit next to God. As for Frack as you call him, Conrad Knight couldn't write his way out of a paper bag, but when you're the grandson of the former governor of California, certain things are given to you." Her dark eyes rolled in support of her remarks. This was more out of amusement than disdain.

"Like guaranteed employment at one of the most prestigious papers in California with little attention to qualifications?" grinned Steward.

With nothing more than a smirky smile and index finger pointing at him, she acknowledged his assessment.

At that moment, Donahue exited his office and called out, "Small conference room. Fleming, Steward, Alunda, Knight."

He carried an aged-looking brown leather folder under one arm. Its small metal clasp swung precariously in the air as he walked. Wasting no time, Alunda returned to her cubicle and grabbed her steno pad off her desk. Steward left his prized Olivetti on his chair and picked up his satchel. He followed Alunda to the opened door next to Donahue's office. G.O whispered, "Good luck!" to Steward as if some darkness were about to rain down on him. A man hurried from the back of the city desk room up the inside aisle toward the conference room's open door. His coffee cup spilled its contents as he went. The conference room was not what Steward would call a conference room. It was more like a large office. There was no table, only a circle of half a dozen black leather chairs with wooden arms. Donahue occupied one of the chairs. The others joined him. Alunda sat directly across from Donahue. A position Steward would learn brought one into direct eye contact with the boss. Not always the most comfortable spot to sit in, Conrad Knight sat two chairs away to Alunda's right. Steward opted for the chair next to Alunda. Steward remembered Knight from his introductory meeting. A pleasant sort, Steward, thought, who specialized in crime stories. Donahue looked up from his opened folder.

"Where's Fleming?" he barked, clearly annoyed that the erudite egotist was not present. There was an awkward silence. No one said anything.

"Let's not waste time, folks. Liz, a source at KHJ-FM, tells me Rudy Steinmann has lined up Timothy Leary for a series of interviews. See what he's got up his sleeve. Rudy sees the world through smoky glasses if you get my meaning."

Alunda nodded, knowing full well the talk show host's reputation as an advocate of legalizing drugs in California.

"Knight, contact Chaplin Edwards at the P.D.'s Ramparts Division. Seems a rash of officer suicides is being kept under wraps."

"Off the record, Jimmy?"

"Yes, until it needs to be for the record. Even chaplains have a code to follow."

"Stewad, …"

Suddenly Fleming rushed into the office. He was scrubbing the sleeve of his Armani coat with a dampened handkerchief. His face was flushed, and his carefully maintained pompadour had been hastily brushed back. He offered his explanation.

"Sorry to be late, but some god damn homeless street trash grabbed my arm outside the parking lot, panhandling for money. God, he was filthy. Why can't the city get rid of that kind of garbage?"

Alunda squirmed in her chair at his complete lack of empathy for those less fortunate. Fleming's demeaning outburst toward some unfortunate soul seethed within her. She loathed Fleming's marginalization of the person as garbage and street trash. Donahue was similarly offended as he remembered growing up listening to stories from his grandfather of how the Irish were treated when they came to America. Donahue closed his folder. He closed his eyes and slowly rubbed his fingers across his brow. Be it retribution or inspiration, he opened his eyes and spoke with surprising enthusiasm in his voice.

"You just may be onto something, Julian. Take your one-time encounter, then multiply it by a hundred, hell, even a thousand times. Can you imagine the blight in the city? People are accosted everywhere they go. With our streets taken over by homeless street trash, think of the effect on tourism, business, property values. I could go on and on. This could be big, Julian. I want you to contact local charities, the city's social services department, the welfare department, the Salvation Army, hell, anyone dealing with this problem. See just how bad this problem is and how bad it could get."

"You're kidding, aren't you? Anyone could write that story." Fleming said, aghast that someone of his ability would be tasked with such an inconsequential topic. He dropped his stranglehold on his expensive Italian coat. "Besides, who's going to be interested in reading about some down and out bum on the city streets? Why not give this to Steward? After all, he is the new guy on staff."

When he made this remark, he looked down on Steward, literally and figuratively. Donahue's eyes reflected his amusement that Fleming had played right into his hands.

"Well, Steward. Think you can handle this assignment?"

"I'll do my best, Jimmy."

"All right then, it's yours. Julian, a friend in the mayor's office, has leaked to *Daily News* that the County Board of Supervisors will support a planned development in the LA foothills without an environmental impact assessment. See what's behind this and whose palms are being greased."

Satisfied he had been given an assignment equal to his perceived status, Julian Fleming smiled. Donahue was about to send them on their way when Steward raised his hand.

"I wonder if I could ask Julian a question?"

It was clearly a rookie move.

"Certainly," responded Fleming.

"Could you describe the person who grabbed at your coat? It might be interesting to talk to the person who is the focal point of this story."

Not attempting to hide his annoyance at such an unnecessary question, Fleming groaned aloud, "Fine. He had on a faded old Army jacket covered with grime, grease, food stains, and god knows what else. There was a torn patch of some kind on the jacket's shoulder, an eagle, I think, and sergeant's stripes. As for his face, it was filthy, partially covered by long stringy hair. Good enough!"

"Thanks, that'll do," smiled Steward.

"All right then, let's go to work," commanded Donahue.

Steward was the last to leave as he hurriedly copied down the description Fleming had given him. It gave Donahue a chance to offer Steward one last piece of advice based on his nearly thirty years in the newspaper business.

"Listen, kid. No story is ever what it seems to be. Treat every story as if it were the Trojan Horse at the gates of Troy. Only a fool thinks otherwise, and we've got enough of those around. Right? If you get my drift."

There was a twinkle in the old Irishman's eyes as Steward nodded in the direction of the recently departed Fleming. *This kid's gonna be alright.* Julian Fleming had seriously underestimated the value of the assignment offered him. A mistake Dylan Steward would not duplicate.

ON THE DRIVE TO work the next day, Steward found himself fixating on Fleming's description of what he called street trash. Not so much the hair, jeans, or the grimy face, but the faded Army jacket. Was there a unit insignia on it? What does the name tag say, if anything? Was the person a displaced veteran struggling with PTSD? All these questions plagued the man who had served in a place called "Nam." He decided to commence his quest at the same site Fleming had encountered the street trash, as he called him, the *Times* parking structure.

With his newly obtained parking permit, Steward pulled into the parking lot, stopping at the barrier. Precariously balanced on his knee was a cup of hot coffee he had purchased at a nearby gas station—a gift for Gus, the overweight and balding attendant. Steward thought he would appreciate the gesture, as the morning was particularly cold. The man stepped out of the ticket booth when he saw Steward approaching.

"I hope that's for me," he said with a smile. This smile did nothing to improve his bloated and rosacea cheeks.

"No one else, Gus," replied Steward, as he handed the attendant the steaming hot cup of coffee. This, too, was a genuine gesture.

As Gus took his first two sips of coffee, Steward asked, "Gus, have you seen a guy hanging around here lately? Probably hitting up anyone he sees for spare change, kinda down and out guy wearing an old Army jacket and ragged clothing."

A line of cars began backing up behind Steward. What Gus didn't need was anyone complaining about having to wait to get into their slot because of a gabby attendant.

"Go ahead and park, then we'll talk," he said. The look of his weathered face told Steward he was concerned about something more than a line of waiting cars. Obediently, Steward pulled ahead and found a slot near the far corner of the first floor. When he got back to the booth, Gus's relief was checking in for the day shift. Steward stood off to the side near the stairwell and waited. Finishing the exchange with his relief, Gus approached Steward, carefully looking left then right before speaking.

"Look, I don't want to get the guy in any trouble," pleaded Gus, who cupped his hot brew with both hands. "Sometimes, he comes around late at night and sleeps behind the dumpster near the loading dock. I feel sorry for the guy, I guess. Even though he is a bum, he doesn't seem like such a bad guy."

Gus's empathy was in stark contrast to Fleming's belittling and dehumanizing description.

"I will not get the guy in trouble. I just want to talk to him. What can you tell me about him? What did this guy look like?" Steward asked. The empathy displayed by Gus piqued his curiosity.

"He had a dirty old gray blanket wrapped around him. His jeans were filthy, covered with stains from you know what! He had on an old pair of black boots with green-colored sides. Oh yeah! And a faded green Army jacket. I remember thinking maybe he was a vet of some kind."

"Did you see him today?"

"No, after his encounter with Fleming yesterday, I think he's probably hiding low for a few days. It's not my place to criticize, but Mr. Fleming sure can be a jerk."

"I know the guy," responded Steward. "He's kind of an asshole; excuse my language."

"Hell yes, he is," affirmed Gus. "Not a day goes by that he doesn't warn me that if anything happens to his prized Mercedes, he'll have my job."

Steward probed the attendant gently. "If you would, tell me about what happened yesterday."

Again, Gus turned to see if anyone was approaching. Satisfied no one was nearby to hear, he began.

"Fleming was headed to the elevator. This guy was sitting on the ground near the door. He put his hand out and said, 'Any spare change?' That's all he said, honest. Then, this Fleming kicks him in the ribs, and the guy grabs Fleming's coat as he falls backward. Fleming kicked him again, and the guy let go of the coat."

Steward seethed at the treatment given such a defenseless soul, much less someone who might be a veteran. His anger drove him to extreme and unusual measures. He reached into his coat pocket and pulled out a small notepad. He hurriedly scribbled down his phone number and handed it to Gus, saying, "If you see this guy again, call me right away." Steward ran to his car, exited the parking lot structure, and slowly began a street-by-street search for the miserable wretch that once was a man.

CHAPTER 17

The downtown area surrounding the Times Building consisted of aging business buildings. Scattered about were restaurants and cafes catering to the workforce of old downtown LA. When his drive proved fruitless, Steward parked his car near the corner of 5th and Albany Street and started a foot search through a maze of alleyways and back streets. He'd hoped to find his quarry feasting on some restaurant throwaways in an alley dumpster or hiding from the prying eyes of a judgmental and hostile public. By 6:00 p.m., all of Steward's efforts were in vain. Darkness had settled on the city, and he was physically and mentally drained from his emotional journey. To his amazement, when he reached the corner of Spring and Atwater, he saw the flashing neon sign to Saltzman's Kosher Deli. Donahue had mentioned the place as being one of his favorite places to eat. Steward crossed the street in haste, hoping to soothe his groaning stomach and call his wife to say that he would be late getting home. Steward had no sooner reached the door to the Deli when the lights went off. He saw through the glass an older man wearing a white apron approaching the door, a set of keys in his hand. Steward quickly rapped on the door to get the man's attention. A look of frustration appeared on the man's face. He opened the door partway and said, "I'm sorry, but I'm closed."

Steward was quick to plead his case. "Jimmy Donahue said this was the best place to get a pastrami on rye west of Chicago. I work with him at the *Times*."

The mention of Donahue's name softened the old store owner.

"Oy! A friend of Jimmy's? Sure, come on in, but I got nothing hot left, only cold cuts." The balding man adjusted his kippot and retired his apron. The sound of his Yiddish accent was but one more reminder of the ethnic diversity of his old San Francisco neighborhood that Steward so loved. "That's not a problem, Mr. Saltzman. Cold pastrami on rye and the use of your phone to call my wife, I'd be grateful."

The old man stared at Steward with a mirthful twinkle in his eye.

"What kind of a putz do you think I am to serve cold pastrami on rye! Have a seat. The phone's on the wall."

Steward headed to the payphone on the wall near the front door while old man Saltzman made his way to the kitchen. It took a few minutes to assure a very worried wife that he was okay and that he'd be getting home later than usual and there would be no need to hold dinner for him. When he returned to his table, Saltzman had steaming hot pastrami on rye on a plate with melting cheese oozing out the edges, a slice of dill pickle, and a glass of Manischewitz wine waiting for him.

"So, why the late hours, Jimmy Donahue's friend?" quipped the old man as he sipped his own glass of Jewish sweetness.

He had long since learned to take unexpected events in stride by this point in his life. In fact, he rather enjoyed them. Embarrassed that he had not introduced himself, Steward quickly finished his first bite of the divine sandwich Saltzman had prepared and said, "Dylan, Dylan Steward, Mr. Saltzman."

"Please, no Mr. Saltzman. It's Abe to my friends," smiled Saltzman, who took another sip of wine. "My wife tells me I drink too much of this, but what does she know!" he chuckled. He was transparent in his desire to please and show goodness to others—a genuine person.

Before answering the old man's question, Steward took another bite of Saltzman's heavenly creation, followed by a bit of the crunchiest dill pickle he had ever tasted. Alternating between bites of sandwich and pickle, Steward told the man of the meeting that afternoon with Donahue and the three other reporters and how he had been given this unusual assignment. Keeping his personal emotions to himself, Steward continued the story of his day, his talk with the parking lot attendant, and his futile search for the object of his inquiry.

"I don't think I would like this Fleming person," Saltzman said, his voice firm, his eyes blank of any visible emotion. The imagery of a defenseless person being kicked over and over evoked Saltzman's own nightmares, the sound of marching black boots echoing through the night streets, striking at panicked people who had been dragged out of their homes. It was an atrocity that had sucked the very life from him. For several moments, Saltzman was silent. He glanced at his watch and then said, "I have a wife also, Dylan Steward. But before I go, I have something for you in the kitchen."

Steward followed Saltzman into the kitchen, where Saltzman picked up a small white bag with Saltzman's Deli printed in green letters on the side.

"This is for your wife for putting up with a schmuck like you," he joked. "Would you help an old man and put this bag of cans in the dumpster out back?"

The two men headed to the back door of the kitchen with Steward toting a large black plastic bag untied and full of aluminum cans and beer bottles. Saltzman pointed to a large green dumpster just to the left of a ragged screen door that hung unevenly thanks to a loose hinge at the top. The alley light above the door cast more shadows than light. Steward swung the bag into the metal receptacle. The contents of the bag banged on the walls of their metal tomb and reverberated into the darkness. The agonizing groan that followed startled Steward. Saltzman froze where he stood. It reminded him of human sounds he had heard long ago—sounds that reflected deep anguish and despair. The groaning sounds echoed again in the darkness. This time more distinct and with more urgency. Steward had heard that before, first when he was in Vietnam and later in his dreams. Shouts of warning, "Incoming! Incoming!" As if he were back there again, his instincts took over. Steward moved cautiously past the screen door. He moved in a semi-crouched position around the front of the dumpster to the other side. That's when he saw it, a figure wrapped in a filthy gray blanket pulled over its head. The figure swayed back and forth. Hands covered with sores and cuts cupped his head like an iron vice. Sobs accompanied body shakes as the warning cries persisted. Now on his hands and knees, Steward spoke to the figure with a sense of urgency.

"It's okay. I'm here. Relief is here!" The cautionary words were repeated over and over until the swaying stopped. Slowly the figure's hands pulled the covering off his head. A head lifted upward. Through the dim light, Steward noticed a jagged scar running across the man's forehead. A single hand brushed away long strands of matted hair that covered its face. Bloodshot eyes reflected off jaundiced skin. A shaking hand rose into the air to shield exhausted eyes from a slice of light from the alley light that had crept over the edge of the dumpster

"Kenny is that you?" a quivering voice muttered.

Steward scooted over to the man's side.

"No, it's me, Sgt. Steward. Second Platoon just got here to relieve you guys. Everything's going to be ok! Stand down, pal!"

His hand reached out and grabbed Steward's arm. His other hand reached for the handle on the dumpster to help him stand. As he righted himself, his protective blanket fell to the ground. The jungle green jacket bore a bald eagle on its shoulders, the insignia for the 101st Airborne Division known as the Screaming Eagles. There was a sense of near panic in his voice.

"Are my guys okay? I've lost track of my men! Have you seen them?"

His left leg nearly buckled as he tried to stand, driven by some mysterious force to find his men, men whose welfare had been entrusted to him. He had to know and now!

Steward tried to restore some sanity to the insanity of the man's nightmare. A nightmare of perpetual warfare that had never ended for him.

"I'll take care of that," he assured the struggling man. "Right now, I need the medics to check you out. I've got one right here. I'll get him."

To complete his ruse, Steward turned around and went back inside the kitchen. He quickly explained his role in Steward's ruse to Saltzman and then returned to the alley. In those few moments when Steward was gone, the stranger disappeared into the night determined to find his men and ensure their safety. When he returned, the alley was empty. Clouds moving slowly in front of the moon cast a patchwork of diaphanous figures moving eerily down the alley.

"Damn it!" Steward yelled when he realized his discovery was missing. His fist slammed against the side of the dumpster to punctuate his frustration. Abe Saltzman knew nothing he could say would remedy the immediate situation, but he could offer hope. He placed a fatherly hand on Steward's shoulder.

"Look, Dylan. You go. Find your friend. If he comes back, God willing, I'll have a little hot soup and warm Challah waiting for him."

Steward looked into Saltzman's eyes. He had lost this guy just like he had lost his best friend, Tommy. The emotions from one tragedy quickly spilled over into the present. His hands gripped the handle of the dumpster as he unsuccessfully tried to contain his emotions. He choked on his words as tears pooled in his eyes.

"I've got to find him, Abe. We don't leave our men alone to die out in the bush. This guy thinks he is still out there."

"Yes, he is like mishpacha. I understand."

Saltzman gently brought the Star of David hanging around his neck to his lips. With the wisdom of an old man, Abe Saltzman replied softly, "Find him, my son. Make sure people know who he was and what he did. The past is full of too many unwritten stories."

PART TWO

Hold fast to dreams, for if dreams die,
life is a broken winged bird that cannot fly.

LANGSTON HUGHES

CHAPTER 18

The following Monday, Donahue's regular routine had a surprise waiting for him. When he picked up his copy of the *New York Times* for his daily dose of Jimmy Breslin, Willis alerted him.

"You got that young boy working overtime, Jimmy?"

Folding his copy of the *Times* under his arm, Donahue responded, "I don't follow you, Willis."

"That new reporter, Steward, he got here just as I was opening up. He said he had to finish his story."

Donahue paused to remember what, if any, deadline he had given Steward at the Thursday meeting—none that he remembered. With a shrug of his shoulders, Donahue replied with a smile, "Rookie eagerness, Willis."

Wiser than his appearance would indicate, Willis said, "I don't think so, Jimmy. He had that look of a bulldog a chewin' on a bone."

Donahue thanked Willis then headed to the elevator. He would soon discover the reason for Dylan Steward's early arrival. When Donahue entered the city desk work area, a solitary head appeared above a cubicle. As Donahue opened the door to his office, he heard a voice call out, "Boss, can I get a minute of your time?"

Without turning around, Donahue answered, "Come on in."

Steward picked up his draft and his cup of coffee from the kiosk in the foyer and marched into Donahue's office. Donahue had barely loosened his tie when Steward began.

"I spent a lot of time after our meeting on Thursday getting into my assignment, as a matter of fact, most of Thursday into the night and Friday as well. I even talked Willow into joining me on Saturday on a drive around."

Handing Donahue his draft, Dylan said, "Jimmy, this barely touches the heart of the story."

Donahue pulled a pair of reading glasses out of his shirt pocket—one arm was bent, and the nose pad was crooked. He settled back in his chair and began reading Steward's draft. He said nothing. Only his eyes moved slowly, line by line, until he was finished.

Street Trash
By Dylan Steward

Have you ever thought about the term street trash? What does it conjure up in your mind? I think of discarded aluminum cans and bottles, thrown away paper products, broken toys, old clothes, soiled diapers, maybe even a bicycle with bent wheels. In effect, street trash is nothing more than the castaways people no longer want or value. I've never thought of a fellow human being as street trash, having no value or importance to anyone. Sadly, that is exactly how I heard a person describe a homeless man asking for help. What did that man get in return for asking for help? He was savagely kicked in the chest over and over. Who was this man that was so repulsive that he deserved such treatment? Yesterday, I went to the location where the encounter between the homeless man and his assailant took place. To my surprise, it was a downtown parking garage. I spoke with a witness who described the men involved and what took place. The witness said the victim was a displaced and forgotten Army veteran who no doubt endured unthinkable horrors and suffered from God knows what type of nightmares. I drove around the streets bordering the parking lot for hours, hoping to catch a glimpse of the man but to no avail. Then, on foot, I scoured the back streets and alleyways for blocks. Finally, when I was about to give up, a chance encounter with the owner of a deli took me to the alley behind his establishment. That's where I found him. Huddled under a blanket next to a dumpster, he cried out over and over, "Incoming! Incoming!" His body shook in abject terror. I knew it was a flashback to the time vets refer to as being 'in county,'— what civilians call combat in Vietnam. I had heard those same cries and felt that same fear during my time there. I attempted to ease the panic in his voice by putting myself in his nightmare. I told him my platoon was there to relieve him, and we were going to get him help. He shook off his blanket and grabbed my hand yelling, "Kenny, is that you? My men, where are they? Are they okay?" What could I tell him? I didn't know his name. I didn't even know his rank. From the insignia of a bald eagle on his jacket, I only knew that he had served with the 101st Airborne Division, known as the Screaming Eagles. Assuring him, I was going to get him medical help, I quickly returned to the deli in the hopes of getting help. When I returned to the dumpster, the man was gone. He had disappeared into the night. He was still trying to find his men.

This man has a name and a story that needs to be told. To find out who he is and tell his story, I need your help. Somewhere in the vast readership of the L.A. Times, there must be someone who had a loved one, a family member, a friend, a friend who knew a friend who served in Vietnam with the 101st Airborne. Maybe that loved one wrote home about him and his friend, Kenny. If that person exists and you read this article, please write the L.A. Times at the following address: L.A. Times, 5 Spring St. Los Angeles,

California or call the following telephone number 415-295 6679. Help me help him.

Donahue reached for a blue pencil from a small leather cup on the corner of his desk. His hand moved quickly across the three-page draft, a mark here, a scribble there until it was newspaper ready. He laid his pencil down and looked up at Steward. "You know you're going to piss some people off when this goes to print."

"Like whom?" asked Steward. "I haven't mentioned anyone by name."

Donahue smiled. "For one, this encounter occurred in the *L.A. Times* parking structure. Many will assume the alleged assailant works at the *Times*. Two, the police may be interested in talking with the witness of this assault. Lastly, some veteran support groups will want to crucify this guy."

The need to be coy with his wording had never occurred to Steward. His disdain for Fleming may have clouded his choice of language. His identification with a possible Army veteran was another emotionally charged issue. However, within his heart, Steward truly felt he had done the right thing. By way of a defense, he responded, "Jimmy, assumptions are the enviable result of anything a reporter writes. Any reporter worth their salt knows the importance of protecting their source of information. As for any fallout from veterans groups, maybe that is something the assailant should worry about."

Donahue's questions were more to test Steward's mettle than a reason to stall the story, which he had no intention of doing. He smiled.

"Okay then, it runs tomorrow and every Sunday for a month."

The following Thursday morning, Dylan got to the *Times* foyer at 7:45 am, fifteen minutes early by his job description but clearly on time by his work ethic. He grabbed a cup of coffee from the kiosk before heading over to Willis Carpenter's newsstand. As he approached the newsstand, Willis called to him, "Mr. Steward, got you a copy of the Progressive right here," holding the liberal rag, as some called it, in his hand. Dylan smiled as he peeled off a five-dollar bill from his money clip. When he handed it to Willis, the old man surprised him with quite the compliment.

"I liked that story you wrote." Then in a whispered voice, he added, "Those boys from Vietnam deserved better when they got home. When you find that young man, tell him thank you for me." His eyes reflected a sense of shame.

Steward reached out to thank the man. With wrinkled old fingers whose knuckles were enlarged by the onset of arthritis, a surprisingly firm grip took hold of Steward's hand. Willis Carpenter struggled to right himself on a crippled left leg. A prideful look came over him. Determination burned in his eyes.

"I was with Patton's Third at the Battle of the Bulge. We kicked the hell out of those Krauts. Got this bum leg from a German 88." He tapped his left knee as if it were a badge of honor.

Time had not healed the raw emotions Steward had from his own war experience, not from his time 'in country' nor his reception at San Francisco International when he returned home. Willis's words answered a long-festering question for Steward, *Did anyone really care what we went through or why?* From at least one person, that question had been answered. In return, for all his friends, those who survived and those who hadn't, Steward said, "Willis, thank you." At that moment, a special kinship was formed. One that Dylan Steward would eventually cling to at the worst time of his life. The two parted with nods of understanding.

When Steward entered the city desk work room, he was greeted by applause from his two new friends, Liz Alunda and Geoffery Roberts, standing in their cubicles.

"Nice job on that story about the homeless guy," smiled Alunda.

Roberts echoed her sentiments and added with surprising

insight, "It seems we ask so much from those guys and kind of ignore them when they return."

The voice of Martha Irons, Donahue's secretary, caught his attention.

"Dylan, before you go in, would you come to my office?" Her tone seemed uncharacteristically pleasant.

"I'd better see what's up, and thanks for the compliment," replied a smiling Steward.

Steward knocked politely though the door to Irons' office was open. Irons was standing in front of a small corner table in her office. She motioned for him to come over. There was a plastic bin on the table. Irons reached inside, pulling out several sheets of paper stapled together.

"Per Mr. Donahue's instructions, you will not be getting any new assignments for a while."

Steward was momentarily crushed. Had he not written a compelling story? Was he being reprimanded for some unforeseen consequence that neither he nor Donahue could have anticipated?"

"Have I done something wrong, Ms. Irons?" he asked, with the naivete of a child addressing his teacher.

A smile formed on Irons' face. "To the contrary, Dylan, you touched a lot of people with that story."

Handing him the papers, she said, "These are the telephone logs of calls made to the paper after your story ran."

She scooped out nearly two dozen envelopes from the plastic bin.

"These are letters from people who read your story. Mr. Donahue is going to rerun your story in the Sunday edition. He expects a dozen times the number of responses. Your job is to return every call, read every letter, and take whatever time is necessary to find our mystery hero."

"Thank you, Ms. Irons. This guy deserves it. Everyone who fought there deserves it," replied an appreciative and obedient Steward.

Steward returned to his cubicle, trying to wrap his head around the enormity of his expanded assignment. He was beginning to feel overwhelmed with the task at hand, not so much from the workload standpoint, but from the realization that people, at least some people, finally cared. The memory of his reception when he had landed at SFO upon his return from Vietnam had never completely gone away. The shouts, the screams, the insults still echoed in the recesses of his mind. Perhaps this time, things would be different for this lost hero.

There was little that Dylan had ever told his wife about his experiences in Vietnam. She knew of his friend Tommy's death, but only in the most generic terms possible. The nightmares he shared with no one. The restless nights went without explanation, though Willow was intuitive enough to guess the source of the disturbances. The accolades he had received from Donahue, Martha Irons, and a few of her peers would change all that. Steward would share at least some of those experiences with his wife when he got home that night. Ironically, Willow Steward would also share some news with her husband when he arrived home, but not everything would be revealed.

WILLOW HAD SOMEHOW MANAGED to get through her teaching day with a minimum of trips to the faculty lady's room. Despite her womanly intuition, Willow had so far put off confirming her suspicions about the cause of her intestinal issues. As she walked home that day, she had decided to put that issue to rest by using the last home pregnancy kit Doctor Henderson had given her before she and Dylan had relocated to Southern California. By midday, the endless Southern California blue skies and warm temperatures had been replaced by gray skies and an uncomfortably cool sea breeze, causing Willow to wish she had taken a light jacket or sweater with her that morning. If that wasn't enough to hasten her pace, thoughts of a lifetime dream coming true certainly were. Even the weight of her woven tote bag full of student reports to go over had not deterred her.

The sight of her front door meant a warm blanket and cup of hot chai tea were soon at hand. More out of habit than curiosity, Willow grabbed several letters that the mailman had placed in the mailbox next to their front door. Once inside, Willow haphazardly tossed the miscellaneous mail on the coffee table along with her tote bag. She first headed to the kitchen to put a flame under the blue and red enamel tea kettle she had received from Mrs. Podesta as a going away gift, then it was off to the bathroom. Willow had surreptitiously placed Doctor Henderson's kit behind the rolls of toilet paper in the bottom drawer, a place she was assured her husband would never look. His voice would bellow from the bathroom, "Honey, is there any more toilet paper!" As she sat on the toilet seat, Willow carefully read the instructions again before opening the kit. With the steps completed, Willow closed her eyes and waited before looking at the results. Staring at the colored stick, Willow seemed frozen in some euphoric state before being startled back to reality by the whistling sound of the tea kettle blaring its ready signal throughout the house. She quickly washed her hands and headed to the kitchen to relieve her tea kettle of its torturous cries. For several minutes, Willow Steward's body was on autopilot. She dunked her tea bag several times, then let the paper label hang over the rim of her cup. She turned off the stove burner and headed to the living room couch. Preferring the knitted quilt that lay across the back of the couch to turning up the heater, Willow snuggled under the weight of the heavy covering. Her mind could barely cope with the speed at which the life within her was taking. Infancy, with its breastfeeding, baths with tepid water in the kitchen sink, quiet times in a rocking chair that her husband would buy her, and first steps lasted but a nano second. Her first day at school and college graduation seemed to occur in consecutive blurs of time, then suddenly there was a wedding. God had answered her dream, and though Willow did not follow any particular denomination, she had a firmly held belief in the existence of God, that the Golden Rule is to be followed, not just recited. That life, any life, is to be cherished. She placed her hand on her stomach and thought of the life to be.

For whatever reason, Willow chose that moment to glance at the mail that lay on the coffee table. She noticed an envelope with Doctor Linda Henderson's return address, Buena Vista Medical Clinic, San Francisco, California. It was addressed to her old address. Scribbled across the front of the envelope was her Venice Beach address in Mrs. Podesta's handwriting. How long Mrs. Podesta kept it before forwarding it to her was anyone's guess. Willow remembered the blood test that Doctor Henderson was going to run to confirm whether or not Willow had some blood disorder that might affect a pregnancy. These must be the results, she thought. She tore off the end of the letter, eager to read its contents. After reading the letter, Willow let it rest on her lap. Tears began to pool in her eyes. She picked up the letter and read its contents again. There they were, the words she was looking for, only ten to twelve percent of women who have this blood disorder face any danger in bearing a child. For the eternally optimistic Willow, that meant ninety-three percent of women with this disorder have no problem whatsoever bearing children. Who wouldn't take those odds!

Relieved that Lady Luck was surely on her side, Willow began to focus on how to break the news to her husband that he was going to be a father. There was no need in her mind to burden Dylan with any statistical probabilities. He was the one who hoped to avoid failure rather than hoping for success. She desperately wanted him to see that the glass was half full.

———

At times, Willow had found Mrs. Podesta's late afternoon interruptions with some dish she had prepared for them a little overbearing. Nonetheless, she took advantage of getting the recipe for whatever Italian delicacy the lady had prepared. Those recipes were carefully hidden away in a small file box in the cupboard above the kitchen stove. Tonight, she would prepare a special meal for Dylan and herself while coyly introducing the idea of having a third person at the kitchen table. The mischievous plan brought a smile to her face as she surveyed the cupboards for the necessary ingredients to make Mrs. Podesta's sausage and tortellini soup.

As she hummed one of her favorite songs, "If you're going to San Francisco" by Scott McKenzie, Willow wistfully read the ingredients off of her recipe card; a small can of diced tomatoes, a can of tomato sauce, a box of Barilla Tortellini, and one small yellow onion. Another lesson learned from Mrs. Podesta was to always have some sweet Italian sausage on hand. Retrieving a saucepan from the wrought iron rack she had convinced Dylan to install over the oven, she began the process. First, she diced a small yellow onion, crushed several cloves of garlic, and sliced the sausage into chunks. Willow drizzled a little olive oil into the saucepan. Once it was hot, she placed the ingredients into the hot oil. As the sausage browned, she added a sprig of thyme from the small herb garden on a shelf over the kitchen sink, a liberal dose of dried oregano, and a sprinkle of salt and pepper. After the ingredients had sautéed for several minutes, their sweet aroma signaled to Willow to add the diced tomatoes and tomato sauce. She lowered the flame on the gas stove to a bare simmer. After taking a glass from the cabinet next to the sink, Willow opened the refrigerator, took out the pitcher of cold tea she was in the habit of preparing each day before she left for work, and poured herself a glass.

Sitting on their small couch in the living room under the protection of a knitted comforter, courtesy of Mrs. Podesta, Willow wondered about the world that awaited the life inside her. Would kindness and charity rule the day? Would service to others be seen as a noble endeavor or some half-baked Pollyanna view of the world? Would her child grow up to be a giver, not a taker, a person who saw value in everyone? Or would she become the "I," "Me," "My" materialistic person Willow so despised, one destined to live in some gated enclave of self-indulgent societal elitists, never giving a thought to those less fortunate? Willow sipped her chilled beverage, hoping to bring her mind back to a more optimistic pursuit. How shall she tell her husband he would soon be a father, a provider, a teacher?

Having received his new assignment from Martha Irons, Steward took the liberty of leaving work early. He took the documents Irons had given him, intending to work from home for an extended period of time. This, of course, would require him to explain to his wife the nature and breadth of the story of a Vietnam war veteran. He hoped he would not have to share much detail of his time there. Willow already knew of his best friend Tommy's death and the toll it had taken on him. That was all he was willing to share with her. When Steward returned home, he never talked of his time in Vietnam to the best of his ability. What he saw there, what he did there, would stay there. He hoped his wife's generous heart would be satisfied, knowing his work was focused on helping a lost and forgotten soul. That concern did nothing to dispel the excitement he felt at the opportunity to restore hope to one who had lost all hope, to give gratitude to one whose sacrifices drew unwarranted condemnation.

Steward thought his new assignment called for some sort of celebration. After all, with no commute to start and end his day, he could sleep in a bit in the morning, perhaps even share breakfast with his wife. Dinner preparation could even be a joint task for the two. On their walks to Venice Beach, the couple had passed Giuseppe's Italian Deli, a relatively small but intimate establishment on the corner of Echo and Venice Boulevard that specialized in imported Italian meats, cheeses, and wines. The place reminded Steward of ethnic specialty stores back in San Francisco. On either side of the glass-door entrance were crates of fresh vegetables protected from the Southern California sun by a large green, red, and white canopy. Entering, you were nearly suffocated by the aroma of an array of Italian cheeses and the fresh-baked bread and pastries that the owner, Giuseppe Grillo, personally took charge of daily. Steward momentarily paused as he entered the deli, allowing his sense of smell to partake in the plethora of olfactory delights. A baritone voice from an older man whom Steward assumed was the owner called out from behind the glass case displaying multiple styles of cheese and sliced meats, "Welcome to Giuseppe's. What can I get you?"

"I'm looking for a special brand of prosecco. I wonder if you carry it. It's called Nino Franco Rustico."

The old man wiped his hands on his apron as he came around from behind the display counter. A broad smile formed on his face.

"I'm a Giuseppe, but call me Joe. Are you from the old country? Nino Franco is a," he struggled for the words in English before saying, "vino molto bello,' (beautiful wine). I no sell much of it here."

Steward smiled at the man's hospitality and compliment of Steward's selection. "No. I'm from San Francisco. Nino Franco is my wife's favorite. She's the Italian one in the family."

"Vieni con me," said Grillo, as he motioned for Steward to follow him. Dylan followed the man to the end of an extended display of wines arranged individually in slots on a dark oak shelf that ran the length of the wall of the deli. He stopped at the end of the rack, reached up, and pulled down a light green bottle. He carefully rotated the bottle in his hands as if to appreciate one last time the exquisite blend of Glera grapes grown in northern Italy.

"Nino Franco!" smiled the owner. "Maybe some cheese or a little prosciutto with'a the vino?"

"No, thank you, Joe. This will do fine," smiled Steward, feeling drawn to the man's caring personality.

The old man proceeded back to the counter. After bagging the bottle of wine, he carefully selected several pieces of finely sliced prosciutto and a couple of slices of Provolone cheese, wrapped them in white butcher paper, placing the small package in the bag with the wine.

"A little something extra," he smiled with a twinkle in his eye. "Please bring'a your wife the next time you drop in."

Steward was about to answer the man when he saw a photograph on the wall behind the counter. It was a Navy officer and an enlisted man standing side by side. It was signed, "Love Pop."

"Your sons?" Steward asked, pointing to the photograph.

As proud as any father could be, the old man replied with the broadest of smiles, "Si, my son Joe," pointing to the one in the officer's uniform. "With my other son, Michael." His fingers graced the photograph of his sons. "They just got back from Vietnam."

Thank God at least one family's sons returned, Steward thought.

"Thank you again, Joe, and yes, I will bring her the next time."

"A Presto!"

Steward left the smiling Grillo and proceeded home to surprise his wife with the wine and extra snacks, compliments of the deli's owner, and his new assignment.

CHAPTER 19

Willow's futuristic journey into motherhood almost caused her to burn the base of her sausage and tortellini soup; only her husband's opening of the front door prevented a disaster.

"Something sure smells good!" he announced upon entering the living room. Willow tossed off the comforter and hurried to her husband's arms.

"Could it possibly be me?" she cooed as she drew his face closer—a more than welcome home embrace. The scent of Yves Saint Laurent's Riva Gauche triggered the primal instincts in Steward. Willow had to push her husband away gently. She struggled to maintain her native urges. "Whoa, Tiger! How about some dinner first?"

Steward inhaled deeply for one last taste of the romantic potion before begrudgingly acquiescing to his wife's request. Turning his head toward the kitchen, Steward said, "It smells like Mrs. Podesta has been here."

Willow straightened her ruffled blouse and headed to the kitchen.

"Her famous sausage and tortellini soup awaits you if I haven't already burned it," Willow decried, taking the scalding pot of sauce off the stove and stirring it vigorously with a large wooden spoon.

Steward unveiled his surprise from the deli bag and proudly announced, "Then a glass of your favorite prosecco will surely calm you down." Willow quickly recognized the light green bottle of Nino Franco.

"My God, Dylan, where did you ever find this!" She was nearly overcome with the anticipation of the fruity sparkling wine crossing her palate.

Taking a wine opener from the kitchen drawer, he replied, "There's a little deli near the boulevard called Giuseppe's Deli. I stopped there before coming home. The owner goes by his American name, Joe. He's quite the character. Anyway, he threw in some complimentary slices of prosciutto and Provolone cheese for us. He said it should pair quite nicely with the wine."

After tasting the sauce and assuring herself she had not ruined it, Willow put a pan of water on the stove to boil. Dylan had retrieved two glasses off the driftwood wine rack and was awaiting her at the kitchen table. Within each, a secret awaited the other. Ironically, it was a proposed toast by Dylan that would reveal one. Most anxious to tell her of his new assignment, Dylan raised his glass to her and announced, "Here's to the two of us."

An impish smile spread across Willow's face. Well attuned to his wife's idiosyncrasies, Steward mused aloud, "And what exactly does that smile mean?"

Willow sipped her wine and daintily dabbed her mouth with a napkin. "Your counting is a bit off."

She sat back and smugly waited for her husband to decipher her meaning. At first, he was bewildered. He comically turned his head left and then right before responding, "Is there someone here I don't see?"

The irony of his words caused Willow to burst out in laughter. "As a matter of fact, yes."

His humorous smile quickly faded as his mind shifted to trying to interpret his wife's cryptic words. As if he were a contestant on some tv game show, Dylan asked, "So there's someone here, but I can't see who it is, right?"

"Right," Willow responded. She stared into her husband's eyes, thoroughly enjoying the mental hijinks she was putting him through.

Never one to enjoy solving riddles, Dylan let his exasperation speak for him. Pleading, he said, "Honey, you know how much I dislike riddles. Can't you please just tell me what you're talking about?"

"If I told you the table isn't going to be big enough for three, would that help?"

Not one to be quick on the uptake, Dylan's mind continued with its momentary short circuit until suddenly the wires connected. Those days when she wasn't feeling good in the morning, or when she had no appetite at all, or if she did, it was for some ungodly concoctions of food items. That had to be it. She was pregnant. He was going to be a father. His mind almost exploded. He jumped to his feet. He stumbled on his words, not believing what he was saying.

"You're kidding! You, I mean, we, I mean, are we going to have a baby!"

At last, he figured it out, she thought. Willow wasn't sure she could keep it to herself much longer.

"Yes, honey. All of the above, You and I, we are going to have a child."

Dylan knelt next to his wife. He placed his hands on her stomach as if he were touching a fine piece of crystal that might crack at the slightest pressure.

"That's our baby, our child!"

His wonderment was more of a question than a statement of fact. At that moment, Dylan Steward became overwhelmed with the future that faced the unborn in his wife's womb. He rested on both knees. Steward peered into the future and saw a holocaust of potential tragedies awaiting his child. His face turned ashen. His eyes reflected abject terror, so much so even Willow was taken aback.

"Sweetheart, what is it? You look so terrified."

Dylan mustered the strength to verbalize his deepest fears.

"What if I can't protect it? What if I can't give our child everything he or she deserves and need? What if I can't shield them from the evils that life will put before them?"

Willow agonized for her husband. She took his hands in hers.

"Look at me, Dylan Steward. You will be a great father, a great provider, and a great protector. You and I will prepare our child to have a great future, one filled with all sorts of possibilities and full of potential for them to pursue their dreams. That, my love, is the greatest gift we could ever give our child."

For the moment, Steward took solace in his wife's commentary. He tried to focus on the present, with all of its joys and elations. Yes, he was going to be a father. A smile appeared on his face. Blissfulness returned to his voice. "Okay then, let's celebrate."

He reached for the bottle of prosecco and topped off his glass. When he held the bottle up to Willow, she placed her hand on top of her glass.

"I think I'll pass, what with the baby and everything."

"Oh yeah. Sure, sure! I understand," Dylan replied, embarrassed that he had not immediately grasped the danger of alcohol to an unborn fetus.

Steward sat back silent in his chair, still in wonderment over the news that he would soon be a father. If not for the slightly acrid odor of a tomato sauce starting to burn, he might have sat there till dawn. Try as he might, the old Dylan slipped back into his old pessimistic, distrustful self. Dare he hope that this foreboding sense of the future was nothing more than his own sense of inadequacies to deal with the unknown?

Willow hastened to the kitchen to save the sauce from ruination. Setting the saucepan aside, she started a pot of water to cook the dried tortellini noodles. Willow sprinkled a few shakes of salt and a quick drizzle of olive oil into the water. Out of the corner of her eye, she caught a sudden motion. When she looked, she saw her husband adjusting the positions of the kitchen tables and chairs. He would get a perplexed look on his face, then rearrange the chairs, another perplexed look, and another repositioning of chairs. She mused as her dream was coming to life. As she added the tortellini noodles to the boiling water, she suddenly felt his arms embrace her from behind.

"Do you know how much I love you?" he whispered, kissing the softness of her auburn hair.

"No, tell me," she answered as she allowed his arms to tighten around her waist.

"Beyond the horizon, past the moon, and into the next galaxy."

The importance of Steward's story paled in comparison to the news of his wife's pregnancy. Still, nonetheless, it was a testament to the faith Jimmy Donahue had in him as a reporter. Still holding her, Steward said, "I've got some news to share too."

Willow felt herself pushing backward into her husband's body.

"Do tell, my love," assuming the physiological reaction to her bodily movements would be an invitation to postpone dinner.

"Jimmy Donahue gave me the green light to dig deeper into the story of the homeless vet. He even said I could work at home if necessary. He really wants this guy's story to be told."

Willow turned to face her husband.

"Oh Dylan, that's fantastic! It just goes to show you what a talented writer you are, and I'll have you close at hand," she added with a smile. As an aside, she said, "Jimmy must have a lot of faith in you to give you that kind of latitude."

"If he does, I sure don't want to disappoint him," sighed Steward.

Tasting one of the noodles for doneness, Willow said, "Would you get me a couple of plates? This pasta is al dente."

After serving up his plate and then hers, Willow said, "Let's hear more about this," as she headed to the kitchen table.

Dylan methodically explained his investigatory process over a steaming bowl of tortellini and sausage soup. First, he would sort all correspondence by city and county. Then a second sort by the Army unit mentioned, if any was given, paying particular attention to the mention of someone named Kenny. Secondly, he'd contact every caller who left a return number, again documenting any reference to a specific Army unit and any reference to a "Kenny."

"I don't think contacting the VA, or the Army's First Division Command will be of any use. My information is too vague at this point. I'll have to have something detailing time and location in Vietnam."

"Honey, I hope doing this piece doesn't bring up too many bad memories?"

Willow made no mention of her husband's friend, Tommy, who died in Vietnam. She knew all she needed to from his stories of Tommy. Dylan's nightmares told another story, one that Willow felt best to leave untold.

Dylan rested his fork and took a somewhat healthy sip of prosecco.

"You know, sweetheart, there are really two stories here. One is about my mystery guy and what happened to him in Nam. The other story is about what happened to him when he came home. I can't do anything about the first story, but maybe I can make a difference in his life now and the lives of others like him."

Willow smiled at him. She didn't need to say anything. Her eyes said it all.

"I love you, Dylan Steward!"

CHAPTER 20

By the end of the first month on his new assignment, Dylan Steward had begun to feel like he was searching for the identity of someone who did not exist. He had read hundreds of letters, all claiming that they had a loved one or knew someone who had served with the 101st in Vietnam. Some wrote on behalf of someone who had served in the Navy, Air Force, or Marines in Vietnam, completely ignoring the fact that Steward had explicitly noted the Army's 101st Infantry Division as his sole focus. No one made a single reference to anyone named Kenny. The phone calls he returned were equally, if not more frustrating and painful. The majority were callers who only wanted to share their grief over the loss of a husband, son, or brother with someone who would listen. They, like Dylan, suffered from their own nightmares; the voice of a child riding off into the distance assuring his mother he would be okay, never to return; or seeing someone in a uniform from a distance and desperately hoping that the faded image was their lost one, miraculously returning home to them. Dylan thought of the countless conversations he had had with Mrs. Podesta about her son, Tommy. Her recollections of his childhood, teaching him to ride a bicycle, watching him play high school baseball, and meeting the girl he took to his high school prom. Toni Bonadetti was an Italian girl from the old neighborhood who Mrs. Podesta thought was the perfect match for her son. It was like driving a stake through his heart. He would scream to himself, *Please, not another damn story about Tommy.* To her, he would only smile, put his arms around her shoulders and say nothing as the woman wept.

STEWARD WOULD REPORT every Monday to Donahue's office to remind the other staff reporters that he still worked there. While he was there, Steward would lay out a carefully detailed report of his work. Donahue's response was always the same. Looking over his reading glasses and peering thoughtfully at Steward, he would state, "You've got a great story here, Dylan. Don't give up hope." Clouds of cigar smoke always punctuated his response.

After one such meeting, Steward had the misfortune of running into Julian Fleming, who was there to discuss an assignment with Donahue. He stood in the door and announced, "Well, if it isn't the golden boy who stole my story." His statement reeked of sarcasm of the most bitter blend.

Jealousy froze Fleming's face in a hateful sneer. His eyes reflected the scalding resentment he felt for Steward and the special treatment he felt Donahue had given the newly hired reporter. Donahue seethed at the allegation of favoritism that spewed out of Fleming's mouth. Despite his desire for a cooperative work environment, he felt duty-bound to respond to this insult.

"As I remember Julian, I offered the lead to this story to you first, and you turned it down. In fact, you thought it was beneath someone of your experience and education. It was you who said, 'Give it to the new guy.' So what's your beef?"

Frustration squeezed Fleming's throat muscles to the point he gagged on his words. Particles of spit flew from his mouth as he spewed out his venomous rage.

"A homeless bum gets Steward privileges no one else gets. That's what gives!" He slurred the last word for emphasis.

Fleming's last remark pushed Steward over the edge. Mustering up every bit of civility he could, Steward replied, "Before I go..."

Believing his nemesis was intent on leaving, Fleming stepped aside. When Steward got to the door, he took hold of the doorknob and closed the door. He turned to face Fleming. Every instinct in his body told him to grab Fleming by the throat and squeeze until his eyes appeared to pop out of their sockets before passing out. As he stepped forward, Julian Fleming took a step backward, suddenly realizing he had released the tiger within Steward. His voice was eerily controlled. Each word seemed to have a sharp, harsh pronunciation designed to emphasize his point.

"Julian, I can call you Julian, can't I?" Steward said. It was Steward's turn to unleash sarcasm on his antagonist.

An audible gulp for air and a nod was Fleming's answer.

Steward smiled. "Good. So, Julian, here's something they didn't teach you in journalism school at Stanford. A lead is like a piece of a jigsaw puzzle. Put enough of them together, and you have the start of a story. The problem is all the pieces are blank. There is no image, color, or shape to help you decide what piece goes where. Like the colors on a palette in the hands of an artist, you will paint those nondescript pieces with whatever sense of humanity lies within you, with whatever sense of compassion for the suffering of others lies within your heart. When you're done, if you are lucky, you will have written a story that the reader will want to read over and over, a story that pushes blood through every vessel of their body until they feel the same empathy you felt when you wrote the story."

Jimmy Donahue sat spellbound by Steward's soliloquy. It was brilliant. It spoke to the essence of what a good reporter, no, what a great reporter must possess. Too bad it was wasted on a reporter like Julian Fleming, whose sense of humanity was defined by, "if it doesn't affect me, so what?" and whose empathy for the suffering of others hung off the wrought iron gate to the entrance of his home in Brentwood Estates. Had he the courage, Julian Fleming would have struck out at the impudence of the boorish, uneducated Steward who dared to think he could preach to him about writing. Who in the hell did he think he was talking to, some student reporter on a high school newspaper? But then courage was not a trait within Julian Fleming's DNA.

He was about to leave when Steward added, "Oh, Julian, there's one more thing that you didn't learn at Stanford or anyplace else for that matter."

Fleming would have agreed to anything just to get Steward out of his face.

"What?" The defiance in his voice spoke volumes about his intent to truly listen.

"The next time you kick a man when he's on the ground, make sure that person doesn't have a friend. Because if he does, that friend might want to give you a taste of your own medicine."

Not one to heed that inner voice telling him to be quiet, Fleming, in a mistaken display of bravado, replied, "Are you threatening me?!"

"Oh no, Julian, a threat is something to come in the future. This is here and now."

With that last explanation, Steward moved so close to him that Fleming could see the hairs in Steward's nose. The heat from Steward's mouth caused Fleming to turn his head aside. If Steward's words didn't convince Fleming of his intent, his eyes indeed did. Without a single blink, the hatred in Steward's eyes might even have frightened Satan himself. Fleming could feel himself losing control of his urinary tract.

"I will find you, Julian, and treat you in a like manner only with more feeling. Understand?"

Fleming had to steady his legs as he moved to open the office door, never once taking his eyes off Steward. He walked out without saying a word. He took short steps; his feet positioned close together. He struggled without success to hide his momentary loss of bladder control. With Fleming gone, Donahue reached for his half-smoked cigar. Taking a small box of matches from his desk's middle drawer, he took one out, lit his cigar, and deeply inhaled, savoring the imported product, but more so, the dressing down that had just taken place.

"That was quite the raking over the coals," he said, with a slow exhale sending a narrow stream of smoke upward. There was just a hint of an appreciative smile on the corner of Donahue's mouth.

"I doubt it will make a dent in his conscience, assuming he has one," replied a non-repentant Steward. "But if it doesn't…"

"That's for another time, Dylan. Let's focus on the task at hand."

Donahue handed Steward a letter he had personally received that morning. The letter would provide answers to Steward's quest for his mystery man and the tragic circumstances surrounding him.

"Several papers, across the nation, reprint articles published in the *Times*, mostly small-town papers that cannot afford full-time reporters. One such paper is the Cut and Shoot Star out of Cut and Shoot Texas, a small town about sixty miles north of Houston, Texas. Their editor, a man named Riley Cotton, sent this to me. You need to read it."

Steward took the envelope from Donahue. He took a seat, staring at the letter in his hand. He was having some difficulty focusing, and his hand shook, the product of the wave of testosterone that had engulfed him.

"Well, go ahead, read it," Donahue said, knowing its contents would result in help for the young man and raise Steward's stock as a gifted writer and reporter. Steward was entirely unprepared for the story that was about to unfold before him.

Dear Jimmy, after reprinting the story by Dylan Steward about that homeless vet in the Times, I received a phone call from the son of a small local rancher. The boy's name is Kenny Maxwell. He had served in Vietnam with the 101st Airborne Division. He lost a leg over there and is thought of as a local hero in these parts. Anyway, he talked about his squad leader, a friend of his by the name of Richie Calhoun. They had served in the same squad together. After being wounded during a battle Kenny referred to as Hamburger Hill, they wound up together at a VA hospital in Palo Alto, California. Kenny lost track of his friend after that. This kid was very emotional when he recounted his story to me. My letter would not do justice to the depth of his feelings and what he and his friend went through. It was thirty days and nights of the most horrific bloodshed any human being could possibly endure. I think your Steward guy needs to talk with him. I've enclosed Kenny's contact information.

Best of Luck, Riley Cotton.
   Kenny Maxwell
   139 Rural Route 17
   Cut and Shoot Texas, 77303
   Telephone # 936-498-3432.

Steward laid the letter on his lap. He bent forward, holding his face in his hands. His breathing became labored. Steward cleared his throat several times before looking up to speak. When he did, tears had pooled in his eyes. Memories that he hoped had faded away forever now burned again. His own personal PTSD had surfaced at an inopportune time. Steward was at the mercy of his own demons, which now struck out from somewhere deep within him, a place he didn't want to acknowledge, let alone visit.

He was unable to control or suppress the emotions it evoked. Tears, so repugnant and shameful in the macho society of the time, began to flow. No amount of resistance could prevent their release.

Then that same inner strength that had enabled him to survive took over. His breathing slowed, and his composure returned.

"I know these guys, Jimmy, not personally, but I was there where they were. I saw the things they saw. This guy Calhoun will bring closure not only to his story but maybe a lot of other stories just like it." His heart raced after he uttered these lines, realizing that he needed that closure as much for himself as for them.

Donahue understood precisely what the young reporter meant. Once a year, surviving members of his old Marine Corps 5th Division who fought on Iwo Jima met at the Marine Corps base in Twenty-Nine Palms for a reunion. Old friends were reunited, old memories were shared once again, and unfortunately, old tears were shed again and again. Donahue often wondered why he put himself through it year after year. *Was closure even possible*, he thought to himself?

Clearing his own throat, the old Irish man said, "I'm getting flak from upstairs about favoritism if you get my drift, so the faster you wrap this up, the better."

The source of Donahue's troubles was self-evident to Steward. *I'll take care of that*, he thought to himself. "Don't worry, Jimmy. I'll handle it." The firmness of his words left Donahue wondering what else besides the story he would handle.

―――

THE THOUGHT of talking with someone who might know Steward's mystery man caused his fingers to stumble twice over the telephone keypad on his cubicle desk before he finally got the number right. He waited anxiously as the phone rang. Finally!

"Y'all reached the Maxwell Cattle Ranch. How kin I help you?"

"My name is Dylan Steward. I'm a reporter with the *Los Angeles Times*. I'm trying to reach a Kenny Maxwell. Can you help me?"

"I do believe Mr. Kenny is here. Let me check for y'all. One sec, please."

There was a brief silence; then Steward heard the voice.

"Kenny Maxwell. Y'all must be that reporter from Los Angeles I heard about. I figured y'all be too busy to call."

Steward could hear the distinct sound of a helicopter over the phone.

"Excuse me, Mr. Maxwell, but are you airborne?"

"Just a little cattle counting, pardner. I'll be on the ground in two 'mikes'."

"I guess I am a little confused. From the editor's letter, I assumed you ran a small cattle ranch, but you need a helicopter to count your chattel?"

Maxwell's audible laugh rose above the static over the telephone.

"Small by Texas standards, maybe. We run about twenty-five hundred head on two thousand acres."

The helicopter's rotors slowed to a dull hum, then stopped.

"Now then, it's a little quieter here on the ground," Maxwell said with a sigh of relief. He walked over to a metal overhang near his landing pad. Once out of the blazing Texas sun, he dipped his hard straw Resistor hat into a two hundred gallon water trough and poured the contents over his head. A blue bandanna around his neck served as a towel to wipe the cooling liquid off his face and neck.

"Is this a good time to talk with you, Mr. Maxwell?" Steward asked.

Steward was mildly annoyed by all these distracting influences but jazzed about the possibility of solving his "puzzle."

"It is now," Maxwell said after placing his bandanna loosely around his neck. "And Mr. Maxwell was my father, I'm Kenny, and you're Dylan, right?"

Relieved with the welcome sense of familiarity, Steward began his quest for information.

"Okay, Kenny, it is. You've read my article?"

Maxwell spoke his words with certainty.

"The guy you're looking for is Richie Calhoun. He was my squad leader. We were in the third squad, weapons platoon, Alpha Company, 2nd Battalion, 1st Brigade of the 101st. If he could stand upright, he'd be about six-foot tall and skinny as a rail. He's got a crooked scar across…"

Steward interrupted him. His anxiety had been piqued. "Did you say a scar?"

"Yeah, really pointed. It ran across his forehead, courtesy of a piece of shrapnel from an RPG that hit our position one night. We spent ten days going up and down that goddamn mountain. A Stars and Stripes reporter called it Hamburger Hill because of the casualties we took."

Maxwell was matter-of-fact about this information, no doubt attempting to hide the emotion it evoked. The mere mention of the name Hamburger Hill caused Maxwell to pause. Steward could hear the man's labored breath over the phone.

"The terrain was terrible. The hill was heavily foliaged with steep ravines that ran down its side like fingers. The night of May 19th, we neared the crest despite heavy weapons, fire and rocket attacks."

Again, he stopped; his pretense at detachment slipped away. When he resumed, there was a panicky tone in his voice, like he was living the past all over again. His words raced.

"Rain like I've never seen poured down from a darkened sky. Suddenly, we were ordered to retreat. An artillery barrage caught us off guard—the earth shook. Artillery flashes lit up the sky. It was like the earth opened up, and the devil screamed for the souls of those of us crawling into mud holes for protection."

There was another long pause. The drawl in his voice increased with every spoken word. Steward hoped reliving this experience would not be too much for his source.

"Sorry," Maxwell said. "No human being should ever have to endure what we did, and of all the luck, I survived that night only to lose my left leg below the knee to a short round from our own mortar team in a counterattack the next day." With every word Maxwell spoke, Steward's breathing was affected. His own memories came back. Their shared horrors would soon become known.

"I know. I was with the 1st. Cav at Duc Pho in 67'."

There was a sudden and relieving sensation in Maxwell, knowing that he was talking with someone who understood, who had been there and endured the suffering and sacrifices he had. Maxwell detailed his history with Richie Calhoun for the next hour or so. They had become best friends in airborne training at Fort Benning, Georgia. Calhoun was from Ann Arbor, Michigan. He was raised in foster care until he aged out and then enlisted in the Army.

"I think he was looking for the family he never really had," Maxwell said.

He and Calhoun had been medevacked to a hospital in Saigon following their extraction over Hill 937, or Hamburger hill, to those who survived the carnage. Then he went to a VA hospital in Palo Alto, California. Maxwell was placed in the rehabilitation wing for amputees while Calhoun was sent to a unit for trauma disorder patients.

"When I was discharged, I tried to find out about Richie. All they would tell me was that he had walked away from the facility. They conducted searches, but no trace of him was ever found."

There was another long pause before Maxwell spoke. When he did, Steward realized he was only getting the tip of the iceberg regarding Maxwell's friend.

"You know, there's a lot more to the story about Richie and what happened over there."

Steward was surprised that a cowboy from Texas could be so captive, but there it was.

"That's the story I need to hear, Kenny. Listen, I need to sit down and talk with you. Taking notes over the phone isn't gonna cut it for me."

Excited about the possibility of telling the whole story about his friend, Kenny Maxwell eagerly replied, "Okay then partna', meet we will. The boys can finish this count. Give me a day or two, and I'll give my new Cessna a test run to LA. What say?"

Steward practically blurted out his phone number, punctuating his excitement with, "Call me the second you land!" He hung up the receiver, both his mind and heart racing.

CHAPTER 21

Dylan Steward's focus was often single-minded, whether playing a jazz standard or researching a story. He was able to ignore most peripheral ongoings. However, the flow of black suits (confirmed by the rumor mill as attorneys for the Times) in and out of Jimmy Donahue's office the past several days could not be overlooked, nor could the change in Donahue's demeanor. His broad smile when greeting people became a simple nod. He ignored questions, offering a grunt as an answer. Those in the city desk room seemed to spend more time questioning anyone and everyone from the janitors to secretaries and as far up the chain of command as they dared risk to find out what was going on. If that wasn't enough to put Steward on edge, every ring of his phone caused him to grab the receiver like a drowning man clutches a life preserver until it was the call for which he had been waiting.

"Dylan Steward?"

"Dylan, Kenny Maxwell. I got into LAX about a half-hour ago. This cabbie here says he can get me up to your place in twenty minutes or so."

"I'll be in the lobby waiting. Oh, and how do I recognize you?"

Steward regretted the question the minute it escaped his mouth. With a burst of laughter, a Texas voice said, "It won't be hard to spot a six foot-four cowboy with a white Stetson and one leg."

With Donahue behind closed doors again, Steward alerted Donahue's secretary of his temporary absence. Twenty minutes seemed like an eternity to Steward until he saw his guest. True to his word, Kenny Maxwell was every bit of six foot-four and not an ounce under two hundred and twenty pounds by Steward's estimation. A pair of alligator skin boots with silver toe tips, tan western slacks secured by a handmade leather belt with a big silver belt buckle, and a long-sleeved western dress shirt with a silver-tipped bolo tie completed his attire.

"Do I even have to ask," said Steward as he approached his quarry?

"Hell no! Kenny Maxwell in the flesh" bellowed the gregarious Texan whose appearance had caught the eyes of those in the lobby.

The strength of his grip surprised Steward. Maybe it shouldn't have, but it did.

"I'm really looking forward to hearing the rest of your story. I've reserved a small conference room for us. Follow me."

Maxwell noted everything about the four-story Times Building. Its expansive lobby, multiple elevators, and a city desk area with office space and cubicles for twenty-some reporters was a far cry from the offices of the Cut and Shoot Star back home. As Steward opened the door to the conference room, Maxwell whistled and marveled, "Y'all got quite a place here!"

Steward nodded appreciatively. "We can talk here. Have a seat."

Maxwell arched his back, then took a few steps before sitting down. "That Cessna 421 lacks a bit of leg room for me."

With a surprising degree of urgency, the tall Texan said, "I've wanted to tell this story for some time so let's not waste any time on formality, shall we, partna'?" The dominant Texas twang only gave the statement more emphasis.

Steward sized up the big Texan. He seemed open and forthright, but one never knows what will happen when the big questions get asked. He tried to be informal and adopted a standard means of broaching the subject matter.

"Normally, I just take notes, but if you don't mind, I'd like to record this. I don't want to miss anything, okay? Let's start with what you know about Kenny's background. You said he was raised as a foster child?"

Maxwell nodded. He took off his Stetson and laid it on the table.

"Yep. The way he described it, it was damned awful. Whenever he started to form a bond with some kid, suddenly they were gone, moved to another placement with no explanation to the other kids in the home. Then there were the abusive parents, the abusive father who beat the kids, or the neglectful mother who ignored them because she was only interested in a paycheck. Like I said earlier, the Army offered him a home with the brothers he never had before. It's one of the things that made him such a great squad leader. He really cared about the guys in his squad. He was always the one to spend time talking to everyone after a firefight. Ya know, to see how they were, especially the new guys. We called them "cherry-boys." He checked with the medics whenever he could on anyone who got hurt. Hell, besides our commanding officer, he even wrote letters home to the families who lost someone in his squad. He was that kind of guy. I told him when we got back to the world, I'd bring him to our ranch and show him what a Texas family was like. He said he couldn't imagine what that was like, but he sure would like to see it."

The slowly turning tape recorder was both a blessing and a curse. It accurately documented every word along with all the emotional intonation that accompanied it— more than a hurried pen scribbling across the page of a notebook could possibly do.

Unfortunately, it also freed Steward from that task, leaving him to focus exclusively on every recollection of the Vietnam vet—every memory when walking point on patrol. The abject terror that gripped every muscle in your body whenever a bush appeared to move or when the night sounds in the jungle ceased—a sign shit was about to happen. It was hell revisited for Dylan Steward. His mind displayed a flashback in response. The squad hunkered down in the jungle, their ponchos not really keeping out that god-awful rain. Their teeth chattering so loudly they were afraid the VC could hear them. There they sat, tired, hungry, and scared shitless. He pressed the stop button on the recorder as much to offer Maxwell a break as it was to mute Steward's brain if that was even possible. Maxwell leaned his head back and closed his eyes. For a minute or so, he stayed in this meditative state. He seemed to be preparing his next words. When he opened his eyes, Steward sensed the final segment was coming. He pressed start again on the recorder.

"The night we came off that hill, I'd lost contact with everyone. You couldn't see your hand in front of your face until the skies lit up with artillery rounds and mortars. The ground was a swampy mess from the rains. It was like trying to run down a slip-n-slide. Our lieutenant found what was left of our squad—me and a guy named Sanders, a blonde Swede from Minnesota, I think. He asked us if we had seen Calhoun. We told him no. That's when he told us that Richie had made it down the hill, but when he couldn't find any of his squad, against direct orders from the Lt, he went back up the hill looking for us. It wasn't until the next day that I learned a company sweeping the hill for survivors had found Richie hovered under a broken tree limb. His poncho was pulled over his head. He was muttering incoherently, 'Where's my guys, where's my guys.' Like I said before, I spent a week or so in a hospital in Saigon before being shipped home to a VA hospital in Palo Alto, California. I asked around and found out that Richie was on the same transport C141 as me and was at the same VA hospital. You know the rest of the story."

Steward reached for the recorder and turned it off.

"I'm sorry you had to go through all of that again, Kenny."

The statement would have sounded ridiculously shallow when uttered by most, but not when spoken by someone who had been in the "Shit." With words, only Steward would understand, "If not now, it would be another dream, tonight or the next night."

The two men sat there, emotionally drained, one from unburdening the past that would haunt him for years to come, the other from revisiting his own haunted memories, neither saying a word to the other. A knock on the door and the voice of Martha Irons brought the two men out of their self-imposed trance. She stuck her head into the room, black-rimmed reading glasses, hair bun, and authoritarian manner on display.

"I'm sorry to interrupt, Dylan, but I think you'd better take this call." She pointed to the phone on the table and added, "I'll transfer it."

Irons left. A minute later, the phone on the conference table rang. Steward picked it up. He was so drained of energy he could barely speak his own name.

"Dylan Steward."

The voice on the other end of the line was all business.

"Mr. Steward, this is Officer Peter Kay. I'm with the LAPD. I believe I may have some information about the man in that article you wrote several weeks ago. Are you still interested in this man?"

Steward answered, "Officer, I'm going to put you on speaker. I have someone here who needs to hear this also."

After pressing the speaker button, Steward said, "Yes, Officer, please tell me what you know."

"Well, I am not sure this pertains to the right guy, but here is the story. Last night, I responded to a call regarding a body found in an industrial park south of Spring St. When I got to the scene, the ambulance was already there. They had the body on a gurney, ready for transport. The only ID they found was a VA card in the pocket of his field jacket. It had the 101st eagle on the shoulders. The card was so worn they couldn't make out a name. I remembered your article and the patch on that man's shoulder and thought I should call you."

Maxwell was shocked back to the present. He leaned forward as if to forcibly draw out every word he wanted to say.

"That's helpful, Officer Kay, but could you describe what the man looked like?"

"Well, sir, I'd guess he was close to six feet tall. His face was covered with sores and bruises. His clothes were filthy. My guess is he'd been homeless for some time. Something else, too, he had this ugly scar across his forehead."

With those words, Kenny Maxwell sank back in his chair. His face turned ashen. His Adam's apple moved rapidly as his throat muscles contracted. Steward froze at the description of the scar. The silence caused the officer to ask, "Are you still there, Mr. Steward?"

"Yes, yes I am, officer." Struggling with his words, Steward added, "Where is the body now, officer?"

The officer's words seemed like he was describing the location of an inanimate object like a building or a monument, not a human being, made of flesh and blood.

"The city morgue. Ask for a John Doe 139C."

Steward struggled to end the conversation without a complete breakdown. His answer was void of any emotion, some robot-like response from a recorded caller.

"Good work. Thank you, Officer Kay." As an afterthought, Steward added, "I have someone here who can make a positive identification if that would help?"

"Yes, it would. We could make family notifications that much sooner."

Maxwell stood up slowly. He walked to the conference room window and looked out over the sprawling city of Los Angeles.

No one should die only to be remembered as a John Doe, especially not his friend. There was a firm resolve in his voice when he turned around. His face reflected the grim determination of a man on a mission.

"Dylan, thank you for your time, but I've got a friend to see and then take home to his family."

"Yeah, and I've got a story to write."

The two men hugged each other; then, each proceeded on their tasks.

THE NEXT MORNING Steward went to his office to begin writing his story. He stared at his Olivetti. He never realized how painful changing a simple verb tense could be. Steward looked at the first page of his draft. Slowly, he found his red pencil. That pencil felt like a ten-pound weight between his fingers. It moved slowly, line by line, until he found the spot. The line started with, "Today, I found out the name of my missing veteran is Richie Calhoun." The red pencil exed out the word 'is' and laboriously printed 'was.' Steward took out a fresh piece of onion skin paper and slipped it into the carriage on his Olivetti. There was no rush of inspiration, no flurry of fingers pounding the keys lest a creative thought get lost, only the slow, steady, methodical sounds of keys striking their target and forming another tragic episode of human loss.

CHAPTER 22

Steward and his colleagues attending Donahue's weekly assignment meetings had noticed a prevailing chill in the air whenever Julian Fleming was a part of those meetings. Fleming avoided any contact with Steward at all cost, never sure when the not-so-subtle undertone of Steward's words might become action. He only attended the meetings because Donahue had ordered him to do so. Even then, there was no word of hello, a glance of acknowledgment, nothing from Fleming. He barely reacted to the enthusiasm of the others when they talked about any progress they were making or the newest lead they had received in pursuit of their assignment. What particularly grated the arrogant Fleming was any praise Steward received for his article on the homeless man. The editor-in-chief, Damon Willard, had personally presented Steward with a plaque for reporter of the month. The Salvation Army and the head of Catholic Charities for Los Angeles gave Steward certificates of appreciation for his humanity to those disenfranchised by society. Fleming would squirm in his chair at the sound of accolades he felt he had deserved. To make matters worse, those in attendance would deliberately take every opportunity to opine on such accolades in the presence of Fleming.

Steward had grown accustomed to Fleming's juvenile behavior and chose to ignore it, that is until the day Julian Fleming crossed a line that even Jimmy Donahue could not tolerate.

Before his Thursday meeting with selected reporters, Jimmy Donahue found his anger almost impossible to contain. He had been in and out of meetings with Legal Affairs and Human Resources for several days. The matter at hand threatened the very foundation of journalistic integrity that had been the cornerstone of the Chandler family's ownership of the *Los Angeles Times* for over twenty-five years. The days when disciplining a reporter would consist of a severe ass-chewing behind closed doors, or even a one-on-one session of parking lot therapy were long gone. The old school Donahue would have preferred either of these alternatives, but the litigious world of employment law called for complex measures. Only Harold Williams, head of Legal Affairs, knew of the private meeting between Jimmy Donahue and Sarah Broadbent, Chair of the Leland Stanford Graduate School of Journalism. No one was going to accuse Jimmy Donahue of acting impulsively or without solid academic and legal precedence to stand on.

The fourth-floor conference room of the Times Building, with its private elevator, afforded those involved the necessary degree of confidentiality warranted by the seriousness of the allegation. Donahue had sent Broadbent a copy of the material in question, asking both for her opinion on the ethics and thoroughness of the author. The meeting day would result in a moment of introspection for Donahue. Was he an aged dinosaur among a newer and more sophisticated breed of newspaper journalists? It also brought Donahue's blood to the boiling point for the embarrassing and unflattering attention brought to the *L.A. Times* and its reporting staff, a staff he, Jimmy Donahue, had personally hired and mentored.

The arrival of Sarah Broadbent evoked the first apology from Donahue. The fiftyish Broadbent was a woman of impeccable appearance with a rather regal presence brought about in part to her six-foot frame. Stylishly attired in an ivory pointelle knit bell-bottom pantsuit, she paused in the doorway of the conference room like a model preparing to walk the runway in a fashion show of Parisian creations. Her stealthy brown eyes scanned the room. Ceiling to floor tinted glass windows overlooked the landscape of greater downtown Los Angeles. Panels of dark mahogany covered three walls. A scarcity of amenities—a refrigerator for cold beverages, a glass credenza with imported crystal tumblers resting in front of expensive liquors, embroidered leather coasters for those carrying their own hot or cold beverages, or those oversized leather high back chairs designed for maximum comfort surrounding the oval conference table—indicated this room was intended for business only. *Not exactly where I envisioned seeing Jimmy Donahue*, she thought, expecting a more personalized environment from the bawdy Irishman. Broadbent had made Donahue's acquaintance at a Hollywood gala fundraiser for the endowment of the Otis Chandler Scholarship at Stanford University held by the Chandler family at their Monticello estate. There, among those who jockeyed for favor with the politically important and wealthy while sipping expensive champagne from fluted glasses with their pinkie finger lifted in the air, Broadbent found Donahue's ribald sense of humor and taste for Irish Whiskey rather refreshing. On seeing her staged to enter the room, Donahue rose from his chair.

"Sarah, I appreciate your coming, and under the circumstances, I do apologize both for the inconvenience the trip caused you and the issue involving one of your esteemed graduates."

"Graduate yes, esteemed remains to be seen," she responded in a most lawyer-like manner as she laid her monogrammed Italian leather valise on the table.

"Which goes to the crux of the issue," replied Donahue, "I need the mind of one of the most respected in academia to guide me."

"Unwarranted flattery is unbecoming to you, James Donahue. I prefer your blarney from that night at Chandler's last year."

Donahue found Broadbent's earthiness one of her more appealing traits. "Then perhaps we can enjoy a glass of Old Bush mill afterward?"

Donahue hoped he had not misinterpreted the seductive way in which her upper teeth grazed her lower lip. He had only a moment to enjoy his tryst into fantasy land before Broadbent announced, "Shall we get to the matter at hand?"

Her no-nonsense approach to business was a bit disappointing given the wistful thoughts of Donahue. Broadbent pulled out a chair near Donahue.

"Have you had a chance to review the documents I sent you?" asked Donahue.

"I'm here, aren't I, James?"

The formality of hearing his given name chilled Donahue to the seriousness of her visit as if he needed reminding.

"What is your assessment? Could it be an inadvertent omission to cite a source? Or something more serious?"

She released the clasp on her valise and took out a large envelope secured with a tie string. Slowly unwinding the string, Broadbent lifted the flap and withdrew several sheets of paper along with a paperback book. She deliberately laid the pieces out side by side, placing the paperback in front of her. Broadbent then went methodically line by line, page by page, noting phraseology, vocabulary, even complete paragraphs in the article she had received identical to passages citing specific page references in the book in front of her.

"It is certainly not inadvertent based on the writer's academic history at Stanford. More to your point," she added with emphasis, "the pattern of plagiarism is, in my opinion, deliberate and pervasive throughout the article. As for the question failing to confirm information from an unnamed source, that violation is of equal magnitude."

Broadbent's analysis confirmed Donahue's worst suspicion, but Donahue was dealing with a master manipulator, and he wanted one more nail to hammer in the proverbial coffin.

"Sarah, what did you mean when you referred to his academic history at Stanford?"

"Your reporter was removed from his position as an editorial writer on the *Stanford Daily* for violations of the code of conduct for student journalists, namely plagiarism."

"Yet somehow, he made it into graduate school and graduated?" asked a bewildered Donahue.

Broadbent stoically picked up her papers and the book and carefully placed them back into her valise. As she stood up, she acknowledged the greatest of all evils while distancing herself from any fault.

"It was before my time, James, but a certain family made a substantial donation to the department's endowment. Need I say more?"

Having gifted Donahue with all the information he would require, Sarah Broadbent made a swift and silent departure, leaving Donahue to strategize his next move.

―――

He slammed his fist down on his desktop, causing his crystal ashtray to bounce in the air, causing a shower of cigar ashes to explode into the air only to fall gently back down on his desk. He still could not believe what he had read for the third time. There were two things Donahue loathed, plagiarism and lying in a story. This reporter had done both. The day of reckoning had arrived for Julian Fleming. He pressed the intercom button with the venom of someone squishing a bug while remembering his dressing down the last time he had called for her.

"Martha, I need to talk with you!"

This time the urgency in his voice was not a command. It was more like a plea. Martha Irons grabbed her steno pad and a pencil and moved quickly to the aid of her distressed boss. As she entered his office, Donahue said, "Shut the door! There's something I want you to see."

Watching her boss as if he were a coiled snake ready to strike, she cautiously took a chair. Her eyes never wavered from Donahue's face, a face flushed red with anger. His jaw clenched so tightly his facial skin appeared to be stretched to the tearing point. A crumbled copy of Julian Fleming's article on the proposed Board of Supervisors approval of an LA foothills development without an environmental impact report was in his fist.

"Would you read this?" Donahue said, barely able to open his mouth to speak.

Flattening the crumbled paper as best she could, Irons took her reading glasses from a lanyard hanging around her neck and began reading. It was an exquisitely written section denying the alleged dangers that unfettered development can have on the environment.

When she finished, Irons looked at her boss.

"Quite well written and surprisingly so, coming from Fleming."

That's when Donahue dropped the bombshell.

"That's because that son-of-a-bitch didn't write it! Here, read this!" Donahue said, handing Irons a detailed report provided to him by Sarah Broadbent.

Again Irons positioned her glasses on the bridge of her nose. She read the selected passage with no reaction other than her green eyes widening till they appeared ready to pop out of their sockets.

"I'm surprised but not shocked," Irons said, "but really, word for word, that's a bit lazy, don't you think?"

"I can only imagine what Rachel Carson's agent at Morris Brothers thought when she read the article, word for word from Carson's, The Silent Spring. She's the one who called me," said Donahue, whose reddened face had subsided somewhat.

"Read what's on the second page."

Dutifully, Irons turned the page and read another circled passage. This one quoted an unidentified source on the California Coastal Commission saying the agency had approved the proposed development in the hills above Palos Verde. Irons set the paper down on Donahue's desk.

"Don't tell me!?" she exclaimed.

"Oh, this time, it's not plagiarism. It's a downright damn lie," bellowed Donahue. "I got this letter from them yesterday. Once the article came out in the *Times*, they started their own internal investigation. Lawyers, affidavits, the whole ball of wax. As it turns out, his unnamed source was a temporary hire in the filing department level by Alice Gordon, niece of none other than Board of Supervisors Chairman Sheldon Martz. She admitted to being contacted by Fleming but claims she told Fleming she had no knowledge of any decision by the Commission regarding the project. Apparently, the Commission's investigators didn't believe her. She's out of a job and is threatening to sue the Times."

"You get him in here, Martha. If I call him, I'll break the damn sound barrier!"

Irons had been Donahue's secretary for more than twenty-five years. There was more than a supervisor-employee relationship between them as far as she was concerned. Donahue would soon realize he felt the same way. Irons picked up the telephone on Donahue's desk and dialed Fleming's extension. When the red button flashed on his phone, Fleming picked it up.

"Julian Fleming."

"Julian, this is Martha. Mr. Donahue wants you in his office, now."

The tone of an order coming from an underling irked Fleming's sense of self-importance. He could not control his rage at being told what to do by a mere clerical employee.

"And this sense of urgency is from who? You, Martha?"

Irons elected not to answer his question directly. *You can deal with the lion and not the messenger*, she thought. Irons hung up the phone and told Donahue of Fleming's response. Donahue was on his feet in a second and rushed to the door of his office.

"Remember the sound barrier, Jimmy," Martha advised him.

"To hell with the sound barrier," Donahue hollered as his blood pressure began to rise. He ripped open the door so hard it bounced off the door stop at the bottom of the wall. Standing in the doorway, Donahue bellowed a command that stopped every typewriter, computer, and phone call in the city desk room.

"Fleming, get your ass in my office, now!"

"I'll call you back," Fleming said to the person on the phone. The demeaning tone in Donahue's voice punctuated with mild profanity did nothing to put Fleming's brain into a "Think before you speak" mode. He moved quickly through the maze of cubicles, eager to confront his summoner.

In a voice loud enough for anyone to hear, Fleming answered with equal venom in his voice. "Try being a little more professional when you address me, Donahue. My tenure on this staff has earned me that much!"

Donahue said nothing as he stepped aside to allow Fleming into his office. The anger that raged inside him caused Donahue's face to freeze. His lips pursed. His jaw clenched so tight his cheek muscles twitched. He pointed to a chair, afraid to open his mouth until he shut the office door.

As Fleming took a seat, he made one last fatal mistake. "Does she need to be here?" He asked, referring to Irons, who was sitting at the table.

Without addressing his question, Donahue adjusted the chair behind his desk and told Irons to get Harold Williams from legal affairs to his office. "Tell him I've got Fleming in my office. That should speed him up."

Irons picked up the phone and dialed Legal Affairs to inform them of Donahue's request. It was the shortest conversation on record for Irons. She hung up the phone and responded, "He's on his way."

The inclusion of an attorney from the Legal Affairs Department created the first chink in Fleming's arrogant attitude. He had lost control of the narrative. The three sat in silence. Irons stared at Fleming with an inner sense of satisfaction at knowing the outcome of the meeting. Donahue picked up a half-smoked cigar and, with deliberate patience, struck a match with his finger and thumb and slowly re-lit his cigar, savoring each inhalation of the Caribbean blend of Cuba's finest and enjoying, even more, a slow exhale.

"Is that really necessary?" asked Fleming, who had long ago expressed his displeasure at having to endure Donahue's penchant for the imported tobacco product in meetings.

"It won't bother you for long. Believe me. It won't!"

His terse response resonated in Fleming a sense of foreboding that he could not ignore.

"What exactly is going on here?" he asked more as a supplicant than an imperative.

A knock on the door would provide Fleming with his answer.

"Come in, Harold," Donahue said.

Harold Williams was a senior member of the Legal Affairs Department of the *L.A. Times*. He was a graduate of Harvard Law and had some twenty years working for the Washington Post before leaving the frigid winters of New England for the sunny climes of California. *What was it about lawyers,* Donahue thought as Williams took a chair amongst the others. They were always in black suits, red or blue ties, with eyes like they were playing Texas Hold'em. With all the participants present, Donahue began his soliloquy on the demise of Julian Fleming. Handing Fleming a copy of the article he penned on the LA hills development with two paragraphs circled in red, Donahue asked, "Did you write this?"

The absurdity of the question distracted Fleming's previously leery train of thought.

"Yes, of course." He couldn't imagine where all this was leading. It would do no good to deny the obvious.

"Then read the highlighted portion in this book," Donahue continued, handing Fleming a copy of Rachel Carson's *The Silent Spring*.

There was no need for Fleming to read anything. The instant his eyes saw the page and title of the book, he knew his plagiarism had been discovered. Never without plausible deniability, Fleming responded, "So, it's a minor oversight on my part that can be corrected with a simple acknowledgment I inadvertently omitted citing Ms. Carson's book as the source."

Feeling secure he had dodged a bullet, Fleming relaxed a bit, sitting back in his chair. He smirked at his accuser as he resumed his arrogant attitude. Donahue then directed Fleming to the portion of his article addressing an unnamed source that told him the Coastal Commission had approved the development in question. Donahue was having difficulty restraining himself despite all his years of dealing with impassioned reporters and inflated egos. He betrayed himself as his eyes widened, and his face grew dark with rage.

"Who was this unnamed source that you were so quick to use as the lynchpin of your story?"

"Is this really necessary? How many other reporters have you put through this type of intense scrutiny?" His normal masculine voice was beginning to rise, octaves.

Undeterred by Fleming's attempt to avoid accountability, Donahue repeated his question with an additional one. He was more determined than ever to expose the prevaricator, no matter what.

"Again, Julian, who was this source, and who else did you interview to confirm what the source told you?"

Ignoring the advice of Mark Twain—if you tell the truth, you don't have to remember anything—his words virtually sputtered as he dug himself deeper into the pit of deception. "She was a high-level staffer in the records division with close ties to the Board of Supervisors. Being so, I did not feel the need to confirm her information with subsequent sources."

Irons could not hide her feelings anymore—she broke into a broad smile. Jimmy Donahue was old school. He stood by the adage, "Lie to me once, shame on you. Lie to me twice. Shame on me."

Turning to the attorney, Donahue said, "Harold, I think this is where you come in."

Having achieved what he set out to do, his features were visibly softening, and no doubt his blood pressure was dropping.

Harold Williams's six-foot-five frame was a most intimidating factor, which he used to his advantage. Having been a Golden Gloves lightweight champion while attending Harvard Law School, he exuded a killer instinct when facing an opponent. As he stood up, he opened a folder he had carried in with him. His green eyes remained focused on Fleming as he took a brown hard-shell glass case from inside his jacket pocket and placed his glasses gently on the bridge of his nose. Then, as if to emphasize the news he was about to deliver, he peered over the top of his glasses directly at Fleming.

"I'm going to explain the legalities we are facing. A single line or two, a phrase here or there, might be excused as an oversight. What we're talking about is over thirty instances of exact phraseology, whole sentences, even complete paragraphs taken word for word from a novel you failed to cite as a reference. That is not an inadvertent omission, sir. That is plagiarism of the worse kind. Your so-called high-level staffer in the records department is, in fact, a temporary hire in the filing department who incidentally is a niece of a member of the Board of Supervisors. If that minor detail was not sufficient for you to confirm her alleged comments, then her relationship to a member of the Board of Supervisors should have certainly alarmed you to seek verification of her statement."

In a desperate attempt to mitigate the appearance of impropriety, Fleming went on the offensive. He rose to his feet and angrily responded, "Aren't we really making a mountain out of a molehill?"

A tone of panic was unmistakably present in his voice. Quickly seeking to divert blame to others, he pointed accusatorily to Irons and then to Donahue.

"What about her? She read the story first. If there were mistakes, why didn't she catch them? And what about Donahue? If I have made any errors, he as my boss has a responsibility to help me correct them and become a better reporter!" His defiant outburst ended with the whimpering tone of a man desperately seeking to avoid the inevitable.

Williams slowly shook his head side to side at the absolute gall of the reporter. He took out a piece of paper from his folder. It was like the last cigarette before the firing squad took over.

"This is how we are going to prevent that molehill you so euphemistically call it from becoming a mountain." Handing him the paper, Williams said, "This is a statement you will sign before I leave this office, stating that you are resigning your position on the staff of the *Los Angeles Times* to seek other professional opportunities. You thank Mr. Donahue, his staff, and your colleagues for all the support they have given you. To the satisfaction of Ms. Carson's attorney, the *Times* will publish a retraction of the article's content without identifying you as the issue. Secondly, Ms. Alice Gordon has agreed to accept monetary compensation in lieu of further legal action on her part."

Williams withdrew a pen from his inner jacket pocket, removed the cap, and handed it to Fleming. There were no options left for Julian Fleming though his brain raced to come up with some last attempt at redemption. He could have asked for forgiveness, but then this was Julian Fleming, not some low-level copy boy they had before them. He held the pen for the longest time before signing the document. His fate was undeniable. Handing the pen and paper to Williams, Fleming turned to Donahue and said, "I'll clear out my desk tomorrow."

Donahue's response could not have said more about his feelings toward Fleming.

"Every trace of you will be gone this afternoon."

Donahue's tone and grim features made it obvious that was the end of Fleming's negotiations.

CHAPTER 23

It was not so much the morning sickness that concerned Willow Steward. That was just an uncomfortable but necessary part of the process of having her dream come true. It was, however, the increased frequency of vaginal discharge. She had not been completely honest with her husband when she told him about her pregnancy. After all, Dr. Henderson had told her only ten to twelve percent of women with her blood disorder ever had any problems with a full-term pregnancy. Certainly, a ninety percent rating for a problem-free pregnancy was nothing to worry about. Only, now, Willow Steward was beginning to have doubts, not enough to cause her to question herself, but significant enough that she felt she needed to consult with a pediatrician. Only then would she tell her husband—if there was news for concerned.

Besides her concerns, Willow had noticed the toll her husband's assignment had been taking on him. There was too much about his past tied to his assignment. The one place where they could both escape from the mental anguish that plagued them both was the weekly session at Pogo's. It was there that Steward could lose himself, playing the music he loved, and it was there that Willow could clearly see the benefit these sessions had on her husband. If there was one subject that Dylan Steward could ramble on and on about, it was music, particularly jazz. Long after their sessions ended, Steward and his friends would talk for hours about the subject, the great musicians that contributed to this genre, from Scott Joplin and Buddy Bolden to Miles Davis, Carlie Parker, Duke Ellington, and others. Willow knew her husband better than he knew himself. If he were to allow himself to dream, Dylan's dream would be to make the music he so loved. The unimaginable was about to cause his dream to evaporate from his future—if he had a future at all.

DYLAN'S FOLLOW-UP article about Army Sergeant Richie Calhoun, the homeless veteran referred to as "street trash," brought both praise and outrage. Outrage from families with loved ones that served in Vietnam. Local and national veteran's groups were infuriated by the treatment returning veterans had received at the hands of the Veterans Administration. Thousands of letters praised the *Times* for addressing returning veterans' experiencing mental health issues, specifically post-traumatic stress disorder. That praise also vindicated Jimmy Donahue's decision to hire Dylan in the first place. Steward had become something of a golden boy reporter for the *Times*. Not only did choice assignments come his way via Donahue's desk, but those unidentified sources that Donahue had relied on for years for leads now started calling Steward directly. Donahue took no offense at the changing paradigm. In fact, he felt an immeasurable sense of pride for the young man and his emerging talent. The future never looked brighter for Dylan. Yet, in the background, events were unfolding which would alter his ascent and test his very core being.

THANKS TO A RIDE from her principal's wife, Terri, Willow was able to get to her appointment with a local female obstetrician, Doctor Helen Casper.

Terri said, "No problem, Willow. It will give me a chance to do some needed shopping."

Doctor Casper was a well-known and respected obstetrician, and the referral from Terri Skaff, a close friend of the doctor, ensured a timely visit. Fortunately, the doctor's office was adjacent to Providence Saint John's Hospital, about a ten-minute drive from Willow's home.

As Willow sat in the doctor's office, filling out several forms the receptionist gave her, her anxiety grew with each glance at the posters on every wall of the waiting room. There were photographs of sonograms at various stages of pregnancy, expectant mothers and fathers in Lamaze classes, and montages of the birth process. Willow's heart swelled with joy at the thought of her baby in one of those photographs, or she and Dylan as parents in birthing classes. But there was still that one dark spot, like that blur on the x-ray of an otherwise clean lung that spoke to potential danger.

The idle chatter amongst the waiting mothers struck a familiar note with Willow. Everything was, "My baby really kicks hard, has to be a boy."

"If only I could get through the night without having to go to the bathroom,"

"From the amount of baby clothes my family sent us, you'd think I was having triplets."

There was nothing but positivity and great expectations. That was Willow's nature, to focus on the silver lining, not the cloud.

The intake process in Doctor Casper's office was quite different than that of the neighborhood free clinic Willow was familiar with back in San Francisco, where volunteer staff from the neighborhood knew you and chatted about anything and everything when you came in. Casper's office was more streamlined and left Willow with a sense of objective coldness. The receptionist feigned a smile when she gave Willow the forms to fill out. The nurse who came into the waiting room and called out her name smiled but quickly shifted her attention to another patient.

"I'm sorry, Mrs. Robbins, the doctor is running a little behind today. This way, Mrs. Steward." Following the nurse with a number of files under her arm down a short hallway, they stopped in front of a door numbered three.

"Please wait here. The doctor will be with you shortly."

With that, the nurse turned around and headed back to the waiting room, leaving Willow to wait again. Willow sat on the edge of an examination chair. The warmth exuded by photos of infants in cribs with a variety of expressions of smiles, cries, and laughter softened the indifference of the assembly-like intake process. Like always, Willow deferred to the positive.

It was just a busy day for the staff. They had to be as tired as their waiting patients.

There was a light knock, and the doctor entered.

Helen Casper was in her early forties and stood nearly six feet tall. She had maintained a youthful figure and Southern California tan by participating in a local beach volleyball club. Her warm personality put Willow at ease.

"Mrs. Steward, please forgive any delay in seeing you. One of my nurses is out sick, and another is on maternity leave. We're all a little stressed. What brings you here?"

Willow told her of her self-diagnosed pregnancy and then handed Casper the letter Doctor Henderson had mailed after her visit to the free clinic in San Francisco. There was a welcome attentiveness from the doctor as she listened to Willow and then read Doctor Henderson's letter. Handing the letter back to Willow, Casper smiled, "Well, Willow, what say we confirm your pregnancy, and then we'll talk about this letter."

"You can do that now?" asked Willow.

"Certainly," smiled Casper. "The nurse will get a urine sample from you, and then I'll do a pelvic exam. It will take no time at all to confirm your pregnancy."

Willow took the small plastic cup the doctor gave her and went to the women's restroom next door. When she returned, a nurse took the sample, and Willow changed into a gown the nurse had given her. After changing, Casper had Willow sit back on the examination table and adjust her feet into stirrups on either end of the table.

"This may be a little uncomfortable, but there will be no pain involved," Casper said as she adjusted her headband light and observation disk to peer through. Casper's head moved slowly from side to side. She lowered her posture to see more directly into the vaginal passage to confirm any abnormalities.

Without looking up, Casper asked, "Have you been having more than normal vaginal bleeding?"

"Isn't some bleeding normal, Doctor?"

Her somewhat evasive answer signaled to Casper that the true answer was yes. There was a brightness in the tissue between the uterus and the vagina. The alignment of the pelvic organs and the ligaments that hold the uterus in place appeared abnormal to the experienced obstetrician. Casper sat up and looked directly at her patient. Recalling the letter Willow had given her from Willow's doctor in San Francisco, Casper said, "I concur with Doctor Henderson's diagnosis of placenta previa, and though yes, the condition has dangerous side effects in about ten to twelve percent of women with the condition, from the condition of your vaginal organs and the position of the placenta in relation to the cervix, you are outside that safety zone."

This was, for the doctor, a routine and objective analysis of a medical condition. She unintentionally lacked any warmth or empathy. The effect in the room's atmosphere was immediate and palpable.

"But doesn't every pregnancy have some risk?" responded Willow, trying not to sound too argumentative.

"Of course," replied the doctor, who had quickly realized her patient had decided to completely ignore any potential harm to both her and her unborn child, "But I would like to see you in a month just as a precaution."

Willow thanked the doctor and assured her she would stop at the receptionist's desk to schedule her next visit. Still, Willow's inner self could not wholly disregard the doctor's words. Her focus on the silver lining now shifted to the cloud, a gray cloud whose hidden contents shook Willow to her core. As Willow exited the medical complex building, she saw Terri Skaff loading several packages into the back of her Subaru Forester from her shopping trip to the Pantry Pride; a store that afforded the bargain shopper the best value for her money. Willow sat patiently in the passenger seat while Skaff meticulously adjusted every bag to ensure nothing spilled on the drive home. A woman's intuition is rarely wrong, and Terri Skaff could tell from the silence as they exited the parking lot that Willow was bothered. She sat silently in the car, staring out the passenger window as Terri Skaff maneuvered across a four-way intersection to return home. The quiet was too much for the older woman to bear.

"So, how did your appointment go?"

Willow would have preferred that the solitude continue, but she felt obligated to answer the question considering Terri had graciously provided her a ride. Willow forced a smile then proceeded with a half-truth.

"Doctor Casper confirmed I am pregnant though I was pretty sure of that even before the appointment. She talked about certain precautions to take, you know, like watching what I eat, get plenty of rest, the standard stuff," Willow answered, almost convincing herself that the foreboding caution from Doctor Casper was nonexistent.

Willow never made eye contact with Terri, confirming the woman's suspicions that there was more to the visit than Willow was willing to divulge. Taking a different tack to a less threatening subject, she said, "My gosh! At some point, Joe's going to have to line up another teacher to cover behind your pregnancy. Ironic. Isn't it? You get hired to fill a pregnancy leave, and now you are pregnant."

A faint smile was all the response Skaff got for her efforts to engage the young woman in conversation. Grateful when at last they pulled up in front of her house, Willow turned to her driver and said, "Thank you so much, Terri. I so appreciate your kindness."

With a grandmotherly smile, Skaff replied, "Nonsense, my child, it was nothing." Then she giggled excitedly, "Oh, can I tell Joe? He'll be so excited for you." Her enthusiasm over revealing the news to her husband was not to be denied. Relieved that it would be one more half-truth she wouldn't have to deliver, Willow smiled graciously and answered, "Sure, that would be fine with me, Terri."

As Skaff pulled away from the curb, the last place Willow wanted to go was inside her home. The confines of the small cottage were not the place to dwell on the emotional enormity of the doctor's words, "You're outside that safety zone." The words raced through her mind over and over.

Willow started the short three-block walk to Venice Beach. An undeveloped lot at the corner of Echo and Venice Beach Boulevard was a tented area where various vendors sold their wares, including handmade jewelry, leather goods, scented candles, perfumes, and paintings. Willow found some peace of mind as she meandered from table to table, admiring the artists' creations. One vendor, in particular, caught her attention. Several small paintings had been arranged on easels in a semi-circle by the artist who sat off one end, watching the gazes of those who admired his work. Willow had a fondness for street artisans from her days of wandering the streets of North Beach and the marina in San Francisco, admiring the artistry of the Bohemian purveyors. She paused in front of a painting that had captured her attention. It depicted a young black woman sitting in a rocker on the wooden porch of a dilapidated shanty house wearing a shawl of pieced together strips of cloth. Burlap bags hung as window coverings, and the faded board and batten walls were broken in places, leaving gaping holes. She was obviously pregnant. Her hands were folded over her extended stomach. The background was a montage of history for African Americans, which included scenes of field workers bent over as they made their way down rows of cotton, a Civil War battle, a parade of white hooded thugs carrying torches, civil rights marchers being attacked by police dogs. Each scene merged into the next. The woman's face was in stark contrast to the bleak imagery of the artist's rendition of the turbulent post-civil war era. She wore a smile that radiated confidence. Her eyes were raised upward, seemingly ignoring the reality of what indeed laid before her. Her fantasy had a different vision for the life within her. Willow saw herself in that woman, the bleakness of the future being held at bay by the sheer force of determined optimism. Even as she spoke, she could not take her eyes off the painting. Her hands instinctively moved slowly across her stomach. The vendor couldn't help but notice.

"How much are you asking for this one?" Willow asked the artist.

The elderly black man used his cane to stand. With his free hand, he removed a sweat-stained straw fedora then wiped his forehead with the sleeve of his shirt.

"Do ya' like it, Missy?" he said with a graveled voice.

"Yes, I do, very much!"

The aged one stood as straight as his bowed shoulders would allow.

"So do I," he said, smiling at the painting. "That's my momma. You take it, call it a gift."

"Oh, I couldn't possibly," Willow pleaded. "Please let me pay you."

Putting his hat back on, he took hold of the painting and

handed it to Willow. He held on for just a second while staring into her eyes.

"My momma, she had a dream for me, and I'm abettin' y'all gotta dream for that little one inside you. Now you just go and take this. Cuz I knows a thing or two about dreams."

Willow tried again to pay the man, but he was determined to make it a gift, not a purchase.

"No, Missy. It's yours; no use a arguin' with me."

Her soul was touched by the old man's kindness. Willow took her gift and headed home. Her mind was at ease. Her heart was calm. The future, no matter what, would not rob Willow Steward of her dream.

CHAPTER 24

For Willow Steward, a dream was much more than some nocturnal journey into the land of fantasy and make-believe. A dream, her real dream, was much more. Dreams allowed her to see the possibilities when others only saw the limitations of this world. She saw dreams as giving her life meaning beyond the day-to-day drudgery of the mundane. It was the reason all humanity was created, to take what is given and dream of what it could be. The life inside Willow was the embodiment of that principle. On the walk home, Willow found solace in the words of the elderly black man who had gifted her with one of his paintings. His mother had a dream for him, and as if by some mystical power, he knew Willow had one for the life yet to be born inside. But it was more than his words that had touched her. It was the look in his eyes and the tone in his voice when he spoke of knowing about dreams that helped abate an unavoidable, and in Willow's mind, unnecessary sense of worry when Doctor Casper spoke of being outside the safety zone. It was the same look her father had given her the day of her first dance recital. A petite six-year-old ballerina dressed in a white tutu and crowned with a silver tiara stood frozen off stage, unable to move to the cue of the piano player. Suddenly, like the proverbial knight in shining armor, her father was by her side. He knelt down next to her. His mere presence was like finding shelter in a thunderstorm. His deep blue eyes shone like a beacon, leading her out of the darkness that had engulfed her. The softest of baritone voices spoke in her ear, "You're going to be just fine, sweetheart." And she was, then and again so now after hearing "I know something about dreams."

She wished she had asked her benefactor's name. Then just before reaching her front door, she realized exactly where to find his name. Every painter puts their name on the canvas. Willow held up the small painting she was carrying. There it was. In the lower right-hand corner of the canvas, barely visible to the casual observer but to the discerning eye, the artist's signature was quite apparent.

Now feeling fatigued from her walk and the emotional nature of her doctor's visit, Willow took a seat on one of two twin teakwood rocking chairs with padded cushions on her front porch, a recent gift from her husband. She set her leather purse, trimmed with turquoise beads, on the porch next to her. It was another gift from her appreciative husband to the mother of his child-to-be. The thick foam rubber cushions wrapped in a sea-green polyester material engulfed Willow's petite body, providing yet another form of protection for her weary psyche. Her feet provided a gentle rocking motion as her right hand gently traced over the artist's name. What an odd name, she thought. The letters filled in with the minute brush strokes read Le Chercheur de Rêves. It must be French, she thought. She fantasized over the possible translation. It was such a childish exercise, but one that brought the spiritually enhanced Willow an immense sense of pleasure.

Her linguistic juggling came to an end with the sputtering sound of her husband's aged Citroen. Its engine was now in the habit of backfiring when the ignition was turned off. Only then did she realize she had forgotten to take anything out of the freezer for dinner. She had stretched their left-over pot roast as far as its mushy carrots and soggy potatoes could go, and there was more to tell her husband than the requisite explanation regarding their newest wall mounting. There was the truth, the whole truth surrounding her pregnancy. Willow had not been completely honest concerning the circumstances of her pregnancy, beginning with her first appointment with Doctor Henderson. Now, after being told by Doctor Casper that she was, in the doctor's words, 'outside the safety zone,' Willow could no longer keep from her husband the potential dangers that came with her medical condition. Willow Steward had always been unconditional in her support of her husband's endeavors. Theirs was never a path taken by one, but by both, and now she needed his support more than ever. Neither could have imagined where that path would take them.

As Dylan pulled up to the curb in front of his home, his aggravation at the Citroen's failing carburation system quickly abated at the sight of his wife sitting on one of their newly purchased twin teakwood rocker chairs. The roughhewn timbers that supported the front porch gave the appearance of a life-size shadow box. Slightly off-center sat the love of his life as if on display in an upscale department store window. At that moment, Willow looked more beautiful and alluring than ever before. The brightness of the afternoon sun produced an angelic aura in the reflection from her auburn hair. When she brushed her hair aside, Dylan caught a glimpse of her radiant smile and hazel eyes. He was sure that God, if there was one, had created the perfect woman. Then an unexplainable eerie feeling came over him as his eyes focused on the empty rocker next to his wife. Dylan quickly dismissed this strange phenomenon as merely hunger pangs playing games with his mind. The pot roast sandwich Willow had made him for lunch hadn't satisfied his ravenous appetite, but it did serve to convince him to avoid having that dish for a third time in twenty-four hours at all cost.

Aside from their evening meal, there was much to share with his wife. To begin with, the unexpected departure of his fellow reporter, Julian Fleming, and the circumstances surrounding his termination. In addition, according to Jimmy Donahue, an editorial decision from none other than Damon Willard himself had been made to do a series of articles on the plight of returning Vietnam veterans. Willard's decision had not been entirely altruistic. Dylan's articles had generated enormous interest and outrage at the treatment of returning Vietnam veterans, like Richie Calhoun dealing with PTSD and a plethora of other physical and mental health issues. That interest translated into increased readership, which translated into increased advertising, which meant increased revenue. Willard had arranged to be photographed with the heads of local charities pledging to do more for the homeless. In contrast, he took the additional steps of hiring a private security firm to ensure that the homeless would not find space in or on any of the *Times* properties. His "Altruism" knew no bounds.

Suddenly, Dylan felt guilty for his self-centeredness. At breakfast that morning, Willow had mentioned in passing that she had a scheduled appointment with an obstetrician that afternoon. Standard procedure for a woman in my condition, she had said. Taking his wife at her word, Dylan had no reason to believe that there was anything for concern outside of the norm. He broached the subject accordingly.

He had taken but a few steps from his car when the small weather-beaten engine produced one last backfire before sputtering as if convulsing to a stop. Walking up to the porch, he felt a rising sense of frustration which distracted him from his original intention to find out about his wife's doctor's appointment. His mounting frustration, ever the pragmatist, was palpable. He slumped into the chair next to Willow. He announced, "I've had it with that car! If it's not one thing, it's another. First, the transmission, now that damn carburation system! Maybe I should just get us a new car?!"

She smiled in her sweet inimitable way throughout his dissertation.

"Sweetheart, do we really need the expense of a new car with the baby on the way? And besides, you've pampered that Citroen for years; a little longer isn't going to hurt. You've fixed it in the past. You can fix it again."

This was an aspect of the couple's marriage that Willow had truly mastered. She knew precisely how to soothe her husband's occasional volcanic episodes. Dylan, mollified, turned to face Willow. Realizing that he should be more sensitive to her primal and immediate concerns, he asked, "Speaking of the baby, how did your appointment go today? Everything as you expected?"

Conflicting thoughts raced through Willow's mind. Should she present the unmitigated facts, with the expectation that Dylan's likelihood of assuming the worst would happen, or should she simply gloss over the episode in the hopes that he would not question her further? Knowing that her husband could at times read her as well as she could him, she attempted to control her expressions.

She gave him her best "everything is okay" smile and said, "My exam went just fine. The doctor wants to see me in another month, and I just need to watch some female stuff. It's no big deal."

Knowing that he was trespassing in a dangerous area, Dylan hesitated before asking, "What exactly is female stuff?"

Willow was typically quite chatty with extraneous details that Dylan often found boring, but not this time. This time she had glossed over the subject calling it female stuff.

"If you must know, we talked about vaginal fluids, the tissue between my uterus and vagina, the alignment of my pelvic organs, and the ligaments that hold the uterus in place. Do you want more details?" There was a cold, almost resentful tone to her voice as if he had invaded secret sacrosanct space between doctor and patient.

To pry deeper would only elicit more resentment from his wife and force him to endure more boring and analytical explanations of the female reproductive system, neither of which Dylan had any inclination to face.

"Nope, I know all I need to know," replied a relieved Dylan now that the term vaginal fluids and such would stay between his wife and her doctor. Desperate to change the subject, he said, "Something else for me to hang on the wall," pointing to the painting resting next to her chair?

Happy to change the subject, Willow smiled appreciatively and said, "Yes, beautiful and insightful."

She held it up for her husband to see. Dylan studied it for several minutes before responding.

"It's a little dark, don't you think, what with all the symbolism?" he said, referring to the Civil War, the cotton fields, and the KKK.

True to his nature, Dylan had missed the point as far as Willow was concerned. Yes, there were dark times, but it was always the light of someone's dream that brightened the future. At opportune moments in the past, Willow had tried without success to get her husband to understand the almost omnipotent power of dreams and what they could accomplish. Oddly enough, it would be Dylan's past that would provide the vehicle for Willow to achieve her goal finally successfully. She gave his hand the softest squeeze, like one heart telling another, it's okay now.

"Honey, when you were in Vietnam and saw all the things you saw, what was the one thing that kept you strong enough to keep going. What enabled you to survive, no matter what?"

Dylan laid the painting on his lap and sat back in his rocker. His feet nervously moved the chair forward and back. He jerked his head backward, then left and then right, desperately to shake the memories away, memories his wife now wanted him to revisit.

Vietnam was in the past, and he never wanted to go then again, never to think about it again, and yet now he was. His eyes stared upward toward the later afternoon clouds. A dense morning fog wove its way through the thick jungle foliage. The cold sucked every ounce of body heat out of you until your teeth rattled, and your body shivered uncontrollably. A torn green poncho provided little protection from the incessant monsoon rains. Every shadow was a VC. Your body tensed up at every noise that traveled through the pitch-black night. Your mind tried desperately to determine which sounds were birds, roving bands of monkeys, or other small animals and which were the sounds of an advancing enemy? In that abyss of a moonless night, you prayed you might live to see the first light of dawn.

By mid-morning, the fog would lift. The chilling cold of the night would be replaced by stifling heat, humidity, and the foulest smells that made you gag. The fear never left you. As you moved through the bush, you wondered if your next step would break a trip wire or land on a punji stake? Could the slightest movement in a tree line be a VC ambush? Could you just get across that rice paddy before an ambush went off from the far tree line? Would the sudden snap of a branch set off a booby-trap that could take someone's life or limb. It was twelve months and twenty-six days of trembling, never-ending fear. His past had engulfed him. Tomorrow was his ETS, but tomorrow never came.

The sight of her near-comatose husband frightened Willow.

"Dylan, can you hear me?"

He stayed focused downward. He dared not look up at her as his tears would reflect the hell had revisited at her request.

"I dreamed about the aroma that filled our house when my mom was cooking Thanksgiving dinner; the touch football games with my friends at the local park on Saturday with a keg of beer riding on the outcome; the scent of my girlfriend's perfume filling my car when we parked in the hills overlooking the city. I dreamed about all those things and more."

"Now, can you understand the dream this woman had for her child and the hope that she had for the world in which that child would grow up? That's what a dream can do. A dream can have almost curative powers, Dylan. It can motivate you to endure terrible things and provide the strength to survive unspeakable tragedy."

The mood of their conversation had darkened measurably, despite her best efforts. The late afternoon skies had unexpectedly turned cloudy. A chill in the air caused Willow to cross her arms.

"It almost smells like rain," she said. "We'd better head inside. I should have thought of something to cover the chairs, honey."

Suddenly, without any warning, there was the roar of thunder from behind gray clouds and the crackling flash of lightning bolts that appeared to shred the darkening horizon.

CHAPTER 25

Sylvia Markham had just poured her second glass of Chateau La Mission's Haut Brion. The prestigious Wine Institute of France had recently given the highly praised Bordeaux Gold Star status. Markham was particularly fond of the bold earthy undertone of the varietal despite its high tannin content. Markham's home was a three-level forties-style Tudor home that sat on an outcropping high on the rim of Turnbull Canyon. The setting offered an unobstructed view of Los Angeles south to the Long Beach Harbor and north to the edge of the Santa Clarita Mountains. The house had been the residence of the eccentric and famous Busby Berkeley, noted Hollywood musical director and choreographer of the 30s and '40s. The home had elements that reflected Berkeley's opulent and self-indulgent imagination.

A tram car carried visitors from the five-car roadside garage on the hillside down to the home. Carved into the side of the mountain alongside the house was a large Roman-style bath, with an overhead waterfall and three sculptured water nymphs with water draining out their mouths. Every bedroom came equipped with a step-down Italian marble bathtub and a dry sauna, unheard of in its day. The marble bathtub in the master bedroom had inset circles designed to hold a Martini glass. A beverage Busby was famous for partaking of while taking a bath. A line of palm trees edged the hillside property. Markham had been particularly drawn to the large living room. The great room resembled something out of a medieval English castle. Large roughhewn beams supported a peaked ceiling. Its most unique feature was a small wooden balcony off of a second-story bedroom that looked down on the great room. Many years traveling in Europe for the *Los Angeles Times* left Sylvia in possession of an extensive collection of artworks that now adorned her medieval abode. Her eclectic array ranged from original paintings by up-and-coming artists to masterful reproductions. Markham was also taken by the artistry of Venice's medieval Murano glass masters. She loved nothing more than to lead guided tours through her home, explaining the history of each and every item.

IF THE FIFTEEN-HOUR flight from France had not left her fatigued, the surprise visitor who awaited her arrival home at two in the morning only added to her state of exhaustion. She tightened the belt on her silk robe as she walked to the double French doors that opened up onto a cobblestone patio to enjoy the majestic view. Her long relaxing soak in her oversized marble bathtub had been most enjoyable after a rather trying day at work. She paused in front of a small Victorian tray on wheels next to the doors, selecting a few squares of Camembert cheese from a blue porcelain cutting stone and placing them on a delicate crystal serving plate engraved with a view of the Bordeaux valley located in southwest France. The wine, the cheese cutting stone, and serving plates had been a gift from a friend. The tactile contrast between the tile squares in her living room and the cobblestone patio caused her to step gingerly until she reached the Bonacina rattan chairs. Her body welcomed the softness of the pale blue cushions. Sylvia placed her plate of cheese squares on a small matching rattan table with a thick glass top set in front of her chair. Markham was a woman of refinement and not ashamed to enjoy the finer things in life. Of course, it helped that Sylvia's grandfather was Henry Markham, former governor of California in the 1900s and wealthy rancher in what was then a pastoral Pasadena, California. Sylvia raised her wine goblet made of Murano glass to the setting sun. With slow swirls, she watched the legs of the fine Bordeaux make their way to the bottom of her glass. The sun's rays reflected through the fine glass and then through the rich Bordeaux creating a subtle velvet-like covering that mesmerized this wine aficionado. It took the voice of her guest to bring her out of her self-induced stupor.

"Hey Syl, how's the vino?"

If ever there were an odd couple, it was Sylvia Markham and Jimmy Donahue. Growing up, Markham loathed the attempts of others to shorten her name, as if "Sylvia" was somehow too tongue-twisting to pronounce. There was a certain elegance to her full name that she was not about to relinquish for the sake of familiarity. That was until she met Jimmy Donahue.

Yes, Jimmy Donahue, the brash, outspoken Irishman whose idea of a fine dinner was a three-inch T-Bone well done, a baked potato, no vegetables, and an ice-cold bottle of beer, had somehow struck a note with the sophisticated and urbane granddaughter of the famous Henry Markham. Beneath his rather gruff exterior lay a man of intense loyalty who subjugated himself to no one's standards other than his own, a man who, when he anointed you with a moniker of his making, was acknowledging you as his friend. He respected honesty above all virtues and expected nothing less from others.

It was a political fundraiser at the Hollywood Hilton for state senator H. L. Richardson—considered a rising star in the Republican Party—that the editorial staff of the *L.A. Times* had been mandated to attend that had brought the two together in a social setting. Richardson had curried the favor of Markham for her opinion on European politics, no doubt hoping for a favorable mention in one of her columns. She found him blatantly transparent as he parlayed every comment she made with, "Yes, I couldn't agree more. We should talk more on this issue."

Donahue had exiled himself from the crowd of political sycophants by seeking sanctuary on the outside patio overlooking the city of angels. He could no longer tolerate the endless rantings of "If only Goldwater had won!" or "Welfare will destroy the initiative of Americans to work!"

When Richardson and his entourage moved on to the next victim of political prey, Markham smoothly glided through the crowded banquet room to the outside patio where fate would place her with Donahue. After several minutes of sharing their mutual disgust with the events of the evening, Markham lamented, "if only there were a place for thoughtful conversation, soft music, and a glass of decent wine."

To her rescue, Jimmy Donahue offered just such a place. The rest of the evening was spent at Lefty's, listening to albums of Sinatra, Nat King Cole, Ella Fitzgerald and discussing a world of "What ifs." Markham was charmed by the Irishman's witticisms and sense of humanity. Donahue marveled at Markham's penchant for collecting art, a subject that previously would have bored Donahue to the nth degree, yet somehow it worked.

"Your selection exceeded expectations, James," responded Markham as the sip of Bordeaux crossed her palate.

"Perhaps I'm learning something?" grinned Donahue, as he settled into his chair, still grasping his crystal tumbler of Jameson Irish Whiskey. Learning the fine wines that would please his paramour would not dissuade Donahue from his beverage of choice.

"Based on last night, I would agree," toyed Markham as her tongue sensually moved across her lower lip.

The old Donahue would have beaten his chest like Tarzan after leaving Jane in a state of euphoric bliss. The new Donahue merely smiled, his inner self dutifully acknowledged by Markham's words.

"You know, Syl, I was looking at that last painting you brought back from France. I swear I've seen that exact scene before."

"I hardly think so, James. That painting is by a relatively unknown young artist named Jean-Paul Menuisier. He's developed quite a following for his landscapes. That particular scene is near the Garonne River outside Bordeaux."

Markham's polite but smug denunciation of Donahue's recollection only served to fuel his determination to remember. His eye for details had not deceived him; he had seen that place before, the same rugged outcropping of granite rocks, the same aged tan stucco building with a red tile roof, windows with flower boxes and trimmed with wooden shutters that hung unevenly. The same sloping green pasture in front of the structure had scattered clusters of chairs and chaise lounges. It was all there, but where, where had he seen it?

Donahue partook of another piece of cheese and sipped his Jameson, now nearly empty.

"It'll come to me," he announced with confidence.

"I'm sure it will, James." Markham smiled at her paramour's dogged determination to prove her wrong. "But in the meantime, shall we consider dinner and that device I bought for you."

A new Weber Kettle Propane BBQ was awaiting Donahue's use, a sign the traditionalist who swore by charcoals and newspaper starter was accepting of change (at least in some regards).

———

As he entered the lobby of the Times Building on Monday morning, the usually jovial and gabby Jimmy Donahue walked with a slower gait. His head hung down so his eyes would not cringe in pain from the bright lobby lights. The ungodly combination of twenty-year-old Jameson Irish Whiskey and a fine

Bordeaux wine whose name he couldn't pronounce were at war in his frontal lobe. The lively banter of Monday morning greetings echoing throughout the lobby felt like lightning bolts exploding inside his head. With no sense of his usual morning urgency, Donahue headed to the newsstand for his morning reading of Jimmy Breslin, a hot cup of coffee from the kiosk in hand.

Willis Carpenter had just finished arranging his daily issues of newspapers. When he saw Donahue approach, he knew exactly what his old friend needed. With a subtle chuckle, he said, "Let me have that coffee, Jimmy. You need a bit of the dog that bit you."

Reaching under the countertop, Willis picked up a small brown paper bag. He carefully folded down the top, trying not to make too much noise to reveal a pint bottle of Hiram Walker Bourbon. His hand shook slightly as he poured a liberal dose of the amber liquid into Donahue's coffee cup. The entire sequence was shielded by the simultaneous exchange of the *New York Post* and a knowing wink. Donahue took one, then two healthy sips of the "curative" beverage. There was no earthly scientific reason why this age-old concoction had the powers it did, but nonetheless, it did. Within a minute or two, the stabbing pain in his forehead began to subside, and with that, bloodshot eyes began to focus more clearly.

"Thanks, Willis, just what the doctor ordered." He managed a subdued smile and then sighed. He took a seat in one of several chairs assigned to two small tables recently added to the area surrounding Willis's stand by the building superintendent. The purpose of this was to provide employees a place to enjoy their morning beverage and choice of reading material before reporting to their offices. It was immediately judged a success by the *Times* employees, who often had every chair filled before Willis even arrived. It was Donahue who had encouraged Willis to hang his paintings around the edges of his newsstand in the hopes of making a sale here and there, nothing too outlandish, perhaps a couple hanging off each end of the newsstand.

As Donahue eased back in his chair, allowing his medicinal

mixture to continue its miracle, he noticed a painting hanging off the end of the stand's frame nearest where he sat. A small display light attached to the edge of the painting shone down on the canvas producing a unique shadow effect. Donahue was strangely mesmerized by the shadowing effect of the lamp. It was as if the sun was slowly rising, its rays exposing a beautiful verdant hillside near a river's edge. By the water's edge, in the vicinity of an outcropping of rocks, was a painter's easel with a white wooden chair next to it. At the top of the slope was a long two-story building. The brilliant use of a deep red to color the tile roof in contrast to the forest green window shutters gave it almost a three-dimensional effect. The front of the building was lined with white chairs and lounges. Donahue found himself leaning forward, focusing more closely on the painting. Then he remembered the painting Markham had recently purchased. It was the same landscape. Except for the addition of the white wooden furniture, everything was the same, down to the exact rock formation. But how? How could Willis Carpenter have painted the exact same landscape as Markham's newest discovery? Donahue got to his feet and walked over to Willis. Without revealing the source of his curiosity, Donahue said, "You need to tell me about this painting, Willis. Where did you ever get the inspiration for it?"

    Donahue watched Willis as he turned to look at his painting. Willis stared at his painting, examining every detail for the millionth time. His eyes brightened. His lips parted into a smile that soon spread across his aged face. His chest heaved with something akin to spiritual contentment. The scene on the canvas was like a magnet drawing him closer to a time and a place that was his Shangri-La. He reached out with the fingers of his right hand and slowly traced over the bottom edge of the painting. Without even looking at Donahue, Willis replied with the kindest, most heartfelt words Donahue had ever heard him utter, "A dream, Jimmy, a dream."

What kind of a dream could create that depth of emotion, thought Donahue as he stared at his friend's face.

"That's a dream that calls for an explanation, Willis."

With his focus still fixed on his creation, Willis answered softly, "I suppose my friend, someday." His words softly faded away, still gazing at the scene before him.

Donahue stared at his friend in wonderment. What dream, what memory could have put the old black man into such a euphoric trance. His curiosity was piqued. The old newspaperman had the scent of a story, and he was not about to give up so easily. Careful not to sound like he was issuing an ultimatum, Donahue said, "Someday the Red Sox are gonna win the World Series too, Willis, but I don't think I'll be alive when that happens, so let's the two of us get together tomorrow, and you tell me your story."

DONAHUE SET his carefully planned strategy in motion as the noon hour approached. He had sent word to Willis to meet him outside the Times Building promptly at noon. Leaving his office, Donahue stopped in to see his secretary.

"Martha, there's a good chance I'll be gone for the rest of the day. If anyone asks, tell them I had a doctor's appointment or whatever BS you want to come up with."

The mischievous twinkle in his eyes told Irons how the afternoon would really go. She tipped her fingers to her forehead, acknowledging her boss's directive. *A long lunch at Lefty's,* she thought.

The thought of learning about the inspiration behind Willis's painting caused Donahue to hasten his stride as he exited the elevator and headed to the sidewalk outside. He found Willis obediently waiting outside, standing against the wall to avoid the noontime foot traffic.

Donahue smiled at his friend. "Are you thirsty?"

Willis removed his tan straw fedora and wiped his forehead with a red bandanna he had withdrawn from his back pocket.

"In this heat?" Willis answered incredulously at the ridiculous question.

Donahue hailed a cab, in deference to Willis to whom the short three block walk to Lefty's would be troublesome with his artificial leg.

As the yellow car responded to his sharp whistle, Donahue opened the passenger rear door and said, "Get my friend. We're headed to an oasis."

He was hoping the quiet intimacy of Lefty's would lend itself to Willis opening up about the background of the painting. He would not be disappointed. As the cab pulled up to the curb in front of Lefty's, Willis said, "Passed this place many times."

"But never went in?" asked Donahue.

Willis straightened up to stretch his back and extend his leg, then gave Donahue a quizzical look and chuckled, "Jimmy! Me? Really?"

That was when Donahue realized the perception of old prejudices dies hard. With absolute conviction, Donahue replied, "This place or at least its owner is different, Willis."

Willis nodded out of politeness, 'but the proof was in the pudding' as the saying went.

As they entered the half-full establishment, both men had to blink several times to adjust to the noir ambiance.

"Got your place all set up, Jimmy. End booth with Maker's Mark waiting for you," Lefty called out from behind the bar. He approached the two with a small bucket of ice and cocktail napkins in hand.

"Lefty, meet Willis Carpenter, a friend of mine from the Times."

With genuine sincerity in his voice, Lefty extended his hand and gave Willis a firm grip saying, "A friend of Jimmy's is a friend of mine. Nice to meet you, Willis."

"Likewise," responded a somewhat skeptical Carpenter.

As the two men seated themselves at the end booth, Lefty explained the presence of the bottle of Maker's Mark, a tradition started by his father, the original Lefty.

"Willis, Maker's Mark is Jimmy's favorite. I set the bottle in front of him, and when he's ready to go, he tells me how much he used, like two shots or three. You get the idea. So what's your drink of choice? The next time you come, it will be waiting for you."

Prepared to test the man, Willis replied, "Hiram Walker, ice on the side."

Moments later, a bottle of the requested blended whiskey with its iconic crest of golden eagles next to a blue shield under a red and gold crown was set before him, along with a small pitcher of ice and a crystal tumbler. Looking around at the items on the table, then at the faces of his patrons, Lefty was satisfied all was well.

"Enjoy, gentlemen," smiled Lefty, returning to his position behind the bar where several new arrivals were waiting to quench their thirst.

"Shall we?" said Jimmy, who poured himself a healthy serving of his selection, dropping several ice cubes into his glass. Following suit, Willis slowly twisted the cork top off his bottle; then passed the open bottle beneath his nose several times. He smiled as the oaken rich boutique stimulated his olfactory sensors. After reaching the halfway point of his tumbler, Willis stopped then added several ice cubes. He raised his glass to Donahue, "To friends, Jimmy." The clink of their glasses symbolized the deep feelings each man felt for the other and introduced a story that would leave Jimmy Donahue in shock and awe.

JIMMY RESTED his head against the back of the red upholstered booth while slowly turning his tumbler with his hands, never once taking his eyes off his friend. Willis was still savoring that first sip of brown nectar, more commonly known as Walker Imperial. A smile spread across Willis's face as his throat muscles held the liquid captive as long as possible before swallowing. This was Donahue's moment. He leaned forward, setting his tumbler off to the side; he folded his hands together and said, "So Willis, tell me about that painting I saw at your stand yesterday. You referred to it as a dream. What's the story there?"

Willis tilted his head back as his Adam's apple moved the last amount of the liquid down his throat. He stared at his crystal tumbler before setting it back on the table. His dark eyes were aged but still glowed with perception.

"Ever had a dream, Jimmy, where you reach out to touch somethin' and you can't? Ya see it. It's real as hell, but ya can't feel it?"

"I guess so," Donahue replied, who was completely unsure where this was going and wasn't inclined to believe such things. Donahue's world was black and white.

Willis smiled. His eyes brightened.

"In my dream, I'm feelin' every blade of grass on the hillside. I'm smellin' the water in the Garonne River. I'm hearin' every bird singin' in the trees."

His long dark fingers stained with blotches of dried paint reached into the bucket of ice cubes on the table. He dropped several fresh ice cubes in his glass, then reached for his bottle of Walker and poured himself a second serving, watching carefully to ensure that the liquid barely covered the frozen cubes. He wiped his wet fingers on the white tablecloth as he did so. That's when he noticed the ice tongs lying next to the ice bucket. Donahue instantly realized his friend's embarrassment at his oversight.

"They're more for show, Willis, and hardly needed when drinking with friends."

His enraptured smile slowly disappeared, replaced by a ghostly stare.

"I can hear them screams too. Horrible, awful wailin' of men beggin' God to end their lives. I can hear my own screamin' too."

Donahue sat there entranced with each word. Despite his earlier skepticism, Donahue was increasingly captivated by the narrative.

"My God, Willis, what kind of a place was that?"

Willis sat frozen with his memories of burned flesh being pulled from his back and the nerve endings in his leg sending excruciating pain through every fiber in his body as antiseptic solutions were poured every few hours on the bloody stump where his left knee used to be, to prevent the spread of infection. When he finally looked up, tears flowed freely down his ancient face.

"It was an Army hospital, Jimmy. The French called it the Chateau Rêves. Before the war, it was a kinda luxury hotel. The Jerry's turned it into their own pleasure palace. When the Allies took over, they turned da place into a hospital for burn patients and amputees. I was both."

Thinking back to the painting, Donahue exclaimed, "That explains the white lounge chairs in your painting."

"Yep, the nurses would wheel us out whenever they could. Some spent a lot of time askin' us about where we come from, our families, things like dat. Tryin' to cheer us up, I guess." His face reflected the failure of their efforts.

Suspecting he knew the reason for the easels near the water's edge, Donahue asked, "The easels were for painting, weren't they? Another way to take your mind off the way things were?"

Willis nodded. "There was a volunteer who had worked in some museum before the war. She knew a lot 'bout art n' stuff. A few of the white GIs gave it a try, but they quit. No touch with a brush." Willis smiled at the opportunity to criticize white men, unheard of in those times and hardly routine in the years following the war.

"Her name was Anastasie. She said it meant resurrection in French. She taught me a lot, Jimmy. How to use different brush strokes, how ta create shadows, even make them look like somethin' alive. She would bring tubes of different colors and show me how to mix dem to make other colors. Tried ta teach me how colors are like feelin's, ya know a happy color, a sad color. I had no idea, Jimmy, how many different feelings colors could make. I spent nearly a year there, paintin' every chance I could. She breathed new life into me. She was so beautiful. I thought about the scar."

Donahue realized that there was a sudden and deep sweetness in Willis' voice. These were memories from his heart, memories as fresh as the day they were created. It was much more than the appreciation of an art student for his teacher; something had happened between this Anastasie and his friend. And now, a scar added only more intrigue. The obvious was not so obvious.

"What's one more scar? After all you'd been through, Willis?"

His friend's misinterpretation—that the scar was his—demanded that the old man recount the senseless savagery that occurred over thirty years ago.

"Like I said, Annie, I called her Annie, worked at a museum. Toward the end of the war, some Jerry colonel was stealin' some really valuable paintin's, and he told Annie if she didn't help him, he'd have her family sent to some kinda' labor camp. The resistance guys said she was some kinda traitor for being a Vichy, so they cut a T for traitor on her left cheek. Nobody at the hospital wanted anything to do with her, but I didn't care, Jimmy. I…" Welled-up emotions paralyzed his throat muscles.

"You loved her," Donahue replied, finishing Willis' words for him.

Making no attempt to wipe the tears flowing freely down both cheeks, Willis leaned to one side as he took out his wallet from his back left pocket. He opened the wallet. Stiff fingers managed to pull out a faded old scalloped edged sepia photograph of a young black GI standing next to a beautiful tall brunette in nurse whites. Her long hair was carefully placed over one side of her face, reminiscent of Veronica Lake. He laid the snapshot lovingly in front of Donahue.

"I loved her with all my heart, Jimmy, and she loved me, but I was me, and she was her. Ain't been a day or a night since I left France I didn't think of her."

There was no need for Donahue to speak his thoughts. He knew there was no way a black man and a white woman would be accepted back in the states at that time. What hypocrisy for a country to ask some of its citizens to fight and shed their blood for it, only to have them return home to a segregated society fraught with racial hatred and discrimination. As a man who always championed the underdog, it sickened Donahue.

As he handed the photo back to Willis, Donahue noticed a note on the back. He read it. Mon Chercheur de Rêve, Anastasie Bouchet,17 Rue Madeleine, Bordeaux, France. Willis saw the pensive glare in his friend's eyes. He answered the question before it could be asked.

"No, Jimmy, I never wrote her. Why? What good would it do? Nothin' had changed. I was still me, and well, you know. But someday, Jimmy, I'm going back. It's where I felt whole, where my heart is."

Donahue nodded as Willis gently put the snapshot back into its sacred place.

The catharsis that had just occurred left both men emotionally spent. Donahue felt the need to fill his glass, this time well past the level of ice cubes, nearly emptying the bottle of choice left by Lefty.

"No need to insult the owner by leaving any," grinned Donahue.

"You payin' for my cab home?" Willis asked, his head cocked to one side, a slight smirk appearing on his face.

"Hell yes!" laughed Donahue. To wit, Willis Carpenter did likewise with his bottle of Imperial Hiram Walker, with a clink of their glasses.

They traded more stories, well into the night.

CHAPTER 26

There was much on Dylan's mind as he made his way through early morning traffic on the I-10 east to work. For one, against Willow's better judgment, Dylan was determined to get a more reliable car than his aged Citroen, which was like a cat on its ninth life, perhaps even a second car. After all, he could fix the Citroen and hope for a few thousand more miles and give the new vehicle to Willow to use. His wife, expecting a new baby, deserved as much.

Then there was the announcement that he was going to be a father. Shy by nature, he cringed at the thought of some office gathering where unwanted advice would be heaped on him by more experienced fathers; everything from horror stories of late-night sessions with a colicky baby to the description of the ungodly odors of a baby's intestinal waste.

He was equally averse to such endless questions as, "Have you picked out a name?"

"Have you had a sonogram, or are you going to be surprised?"

"Do you want a boy or a girl?"

However, Dylan felt obligated to share his news with his boss. In many ways, Jimmy Donahue was like a father figure to Dylan, and not just because Donahue had hired him in the first place. Donahue had been instrumental in finding them a place to live and finding a teaching position for his wife. Dylan also knew that much of the praise he had received for his series on veterans was the direct result of the guidance and encouragement he had received from the experienced newspaperman.

He parked his car in the underground lot. He got yet another "Thank you" from Gus, the attendant who had—incorrectly—given Dylan credit for ridding him of the obnoxious Julian Fleming. Dylan's first stop was the lobby, where he picked up his daily copy of the *Progressive* from the newsstand operated by Willis Carpenter. This particular morning Steward seemed more cheerful than usual. There was a new pep in his walk. He smiled at several people sitting near the newsstand and then quizzed the old man instead of the other way around. Beaming with childlike excitement, he boldly proclaimed, "It's a great day, isn't it, Willis! How was your weekend? Do anything exciting?"

Unaccustomed to revealing his personal life, Willis gave Steward a smiling pause. The old man's secrecy gave rise to another question.

"Come on, Willis, you must do something when you're away from this place."

True to himself, Willis replied, "Down by the ocean, sellin' some of these paintin's," as he nodded toward a few of his works hanging from the end of his stand.

Willis Carpenter had spent nearly thirty years watching people pass his way on a daily basis. He could tell by the way they held their head, the stride in the step, the smiles or frowns on their faces what joys or burdens they carried with them. He studied the young man standing before him.

He started to chuckle. "Okay, son. You tell ole Willis what's really goin' on. You actin' like you standing in tall cotton and just shot yo' self a big fat jackrabbit!" His self-amusement caused him to cough several times.

So quickly was Dylan taken aback that he answered immediately and truthfully, "I'm going to be a father, Willis. My wife is pregnant with our first child!"

"Lordy, you gonna be a papa, son!" responded Willis, slapping his two hands together and stomping the floor with his good leg. Their unrestrained exuberance brought several unsolicited congratulations from those sitting nearby. Wishing he had been more discreet in his announcement, Dylan sheepishly nodded to the acknowledgments. Eager to be in a more private place, Dylan said rather awkwardly, "I'd better go. I don't want to be late."

He handed Willis a ten spot and said, "Keep the change, Willis."

Standing off to the side of the main elevator was Jimmy Donahue and a man Dylan did not recognize. As he approached them, he greeted Donahue, "Good morning, Jimmy."

"Morning."

The terse reply told Dylan he was interrupting a private conversation. Not wanting to be a further distraction, he said, "I'll see you upstairs, boss," and entered the opened elevator doors.

"You're sure it was him?" asked Donahue, nodding in the direction of the departed young reporter.

"Absolutely, Jimmy," replied Buddy Feldman, the beat writer for the *L.A. Times* covering the music scene in Southern California. "I recognized him the minute I saw him from a photograph of him and Willard in the lobby."

For a man who stood barely five-feet five, with a balding head resembling a modern-day equivalent of Friar Tuck and bushy black eyebrows, the unsightly Feldman had a reputation of being something of a career-maker for up and coming musicians in Southern California. He was famously known for using anonymous references such as, "An unknown pianist is packing them in at Al's in San Pedro," or "nobody sings like the tiny tenor at Benny's Lounge in Reseda, " drawing people to certain clubs. But if he mentioned you by name and wrote more than a passing line or two, there was no telling what the future held. Donahue was amazed at the revelation about his protegee. Beyond knowing his wife's name and that she was a teacher, he knew little about the young man's personal life.

"It just goes to show you never know," replied Donahue with a suspicious grin forming on his face.

I wonder what else I don't know about him.

"Well, you can imagine my surprise, Jimmy. Like I said, I had heard from a friend's wife. Her husband runs a place in Venice where he allows some friends who are jazz musicians to play privately. As the story goes, at first only family and close friends came to listen to the impromptu sessions. Word of mouth soon spread about the sessions, particularly about a new guy who was something of a Svengali on a jazz guitar, and the owner realized he was missing an opportunity to make a few bucks. So he decided to open the place on Monday nights, charge ten bucks a head, beer, and wine but not food. The first night I went, Jimmy, I couldn't believe it. It was like the old days on the "Strip" when clubs would close for after-hours gatherings. You remember what it was like at the Trocadero and Billy Berg's, the greatest of the greats met to make unbelievable music. God, I wish those days were back!"

His reminiscing led Feldman off-topic, much to the chagrin of Donahue.

"Buddy, back to your point," urged Donahue.

"Yeah, sorry. Listen, Jimmy, I've covered the music scene in LA for over twenty years, and I'm telling you I've never heard anyone play jazz the way this kid does. He worked the pentatonic scale like he invented it. He would prolong his bends to the point you thought the note would never end like the B.B. used to do. His fingers were so nimble you could hardly see his hammers and slides. If there's one thing I've learned about musicians, Jimmy, it's that the good ones, the great ones, make everyone who plays with them better. Most musicians like to play within their comfort zone, but when they're playing with someone special, they'll try different things, you know what I mean. Riffs they never would attempt playing with someone else, transposing songs into different keys on the fly, that kind of stuff. You could tell by the look on their faces that the ones playing with him surprised themselves with what they could do. Listen, Jimmy, few jazz musicians would even attempt John Coltrane's "Giant Steps," but this kid did a guitar arrangement that defied the jazz gods. You have got to come and hear him. You won't regret it, I promise," pleaded Feldman.

Knowing Feldman would not take no for an answer, Donahue said, "Okay, Buddy, where's he playing?"

Feldman grabbed the elevator door before it could close and said, "A place called Pogo's in Venice Beach on the Boulevard. The place looks like a speakeasy from the twenties. You can't miss it. See ya there."

When he got to his office, Donahue was more than intrigued about Feldman's revelations. How had he misread his latest hire? Donahue knew something personal about all his staff through innuendo, office gossip, or direct questioning. But when it came to Steward, Donahue had missed the boat. Maybe it was the whole "this is your last time doing the hiring" edict from Damone Willard that threw the usually inquisitive Donahue off track. Steward's sudden rise to fame with the articles on the homeless veteran or the fiasco with Julian Fleming were equally distracting in his mind. He mused over his next decision. Discretion was not in Jimmy Donahue's vocabulary. When asked, he spoke his mind, and consequences be damned, but now there was someone else to consider. Fraternization was not officially frowned on at the *Times*, but why knowingly make yourself an object of gossip? Donahue picked up his phone and punched in her number. The official-sounding voice of his secrete love interest gave him pause.

"This is Sylvia Markham."

"Listen, how about we go out this Monday night for a bite to eat and listen to some good music?"

The ensuing hesitation caused Donahue to think maybe the time was not right. Then he heard her deep sultry voice, "Why James, that would be lovely."

DESPITE THE ATTENTION his articles had brought him, Dylan Steward did not assume it gave him carte blanche to enter his boss's office at will. With a polite knock on the door, he poked his head inside, asking, "Got a minute, Jimmy?"

Donahue waved him in as he ended his call. "Talk to you later."

"I'm not interrupting anything, am I?" asked Steward, hoping to get a private minute with his boss.

"Naw, I've always got time for my ace reporter," grinned a truly proud Donahue.

Steward entered, shutting the door behind him. The kid had a tell about him that alerted Donahue. Not only did he stay standing, but he also had a nervous manner with his hands. His fingers worked back and forth together. He brushed back his long brown hair as if to straighten the perpetual snaggle. Then one hand smoothed his brow. He cleared his throat a couple of times. Finally, "I've got something to tell you, Jimmy."

"Gee, kid, I would have never guessed. Sit!" The sarcasm twinkled in the Irishman's eyes.

He fumbled, reaching for a chair, nearly knocking it over. After righting it, he managed to sit down before blurting out, "Willow and I are expecting our first child."

Donahue's eyes widened as he leaned back in his chair. His evolving relationship had spawned a new sensitivity to the dynamics between two people in love. That emerging sensitivity had Donahue wishing in some ways that he had acted much earlier on his feelings when a certain someone had come on board from the *Chicago Tribune* years earlier. This was not the news he had expected to hear. Based on his earlier conversation with

Buddy Feldman, Donahue was expecting to get a two-week notice from the kid so he could launch his musical career. Donahue stood up and came around his desk. Steward likewise stood up, expecting a hardy handshake and pat on the back. Instead, the thick chested Irishman put a bear hug on his young reporter. Unaccustomed to such a personal display of affection, Steward stood helpless as the man's arms engulfed him, his arms hanging helplessly at his side. Realizing how awkward his captive must be feeling, Donahue quickly released him.

"That's great news, kid. I couldn't be happier for you!"

The genuineness of Donahue's feelings amplified the broad smile that now spread across his face. The announcement had touched the deepening affection that Donahue had developed for the young man. He saw a bit of himself in Steward, or at least the self that might have been. A twinge of envy found its way into Donahue's heart. He turned and walked back to his desk. He opened the bottom right-hand drawer and took out a box of Arturo Fuente cigars, the cellophane wrapping still intact. He held it up with pride and announced, "When the time comes, kid, I'll open this!" referring to the birth still months ahead.

Surprised that Donahue appeared to be abstaining from his favorite habit, Dylan said, "You go ahead now if you want, Jimmy. I never really developed a taste for those."

"Actually, I'm going cold turkey," he said as he raised the unopened box to his nose for a symbolic sniff of the Cuban imports. Donahue set the box on his desk. With a whimsical smile, he said, "A friend told me I needed to quit. You know that whole health and smell line."

"Now that's a surprise to me," said Dylan, knowing Donahue's passion for the box's contents. "Sounds more like a wife than a friend," he joked.

Donahue smiled as he fantasized about that possibility. Seeing the smile, Dylan took the opportunity to ask for a favor.

"Jimmy, would it be okay if I took the rest of the day off?

Willow's got an appointment with her obstetrician this afternoon, and I'd like to go with her. You know, to hear firsthand what's going on."

Donahue's generosity was more than Dylan expected.

"It's Wednesday, kid. Take the rest of the week off."

CHAPTER 27

Willow busied herself as she got ready for her appointment.

"You're sure you want to come with me, honey? Doctor Casper said the dizzy spells are normal at my stage of the pregnancy." In truth, for well over a month, Willow had been experiencing light-headedness and dizzy spells. Her husband had suddenly become very protective after Willow's second fainting spell in as many weeks, and these were only the ones he had witnessed. On the one hand, she found his new attentiveness an endearing trait. On the other hand, Willow had always been the independent sort, and now to be treated like she was some fragile china doll that needed to be kept in a display case was annoying, to say the least.

"Yes, I do," Dylan responded in a firm-sounding tone. There had been a noticeable change in Willow's behavior of late. She seemed lethargic with not nearly the energy she used to have, and she had trouble concentrating on the schoolwork she brought home daily. On more than one occasion, Dylan noticed her rubbing her eyes, complaining her vision was bothering her. It was difficult to hide his annoyance with her continual evasiveness whenever he questioned her about these occurrences. A stiffening of her posture alerted Dylan that he had breached that highly emotional zone in a pregnant woman.

"I'm sorry, sweetheart, I didn't mean to snap like that. I think I just need to hear from Doctor Casper herself. After all, I am a reporter, you know. I always confirm what a source tells me; it's what I do for a living, right!"

His attempt at levity failed miserably.

"Oh, is that what I am now, a source of information!"

With her arms crossed tightly across her chest, her lips pursed, and jaw clenched tight, the tears welling in her eyes were not to be mistaken for a sign of weakness. On the contrary, Willow was genuinely angry. Dylan knew his wife well enough to realize that rewording his statement would be useless. A more indirect approach would best be served. Speaking to her back, he said, "Sweetheart, in every sense of the word, you are my source. My source of joy, happiness, the fulfillment of everything I've ever dreamed of. This life growing inside you is an extension of us, and I want to know everything about it, to cherish and adore it. I'm sorry for using such a poor choice of words to describe how much you mean to me."

Her glacial-like posture began to soften. Her arms unfolded as she needed to wipe away the stream of tears now flowing down her cheeks. She turned to face Dylan and buried herself into his chest without a word. Her arms encircled his neck as she whispered, "I want you to know everything too, sweetheart."

With his arms around her, Willow felt an impulse to tell him everything, from the first indication of a potential problem when she saw Doctor Henderson at the free clinic in San Francisco to the latest ominous words of Doctor Casper that she was "outside the safety zone." But she knew him better than he knew himself. Dylan needed a sense of security when looking at the future. In his mind, there was no such thing as a small problem or a potential problem. There were only problems, and they would become bigger than life the more he thought about them. There was no way humanly possible for him to deal with the details of her condition or the possible outcome without completely losing his mind in worry for her. No, it would be best to shield him from himself.

"I'm sure Doctor Casper will tell you everything after my appointment."

DOCTOR CASPER'S waiting room was not the clinical setting Steward had imagined. A soft azure paint, more pleasing to the eye and the mind, replaced the more typical sterile white latex coating. Dylan was sure the cacophony of sounds was the perfect contraceptive for a young couple contemplating having children. Young mothers with stomachs hyperextended from a late-term pregnancy constantly shifted in their chairs, trying to find some measure of relief while emitting subtle groans of discomfort. If that visual was not sufficient to give pause to any mother-to-be, then the absolute chaos created by unattended toddlers screeching in delight as they used unoccupied chairs as trampolines or considered the magazine table tops as percussion points for any number of plastic or metal toys created fertile grounds for a migraine headache. One thing was for sure, no child of Dylan Steward's would act like these miniature rapscallions.

On the other hand, Willow judged the scene before her as a magical collage. This was just a cycle of life, and those on the verge of beginning their life journey were announcing, with every grimace and moan created in the womb, that they were ready to enter the world. Willow seemed quite at home amid everything. She viewed the spontaneous activity of the little ones as a Montessori type learning experience for young minds exploring the world as it exists before them. This was her dream playing out before her very eyes.

With an announcement, "Willow Steward, Doctor Casper is ready for you," from a nurse, Dylan gave a sigh of relief. He stood up to follow in the direction pointed out by the nurse when she said, "Oh, Mr. Steward. You'll need to wait here. The doctor will speak with you once she's finished with your wife."

The matronly-looking woman who appeared to be in her late fifties with tightly wrapped gray hair was all business in her approach. Dylan noticed her name tag, Agnes Madison, and thought a more personal approach would help.

"But Agnes, I thought I could be there too, please?" Dylan interjected.

Looking as if she was breaking some official medical protocol, the authoritative nurse frowned, then acquiesced. "If you like Mr. Steward, you can wait in the doctor's office. Follow us," said the nurse. Trying to look reassuring, Willow said, "Honey, this won't take long."

Doctor Casper came out of her office as they stepped into the hallway.

"Willow, It's good to see you, and this must be your husband. I'm Helen Casper, Mr. Steward." Her pleasant smile and warm voice seemed a stark contrast to the stern Nurse Madison.

"Yes, Doctor. I'm Dylan Steward. I was hoping I would have a chance to talk with you. You know a first-time father has lots of questions.," he said with a nervous smile.

Dylan did not attempt to hide his discomfort with these new circumstances.

"Certainly, Mr. Steward. Why don't you wait here in my office? When I've completed my examination of Willow, the three of us can chat. Feel free to turn on the TV if you like."

"I have you set up for exam room #3, Doctor," said Madison, all smiles in the doctor's presence.

"Let's see how our new mother-to-be is doing, shall we?" said Casper.

Sensing that her husband was less than happy at being

excluded from the examination room, Willow took her husband's hand and, with a loving squeeze, said, "Honey, I promise there'll be plenty of time for you to ask Doctor Casper whatever you want."

With an uneasy smile, Dylan replied, "Okay, but I've got lots of questions."

His nervousness was ramping up. It was evident that Willow's reassurance was to no avail. He watched as the three headed into the examination room a short distance down the hallway before entering the doctor's office. Casper's office was furnished with patient comfort in mind. There were two ergonomically designed chairs on rollers and levers to adjust the thickly cushioned back. Next to one wall was a midsize sofa with several large back pillows. An attractive wrought iron glass table rested under a large screen TV on the opposite wall. On the tabletop was a rectangular wicker basket with an assortment of fresh fruit, several water bottles, and a printed card that read, "Eat and drink healthy." Next to the basket lay the TV's remote control. Numerous large prints of well-known California landmarks like Yosemite Valley, the rugged Northern California coast, and the iconic Death Valley replaced the standard array of certificates, degrees, bookcases, and medical information. Soft pastel colors on the walls, in combination with a small rock waterfall on a corner table, created a calming meditative state.

Dylan did his best to put aside his anxiety. He grabbed one of the Gala apples from the fruit basket, the remote control, and settled back on the sofa, choosing to ignore the pediatric magazines such as "Young Mothers" and "Raising Your Child" that lay on a small table in front of the sofa. Surfing through the channels on the TV, Dylan settled on a documentary channel airing a segment on the history of jazz in America. With his first bite of the apple and the melodic sound of the narrator speaking of the pioneering influence of Scott Joplin and Jelly Roll Morton to the world of jazz, Dylan finally found temporary peace of mind. Down the hallway, a dream was about to unravel. The first sign of trouble was the distant sound of a siren drawing closer. It was unsettling to Steward, whose nerves were already on edge.

How such a routine vaginal examination could have gone so wrong so fast had rattled the normally unflappable doctor. Her attending nurse recognized immediately the dire circumstances they were facing.

"Please get Mr. Steward over to the ER right away," said Doctor Casper, trying hard not to convey her uneasiness to her attending nurse, "I'm going with paramedics."

Two paramedics hastily pushed a gurney carrying Willow Steward down the hallway through the exit doors and across a short parking lot to the emergency room at Providence Saint John's Hospital. The nurse proceeded post-haste in the opposite direction toward Doctor Casper's office to deliver the news to the waiting husband. The urgency of her mission left little room for any explanation of what had taken place. Madison pushed open the door to the Doctor's office and announced forcefully, "Doctor Casper wants you to come with me to the ER at the hospital across the parking lot, now. There was a slight problem during the examination."

The blurring of the siren told Steward the problem was anything but slight. The news hit the already anxious husband like a bolt of lightning. Steward leaped to his feet.

"What do you mean there was a slight problem? This was supposed to be a normal examination! How is my wife?"

Dylan Steward's personal mantra was unfolding before his very eyes. If something could go wrong, it would go wrong. If there had been a slight problem, why the rush to the emergency room? Willow had never given him the slightest cause to worry. What was it she had said, "just normal female stuff." There was nothing normal about what was taking place as far as Dylan Steward was concerned. Offering little by way of additional information, the rigid nurse stated authoritatively, "The doctor will explain everything when you get there. Now please come with me!"

"Which way!" he demanded, leaping to his feet. His voice was filled with equal measures of anger and panic. Steward pushed his way past the nurse into the hallway. He had no intention of waiting for the middle-aged, overweight nurse to lead the way.

"Down the hallway and through the exit doors, the ER is directly across the parking lot," responded Madison, completely losing control of the situation.

Fortunately, the paramedics had left the door ajar, or Steward would have torn it off its hinges as he shoved it open in his sprint to get to the ER. He bolted across the sidewalk and through the slow-moving traffic in front of the ER entrance. He ran with fearless abandonment. His wife was his only focus. The security guard on duty had just returned from his lunch break and was hurriedly trying to wipe up the spilled mustard from his hotdog off his uniform shirt. The retired police officer still maintained a sense of pride in upholding a professional appearance. He saw Steward moving quickly through the door and had the good sense not to question him for details as he blurted out in a panic, "My wife, they just brought her in from the doctor's office!" He held the door open and said, "Check at the desk to your left!"

Ignoring the police officer standing at the desk in casual conversation with the nurse, Steward interrupted their conversation. His voice cracked with emotion causing his words to tumble out. The nurse could see the fear reflected in his eyes.

"The... the.. paramedics just admitted my wife! Her name... is Willow... Willow Steward! Please God, can you tell me where she is!?"

The officer stepped aside and let the nurse address Steward's panicked plea. Five years working in the ER had taught Kristin

Andrews that reacting to a visitor's anxiety with anything but a calm, confident demeanor only exacerbates the situation. Glancing at her intake chart lying on the countertop, the stately five foot six blonde often referred to as the Sharon Stone of the ER replied, "Yes, your wife is in with the doctors now, Mr. Steward. Why don't you have a seat in the waiting area across the hallway, and I'll see if I can get someone to see you." Her pleasant smile and accommodating demeanor were in stark contrast to the iron-willed Nurse Madison.

Andrews moved rapidly from behind the counter, down a short hallway, and into an ER room. Steward had no intention of staying put. Adrenaline overpowered any inclination to obey the nurse's instructions.

"No! I'm coming with you!"

Andrews mustered up every bit of professionalism she had to deal with the concerned husband now on the verge of losing all control. She stood firmly in front of Steward, speaking with complete poise and calm.

"Mr. Steward, you will not help your wife's situation by barging into her room. The best thing you can do is let the doctor do her job without interference. For your own good, please have a seat in the waiting room. I'm sure the doctor will be out soon to talk with you."

The officer who had been talking with Andrews had positioned himself behind Steward in case physical intervention was necessary. Something reassuring in the nurse's voice caused Steward to pause. But the confidence that radiated from her hazel eyes that seemed to say, "She's going to be fine" was the hope Steward desperately needed to feel.

"This officer will show you to the waiting area, Mr. Steward."

Reluctantly, Steward turned and followed the officer back to the waiting area. The large waiting area was nearly empty. Steward had no problem finding a chair against the far wall. A middle-aged couple sat in one corner. The man's arms were over the woman's shoulders as she wept uncontrollably while her fingers struggled with her rosary beads. Nearby another woman sat rocking a young boy about six years old in her arms, assuring the youngster that "Daddy's going to be okay." Steward took a seat as far away from them as possible. He had his own fears to focus on.

After several minutes, Doctor Casper appeared in the hallway. Upon seeing her, Steward suddenly heard nothing, not the sobbing woman nor the reassuring mother, only deadly silence as the doctor moved quickly to his side, taking the seat next to him. He tried to speak, but it was as if his vocal cords had been cut. He felt like he was in the eye of a hurricane. He managed a few unintelligible grunts. His lungs struggled for air as the doctor interrupted him. Seeing that his eyes were frozen in a ghastly stare as if he was looking death in the face, the doctor spoke calmly and slowly to the nearly incapacitated man. She placed her hands on his, giving him a reassuring squeeze. She had the smile of a mother comforting a scared child.

"Mr. Steward, your wife should be just fine. During the digital pelvic examination, she began to experience unusually heavy vaginal hemorrhaging. It was important to stop the bleeding as quickly as possible. My office does not have the necessary equipment, so I called the paramedics. Additionally, we are stabilizing her blood pressure which was unusually low. She should be just fine in an hour or so."

Now was not the time to explain to him that during the digital examination of his wife, Casper, had to attend to an emergency telephone call. She had directed the attending nurse to perform a transvaginal ultrasound to determine the placenta location, which the nurse failed to do. Compounding that error, Willow had jerked her hips when the attending nurse had inserted the speculum in the vaginal cavity. The insertion of the speculum is not a comfortable feeling, and in most cases, such a reaction would have been harmless. However, with a woman suffering from placenta previa, the combination of sudden movement as the speculum comes in contact with the uterus can cause sudden vaginal bleeding that can be life-threatening.

The focus seemed to reappear in his eyes. His breathing, though labored, had returned. Steward leaned back in his chair, somewhat comforted by Casper's reassurances that his wife would be okay. Then he remembered.

"Doctor, the baby. Is the baby okay? The baby means everything to Willow!"

It would be premature and an unnecessary burden to tell the husband at this time that Willow had been adamant when she was wheeled into the examination room. Nothing, and she meant nothing, was to be done to endanger her pregnancy. Dangerously low blood pressure coupled with a dramatic blood loss would not bode well for the unborn child.

Giving him another reassuring hand squeeze, Casper completely ignored his question and answered instead, "Yes, Mr. Steward, Willow made it quite clear how important this baby is to her and you. We're doing everything we can to attend to both mother and child. Now, I've got to get back to your wife."

In a parting gesture to reassure him, the doctor cupped his hands in her and said, "Your wife has the best staff looking after her," She rose and walked down the hallway to the treatment room.

Despite her best efforts, Casper's words did little to lessen the deep-seated fears roiling within him. Anxiety made it impossible to sit still. He began pacing back and forth between the hallway and the windows overlooking the parking lot. He forced himself to focus on the doctor's words in the hopes of slowing down his heartbeat. His eyes darted everywhere, trying to find a safe haven from the emotional terror that now controlled him. The sight of an approaching doctor caused Steward to stop his pacing. The silver-haired doctor dressed in green hospital scrubs walked over to the elderly couple in the corner. On seeing him, the woman placed her rosary beads over her heart and gasped, "Dios Mio!"

The doctor took a seat next to the woman whose husband now had his arms around his wife.

"Mr. and Mrs. Morales, your son is going to be fine. He suffered a broken leg and bruised ribs from the motorcycle crash, but he'll make a full recovery. He's being moved to room 219 if you want to go up to see him."

The woman fell into her husband's arms, sobbing in gratitude and mumbling something unintelligible in Spanish to the doctor. The husband looked up at his son's savior and said, "How can we ever thank you, Doctor James?"

The doctor smiled and said, "Keep your son off that motorcycle. That will be thanks enough."

The father nodded at what was a foregone conclusion, then kissed his wife on the forehead as they stood up to go and see their son. Steward felt jealous, almost cheated at the good news the couple had received. Had his wife been there with him, she would have said, "See, I told you things would work out." But Willow wasn't there. No one was there for him, only gut-wrenching fear. The hands of the clock on the wall moved laboriously slowly as Steward recalled the doctor saying everything should be fine in about an hour. The screech of the small boy yelling, "Daddy, daddy," ended Steward's preoccupation with his wife's condition. He looked up to see a nurse wheeling a man in a wheelchair into the waiting room area. A large bandage covered his forehead. The nurse stopped the chair in front of the wife and the children.

"Feed him soft foods for a week or so until his stomach muscles heal from the hernia surgery, and your husband will be fine, Mrs. Jameson. And no heavy lifting for you, Mr. Jameson."

The man smiled sheepishly at the admonition, knowing he had brought on his injury by working out at the gym without a weight belt. The young boy ran to his father, who gingerly bent over to hug him. As the happy family rolled away, Steward thought of his wife's words. Could his Pollyanna-like wife actually be right? Good things come in threes, according to her and the adage

Steward remembered as a child. He was alone in the waiting room. He walked over to an empty chair and sat down, wondering if fate would reward him accordingly. That's when he noticed Doctor Casper coming down the hallway. She walked slowly as if burdened by some invisible weight on her shoulders. She pulled off her head wrap, exposing her salt and pepper layered brunette hair, more salt than the middle-aged doctor's ego would like to admit. Steward felt more than uncomfortable as the doctor's stare penetrated his very soul. She took a seat next to him. With the first words out of her mouth, Steward's body jerked backward, his head slamming against the wall.

"Mr. Steward, we did everything we could, but your wife lost too much blood."

He pushed himself harder against the wall, hoping to disappear somehow and escape the doctor's stare. The wall held fast, and Dylan Steward was forced to accept his wife's fate.

"We were unable to stop the vaginal bleeding, which was only made worse by placenta previa, a condition with which she was previously diagnosed. Your wife went into hypovolemic shock, and we lost her. My God, I am so sorry!"

With that acclimation, Casper, the woman, broke down in tears. It was the first patient Doctor Casper had ever lost, and all the years of professional training failed her miserably in dealing with her own emotions.

His head twitched nervously side to side as if to deny what he had just heard. His hands had a death grip on the wooden arms of the chair. No! No! The look in his eyes told Casper he did not believe a word of what she had told him. No, there had to be some kind of mistake. Not my wife! Not my Willow! She can't be gone! Then it came—a god-awful wail like the damned calling out from hell. It resounded off the walls and echoed throughout the entire ER area. The last time Dylan Steward had screamed like that was the day in Vietnam when he had held his friend, Tommy Podesta, in his arms, imploring God to keep him alive even as the boys' lifeblood poured out from a gaping stomach wound.

The volume and intensity brought the security guard and ER nurse, Andrews, running to the waiting area. Even a paramedic team from outside the ER came in to investigate. Steward stood back at a distance, momentarily watching the surge of medical personnel attend to the body slumped over in a chair. Turning back to the chaotic scene in the waiting room, Steward heard a paramedic reading off a blood pressure dial, "One fifteen over seventy-five and rising!" A nurse maintained pressure on the oxygen mask fitted firmly on the man's face. When the nurse removed the oxygen mask, Steward saw the face of the victim. Abject terror seized every muscle in his body, and he froze where he stood. A strange magnetic force was drawing him forward. Steward fought back with every fiber in his body. He was determined to go down the hallway to be with his wife, but he couldn't overcome the eerie force drawing him forward to the body in the chair. He screamed, but no one heard a word. All their attention was focused on the body in the chair. It was him.

Doctor Casper moved her small flashlight back and forth over the man's eyes then put the light back in her coat pocket.

"He went into shock. He's going to be ok but let's keep an eye on him for the next ten to fifteen minutes. We don't need to lose the husband as well."

CHAPTER 28

In the days following the sudden and tragic death of Steward's wife, the city room of the *L.A. Times* was shrouded in distinct shades of emotions. There was open sadness among Steward's few friends like G.O Roberts and Liz Alunda. In contrast, others whispered with speculation that there would be a multi-million dollar lawsuit for medical malpractice against the doctor and the hospital. Steward's desk was heaped with sympathy cards from Damon Willard, the managing editor, and his executive staff. Many at the *Times* had sent their regards even if they knew him only by reputation.

Steward's life had been in a tailspin for months following the death of his wife; nightly battles with alcohol to erase the memories of the hospital, and terrifying nightmares when he awoke in a cold sweat from nightmares screaming at seeing her image fade into a distant light. Steward's return to work would be eased by his unique relationship with G.O. Roberts and Liz Alunda.

Of all the reporters at the *Times*, G.O Roberts was the least gifted. Roberts worked hard at his craft, but unlike Dylan Steward, he did not have that spontaneous creative mind to produce long flowing paragraphs, neatly connected with exquisite descriptive language. Roberts would often ask Steward to look over an article he was working on, seeking advice on word usage or storyline. Steward always obliged his request, but with the gracious caveat, "Remember G.O, these are only my recommendations," hoping not to quash the man's ego.

Liz Alunda found a kindred spirit in Steward as they were both left of center on social issues and politics. Steward gained her lasting loyalty when he put to shame one of their colleagues over his disdain for the current review of the Civil Rights movement on television and in the newspapers brought on by the anniversary of the assassination of Martin Luther King.

However, the unpleasant discovery of a new addition to the staff did nothing to assuage the raw nerves of the grieving widower. Phil Johnson, formerly of the *Orange County Register,* had been forced on Donahue as a visiting columnist. Damon Willard had demanded it as a favor to the Register's owner-editor, Harold Stiverson. Johnson, who was white, had been quite vocal in voicing his displeasure over being passed over for a promotion in favor of a black female. No longer viewed as a team player, Johnson became expendable. However, as the brother-in-law of Barry Goldwater, Johnson had to be handled with "kid gloves," as the expression goes. Hence the sudden opportunity to work for the *L.A. Times* and the riddance of a problem for the *Register*. Unfortunately for Johnson, his political viewpoints and family ties preceded him when his hiring was first announced by Donahue.

Perpetuating his perception of a misplaced focus on history did nothing to endear him to some of the staff, who soon had become tired of his persistent diatribes on the imbalance of racial history as he saw it. After all, he was famous for pointing out, "The North won the Civil War and ended slavery. And what about Johnson signing the Civil Rights Act of 1964? Really, how much more do these people want!" It made Alunda's skin crawl, "these people." Before her anger exploded with her own brand of racial prejudice, Steward said, "These people! Did you really just say, these people, Phil?" Steward leaned forward like a leopard about to leap at his prey. Even Donahue feared that Seward was about to lose it after the racially insensitive remark by Johnson. Steward chose language over his fist in response. Keeping a steely focus on the man, Steward asked, "Do you read much, Phil?"

Never one to be shy about pontificating his own attributes, Johnson announced, "As a matter of fact, I consider myself quite a voracious reader. Why?"

"Then perhaps you should read John Howard Griffin's 'Black Like Me,' a *New York Times* Best Seller, by the way, before you bore us to death with any more of your soliloquies on the history of race in America. You just might gain an iota of understanding of what 'These People' went through." His emphasis on "these people" only added to his disgust for the man.

Alunda did not attempt to stifle her joy at Johnson's squirming in the chair as he struggled to respond before proclaiming to Donahue, "Well, I have never been lectured to in such a manner before!"

Before Donahue could intercede and squelch any further acrimonious dialogue, Steward continued, "And you won't again, Phil, at least not by me, if you'll think about the shoes someone else walks in; instead of your family issued Gucci's."

Though Donahue had no love for Johnson, he felt sorry for him after Steward's evisceration, which he felt had gone too far. To emphasize his point, he slammed the cover of his notebook and announced authoritatively, "Like each other or not, Steward, let's keep things civil!"

Steward had gained a friend for life in Liz Alunda.

———

WILLOW STEWARD WAS AS MUCH a nonconformist in death as she was in life. She had instructed her husband that should she be the first to die, she wanted to be cremated and have her ashes scattered into the air from an overhead plane.

"Who knows, Dylan, where my ashes will land? On what tree or bush that might grow taller or greener or on what person who might be mysteriously inspired to write a great book or achieve some medical discovery."

Steward humored his ethereal wife, never thinking at the time that he would be faced with making her wish a reality. With the help of Joe Skaff, Willow's principal, whose son owned a small Cessna, the arrangements were made to do as she had requested. It was a very private ceremony with only the closest acquaintances invited. Shortly after daybreak on a day when the sun rose with unusual brilliance, Steward stood on the grassy lawn, wet with the morning dew, outside the Griffith Observatory, high above the city of Los Angeles. Jimmy Donahue, Liz Alunda, G.O Roberts, Joe Skaff, and his wife Terri were at his side. The grass was damp from the morning dew, and the air held a brisk chill from the winds coming inward from the ocean.

"There he is now," said Skaff pointing to his left. The bright yellow single-engine Piper Cub, piloted by his son, David, approached from the north. It flew low enough for the call letter on the fuselage to be clearly visible. The plane made one pass over the observatory grounds, dipping its wings to signify the pilot had seen them. Then it made a slow sweeping turn eastward until it was headed due west directly over the Southern California landmark Griffith Park. The contents of the cremation urn formed a faint brown trail as the pilot held it out the cockpit window. Within seconds, the cloud and its contents dissipated into nothingness, seemingly absorbed into the mystic sky illuminated by the rising sun. It was as Willow Steward would have wished. She would be everywhere, touching everything.

When the plane had disappeared from sight, Steward turned to those around him. The dark bags under his eyes were a sign of the sleepless nights since his wife's death. The bright red capillaries that surrounded his eyes screamed of the crying jags that filled his sleepless nights. Steward wanted to thank those with him but the raw emotions still roiling inside him stole his voice. His eyes told them what his voice could not.

"Is there anything you need, kid?" asked Donahue, whose feelings toward Steward had become almost fatherly.

Steward shook his head then managed to mutter, "I miss her, Jimmy."

Donahue's late-in-life relationship caused him to wonder how he would feel if this had happened to him. He couldn't imagine the pain his protegee was going through. How would he handle it? Would he stand stoical and strong, or would he become a weeping soul longing for a lost love? His response was sincere and well-meaning but provided little consolation to the grieving widower.

"There are no words that will take away the pain, kid. You got dealt a shitty hand, and there's no sugar-coating it. Harsh as this may sound, you've got to find a way to deal with it, or that pain will suck the life out of you. I'm here for you. The job's here for you."

Dylan gave a slight smile. Echoing similar sentiments, Alunda said, "So are we, Dylan," referring to her and Roberts. "Another shoulder to lean on when needed." Roberts offered his own type of support. "Maybe we can get a beer sometime at work?" Joe Skaff and his wife had their heads bowed. The deeply religious couple were concluding their private conversation with the Almighty.

JIMMY DONAHUE WAS ill-prepared for the news that greeted him when he went to work the day after Willow Steward's dramatic and impactful ceremony in the skies above the Griffith Observatory. He had slept little the night before, unaware how much he was affected by the sudden passing of Steward's wife. He had awakened several times in a cold sweat, finding relief only when he reached over and found the body sleeping next to him was still there.

As always, Willis Carpenter had Donahue's copy of the *New York Post* waiting for him when he entered the lobby of the Times Building. He also had something else for him.

"It's a damn shame bout that po boy's wife, Jimmy. Pain like dat is hard to live with. Would you mind given' him this? It might help a bit?" Next to the end of the counter was a painting wrapped with brown butcher paper and tied loosely with a long piece of twine. Willis picked up the painting and handed it to Donahue.

"One of Willis Carpenter's originals?" joked Donahue, who desperately needed something to lift his spirits. Willis laughed then answered with the obvious, "Ain't they all, Jimmy! See for yourself. Something I had to learn, and so will he." Willis loosened the twine and carefully pulled the butcher paper off the painting. Donahue took the painting from Willis then turned, so the fullness of the overhead lighting covered the painting. He stared at it for several minutes. At first, he was confused by its simplicity, but then Donahue was overwhelmed by the depth of its meaning. On a small stage against the backdrop of a black curtain was a painter's easel. On the easel was a blank white canvas. Its whiteness was magnified by the contrasting black background. Hanging off one leg of the easel was a can with a dozen or so used paintbrushes, and next to the can was a palette with countless swatches of colors. Leaning against the other side of the easel was an old guitar, a classic Gibson Donahue had to guess. A pick was squeezed between three strings at the top fret, and a capo was clamped above the tuning knobs. Donahue slowly turned his head side to side in absolute wonderment. How and where the old man drew his inspiration was a mystery to Jimmy Donahue, but he did not doubt that Willis Carpenter had talent the world needed to appreciate. His mouth was agape. His eyes glistened as if he was holding a priceless treasure.

As he started to say, "How...?" Willis said, "I overheard you and Buddy talking that day about the boy. One night I made it to the place and listened to him play. He's sweet, so sweet, Jimmy!"

Yes, he is, thought Donahue, who remembered the night he and Markham had sat in the back at Pogo's unnoticed by those on stage and listened to the sheer genius of the young jazz guitarist. Replacing the paper wrapping, Donahue smiled and said, "Thanks, Willis, I'll make sure he gets this."

"Jimmy, one more thing," said Willis, "Could ya come over here?" nodding to a space behind his newsstand. Willis wanted a private setting to share his news. There, hidden behind the newsstand and away from the ears of those enjoying their morning coffee, Willis said to his longtime friend, "Jimmy, I'm leavin'. Thirty years and it's time. I'm tired of dreamin' the dream. I want ta live the dream, one mo' time."

The idea that Willis Carpenter would no longer be there in the morning with a smile and a copy of the *New York Post* was absolutely appalling to Donahue. There was a certain rightness to the universe, and that rightness started with a daily smile from Willis and a column by Jimmy Breslin. As he tried to wrap his head around the announcement, Donahue remembered their lengthy, liquor-stimulated conversation at Lefty's. A warmth of happiness swept over him for his friend and a deep sense of appreciation for the years he had considered Willis Carpenter his friend swelled within Donahue. He looked at his dear comrade and said, "It's the Chateau Rêves. You're going back."

A peculiar and new illumination shone in Willis Carpenter's dark eyes. The broadest smile Donahue had ever seen spread across his ancient friend's face. A simple nod was Carpenter's answer. Donahue nodded his head slowly in silent affirmation of his friend's decision. For the longest time, two old friends held each other in their arms. Unseen tears of joy would be stealthily wiped away before they parted. By the time he got to his office, Donahue could hardly have expected to be greeted by more surprising news. He rushed to answer his ringing telephone.

"Are you sure, absolutely sure?" said Donahue, incredulous at the news he had just received.

"Yes, I am!" said Markham, whose excitement caused her to choke slightly. "After you told me Willis's story and the name of the woman on the back of the photograph, I made a phone call to a friend of mine at the Museum of Beaux-Arts. When I mentioned the woman's name, she knew exactly who I was referring to. Apparently, she's worked there for years, categorizing the works of post-World War II artists and giving art lessons on the side. She even lives at the same address, a small cottage on the outskirts of Bordeaux near the Chateau Rêves."

"Thanks, Syl. I'll talk with you later."

Hanging up the phone, Jimmy Donahue swiveled his chair to face the window, the painting still in his arms. He leaned back in his chair, struck by the irony of the moment. One man was enduring the unspeakable pain of lost love, while another man would soon cherish a love once lost. Donahue never imagined when he told Markham about the name written on the back of the snapshot that she would actually be able to track the woman down. He had hoped that she would be able to find out some information about the woman, with her European connections in the art world, but certainly not to this degree. The enormity of Markham's discovery would spawn an idea that would gratify the longings in one life and save another.

CHAPTER 29

For the moment, Donahue's concern for the absent Dylan Steward was temporarily interrupted by the plans taking place for Willis Carpenter's goodbye celebration. Though not an official employee of the *L.A. Times*, Willis was as important to the start of the day at the metropolitan newspaper as the press operators, the reporters, secretaries, and the like. No matter how poorly you slept the night before or what troubles you were dealing with at home when you entered the lobby of the L.A. Times Building, you could count on the welcoming voice of Willis Carpenter calling out your name. "Hey, Mr…"

If you were a reader, he had your favorite newspaper or magazine in his hand for you. "Here's your copy of the…."

Willis knew your favorite team and their latest success or failure if you were a sports fan. "Tough break for your Dodgers the other night! Mr. Alston's gonna right the ship, don't ya worry."

Or if your son played college sports, Willis seemed to know more about the kid, the team, its players, and record than the school's own sports information director. As much as the family name Chandler, Willis Carpenter was an institution at the *Los Angeles Times*, sadly an institution whose time had finally come.

A large sign had been posted near the elevator doors announcing that contributions toward a going away gift for Willis could be left with the assignment editor, Jimmy Donahue. Most surprising to all who worked at the *Times* was the vast array of paintings that were on display throughout the entire first-floor lobby, dozens and dozens of inspired works that presented the dreams and experiences of a simple man who sold newspapers and magazines. They were simple only in appearance but complex in his interpretations with a brush. The inspiration of Sylvia Markham, the impromptu art gallery showing of Willis's works, drew as much attention from the general public as employees, thanks to a rave review of the artist's works by Rosalind Krauss, noted art critic and a personal friend of Sylvia Markham.

The heap of envelopes on the table his secretary had set up in his office confirmed the depth of feelings for Willis among the *Times* employees and warmed the soul of the sentimental Irishman. When he turned his focus from the piles of congratulatory envelopes to the open door of his office, his mood changed in an instant. The sight of the empty cubicle where Dylan Steward used to sit was like a dose of reality to Donahue's consciousness, announcing with agonizing irony that life can be so wonderfully rewarding for one person and yet terrorizing and painful for another.

THE CAR DROVE along the Southern California freeway as if led by some remote guidance system. Certainly, the driver had no conscious control of the vehicle. Involuntary reflexes caused him to speed or slow down to match the flow of traffic and finally to the off-ramp and into the parking lot at work, all without a nanosecond of conscious awareness of where he was or what he was doing. His first voluntary reaction was to respond to the morning greeting from Gus, the parking lot attendant.

"Good morning, Mr. Steward. It's good to see you back at work. I was so sorry to hear about your wife."

The rotund security guard said this with the utmost sincerity, his squinty eyes nearly tearing up. Gus had never lost his appreciation for Steward and his articles on the homeless veteran or his handling of Julian Fleming. Rumors of their volatile confrontation in Donahue's office had made their way to Gus's ears via the multitude of people who had despised Julian Fleming. Steward had grown painfully tired of responding to that oft-repeated sentiment over the last week, but in Steward's mind, the old man deserved an equal amount of sincerity.

Bloodshot eyes and a shallow face, visibly aged with grief, he managed to say, "Thank you, Gus. I appreciate it."

Steward proceeded to his assigned slot and listened to the tired Citroen's engine come to a noisy stop. He entered the lobby, hoping he could make it to his office without making human contact. He kept his eyes focused on the elevator doors, trying to ignore the crowd of people by the newsstand partaking in obvious merriment—an emotion Steward hardly felt like experiencing. Nor did he take notice of the small groups of individuals moving slowly through the lobby admiring a multitude of paintings on display. Fortunately, he went unnoticed to the elevator and up to the third floor, no doubt aided by the stubbled unkempt beard, dark sunglasses, and a rumpled corduroy jacket that had served as a pillow the night before. However, the scent of perfume from a female in the crowded elevator nearly brought Steward to his knees. It was Adagio, Willow's favorite. He inhaled its sweet fragrance with every goodbye kiss he gave her in the morning before he left for work. He grabbed the metal bar against his back for support, praying for the elevator to open and free him from the torturous reminder.

Steward decided the men's room should be his first destination. The searing brightness of the ceiling lights sent stabbing sensations through the crimson capillaries of his bloodshot eyes as he pushed open the door. It caused him to lower his head and blink several times. When his focus returned, he walked over to a line of shiny white porcelain sinks. Standing in front of the first one next to the towel dispenser, Steward turned on the cold water handle. He let the cooling liquid flow through the fingers of his hands before bending over and bringing several handfuls up to his face. He then ran his wet hands through his long brown locks several times. This feeble attempt at styling did little to enhance the appearance of his unkempt tresses. He straightened up slowly, not wanting to send a rush of blood to his already aching head and exacerbate the pain of his hangover. He stared into the mirror and saw an image he barely recognized. His face had not seen a razor in nearly two weeks, and the resulting facial growth gave a now gaunt face a trace of fullness and definition. Brown eyes that once twinkled with mirthful childishness had become expressionless orbs sunken further into their sockets. With no one to remind him to brush his hair before he left for work in the morning, Steward's long brown mane resembled the frayed ends of a dirty well-used mop. He was about to scream at the reflection in the mirror, "What the hell are you looking at!?" when the flushing sound from a nearby stall caused him to blink. The image in the mirror disappeared. A familiar voice echoed off the tiled walls of the long narrow lavatory.

"Dylan, man, is it good to see you!"

A smiling G.O Roberts stood next to him. His enthusiasm was sincere as he had sorely missed Dylan's way with words and language, a trait Roberts had found most desirable. Also, he was growing tired of listening to Liz Alunda's running commentary on hotbed issues arising from the Equal Rights Amendment passed three years earlier. Steward would have enjoyed playing the devil's advocate to Alunda's passionate orations. Almost shamefully, Steward answered, "Thanks, G.O," as he pulled a brown paper towel from the dispenser. Then came the inevitable words of sympathy. With puppy-like brown eyes and heartfelt sincerity

Roberts said, "Dylan, you know we, I mean me, Liz, we were devastated when we heard of what happened to Willow. I... I don't know what to say," as he too grabbed a couple of towels following a quick wash of his hands.

"Say nothing," replied a stone-faced Steward.

From the hurt expression on Robert's face, Steward realized his answer was a bit blunt and hurtful. He quickly tried to make amends. "Knowing you and Liz care is plenty said."

As the two made the short walk out of the men's room and down the hall to the city room, Steward could only hope that any other such expressions of sympathy would be at a minimum. As it was, he could barely control his emotions at the mere mention of his wife. Any hope of that happening soon would vanish. They headed down the far aisle of the city room to Donahue's office. As they neared the closed door, it opened. Steward could hear his boss thanking those inside the room for their input. In typical Jimmy Donahue enthusiasm, he heard, "I think this has the potential to become a serialized topic. Let's get to work!"

Nearly bumping into Steward as he backed out of the office, a startled Conrad Knight said, "Steward, I didn't see you. Listen, I am sincerely sorry to hear about your wife." And as an afterthought added, "Please accept my heartfelt sympathy."

Knight's flair for insincerity was never better. He sounded like he was reading a sympathy card from Hallmark. He gave Steward a polite tap on his shoulder, then quickly moved on, leaving three more staff members to respond similarly as they exited the room. The last was Liz Alunda, who, thank God, said nothing as she hugged Steward. The silence in her response steadied a shaky Steward. He whispered, "Thanks, Liz."

With Alunda returning to her cubicle, Steward was left face to face with his boss, Jimmy Donahue. "Come on in, kid. I've missed you."

Any words of condolence would take place in private. Steward went in and closed the door behind him. The anxiety of returning to work and painfully enduring countless offerings of well-intended condolences began to ease as Steward entered the confines of Donahue's office. His reporter's eye began to notice subtle changes. Steward had only been away from work for a couple of weeks, but Donahue looked slimmer than he had remembered. Another difference immediately struck Steward, the stark absence of Jimmy Donahue's trademark, the aroma of cigar smoke. As Steward glanced around the unpretentious office looking for other changes, he said as though speaking to no one in particular, "You give up those Havanas?"

With no more than a passing shrug of one shoulder, Donahue said, "Yeah, a friend convinced me to quit."

Donahue's terse answer was diametrically opposite to how he had previously responded when given such advice. "Hell, everybody dies of something," followed by a hearty laugh. The appearance of weight loss elicited another question from Steward. "Have you lost some weight around the middle, Jimmy?" A smile of self-satisfaction came over Donahue's face along with a boastful tug at his waistline to show his looser-fitting black slacks. "A friend said a fewer pounds would help the old ticker."

"Same friend who got you to quit the stogies?" grinned Steward.

"Enough with the questions, kid," replied Donahue, uneasy with the questions and even more uneasy that the reason for his recent lifestyle changes would be revealed. "Let's talk."

Donahue took a chair and pointed for Steward to take an empty one next to him. As he sat down, Steward expected the usual string of platitudes about recovering from the loss of a loved one. What he got was the exact opposite. Donahue sat there looking directly at Steward and said nothing. No doubt the man cared, from the warm, engaging smile on his face and the gentle expression in his eyes, but as he sat there, not a word came out of him.

Unaccustomed to the sudden silence from a man whose modus

operandi was to speak decisively, giving multiple directions to those at hand, Steward's discomfort was evident as he squirmed in his chair. Nervously brushing his hair to the side, he avoided eye contact with Donahue. It was Steward who broke the ice.

"So, you're the one who said 'let's talk,'" his tone was impatient, even a bit argumentative. It was a defensive gesture. He was clearly ill at ease.

Jimmy Donahue had conducted thousands of interviews over the years. He knew how to read the interviewee, their body language, and their physical appearance. He knew what to ask, and more importantly, he knew when to ask. He knew exactly how to play Steward.

It's odd what you remember as a child and how it affects you later in life, like listening to your father on the banks of a mountain stream. He's pointing to a spot across a current of swiftly moving water cascading over exposed rocks and boulders to a clump of green willows casting their protective branches over a deep pool. Then he says, smiling, "See that spot upstream from those willows where the current starts to slow? Watch me. Then you can try."

He brought his arm back and gently cast his line across the current upstream from the intended prey. The tri-tipped golden snare screwed through a squiggly nightcrawler guaranteed to lure the prey sparkled in the air before landing where the current started to slow down.

"Oh, I didn't mean me, Dylan. I meant you."

Piercing eyes followed the bait as the current sent it traveling downstream from the fast-moving current into a stretch of calm, slower-moving water under the willow branches. Nothing.

Steward straightened himself in his chair, shifting his focus to the traffic on the freeway visible from Donahue's office. When he looked back at Donahue, there was a patient calmness about the man. He was at ease, not tense, and self-assured in his posture.

With slow, deliberate turns of the handle on his reel, the older man retrieved his line and spoke to the boy at his side with supreme confidence. "He's there, and he's hungry."

Thinking that humor might free him from the inevitable and awkward conversation, Steward said through a forced smile, "C'mon Jimmy. I work for you, remember? You talk, and I listen. Wasn't that what you taught me?"

Donahue's professorial demeanor was not challenged in the slightest. "The exact phrase was 'Let's talk,' and the implied subject was you."

Once again, the golden snare floated through the air. The boy was amazed how it landed in precisely the same spot as before. The old man watched intently as the loose line that laid on the water's surface slowly straightened. His hand moved stealthily to the reel's handle. He was ready. Then it came—a quick tap, then a second tap, then nothing. You're a smart one, the old man said to himself, giving his prey its due.

His emotions were already frayed, and his ordinarily subdued temper now had a hair-trigger. He was tired of whatever game his boss was playing. "Alright, Jimmy, I give. Just what the hell am I supposed to talk about!?" he snapped.

For a third time, the old man cast his line. This time as soon as it hit the water, the man took up the slack in his line. He watched, preparing himself for the moment his line approached the overhanging willows.

Donahue leaned forward, his elbows resting on his knees. Steward could not avoid the penetrating glare of Donahue's steel blue eyes as he said, "You know that better than I, kid."

At that moment, the tip of the old man's rod suddenly plunged downward, and he gave the rod a quick snap of his wrist. The spasmodic movements of the rod told him the bait had been taken. The boy almost fell backward when the leaping twisting rainbow trout broke water and performed an acrobatic routine designed to free it from the golden prongs embedded in its jaw.

Whatever type of game Donahue was playing, Steward had had his fill. Between his pent-up emotions and the frustration of inane questions from his boss, Steward snapped. He leaped to his feet. His eyes were on fire, his voice hoarse, his throat muscles cramping from the hurt and pain about to erupt.

"Fine, Dammit. You want me to talk, I'll talk, for all the good it will do."

Steward turned and stormed to the window behind Donahue's desk. He stood there for several minutes. Donahue could tell from the jerking motion of Steward's chest the young man was losing control of his emotions. When he turned back to face Donahue, the pooling tears began to flow down both cheeks. His lungs could not control his breathing between the sobs of a broken heart. He spoke in short clusters of words.

"Every night... it's the same nightmare... over and over. I hear the nurse say I can see my wife, but there's an empty bed when I get to her room. I scream, but... I can't hear anything. It's terrifying, Jimmy. I cry out, 'Where is she, where's my wife,' but people pass me by like... like I'm invisible."

Steward could no longer be strong. He could no longer fight to maintain control. The emotional burden was too painful to keep inside any longer. He stood staring helplessly at Donahue, crying uncontrollably. His arms hung useless by his side until his legs suddenly buckled. He grabbed the edge of Donahue's desk. That involuntary reaction to counter the force of gravity and stop himself from falling jerked Steward out of the emotional watershed that had engulfed him. Using the palm of his hand to wipe away the tears, and with his breathing semi-under control, he said apologetically, "Sorry, Jimmy, that won't happen again."

That announcement brought Donahue to his feet. He knew that was a lie. He also knew that he was powerless to stop the process his young protege was going through, but he would be there to support him. Donahue walked over to Steward, who had arched his back like a man adjusting a heavy weight that lay across his shoulders. He put his arms around Steward like the father figure he had become. Donahue's thick torso absorbed the total weight of Steward's body against his.

"Yes, it will, Dylan. You need it to happen."

Emotionally spent, Steward could offer no resistance to the

advice he had received. As Donahue eased his hold of support, Dylan said, "If you say so, Jimmy." There, he said it. He told his boss what he needed to hear.

Having done all he could for the moment, Donahue's normal directness returned. Some might call it tough love. A wry smile formed on the Irishman's face, recognizing that he had done all he could to bolster Steward's spirits. He turned around and walked back to his desk. He unbuttoned the cuffs of his long sleeve shirt and began rolling up the sleeves.

"Alright then. I've got work to do, and so do you."

Steward nodded. On his way to the door, he paused. There was more on his mind. "Jimmy..." Before he could finish, Donahue added, "By the way, there's a project coming your way that's right up your alley. We'll talk about it tomorrow."

Work was not his ally. Steward's refuge took a different form. Without even turning around, Steward said, "Sure thing, boss."

CHAPTER 30

With each telephone ring, searing pain shot through his brain. One arm pulled the pillow over his head while his other arm flailed about blindly, knocking the receiver off its cradle. A voice on the other end pleaded several times, "Dylan, it's me, G.O. For God's sake, talk to me. I can't stall Donahue much longer!"

His hand fumbled along the floor until he found the coiled phone line. He brought the receiver to his ear with his head still buried into his pillow. His head throbbed from a losing battle with a bottle of Ten High Whiskey. His mouth felt like a giant cotton ball. He brought the receiver to the side of his face, laid it on the pillow, and mumbled, "Shit, G.O. Why the early call?"

"Early, are you kidding me!" G.O. hollered, causing Steward's head to jerk away from the phone lying on his pillow. "It's 9:30, dammit, and Donahue's been asking about you. I made up some lame excuse about the traffic on the 10 East, but you'd better get your ass in here and fast."

THE COLD WATER that had poured over him from a hasty shower had at least partially restored Steward's brain to a functional organ. He hoped a large black coffee purchased at the drive-thru of a nearby Bob's Big Boy would do the rest to prepare him to face his boss. Driving on the LA freeway with the window down was not a good way to dry or style his long mane of unruly brown hair. His slacks and shirt that had laid crumpled in a pile on the floor next to his bed should have had more than a good shake to make them presentable to wear to work. His bloodshot eyes never noticed the stains of spilled food and drink as he hurried to get dressed.

Dylan Steward's days were filled with self-deception. Where two or more women were talking, he imagined he heard Willow's voice. Did every woman he pass wear the same perfume that Willow adored, Adagio, or was it just his imagination at work? Once, he thought he had seen her crossing a street, only to disappear in a maze of humanity on the other side. Another time he saw a woman walking down the aisle at the local grocery store wearing Willow's woolen scarf and matching cap. She turned around when he hollered out her name. A stranger's face looked back at him. Nights were the worst. Anesthetizing himself with cheap whiskey would only fend off the nightmares for so long. They came with a vengeance. He would reach down to pick up his smiling toddler from his wife's arms only to have the infant disappear as his hands reached out. He would roll over in bed at the sensual touch of her hand on his back only to find an empty space. Sometimes he saw her in a meadow or on the beach at the shoreline. She would be waving for him to come to her. She was more beautiful than ever, more desirable than he ever imagined. She glided farther and farther away as he hurried to her, calling out her name. The more he ran, the farther she disappeared into the distance until he fell to his knees, screaming out her name while sobbing hysterically. This rollercoaster of nocturnal horrors and daylight mind games left Steward mentally and physically exhausted to the point he looked and acted like a zombie.

The urgency of Robert's phone call had Steward playing his own mind game as to what to tell his boss. How many times can the alarm clock not go off? How many times can an accident bring traffic to a crawl at the very time he's driving to work? How often can his tardiness or absences be something or someone else's fault? Just how much patience did Donahue have for his errant young reporter? Fortunately for Steward, the well was not completely dry.

THE DOOR to Donahue's office was ajar, allowing Steward to expose only his head in anticipation of a barrage of profanity-laced frustrations from his boss. He couldn't have been more wrong.

"Sorry, Jimmy, I couldn't help this one."

His smile intended to appease his boss. The new, slimmer, more health-conscious Donahue greeted him warmly.

"Hi kid, come on in. It must have been one hell of an accident. Roberts told me that traffic was holding you up."

Compounding his colleague's lie and his boss's false assumption, Steward answered, "A motorcycle," careful not to embellish one lie with more lies.

"I hope the poor son-of-bitch makes it," replied Donahue with heartfelt sincerity.

Steward nodded, grateful his story had passed the smell test.

"I've got a story that needs that Dylan Steward touch," smiled Donahue as he took a seat behind a strangely well-organized desk.

Following suit, Steward took a chair and sat down. Feeling comfortable by how easily his moral lapse was accepted, Steward grinned and asked, "Just what is that Dylan Steward touch."

A little more stroking, Donahue thought. "Are you a good writer or not, kid, because that's what this story needs, a good writer."

He had spent too much time wallowing in self-pity to realize that he was being played. Wanting to stay on his boss's good side caused Steward to reply with smug self-confidence, "I work for the *L.A. Times*, don't I?"

"Good!" responded Donahue, "Have you seen the movie "Chinatown?" It came out last year."

"I'm not much of a movie guy, Jimmy, but Wil...." He couldn't finish his words. That stabbing pain in his heart caused him to nearly double over.

Donahue gave Steward a few minutes to compose himself before continuing.

"For starters, suffice it to say Hollywood played fast and loose with Southern California history as far as the granddaughter of William Mulholland is concerned. You do know the name, Mulholland?"

"Like the drive?"

"One and the same, kid. You need to see the movie to get Hollywood's take on history. Then do a little digging into William Mulholland and the 'California Water Wars' as the press called them at the time. Contact Hillary Mulholland Preston, old man Mulholland's granddaughter, when you are done with that. She feels her grandfather was horribly misrepresented in the movie."

This was the old Donahue, quick and succinct directions, sequenced, orderly, and no-nonsense. What came next shocked Steward—more directions, stinging, painful, but accurate, and something he needed to hear.

"Oh, and Dylan, another thing. Either buy a new razor and comb or see a barber, your choice and learn how to wash and iron your clothes or buy new ones, again your choice. When you step foot in my office, you represent the *L.A. Times*, which means you represent me. Do I make myself clear?"

Steward stood there momentarily frozen by the harshness of his bosses' remark. Shame is a powerful emotion. It can evoke anger and resentment when unfairly placed or render one mute when it fits like a well-tailored suit. It remained to be seen if

Donahue's parting words would affect Steward. Would he succumb to the all too human reaction of resentment and anger, or would he embrace them as the small steps necessary for turning his life around?

NOT REALIZING that his boss had handed him a life preserver, Steward returned to his cubicle where he faced the stark reminder of the tragedy that had befallen him, more sympathy cards. A handwritten reply was the gracious thing to do, the type of thing that Willow would have done, but hardly the type of response Steward was capable of at this time. Where he had to, he opened each envelope to identify the sender; otherwise, he scanned the upper left-hand corner. He kept a running list of those he needed to respond to later. Having documented the nearly two dozen senders, Steward considered the directions Donahue had given him for his new assignment. The thought of sitting in a movie theater surrounded by husbands with their wives, boyfriends with their girlfriends with all the intimacy that takes place in a darkened theater was pure torture for the young widower. Steward picked up his phone and called the archives department.

"Archives, this is Marilyn. How may I help you?"

"Marilyn, this is Dylan Steward. I was wondering if you could pull some resource material for me?"

Marilyn Carrington was the unseen heroine for many a reporter at the *Times*. Unseen by most because of the basement archive storage area but appreciated by all, she had been at the *Times* nearly as long as Jimmy Donahue. The credit for the historical and factual accuracy needed by any reporter lay at her footsteps as she had meticulously cataloged and cross-referenced every bit of microfiche data for decades. Her undeniable sultry southern accent left many a caller to ponder what exotic creature was on the other end of the line. Grabbing a pencil and a piece of paper, she said, "Absolutely, Mr. Steward. Tell me what you need. Oh, and by the way, I was so sorry to hear about your wife's passing. I lost my Henry several years ago. It's still hard."

Steward couldn't help but think that he needed to find a new job, somewhere where no one knew him, somewhere he would never be reminded about his wife again. In that pensive pause, Carrington repeated her question.

"Mr. Steward, are you still there? What materials would you like?"

"Oh, sorry, Marilyn," Steward replied, ending his fantasy abruptly. "I'm looking for a review on the movie "Chinatown" and anything you can dig up on the California Water Wars."

"That's not going to be a problem, Mr. Steward. I'll have those materials sent up to you by the end of business today," replied Carrington, supremely confident in her research ability.

Having addressed two of his boss's three directives, Steward decided to consider Donahue's parting remarks. They had left a bitter taste in Steward's mouth. He saw them as ultimatums, not choices. Looking down at his tan slacks with crease lines that resemble the imprint of a pile of pickup sticks, the result of several nights of randomly landing on his bedroom floor, he realized his boss's remark had some merit. Moving his stare to the front of his light blue shirt, Steward saw further confirmation of his boss's critique, crumbles of day-old pizza sauce or a morning muffin; he wasn't sure which. The multiple stains were equally unidentifiable, could be beer, wine, or bourbon, depending on the beverage of the night. With his decision made, Steward stood up and walked across the aisle to Martha Irons' office. Knocking first, he opened the door slowly and poked his head inside.

"Yes," came the dry response from the secretary, not bothering to look up from her Remington Electric typewriter.

"Martha, could you let the boss know that I'm going shopping. He'll understand. Oh, and tell him I'll be at the Orpheum Theater after that."

The men's clothing department at J.C. Penny had never failed Willow when she shopped for her husband, and he hoped he would have the same success. Steward felt somewhat out of place walking alone through display after display of men's clothing. He was used to following Willow as she discreetly eyed the sales racks for the right shirt and pants at just the right price. Now it was his eyes doing the searching. No doubt it was the deer in the headlights look that caused a saleswoman to approach him and ask pleasantly, "Is there something, in particular, you're looking for?"

The well-dressed saleswoman in her early thirties wore a form-fitting black skirt with a white chiffon blouse intended to display her natural endowments as much as complement her skirt and five-inch black heels. Gold-rimmed glasses hung from a lanyard around her neck and rested provocatively above the third button on her semi-opened blouse. Her name tag read, "Heather."

"My directions, Heather, are to get some shirts and slacks for work, preferably something that doesn't require ironing. Oh, and if they would go with either a brown corduroy jacket or a blue blazer, all the better."

Mistakenly taking the use of her first name as flirtatious, the woman ran her tongue slowly over her bottom lip and said, "Come with me, and we'll see what we can find."

Their first destination was men's slacks. For Steward, slacks were slacks. He was about to learn how wrong he was. Cuff or no cuff, straight leg or bell bottom, Khaki or Hagger's, cotton, or polyester. Shirts had their own endless possibilities. Button-down collar or plain, short sleeve or long sleeve, cotton or twill, poplin, on and on. It was no wonder Willow guided him through the process. His annoyance with Donahue's orders grew with every possibility the attractive Heather put before him. On the verge of sounding unappreciative of her efforts, Steward said, "Heather, would you mind picking out, say, three types of slacks and four or five shirts to go with them. My mind is a blur right now."

"Let's look at the permanent press and wrinkle-free combinations. It will be less work for your wife. Believe it or not, many men bring their wives with them to help for that very reason. We're having a sale of men's and women's apparel next week. You should bring your wife. Put these decisions on her shoulders," she said, smiling.

Steward heard little after that. He shook his head when asked if he wanted to try on the pants. He stared blankly at the prints of surfers on the wall behind the cash register as Heather rang up the sale of the day.

"I look forward to seeing you again, Mr..." said Heather, hoping to get a first name.

Steward struggled to maintain his composure. The slightest twitch off his left cheek was all the smile he could muster. He turned to leave, remaining nameless to the salesclerk.

CHAPTER 31

At day's end, Dylan had all the emotional fatigue of a heavyweight boxer who had endured fifteen savage rounds of pounding body blows. Between the explicit references about his wife made by well-meaning people, there were the equally excruciatingly painful moments when Steward imagined seeing her disappear into a crowded street, hearing the sweet laughter of her voice in some passing conversation, or becoming intoxicated by the smell of her perfume on a nearby woman. If this was the extent of his daylight experiences, the thought of the approaching nightfall with its unavoidable tortuous nightmares caused the grieving widower to seek refuge in the sweet mixture of brandy and amaretto. With each swallow of the potent elixir, the pain of Willow's memory dulled. Steward rested. His relief would be temporary. The alcoholic defense would be no match for the haunting memories that awaited him.

THE NEATNESS and cleanliness of their home that had been an endearing characteristic of Willow's attention to the slightest of domestic details were not traits at the forefront of Steward's consciousness. There was an ever-present stack of dishes in the kitchen sink, though at least they had been partially wiped off. TV dinners eliminated the need to use Willow's favorite pots and pans. Thanks to the generosity of Joe Skaff and his wife, Terri, the refrigerator was full of more casseroles than Steward could eat in a month of Sundays. The backs of the kitchen chairs, two end tables, and any doorknob in reach had replaced the need to use their bedroom closet for hanging clothes. More often than not, the sofa, with Willow's handmade knitted Afghan used as a cover, was his nightly resting place. The emptiness of their queen-size bed was yet another reminder of his loss.

There was one place he could go, one thing he could do where he could fend off the paralyzing thought of her memory. The spare bedroom with his collections of instruments, mostly his prized Gibson, was akin to a recording studio insulated from all the world's outside sounds and distractions. There, with his collection of records playing in the background, he could accompany the legends themselves. Ella Fitzgerald's *Let's Do it*, Billie Holiday's *Love is Here To Stay,* Hoagy Carmichael's *The Nearness of You*, Anita O'Day's *Angel Eyes,* and one of Willow's favorites, Getz and Burton's *Little Girl Blue*. For a brief period of time, music seemed to co-exist with the memory of his dead wife until it couldn't.

―――

G.O. FOUND himself working late that afternoon when a very young-looking archives clerk arrived with several envelopes. The clerk's eyes roamed the area for a face he didn't know. It was fortuitous for Steward, who had left early that day, that the clerk stopped at Robert's cubicle.

"Excuse me, but can you tell me where I can find Dylan Steward? I've got some material he requested from the archives department."

"He's gone for the day," said Roberts, not bothering to look up from his typewriter.

The young gift bearer, looking rather helpless, said, "Should I leave these with his boss?"

That announcement caused Roberts to become more attentive. Steward had told him earlier that he was leaving for the day and obviously without Donahue's knowledge. There was no reason to alert Donahue of another unauthorized absence.

"You can leave them with me. I'll make sure he gets them," replied Roberts, sounding accommodating to put the young clerical at ease.

"Are you sure? Ms. Carrington said to deliver these directly to Mr. Steward?"

Roberts took a pen from his shirt pocket. "It's not a problem, trust me. I'll sign for them if that will help you out."

"Well, I guess that will be okay," said the young man tentatively, handing Roberts a clipboard with a receipt on it.

Roberts quickly scribbled his name on the receipt, hoping to send the young man on his way before Donahue stepped out of his office. Roberts had nothing but good intentions once he took possession of the materials from the young clerk. He was protecting a person he considered a friend, someone who had helped him many times in the past, and now it was his turn to return the favor. Unfortunately for Roberts, like the road to hell, which is paved with good intentions, the path he was headed down would bring him perilously close to losing his job.

―――

FRUSTRATED after knocking several times without getting a response, G.O. slowly turned the doorknob and opened the door to Dylan Steward's house. Straddling the threshold before entering the house, he tried one more time. "Dylan, it's me, G.O.; are you home?"

Roberts had seen Steward's car in the driveway. It was only natural to assume he was home. Roberts slowly pushed open the door and made his way inside. For a moment, he thought he was back in his fraternity house. The stale odor of alcohol permeated the air, coupled with the acerbic smell of burned food. He cupped his hand over his mouth until air movement from the opened door could remove the foulness in the air. A stack of unopened mail scattered about on a small coffee table in front of the sofa. Judging from the empty food containers dispersed about the living room and kitchen table, his friend had feasted on Chinese food, pizza, and multiple Hungry Man TV dinners at some time in the past few days. Two large bags from J.C. Penny lay on the floor. Their contents appeared to have been thrown about the living room. Several new shirts still in their Penny's packages and several new slacks still clipped to their hangers made Roberts tread carefully. The sight of the kitchen caused Roberts to mutter, "Jesus, Dylan, how can you live like this!" A large brown bag serving as a trash collector had been tipped over. A colony of ants feasted on its contents. The kitchen sink was full of unwashed dishes, crumbs of food now crusted permanently on them. What the sink could not hold the countertops did. The sordid conditions caused Roberts to fear for his friend's safety suddenly. Decorum be damned, he yelled, "Dylan, where the hell are you!?" The answer would do nothing to dispel Roberts' fears.

ROBERTS HEARD a loud thud coming from the hallway, followed by a "Son-of-a-bitch". He moved cautiously down the short hallway until he heard scuffling from behind a closed door. He called out, "Dylan, is that you?"

The door opened to a shocking picture of his friend. Blurry-eyed and reeking of booze, a completely disoriented Steward stood before him, trying to maintain his balance. Empty album sleeves were strewn over the floor. Next to them lay a few of Steward's prized collection of guitars. Discarded food wrappers from a nearby Bob's Big Boy had apparently been bounced on the walls, ketchup smears leaving a trail of their impact. The arm of a phonograph moved and returned, moved, and returned in the absence of a new track where its needle could rest. Steward's prized Gibson lay atop a sheet of scribbled chords and lyrics. A half-empty bottle of brandy came rolling to rest near the door.

"Dylan, are you okay?" asked his concerned friend, shocked at what his friend had become. His friend's hair was a cluster of unmanageable tresses matted together. His once piercing eyes now had a faraway stare. His face looked fatigued as if he hadn't slept in days.

"Don't I look okay?" was Steward's defiant response. His eyes blinked to gain clear focus, the results of a drunken stupor from which he had been abruptly awakened.

There was a time when that kind of sarcasm would have caused the timid Roberts to retreat from such a confronting question. However, his concern for his friend gave Roberts a newfound strength. Ignoring the hand holding the doorknob, Roberts forced his way around Steward and stood in the middle of the room, shaking his head in disappointment at the scene laid out before him. Unwilling to ignore the evidence of his friend's self-destructive behavior, Roberts confronted the beast that had formerly been his friend.

"Does this look okay to you?" he demanded, spreading his arms to emphasize the question. Continuing his rant, Roberts said, "And to answer your question, no, you don't look okay. As a matter of fact, you look like hell!"

Unaccustomed to having such aggressiveness directed at him, Steward countered defensively, "Who in the hell do you think you're talking to?" slamming the bedroom door shut, leaving the two to face each other like fighters in the middle of the ring.

Wearing only one shoe, Steward stood off balance. The effects of the brandy had not completely worn off, adding to his equilibrium problem.

He swayed slightly as he eyed his perceived opponent through bloodshot eyes. The months since his wife's passing had not been kind to Steward. Days spent wallowing in grief and nights immersed in alcohol to numb the pain had rendered Steward a pathetic sight. So much so that Roberts's initial anger at his friend's condition now took on a more conciliatory tone.

"Listen, Dylan. I can't imagine what it would be like to lose my wife. And frankly, if I lost mine, I don't know if I'd act any differently than you. But if I did, if I tried to drown myself in alcohol, I hope I'd have at least one friend try to help me. That's all I'm doing, Dylan. I'm just trying to help."

Still defiant, Steward answered, "Did I ask for your help?"

Remembering his friend the way he was, Roberts was momentarily at a loss for words. Part of him wanted to answer with as much aggression as Steward deserved. Part of him felt nothing but pity for the friend. Somberly, Roberts replied, "The question isn't did you ask for help, Dylan. The question is do you need help?"

There was nothing more Roberts could do. He turned to walk away. Steward found some small shred of dignity to cling to in that nanosecond. A plaintive voice called out, "G.O., wait. Could you help me with a little cleaning?"

———

ROBERTS STOOD in the living room surveying the surroundings.

"First things first," he said, walking over to the double French doors in the dining area. Opening them, he said authoritatively, "Let's get some fresh air in here,"

Steward sat on the sofa, rubbing the bottom of his foot that still ached from stepping on the empty brandy bottle before putting on his shoe. Quietly resigned to the fact that he needed help, he was in no position to argue with the man who had answered his plea, nor was he inclined. In his more sober moments, which had been few and far between lately, even he had come to hate the slovenliness of his home. He rose slowly, not wanting to aggravate a pounding headache or a stomach on the verge of eruption. Walking slowly to the front door, he opened it and asked, "I guess a little cross ventilation wouldn't hurt." With something of an able partner, Roberts began with the simplest of tasks.

"Dylan, can you get your garbage can and put it on the patio near those French doors and tell me where Willow keeps the vacuum cleaner?" Instantly, Roberts realized what he had said. He was absolutely petrified of the effect this remark would have on Steward.

"I'm sorry, Dylan, it just came out. I wasn't thinking." He was genuinely remorseful.

It was hard to be angry at his friend for something he thought or did himself regularly. The mere thought of his recently deceased wife, much less hearing the sound of her name, would have ordinarily have caused Steward to reach for some liquid relief. Something deep inside him told him not to do that. For the moment, he resisted the urge.

Answering slowly and with a breaking voice, he said, "It happens, G.O.," fully appreciating his friend's sentiment. No further judgment was made or needed. As Steward headed out the French doors to retrieve the garbage can near the garage, he said, "Hall closet. Her Electrolux is in there. It was a gift from her mother." He had no idea why he had said the last sentence.

There was a cardboard box with cleaning rags, several aerosol cans for dust removal and window cleaning, and a broom and dustpan on the small hall closet floor. In the corner of the closet was the oblong Electrolux resting on end with its hose and attachments neatly stacked next to it. No stranger to a vacuum cleaner since his wife, Suzanne, insisted housework had no gender exclusivity, Roberts soon had the machine plugged in and ready to go when Steward returned. It seemed odd to see Willow's prized vacuum cleaner in the hands of his friend. Roberts saw the blank expression on his friend's face.

"What? You never saw a man use a vacuum cleaner?" he asked quizzically.

"Actually, I took care of the outside stuff. Willow handled the inside."

"Well, watch and learn, my friend, while you fill up that garbage can with all this," he said, pointing to empty beer and whiskey bottles, half-eaten boxes of takeout Chinese food, hamburger wrappers, and French fry boxes from Bob's Big Boy, old newspapers, and a pizza box with half-eaten pizza slices inside. "And don't forget the trash on the kitchen floor!"

Having barked his final order, Roberts hit the start button on the vacuum with his foot and began a neat and orderly pattern of back and forth motions over the living room floor, under the sofa, and the coffee table. The high-pitched drone of the vacuum cleaner resonated inside Steward's brain like fingernails across a blackboard, giving him the extra impetus to complete his tasks as soon as possible. What started as a one-and-a-half-man cleaning team soon grew to full strength as Steward's splitting headache began to subside and his stomach settled with the flow of fresh air throughout the house. Once the trash was removed and the vacuuming done, Steward and Roberts tackled the kitchen. With liberal use of SOS pads and Ajax cleanser, dirty pots and pans became clean, and the seafoam green tiles of the countertops became visible. Wiping his hands on a dishtowel slung over his shoulder, Roberts commented with pride, "Not bad if I do say so!"

Steward surveyed their work. Yes, it looked better. Willow would have been proud of him, and that thought stabbed suddenly at the rawness of his emotions.

"Let's take a break outside on the patio, G.O.," Steward said.

Willow's presence seemed to be overpowering in the cleanliness of their work.

"Sure," replied Roberts, who would have preferred to complete all the work before stopping.

"What can I get you, G.O.?" Steward asked as he headed to the kitchen refrigerator.

"A soda would be good," replied the easy-to-please friend.

Willow was never much for alcohol, so their refrigerator was amply stocked with her favorite soda, Dr. Pepper. Steward bypassed the last remaining bottle of Budweiser and grabbed two cans. No need to agitate his friend, he thought. Roberts had settled on one of two folding aluminum chairs admiring the small vegetable garden that had been Willow's pride and joy.

Remember dummy! Don't say anything about it. He reminded himself.

Handing Roberts his Dr. Pepper, Steward lowered himself onto an unsteady folding chair, thanks to an uneven red brick patio. He held the cold can of soda to his temple. The chilling sensation put an end to the last of his headache. It was time to express his gratitude and question the purpose of his friend's surprise visit. He took the first sip of his soda to clear his throat.

"You know, G.O., I really do appreciate your help today. I haven't been able to think of anything lately but her and wondering why, why her?" Using the feminine pronoun 'her' without falling apart was a small step forward for Steward.

"I'm no theologian, Dylan. Why bad things happen to good people is a question for smarter people than me to figure out. What I do know is that you have to seize every moment for the good that comes with it because bumps in the road are inevitable."

Not quite ready to accept his friend's platitude, Steward said, "With bumps like this, I'm not sure I want to travel this road."

"You know something, Dylan; you don't have to. You can travel any road you want to."

The simple truth of his friend's statement escaped Steward for the moment. Steward had little time for introspection between his wife's tragic and sudden death and the unabated shame he felt at his friend's unexpected arrival. Hoping to give his friend something to divert his attention from his present situation, Roberts leaned forward in his chair and said with a sincere expression on his face, "I took the liberty of signing for some material the archives section sent up for you yesterday. The clerk was going to give it to the boss because you weren't there, but I thought it would be better if I signed for it."

Realizing his friend had extended himself again on his behalf, Steward replied, "Thanks again, G.O., Jimmy wants me to prepare for an article on the California Water Wars. He thinks watching some movie called "Chinatown" will help. Apparently, some relative of a guy named Mulholland thinks the movie did her great grandfather a disservice. I never saw the movie, and I don't have a clue about these so-called Water Wars."

There was a gleam of excitement in Roberts' voice. His demeanor instantly shifted as he replied emphatically, "Damn, Dylan, that was a great movie. Jack Nicholson should have got the Oscar for his role! And I can tell you a thing or two about those Water Wars. According to my grandfather, my family lost their cattle ranch in the Owens Valley thanks to some son-of-a-bitch named Fred Eaton!"

"It sounds like Jimmy should have given this assignment to you, G.O.," groaned Steward, who obviously was not looking forward to a project of that magnitude.

His sympathy for his friend motivated Roberts to offer his help.

"Look, Dylan, I loved that movie, and with my family's history, I think I could put together something for you to examine. At least it would give you a little more time to, you know, get things more together around here and get your mind clear."

In addition to the Water Wars assignment, Steward had only completed half of his boss's other directives. With the remaining cleanup that needed to be done and completing Donahue's directives improving his wardrobe and appearance, the temptation to accept his friend's offer was something he couldn't pass up.

"I'd really appreciate that, G.O. Those healing hands of time aren't working quite as fast as some would hope."

For Dylan Steward, alcohol had temporarily lost its grip on him.

CHAPTER 32

Punctuality had always been a trademark of Dylan Steward's work ethic. If the workday started at 8 a.m., that meant 7:45 for Steward. 4:30 p.m. didn't mean stop work. For Steward, it meant to finish what you're working on, then leave. He took pride in being the first at his desk and the last one to be gone. In recent weeks, meeting times and deadlines had become things to shoot for, not adhere to.

Jimmy Donahue was a patient man, but the patience of a saint he didn't have. As much as he liked Steward and sympathized with his circumstances, Donahue had grown weary of hearing, "He's on his way, boss," or delaying the start of a meeting due to Steward's tardiness. Though the California Water Wars assignment was more of a historical analysis of possible inaccuracies and not that probing inquiry into some scandalous or salacious political issue so sought after by any reporter, Donahue had hoped it would rejuvenate his young reporter's spirits. After sharing his concerns with the person who had become his "Voice of Reason," he was looking forward to seeing the draft Steward had promised him he would have in a few days.

"There's real meat in this story, Syl, if only he delves into it," Donahue said, as he and Markham shared a cocktail on the patio of Markham's Hollywood Hills home. The two had just enjoyed a relaxing soak in the marble hot tub before grilling two steaks on Markham's new Weber, a Friday night tradition initiated by the arrival of Jimmy Donahue in her life. The setting sun provided an ambiance destined to elicit feelings of intimacy. Donahue reached across their adjoining wicker lounge chairs and placed his hand on Markham's thigh. Markham offered her own bit of flirtatious behavior. She slowly moved the crystal stir stick between the ice cubes of her Manhattan on the rocks, a beverage she had come to enjoy thanks to Donahue's influence. She removed the crystal piece from her drink and placed it in her mouth, slowly drawing it out after savoring the sweetness of the grenadine in her Manhattan.

"Indeed, that may be James, but Dylan strikes me as a person who needs to see himself in the story. There must be a parallel between his situation and the object of the story to bring out his special gift. I'm not sure a treatise on the California Waters Wars and the righting of a perceived slight by Hollywood screenwriters of William Mulholland is the proper vehicle to achieve that end."

Of the attributes that had served Jimmy Donahue well over his nearly thirty years at the *L.A. Times*, it was knowing when to be the "Voice of Reason" and when to listen to the "Voice of Reason." The person sitting next to him had become his "Voice of Reason."

"Well, time will tell if this assignment is the right fit. If it's wrong, Syl, I hope some sort of miracle happens because I can't continue to turn a blind eye to his work, or lack thereof."

Neither realized the miracle Steward was about to discover, the unimaginable power of dreams.

ANTICIPATING the start of their Thursday meeting with Donahue, G.O. Roberts was more anxious than usual. The perspiration on his forehead was a testament to his condition. A nervous dryness in his throat caused a persistent clearing sound. He followed Liz Alunda into Donahue's office, anxiously peering over his shoulder, hoping to see Steward behind him. Roberts had exhausted himself over the two days preparing the material for Steward. Lists of telephone calls to family members, recollections of summer vacations camping at Upper Lake, and hours spent pouring over old newspapers and family letters kept in his father's garage had given Roberts a wealth of information on the California Water Wars—all the information that never made its way into the public records of the day. He clutched the manila folder containing the material under his arm as if it held top-secret documents from the halls of the FBI. Uncharacteristically, Donahue was late for his own meeting. His absence allowed Alunda time to ask Roberts about Steward.

"Is he coming?" she whispered, keeping one eye on the open door of Donahue's office.

"God, I hope so!" sighed Roberts, "He really needs to go over this stuff," pointing to the folder under his arm. At that moment, the tardy reporter arrived. From his appearance, it was evident that Robert's visit had had some effect on Steward, at least on the outside. He wore a freshly pressed shirt and tie. Even his tan dockers had the appearance of being ironed. His shoulder-length hair was neatly tied in a ponytail. Inwardly, Steward still struggled. He paid no attention to Roberts or Alunda as he took a chair next to them, not a smile or even a nod of acknowledgment.

"Jesus, Dylan, could you possibly call it any closer!" groaned an exasperated Roberts as he shoved the material he had worked on into Steward's hands. Taking the material with barely the slightest acknowledgment of the work Roberts had done, a coldness came across Steward's face, and with a shrug of his shoulders, he seemed to say, "I'm here, aren't I?"

Roberts could not hide his disappointment, not in his friend's late arrival, but the liquored breath that came out of Steward's mouth. Seeing his disdain, Steward snapped, "What?"

"Nothing," replied a disgusted Roberts, "I just thought that after coming over to see you, things would change."

"I'm trying," was the robotic reply.

Alunda shook her head disapprovingly. She leaned toward him aggressively and said, "You can't keep pushing the envelope like this, Dylan," she said, scolding her nearly tardy colleague.

Steward had done his best to adhere to Donahue's previous grooming and apparel directives. His long unruly, shoulder-length brown mane was now secured in a tightly bound ponytail. A newly purchased Norelco reduced his slovenly beard to an acceptable five o'clock shadow. Now sporting a long sleeve pale blue shirt with a loose-fitting dark blue and white striped tie and tan dockers, Steward might have passed for a grad student at UCLA. On the outside, he looked like a new man. On the inside, the battle for his sanity was raging, with depression and despair still winning. He had lazily adjusted his tie when Donahue entered, accompanied by Conrad Knight.

"My apologies, folks. Conrad had an urgent matter that he felt needed my immediate attention. Let's get started, shall we?"

It was apparent that Donahue had been frustrated with Conrad's self-serving request for a private audience. Alunda smirked at the thought that the office sycophant had anything meaningful to see Donahue about except to kiss his ass. Turning to Alunda, he said,

"Liz, have you heard of Earl Graves?"

"Are you kidding me!" Alunda said. "In my community, he's a savior." The excitement in her voice was genuine.

"Good. I'd like you to set up an interview with Earl Graves. Get his slant on the difficulties that black entrepreneurs face today."

Earl Graves first published Black Enterprise in 1970 as a springboard for venture capitalists looking at minority-run businesses.

Alunda was more than pleased with the assignment. The African American reporter had long harbored dreams of owning her own black-run publishing company, and she wasn't above using an assignment to promote her ambitions.

"Conrad, the Downtown Men's Club had asked for a speaker for their monthly meeting next week at the Beverly Hilton. I recommended you. I thought you could speak about your grandfather's accomplishments as governor. It's a very Republican-based group, you know."

"Thank you, Jimmy. I've always thought my grandfather never got the credit he deserved." An almost naive blush spread over Conrad's face.

Donahue smiled, inwardly thinking, this is an assignment even Conrad couldn't screw up.

Pleased to see a nicely groomed and well-dressed Steward, Donahue said, "Nice choices." Jimmy was never one for long-winded compliments. Seeing the folder in Steward's hand, he asked, "Is that the stuff on the Water Wars assignment? That Preston woman called yesterday asking again when you were going to interview her."

Donahue had made it clear this was a time-sensitive issue. Descendants of William Mulholland still carried considerable influence in Southern California, and Donahue wanted to rid himself of the annoying granddaughter. The previous night's battle with a bottle and the nightmares that had become commonplace left Steward ill-prepared to play mental games with his boss. Steward had not even had time to see what Roberts had put together. He awkwardly stalled for time as he certainly could not reveal that his friend had produced the work. Steward felt his face start to blush. His throat was dry as he made a feeble attempt to buy time.

"It's only a draft, Jimmy."

Alunda tried to hide her surprise at Steward's excuse. He was one who always had the finished product when asked. She always thought Steward had too much pride to bring a draft to a meeting. Another thing that bothered her, Roberts suddenly hung his head, avoiding any eye contact with Donahue or Steward. Alunda knew something was not kosher. Suddenly, she thought of the fiasco with Julian Fleming. No way would Steward be a party to that type of chicanery.

"Time is precious on this issue, Dylan. Let me see what you've got."

"Like I said, Jimmy, it's a draft. I want a chance to clean this up first," said Steward, who sounded more belligerent than supplicant.

His eyes focused directly on his reluctant reporter.

Why the hesitation and why the sudden attitude, Donahue thought.

Though sensitive to what Steward had been through recently, Donahue had a deadline to meet, and his patience ended abruptly. With a no-nonsense tone in his voice, Donahue stated, "I'm the assignment editor, Dylan. Reviewing drafts is what I do for a living, so leave the draft with me, and I'll get it back to you when I'm done! Okay, everyone, let's get to work!"

His emphatic directive left little room for further discussion. The four reporters rose and headed for the door. Without so much as a word, Steward dropped the requested material on Donahue's desk and turned away. His eyes betrayed the hopelessness that swept over him. He didn't care anymore, not about his assignment, his job, nothing. All that occupied his life was the haunting memory of his wife.

With his office empty, Donahue took a few moments to compose himself. He had felt his anger rising to an unacceptable level. Being firm and direct was part of the job, but after twenty years as the assignment editor, Donahue felt uncomfortable with these often necessary traits. He wondered if he was getting too old for the job. He picked up the folder Steward had unceremoniously dropped on his desk and opened it. Out of sheer habit, he reached for the ever-present red pencil lying on his desk and started reading. The editor's sword twirled endlessly between his fingers, never once striking out a word as Donahue perused the multipage document.

It had been Steward's writing style that first caught Jimmy Donahue's attention. His article on the Pentagon Papers was not only factually correct but was enhanced with subtle nuances and asides in his descriptive language of people and scenes. This material had none of the latter. Yes, it was well written. Its inferences were logical, leaving little room to dispute its conclusions and by any measure deserving of being published. But it lacked that certain "Yes, I know exactly what he means" reaction Donahue was used to feeling when reading Steward's previous works. Donahue tried to avoid a rush to judgment. He had witnessed the freefall Steward had been in after his wife's passing, and after seeing the efforts put forth to clean up his appearance, Donahue felt the young reporter was on something of a comeback. The telephone call Donahue was about to receive threatened whatever confidence he had left for Steward.

———

"DONAHUE."

"Jimmy, this is Marilyn from the archives calling. Have you got a minute?"

"Anything for you, Scarlett," mocked Donahue, referencing "Gone With The Wind," Marilyn Carrington's favorite movie.

"Remember Rhett, it's Ashley I love, not you, so can we get down to business?"

"Touché, Marilyn. How can I help you?"

"I've been checking over the paperwork of my newest intern. It seems your reporter, Dylan Steward, requested some material, but my intern carelessly had a G.O. Roberts sign for it. I want to make sure Steward got the material he requested. Did he?"

"Just a second, Marilyn," Donahue said as he hastily laid out several pages of Steward's draft side by side across his desk. His focus moved quickly, catching again those minor anomalies that had caught his editor's eye on his first reading.

"Well, I'll be damned," he muttered.

"What was that, Jimmy?"

"Sorry, Marilyn. Yeah, Steward got the material he requested. Thanks for the heads up."

Donahue stood up and walked over to the window. The moving traffic offered a momentary distraction for the ethical and professional dilemma that now faced him. Donahue remembered the words of his first boss when he became the assignment editor. "Jimmy, doing the right thing is easy. The hard part is knowing what the right thing to do is." His brow furrowed as his mind sifted through his options. Each option swayed the scales one way then the other. But how could he ignore what the young man had gone through recently? That alone would cause anyone's moral compass to vary a few degrees. Jimmy Donahue had made a judgment about Steward when he hired him. Despite evidence seemingly to the contrary, Donahue found himself standing by his reporter's intuition. He returned to his desk and picked up his red pencil. He made a quick note on the first page. He walked out of his office to the array of cubicles. He stopped where Steward and Roberts worked.

Never one to be a clock watcher, G.O. Roberts watched the agonizingly slow-moving hands on the clock on the wall near his cubicle approaching 4:30 p.m. Escaping his workplace was a pitiful but effective way to deal with angst that roiled inside him from the exchange between Donahue and Steward in their meeting. At what point would Steward reveal that Roberts had written the draft and not him? His Catholic upbringing searched for justification, the theological nether land where a white lie is okay, and a fib is not really a lie. It was a draft. After all, what did it really matter who wrote it? The sound of Donahue's voice disrupted his moral quandary.

"Glad to see you two are still here," Donahue said, standing near the wall that separated their adjoining cubicles. He had that "I know what's going on here" look on his face like a parent confronting their guilty child whose hands were smudged with chocolate from a missing cookie off the cooling tray.

"Nice job on this draft, Dylan. Actually, it's much better than a draft. I only made one change. It runs tomorrow. I want you to take it to the copy department for formatting."

Steward stood and extended his hand, expecting to receive the document. Donahue had written across the front of the folder, "Run it," with the initials, "J.D." Curious as to the one change Donahue had felt compelled to make, Steward opened the folder. He immediately knew that Donahue deserved an explanation.

"Jimmy, I can explain," Steward said.

Donahue's stare was that of disappointment, a look that Steward had seen all too frequently lately.

"Can you?"

With that terse response, Donahue returned to his office, leaving Steward wondering what explanation would satisfy his boss. Roberts knew the ruse had been discovered from the look on Steward's ashen face. He had a sinking feeling in his stomach as he pondered what it would be like to be unemployed. In desperation, he tried reaching out to his friend. His voice cracked as he nervously looked around to see who might be near enough to hear.

"Dylan, what's happening?"

Without speaking, Steward handed his friend the folder. Roberts' hand shook as he took the folder from Steward. He stared at Steward. His face was flushed, and his eyes blinked spasmodically, absolutely sure that when he opened the folder, he'd see,

"You're Fired!" in bold red-penciled letters. Roberts opened the folder. He was stunned. Was this some sort of game his boss was playing with him? There it was in big, bold print beneath the title, "The California Water Wars." Donahue had lined through Steward's name and printed G.O. Roberts, neatly underlined twice.

CHAPTER 33

For several days, not a word was spoken between the assignment editor and the reporter. Steward occupied himself with mindless paperwork required by the personnel department for his absence following Willow's death. He declined Liz Alunda's request to strategize her assignment on Earl Graves. And then there was G.O. Roberts, the innocent partner in the thoughtless conspiracy. What was he, collateral damage to Steward's thoughtlessness? Steward was like a zombie. His eyes often stared aimlessly off into space. His gait was robotic as if controlled by someone from afar. There was little he cared about. At any moment, he thought the inevitable would happen, that call Donahue's office to be given his walking papers, not that he would blame Donahue for firing him. The truth should not have been that difficult to tell, but that would require that the truth mattered. For Dylan Steward, all that mattered in his life was now gone. If that wasn't enough to deal with, Willow's principal, Joe Skaff, had cleared Willow's classroom of her personal belongings along with notes of sympathy from many of her students and colleagues. That box, with all its painful memories, waited for Steward at home. If there was a purpose to his life, Steward didn't see it. If there was a reason to care about anything, the circumstances of his life had numbed him to that reality. One person would hold the keys to Dylan Steward's salvation, and that person was a complete stranger.

Donahue leaned against the end stone pillar supporting the patio covering, staring out over the panoramic view of the City of Angels. His eyes slowly followed an airplane rising out of the valley smog headed toward some unknown and perhaps exotic destination. He thought about his problematic reporter and wondered if he would answer the call to his destiny. When she had first suggested the idea, he thought it was preposterous. How could he justify the cost of sending a reporter across the Atlantic to interview a woman on the whereabouts of a man who once sold newspapers in the lobby of the L.A. Times Building? A man who had been gone for nearly six months and remembered by few. Accounting would laugh the moment the travel request hit their desk. He could hear the skepticism in their voice. "If you're looking for a human interest story, find one closer and less expensive. Wait till the boss sees this!" And they would be correct, but this was more than a human interest story. The story this woman might tell could literally save a man's life.

The last part of the setting sun had dipped below the horizon, and with it, he let out an audible sigh. As he walked the length of the patio to the two lounge chairs where he had left Markham sitting, there was a confidence in his stride and the look of satisfaction in his eyes. He picked up the bottle of Haut Brion Bordeaux, first offering to top off Markham's half-full glass and then a second full pour for himself. The change from an ice-cold bottle of Budweiser to a glass of French wine was but the first of many changes in Jimmy Donahue. With a nod from Markham, Jimmy filled her glass then did the same to his. Setting the now nearly empty bottle down on the glass-topped wicker table between their chairs, he congratulated his companion.

"Syl, that idea was pure genius."

He raised his glass to her in acknowledgment. Ever humble in receiving praise, Markham merely smiled and tilted her glass in Donahue's direction.

Inwardly, she thought, *Yes, you can lead a horse to water, and yes, you can make him drink. You just have to know the horse.*

Donohue had but a moment to enjoy his scheme when he realized who had the final approval. "I'll never get Willard's okay on this," he groaned as he twirled his glass by the stem, watching the richness of the Bordeaux grapes slowly circle his glass.

Again, Markham offered just the right bait.

"You know, James, you do have that discretionary fund you could use. Discretionary means just that, doesn't it," smiled Markham.

The woman's wisdom fed the Irishman's mischievous ways of getting what he wanted.

―――

THE NEXT DAY upon his arrival at work, Donahue's first task was to call an old friend in the disbursement office.

"Dolores, this is Jimmy Donahue. Can you tell me how much I have left in my discretionary fund?"

Dolores McCann, Dee to her friends, was a married woman in her mid-fifties with traces of gray in her jet black hair. A combination of good genes, clean living, and exercise had fended off the typical signs of aging. This left the still, very attractive woman with creamy skin, radiant hazel eyes, and shapely legs to suffer the unwanted advances of those trying to test the moral fiber of the still-married woman. She and Donohue had formed a special friendship over the years. Donohue hated being constrained by what he felt were the obituary rules set by Business Services on the use of his discretionary funds. McCann's knowledge of those rules and the manipulation thereof was a perfect match for the scheming Irishman.

"That will take me a minute, Jimmy. By the way, how are things going with you and Sylvia?"

Stunned his secret relationship was no longer so secret, Donahue mumbled, "What Sylvia?"

The wily McCann, herself the recipient of flirtatious winks, suggestive smiles, and other mating gestures from her testosterone-driven co-workers, had correctly interpreted the subtle and not so subtle interactions between Donahue and Markham at work.

"Oh, please, Jimmy!" she answered with comic exasperation in her voice. "Remember what Abraham Lincoln said about fooling people?"

Donahue had participated in enough water cooler rumors during his younger years about who was seeing who and who was the next conquest for so and so. He was determined not to be the subject of such copulative speculation. He nervously tried to assess the damage.

"Have we been that obvious?"

McCann felt sorry for the man who had obviously tried to keep his relationship a secret, a trait all too uncommon among the chest-beating Neanderthals who pestered the attractive divorcee. Hoping to ease his anxiety, McCann said, "Not really, Jimmy. I happen to believe in the attraction of opposites. The oddity of such a combination as you and Sylvia would immediately squash any such rumors in the minds of most. I would never participate in such muckraking! I am in the minority around here to your eternal good luck."

McCann could hear the man sigh over the phone. While talking to Donahue, McCann had deftly pulled out a sliding tray labeled "D" and sorted through her alphabetical card listing until she found Donahue's account card.

"Well, it looks like you've been a little overboard in your spending, Jimmy. You've got a little over two hundred dollars left out of your two thousand annual allotment left for the year." Unfortunately, Donahue had done a little research before calling McCann. He would need nearly fifteen hundred dollars to bring his plan to fruition. He muttered his disappointment out loud.

"Damn!"

"Damn what?" asked McCann as she pushed the sliding tray of account cards back into its slot.

Without revealing all of his plans, Donahue said, "Dee, I need about fifteen hundred for what I want to do."

Dolores McCann had a mind for numbers, and as a trained accountant, she knew the rules inside and out as they pertained to the *L.A. Times* financial operations. Without asking for the details of Donahue's plan, McCann said, "Have you considered getting temporary authorization to draw on next year's allotment to get the amount you need?"

"And who would that be?" said Donahue, quickly seeing his plan fade into oblivion.

"That would be the head of the disbursement office, Jimmy, one Dolores McCann. Of course, the big A-hole upstairs (referring to Damon Willard) won't like it. If you'll excuse the expression, he's got a hard-on for you. I get regular requests from him on you and a couple of other assistant editors on spending habits. You know how he likes control, but like the saying goes, 'Better to get forgiveness than permission.'"

A resounding "Yes" was heard outside Donahue's office.

STEWARD ACTUALLY HEARD THE AM/FM alarm clock going off for the first time in weeks. There was no residual alcohol haze to work through, no body craving for sleep after fighting through nightmares chasing the image of his wife fading into the distance. He might as well have endured both for all the energy he had. His daily routine was done like a man facing his execution. There was no need to hurry, no sense of urgency. The pulsating shower head did little to invigorate the body standing under it. He dressed out of habit with no sense of pride in how he looked.

DYLAN STEWARD HAD nothing but respect for Jimmy Donahue as his boss and as a man. He had failed Donahue and all that he stood for, and he had no intention of groveling before him with some lame excuse for submitting Roberts' work as his own, draft or no draft. Weirdly, Steward felt a sense of relief as he made his way through the morning traffic on Highway 10 East to work for what he entirely expected to be the last time.

HIS FIRST TWINGE of regret came as he slowly approached the parking lot booth. Gus's smiling face and raspy voice was there to greet him for the last time. Uncharacteristically, Gus came out of his booth and walked over to the slot where Steward parked his decrepit but lovable Citroen. As Steward got out of his car, Gus extended his hand and said warmly, "I just wanted to say I won't be seeing you anymore after this week, Mr. Steward. The wife and I are moving to Temecula to be closer to our son and his family. He's stationed at March Air Force Base. We got us a small home in a place called Sun City."

Steward grinned, genuinely happy for the man whose smiling face was the first thing folks saw as they arrived at work in the morning and the last thing they saw as they headed home at the end of the day.

"That's great, Gus. I wish you and the Mrs. all the best."

Steward had not the heart to tell him his own exodus was on the horizon as well.

Steward took the stairs. The elevator would have been faster but then why speed up the inevitable. Opening the stairwell door on the third floor, Steward melded into a flow of people scurrying to their workplace. To those who greeted him, he smiled and nodded. He was really not in the mood for any casual good morning-type conversation. He entered the city desk room and was relieved to see the door to Donahue's office ajar. Neither Alunda nor Roberts had arrived yet, so there was another conversation he could avoid. Perhaps after getting his walking papers, he might even avoid them and escape any further discussion. As he got to Donahue's door, he paused to compose himself, took a deep breath, and knocked twice.

"Come in."

Entering, Steward closed the door behind him. Donahue was standing at the window gazing down on the slow-flowing vehicles transporting themselves to a thousand different destinations. Without turning around, Donahue said, "Have a seat, Dylan." The fatalism in Donohue's voice was inescapable. No good news could follow, Steward thought. He hoped the unpleasantness would soon be over.

"Do you mind if I stand, Jimmy?"

"Yeah, I do," came the terse response.

One thing Steward had learned about Donahue in the relatively short time he had worked at the *Times* was there was a specific tone to Donahue's voice that said there's nothing more to discuss. This was one of those tones. He took a chair facing Donahue's desk and sat down. Donahue ran his thumbs around the waist of his pants, gently hoisting up his black slacks. Then he ran both hands up both suspender straps letting them snap back against his chest. With his apparel suitably adjusted, Donahue turned around and took his seat facing Steward. He had the look of someone restraining the excitement inside him.

"When you took that assignment about the homeless guy, did you have any idea where that would lead you?"

This was hardly the lead-in that Steward expected. He assumed it would be something more like, "How stupid could you be!" or "Did you really think I wouldn't notice?" Steward was at a loss for words. He knew he had to say something, but the after-effects of alcohol had addled his thought process.

"Well, did you?" Donahue said, slightly annoyed at having to repeat the question.

Steward stammered out his answer. "Uh, no, Jimmy, I didn't." Uncharacteristically, he began to sweat profusely.

Donahue studied his subordinate for a moment. There was a pause that further unsettled Steward.

"Well, I did, kid, and we're going down that path again."

Donahue handed Steward an envelope.

"Open it."

Steward stared at the envelope.

Was it really necessary to drag this out, he thought. Can you just tell me, I'm fired."

After opening the envelope, Steward had no comprehension of what he held in his hand. He stared at a piece of paper with a name written on it, Anastasie Bouchet, an address in Bordeaux, France, and an airline ticket to Paris, France. He looked up at Donahue, then back at the contents of the envelope, and back to Donahue again. He might as well have been looking at some theoretical physics equation by Stephen Hawking. In complete honesty, he said, "I don't understand, I thought…."

"I know. You thought I was going to fire you."

Steward let his hand rest on his lap. "Yeah, I did."

"Well, to be honest, I thought about it," said Donahue, "But then I got this idea. I heard a story that I thought would be the perfect assignment for Steward. I wasn't going to give this to anyone but you."

"You saved this assignment for me?

"No, kid, I'm saving you with this assignment."

The nuance of Donahue's words was lost on Steward. He was completely dumbfounded. A name he couldn't even pronounce, a name he recognized, Willis Carpenter, and a ticket to a country he'd never been to. *What the hell was going on*, he thought to himself. His reporter's brain began to kick in. He looked again at the name on the paper.

"Who's this person?"

"Her name is Anastasie Bouchet. She lives in a small town outside of Bordeaux, France. She's got a story about a man named Le Chercheur de Rêves. I want you to find out who she is, who he is, and what's their connection, if any."

"That's it?" questioned Steward, whose reporter's intuition told him there was more to the story than what Donahue was telling him.

Donahue was not completely honest with his young reporter. He did know something about Anastasie Bouchet, and the man known as Le Chercheur de Rêves. Jimmy Donahue had survived seven years of Catholic education at All Saints Elementary in Reseda, California, and had avoided the wrath of Sister Angus's severe corporal punishment measures by being well-versed in the distinction between a lie, a white lie, and a fib. The connection between the stranger and the woman would be Steward's salvation, or so Donahue hoped.

"You do know I don't speak a word of French," said Steward, with a quizzical look on his face.

"Buy an English-French dictionary at the airport, kid. They're not that expensive," smiled Donahue.

The journey on which Dylan Steward was about to embark would change his life forever.

PART THREE

A person often meets his destiny on the road he took to avoid it.

JEAN LA FONTAINE

CHAPTER 34

He dropped his luggage in front of the couch and let his corduroy sport coat and shoulder bag fall hapless on the coffee table. He slumped onto the couch. He had not bought into Donahue's enthusiasm for the story. In some ways, Steward had hoped that his boss would have terminated him. At least then, it would have been a new unknown, a new destination, just the way Willow would have addressed life. Staring at the ceiling in their living room, Steward tried to make sense of his assignment. He strained his brain, trying to remember if he had ever heard of or met someone named Anastasie Bouchet. As for the name Le Chercheur de Rêves, barely passing two years of high school Spanish was hardly a solid linguistic foundation for understanding French. His focus shifted to the painting hanging on the wall above the TV. Willow had been insistent that it be centered precisely in the middle of the wall—her sense of feng shui— and the TV would have to be moved. Steward rose and walked over to the painting. Willow loved that painting and staring at it only brought back the agonizing memory of her death. Still, it meant so much to her, and for that reason, Steward forced himself to look at it. Whoever had painted it had certainly captured the racial theme of American history and the hope for a better life by the oppressed. The unusual lines in the bottom right corner of the painting appeared to be letters, though Steward gave them little mind as the theme of hope for an unborn child rendered him on the verge of crying uncontrollably.

Finding his passport, selecting what clothes to take, and sundry hygiene articles all without Willow's help had been a daunting task. If he had time, he might have unwrapped the package Donahue had given him in the office that day. The itinerary Donahue had given him gave little time for that. The package leaned against the wall next to the TV stand, still wrapped in butcher paper and tightly bound with twine. Steward glanced at his wristwatch. Roberts would be arriving any minute to drive him to LAX. He had one last chance to go over everything. Steward walked back to the couch, picked up his shoulder bag, and opened it. Everything was there: passport, tickets from LAX to New York City and then a connecting flight to Paris, France, a woman's name, and the address of the Musee de Beaux Arts, in Bordeaux, France. Lodging was left for Steward to determine. Considering the bare minimum per diem allowed by the *Time*s, a very inexpensive hostel would be the best accommodation possible. Three quick honks of a car horn alerted Steward that Roberts was outside waiting. He slipped on his jacket, slung his bag over his shoulder, and picked up his suitcase. As he left the house that he had shared with his deceased wife, Dylan Steward began a journey that would lead him to the fulfillment of a dream, a dream his wife, Willow, had shared with him.

―――

EXHAUSTED from the nearly fifteen-hour flight from Los Angeles to Paris, including a two-hour stopover in New York City, Steward desperately needed some rest. His nearly six-foot-two frame had been cramped into a less than roomy coach seat in the back of the

Boeing 707. Sleep was virtually impossible thanks to a continuous line of passengers waiting to use the restrooms and flight attendants preparing trays of drinks, snacks, and meals for their passengers. With his one piece of carry-on luggage, Steward avoided the organized confusion that surrounds a complex of luggage carousels. As he made his way to the arrival and departure area, his luck continued. A plethora of signs in English, French, German, and Italian directed new arrivals to taxis, trains, and shuttles. Much to his surprise, most French spoke English as a second language. That was a Godsend considering Steward's lack of fluency in the language of love. A very amenable employee operating an information stand was more than helpful in advising Steward to purchase an inexpensive Eurail pass to Bordeaux and even selected an equally affordable hostel, Bordeaux Ville, for his stay there. With directions to take any one of many taxis lined up outside the terminal to the train station, Steward bid adieu to the helpful attendant whose name tag read, "Jacques."

Inexplicably, Steward found himself amused by the dichotomy of humanity that surrounded him outside the world's second-largest airport. Many, most probably tourists, would stop their walking and suddenly stare intently at a pamphlet or brochure they were holding, then gaze upward at a sea of overhead signs, then resume their walk or completely change directions, all the while muttering some mild expletive. Those who knew where they were going and how to get there maneuvered their way through the throng of stop-and-go human traffic with the ease of a maze walker with a map. The Eurail pass in his hand was an obvious clue to Steward's first stop.

"Train station, right here! Mon Ami!" called out a taxi driver holding open the door to a Renault sedan.

"Yes, Bordeaux," Steward replied, handing the driver his luggage, who promptly hurled it into the back seat.

"Sit up front. It is easier to converse," he said, smiling at the opportunity to talk with an American. The last thing Steward wanted was to get involved in some long boring conversation when all he craved was sleep, but the man's exuberant personality was infectious. Steward found himself warming to the possibility of conversation. The driver reminded Steward of himself. He had a stubble of a beard considered fashionable by Europeans. His black hair was long but neatly trimmed around the ears and nape of his neck. An earring and a powder blue scarf completed his Parisian attire. Steward noticed the driver's taxi license read, "Gabriel."

"What brings you to Paris, my friend?" asked the inquisitive driver as he looked at his side mirror for an opening in the flow of traffic.

Steward shifted his body awkwardly, his knees pushing against the dashboard of the smallish Renault. The driver noticed Steward's movement and commented, "Oui, our French cars are not so roomy, no? The lever is on your right side to adjust the seat."

With an upward tug on the lever located at the bottom right side of his seat, the seat moved backward, bringing instant relief to legs on the verge of cramping.

"I'm a reporter for the *Los Angeles Times*, a newspaper in California. My editor sent me here on assignment," Steward replied with a sigh of relief.

"Aah! No doubt to write about the wonderful wines of the Bordeaux Valley. You know Bordeaux is quite famous for its fine wines." Gabriel seemed genuinely proud of his country's reputation for fine wines.

"No, actually, I was sent here on a human interest story, as we say in the newspaper business."

"In France, we would say a love story."

"Perhaps so," replied Steward, offering no more details to the driver. The driver's insight would prove to be remarkably accurate.

Sleep deprivation limited Steward's contribution to any mutual conversation to a minimum as his eyelids struggled to remain open. He had lost track of time when he heard Gabriel say, "Monsieur, we are here."

After pulling up to the curb, Gabriel hastily exited his taxi and hurried around to the passenger side. He opened the back door, removed Steward's luggage, and opened the passenger side door. He was as vociferous in his farewell as he was in his greeting.

"Have a wonderful time in Bordeaux, Mon Ami. Enjoy the food and wine and write a most intriguing story. You will take train number 4 to Bordeaux. The boarding area is straight through that gate," pointing to a turnstile to his right.

Steward peeled off several francs he had procured at the currency exchange booth at the airport and handed them to the driver.

"I hope this covers everything, Gabriel. It's been a pleasure meeting you."

Steward's compliment was somewhat contrived as he had barely heard much of the man's nonstop conversation, though he did find the driver's personality engaging. Seeing that he had been overpaid, the driver said most graciously. "Please, call me Gabby. My friends do. I hope to see you again, monsieur."

Steward smiled, picked up his luggage, and proceeded through the turnstile to the waiting number 4 train. A very proper-looking conductor, short in stature and balding, with a pencil-thin mustache, greeted Steward at the steps to the train. He was dressed in black pants, a matching coat with brass buttons, reminding Steward of Agatha Christie's police inspector, Hercule Poirot, of the Orient Express. The conductor examined Steward's Eurail pass with stern eyes that peered over rimless glasses that rested on the bridge of his nose, then directed him to the economy cars to the rear of the train. Thinking himself lucky to find a nearly empty car, Steward slid into a wooden slat seat. Using his shoulder bag as a pillow between the glass window and his head, he closed his eyes and was fast asleep as the train pulled slowly out of the station. The gentle jostling of the conductor's hand on his shoulder woke Steward from a dreamless visit to Lala land.

"Monsieur, we are coming into Bordeaux," said the conductor who had shed his previous rigid demeanor and now appeared with a smile on his face.

Steward rubbed his tired eyes to refocus from his blissful rest.

"Thank you," he said as he made small circles with his head to clear his mind.

One last stop, he thought as he surveyed the contents of his shoulder bag for the name and address of the hostel had been given at the Paris Airport. Once he found it, he slipped his bag over his shoulder, grabbed his luggage, and waited for the train to come to a complete stop. The conductor had assumed his post at the car exit, politely tipping his hat to the three passengers ahead of Steward in line. As Steward approached him, he caught a glimpse of the man's shiny brass name tag.

"Excuse me, Francois, but could you by chance direct me to the Bordeaux Ville? I'll be staying there while in Bordeaux."

"Oui monsieur, I know it well. When you leave the station, take Le Rue Fontaine two blocks to Le Boulevard de Arts, then turn right. The Bordeaux Ville will be in the middle of the block. Please tell the owner that Francois said hello. She is my cousin."

Steward smiled at the unexpected familiarity from the conductor.

"I sure will, and thank you again, Francois."

With a polite bow at the waist and the tip of his finger to his fez, Francois said, "It was my pleasure, monsieur."

The sleep during the five-hour train ride from Paris to Bordeaux had somewhat refreshed Steward, who now welcomed the thought of a brief walk to complete his rejuvenation. The six or seven city blocks to the south of the train station had somehow escaped the vast modernization that swept much of post-WWII France. There was a quaintness of the area known as Les Vieux Bordeaux. The walk down Le Rue Fontaine was like a trip back in time. The narrow cobblestone street was lined with small shops. One sold fresh fruits and vegetables displayed in wooden crates tilted against the building walls. Another was a bakery that displayed a vast array of chocolates and custom-designed pastries. The aroma of the chocolatier's creations caused Steward to stop and inhale deeply before moving on. He walked casually, taking note of a small dress shop, an intriguing bookstore, and a shop selling musical instruments. A vintage Hagstrom hanging side by side with a Les Paul Gibson brought back memories of playing at Pogo's, memories of music, and his wife, the two loves of his life. Those parking on the street paid little attention to the curbs as any number of Citroens, Renaults, and Peugeots were parked half on the sidewalk and half in the street. Where they could, an occasional Vespa driver found space between vehicles. Tall buildings with tiled roofs towered over sidewalks barely wide enough for two people to walk side by side. Some apartment dwellers had their windows open to enjoy a rare noon breeze. Others took advantage of the weather to hang various articles of clothing to dry on the wrought iron rails of the narrowest of balconies. True to Francoise's word, the Bordeaux Ville was located in the middle of the block.

A sign in Olde English lettering hung over the doorway. In small letters, under Bordeaux Ville, was the word 'hostel.' Perhaps it was the owner's way of convincing prospective guests their lodgings were more upscale than that of a low-cost youth hostel, which it was. Steward opened the lower half of the Dutch-door entrance and entered a small lobby. To his left were narrow stairs leading to the second and third floors. The faded plaster walls of the small lobby had prints of Vincent Van Gogh and Renoir. Straight ahead was a small dark mahogany reception counter and a nearby sitting area. From the number of keys hanging on brass hooks on the wall behind the desk, Steward guesstimated there were maybe a dozen rooms available. Steward gently tapped a silver bell on the counter. A tall, slender woman soon appeared from behind drawn curtains. She had stunning eyes with only the slightest appearance of crow's feet at the corners to indicate her age. Her hair had turned completely silver in contrast to her complexion, which seemed to defy aging. She had full lips seductively defined with a blush red lipstick and a creamy tone to her cheeks. Steward was hard-pressed to believe that she was not some exotic French movie star who had somehow escaped discovery by Hollywood in the 40s and 50s until he noticed her right arm ended at the elbow.

"My name is Gabriella, and Welcome to the Bordeaux Ville, Monsieur. Do you wish to have a room?" Her smile was enchanting, and her broken English was as seductive as that of a sea nymph calling sailors to their doom.

"Yes, I would," replied Steward, trying not to stare at the angelic face behind the voice.

The woman placed a slip of paper in front of Steward along with a pencil.

"If you please fill this form out and tell me how many nights you will be our guest?"

The barest of information was needed, name, country of origin, and occupation.

"I'm not exactly sure how long I'll be staying. I'm on an assignment from my newspaper. There are people I need to locate, if I can, and interview them. I imagine two to three days, maybe more."

She smiled at Steward as she took his information, then laid a key on the countertop. "That should not be a problem, Monsieur Steward," glancing at his name. "I have several one and two-bedroom rooms that should afford you privacy. It is our off-season, you know. There is a small locker for your use, but you must have your own lock."

Steward smiled then added, "By the way, the conductor on the train from Paris said to mention his name. He said he was your cousin; his name is Francois."

"Ah, you've met Hercule," she smiled and laughed. "That's a nickname I gave him years ago after Inspector Hercule Perot. He hates it!"

"I suspect he does," replied Steward as he took the key to his room.

"Oh, one more thing." Steward opened his shoulder bag and withdrew a slip of paper from his notebook.

"My French is terrible," handing the woman the paper; he asked, "I need to go to this museum and then to the address below it. Could you possibly help me?"

"If you intend to go by foot, that is much too far to walk, Monsieur Steward. The Musee des Beaux Arts is about six kilometers from here, and 17 Rue Madeleine is on the other side of Bordeaux near the Garonne River. I will arrange for a taxi tomorrow morning at 9 a.m. if that is convenient for you?"

"I'd appreciate that, Gabriella. One last thing, do you know where I can get something to eat? It has been a while since I had anything but airline food."

A perplexed look came over Gabriella's face, then a smile.

"Most restaurants do not open until much later, but I can have a small complementary plate of cheese, and a glass of Bordeaux prepared for you by our staff."

"That would be more than enough," smiled Steward, eager to ease hunger pangs emanating from his stomach.

"Good, then expect a knock on your door in about twenty minutes, Monsieur."

THANKS to three flights of narrow curving stairs and awkwardly spaced stair treads, the lack of an elevator taxed Steward more than he thought. By any standards, the room was small. Two single beds were separated by two tall narrow armoires for personal belongings. A small window cranked open provided the only ventilation. Oddly patterned cracks in the aged, plastered wall, not faux prints of famous French painters, provided the only visual stimulation. Steward had no sooner taken off his shoes and shirt when there was a knock at his door.

"One moment," he called out as he hurriedly put back on his shirt. When he opened the door, an elderly man, in a rumpled white shirt and baggy pants and breathing heavily, held out a tray with a small carafe of red wine, a bottle of La Francaise water, several slices of cheese, and a small oval-shaped loaf of bread.

"Compliments of Mademoiselle Gabrielle."

Feeling sorry for the old man, Steward said, "Just a moment." He took out his wallet and put several francs in the man's hand to show his appreciation for the man's trek up the stairs. "I'll take the water. You may keep the wine," said Steward, not wanting to tempt his newfound sobriety.

Looking astounded at this unexpected gratuity, the man bowed slightly at the waist and, with eyes looking downward, backed up saying, "Merci, Monsieur, Merci."

Steward took one of two chairs in the room and moved it to the opened window. He poured his glass of water and carefully balanced it on the narrow windowsill. He placed the small plate with the bread and cheese slices on his lap. Breaking the bread and cheese slices into several pieces, he combined bread and cheese into small, controlled bits, savoring the freshly baked rosemary bread and the mellow samples of brie and gruyere cheese. Between bites, Steward surveyed the street below. Street traffic consisted of an occasional delivery truck for the small businesses on the avenue. Now and then, a Vespa sped down the street, perhaps frustrated at the lack of a parking spot. The laughter of a young voice from the sidewalk below brought Steward to his feet. It couldn't be, he thought, as his eyes scanned the street below. Two young women passed beneath his window, giggling and jostling each other with humorous banter. The same charming banter in which he and Willow would often partake. He watched them pass from view then eased back into his chair. His heartbeat slowly returned to normal. The tasty repast of bread and cheese mellowed Steward's hunger and resurrected the question that had nagged at him since he boarded his plane in Los Angeles. Why on earth had his boss sent him to Europe to chase down some mythical person known as Le Chercheur de Rêve, and what possible connection could this person have with a woman who worked in a museum there? The light of day would lead Dylan Steward to the crossroads of his future.

———

Early morning traffic woke Steward from a sound sleep, an occurrence that had escaped him for weeks. The unexpected amenity of a shared bathroom across the hallway afforded Steward the opportunity for a quick shower and shave. After dressing in fresh jeans, a pullover sweater, and his corduroy sports coat, he made his way down the twisted stairway to the quaint lobby where the hostel owner had a tray of croissants and an urn of freshly brewed coffee. Standing at the table was a young man who appeared to be in his early twenties. He was helping himself to one of the croissants. When he saw Steward appear, he quickly wiped his mouth with one of the napkins on the table. He gulped down the last morsel of the delicious pastry, then said, "Please do not tell my aunt, but I can't keep away from these. My name is Rene. You are Dion, no? My aunt asked me to provide you with transportation today."

Steward smiled, not bothering to correct the young man's mispronunciation of his name though his command of English was generally very good.

"Yes, I mean oui, but I was expecting a taxi."

Rene smiled. "My aunt is trying very hard to impress her guests with such extra, how do you say in English, peeks."

"That would be perks," chuckled Steward.

"Aah, yes, perks!" smiled Rene as he corrected himself. "Whenever you are ready, Monsieur Dion, but my aunt would be very disappointed if you did not try one of these," pointing to the croissants.

Using a napkin, Steward picked up one with shaved almond slices on top and said with a wink of his eye, "I'll tell Gabriella I took two."

Rene laughed at Steward's complicity in deceiving his aunt about who took what and how many.

"Let us go to your first destination."

CHAPTER 35

The quaintness of old Bordeaux with its narrow streets, shops, and bistros soon faded into the cosmopolitan center of Bordeaux as Rene merged his Renault sedan onto a turnabout and then on to a wide four-lane street crowded with electric buses, morning commute traffic, and double-deck tourist buses blaring out points of interest to its riders in multiple languages. Steward's feet pressed hard against the floorboard as he gripped his door handle like a vice as Gabriella's nephew alternated between his horn and brakes as he raced through traffic like some downhill slalom skier. Adjusting to Rene's erratic driving was not easy, but Steward managed to finish his croissant with a minimum of crumbs on his lap. He had taken his last bite when Rene pulled in front of the Musee de Beaux Arts.

By American standards, the four-story building with two extensions to its left and right did not rival the towering structures of downtown Los Angeles. Nevertheless, there was something impressive in the building which dated back to the early thirties. Stained glass windows with wide ledges served as resting places to hundreds of pigeons. Wide stairways led up to three main entrances, each trimmed with ornate stone columns. An intricate maze of carefully trimmed Judas trees, Iris, Jonquil, and yellow Gentian was next to each side of the steps. Before Steward could exit the cramped Renault, Rene had already opened the door for him. He pointed toward the thirty steps.

"Monsieur Dion, there are guides at each entrance that can direct you to your area of interest. I will be parked in the back of the Musee. My red Renault is not hard to see."

AT THE CENTER and far-right entrances, there were lines of visitors behind the guide stands, each seeking their particular areas of interest. The Musee des Beaux Arts was well known for its seventeenth-century Italian, Flemish, and Italian collections. The north wing was devoted to nineteenth-century artists known for romanticism, landscapes, and realism. Since the entrance guide at the far left had fewer visitors to direct, Steward took the steps two at a time to get there quickly. An older man leaned against a tall stool. He wore a brown beret and a dark green muffler around the collar of a well-worn tweed coat. The cool morning air seemed particularly uncomfortable for the man as he patted his arms around his torso.

"Excuse me, but do you know where I might find a woman by the name of Anastasie Bouchet? I understand she works here."

The man seemed startled by Steward's question as if he had not heard him correctly.

"Did you say, Bouchet, Monsieur, Anastasie Bouchet?"

"Yes, I did," replied Steward, wondering if he had mispronounced the woman's name, causing the old man to become confused. "I'm sorry, but my French is not very good," he added apologetically.

"When you enter the Musee, please ask the usher at the desk for Monsieur Menuisier. He will be able to help you."

"Thank you," replied Steward.

"Merci, Monsieur," answered the old man with a look of sadness in his eyes.

Steward crossed the wide granite entrance area and proceeded through a glass turnstile door. Immediately he came upon an older woman, sitting behind a small Victorian desk. Her plump body seemed oddly out of place in a navy blue jacket trimmed with gold braids on each cuff, a black tie, and black pants with a single gold stripe down the seam. A gold name tag pinned over her left breast read, "Marie." Her gray hair was pulled into a tight bun. To Steward, she looked more like a senior naval officer than a museum usher. She looked up at Steward and said rather officiously, "Good day, Monsieur, how may I help you?"

"Excuse me, but can you direct me to Mr. Menuisier?"

The woman looked surprised that a stranger, especially an American, would ask for a man who had only arrived at the Musee a few days ago. She would not give out any details without knowing more information.

"May I ask the nature of your call?"

"Yes, of course," replied Steward. "My name is Dylan Steward. I'm here to see Mr. Menuisier regarding a woman by the name of Anastasie Bouchet."

At the mention of the name, the usher gasped. One hand cupped her mouth as she sat back in her chair. Her startled eyes began to dampen with tears. She reached for the gold-handled phone on her desk and dialed a three-number extension. The woman took both hands to steady the shaking phone in her grasp.

"Monsieur Menuisier, il y a vous à propos de votre mère. Son nom est Steward, Dion Steward."

"Oui, Marie, je vais lui dire."

Returning the phone to its cradle, the woman said, "Monsieur Menuisier will see you. You may wait by the stairwell to my right if you please."

Steward chuckled to himself at what was a common mispronunciation of his name. A wide stairwell descended from the second floor. A highly polished brass handrail reflected the light coming through stained glass windows on its smooth white marble steps. Soon Steward heard footsteps coming down the stairwell. He turned to see a man in his early forties. His short black hair had traces of gray in his temples. He was tall and quite tan and carried himself like a man who prided himself on his appearance. Steely blue eyes and a chiseled jawline added to his movie star appearance. He approached Steward with a smile and extended his hand. He had a most puzzled look on his face. Though formal in tone, the man spoke perfect English.

"Monsieur Steward, I am Jean-Paul Menuisier. How is it that you are here to see me?"

"My French is not very good, so may I call you Jean-Paul?"

Menuisier smiled, displaying pearly white teeth, and replied, "But of course, call me Jean-Paul."

"Well, Jean-Paul, I am a reporter. My editor sent me on this assignment to interview this woman, Anastasie Bouchet. When I mentioned this to the guide outside, I was told to ask for you. It seems that my editor believes that there is some kind of connection between her, and someone called, let me spell it for you, M o n C h e r c h e u r de R ê v e, that would be of great human interest to our readers."

At the end of the spelling of the name, the usher, Marie, sobbed audibly, moaning out loud, "Mon Chercheur de Rêve".

Menuisier himself seemed shaken. His eyes darted to the woman dabbing both eyes with a small lace handkerchief she had taken from her jacket pocket. The woman looked at him and shook her head from side to side in dismay. Menuisier tilted his head to the side and steadied his eye on Steward as if to examine him for the hidden motive to his question. Who outside his immediate family and closest friends would know of Mon Chercheur Rêve? Menuisier answered without believing a word of Steward's explanation, "Of course. A human interest story. Perhaps then we should sit and talk. Follow me, please."

Steward followed Menuisier up the stairs to the top of the landing. They came upon a large open area with several small tables and chairs. Against a wall were several undersized easels with views of a carefully sculpted garden on the grounds below. Against another wall were several large storage cabinets. All were open and in the process of being cleaned out. An open door led to what appeared to be an office/storage area. Several cardboard boxes were stacked atop each other, holding the door open.

Holding his arm out, Menuisier said, "We can talk in here, Monsieur Steward. Please excuse the disorganization. I am trying to clear out everything for the next teacher."

Hoping a side topic might help with his quest for information, Steward asked, "What happened to the last teacher?"

"That would be the person whom you are inquiring about."

"Anastasie Bouchet was a teacher here?"

"For over thirty years, Monsieur, Mademoiselle Bouchet taught thousands of children the joy of painting and the beauty of art— that the brush is but an extension of the heart… Please excuse me for my rambling," said an emotional Menuisier.

Steward was struck by the state of disorganization before him. To his left and right against the adjoining walls were large, long tables covered with scattered stacks of drawing paper. Some looked to be pencil sketches, others covered with shapes of multicolor. Underneath both tables were dozens of small plastic pails with paint brushes, miniature pallets, and trays with pieces of colored chalk, with small tubes squeezed from use and smeared with the color of their contents. The white marble floor badly needed mopping. It was covered with a crisscross of small footprints that had tracked smears of paint everywhere. Against a large glass window overlooking the gardens below was a full-size easel with a cloth bag of brushes hanging from its frame. In front of the easel was a wooden stool with an ecru-colored smock laying on the seat. Next to the easel was a simple secretary desk with a brass name plate that read, "Anastasie Bouchet." Two cushioned chairs on rollers served as hangers for several smocks and hand towels. Menuisier cleared the smocks and towels from the chairs and casually laid them on the closest table.

"She must have been quite the teacher," responded Steward.

"Oui, she was. Please, have a seat."

Steward opened his shoulder bag and took out his notepad. As he sat down, he noticed that the gray, faded barn wood walls were covered with drawings and paintings. Many were childlike in design with no rhyme or reason for shape or color. Others showed more thought and detail in their construction.

Menuisier appeared curiously guarded. He sat erect, his hands folded across his lap as if he was going to be interrogated. Sensing the man's barriers were up, Steward sought to put the man at ease. He smiled politely and said, "Do you mind if I take notes? I'm not much for remembering everything in detail."

"But of course."

"Good. Well, as I said downstairs, I'm a reporter, and my editor has a passion for human interest stories. Quite honestly, Mr. Menuisier, I have no idea where he got this woman's name or what connection, if any, she has to something, or someone named whatever I said downstairs." Steward offered a self-deprecating laugh at his linguistic failings.

Still formal and somewhat rigid, Menuisier replied, "What you said downstairs, Monsieur, was 'the Dream Seeker.'"

"The Dream Seeker. Hum, I guess I should have used that pocket dictionary I bought at the airport on the way over here."

Dispensing with pleasantries, Menuisier, who had grown annoyed at being interrupted from whatever he was doing, said, "Monsieur, please allow me to ask you a question. How would your editor know of a woman who has never been outside of France?"

Closing his notepad, Steward answered, "Jean-Paul, let me start from the beginning. I'm a reporter for the *Los Angeles Times*. My editor, Mr. Jimmy Donahue…" was as far as Steward got.

Menuisier's demeanor changed immediately. A smile suddenly spread across his face. His eyes brightened as he brought his hands together. He cried out, "Mon Dieu, I do not believe this! This cannot be true! You know Monsieur Donahue, Monsieur Jimmy Donahue!"

Steward almost fell backward out of his chair at the man's sudden and explosive outburst. He fumbled to maintain control of his notepad.

"Yes, Jimmy Donahue. He is my assignment editor. Why?"

In that instant, as both men stared at each other, they realized that their mutual mystery was about to be revealed. With the excitement of someone revealing part of a fascinating secret, Jean-Paul nearly shouted, "Then you must know Willis Carpenter! He worked there for many, many years. Monsieur Donahue was his very good friend!"

The shock of hearing the name Willis Carpenter from Menuisier's mouth caused Steward to slump back in his chair. How could this man possibly know Willis? The Willis Carpenter who had greeted Steward warmly every day he came to work at the *Time*s. The Willis Carpenter who had been genuinely overjoyed at hearing that Steward was going to be a father.

What the hell's going on here? He thought to himself.

Tentatively he asked, "Of Course, I know Willis, but how do you know Willis?"

The broadest of smiles came across Jean-Paul's face. His eyes lit up with pride. His voice choked with emotion as he slowly stated, "Willis Carpenter was my father!"

Steward sat there. His mouth agape, his eyes wide open in disbelief at what he had just heard. His pen fell from his hand, and his notepad flopped onto the floor. Steward could not believe it. What kind of assignment had Donahue sent him on? It was then his reporter's brain found itself. Menuisier had said Willis

Carpenter was his father. Steward's mental pencil began to connect the dots. It was not a difficult connection to make.

"So, then I assume that Anastasie Bouchet was your mother?"

This time with tears welling in his eyes, Jean-Paul's chest heaved with emotion as he replied, "Oui, our beloved teacher was Anastasie Bouchet, my mere."

CHAPTER 36

The story behind Jean-Paul Menuisier's exuberant reaction upon hearing the name, Jimmy Donahue, would cause Dylan Steward's pen to move in quick, rapid strokes, only pausing when he asked another question. For the first time in ages, this was feeling good and natural. It was what he had trained himself to do; this was his life's work in action.

"So, as I understand it, Anastasie Bouchet, your mother, met Willis Carpenter when he was recovering from wounds at a US army hospital here in Bordeaux?"

"Oui, I mean yes!" said Jean-Paul, now as excited as a young child who did well on a test at school and was eager to tell his parents. "It was called the Chateau Rêves. It was Christmas, 1944, when the hospital in Bordeaux was flooded with American casualties. My mother spent much time at the hospital."

"Was she a nurse?"

"Oui, Monsieur Steward. My mother was a nurse, but she was not allowed to work at the hospital because of what happened at the Musee des Arts."

Steward's pen continued to move even as he asked the obvious. He was trying to imagine what event could have possibly happened that prevented a trained nurse from helping those in desperate need.

"My mother assisted at the Musee, cataloging priceless works of art. The German commander, a man named Koffler, forced my mother to assist him in stealing a number of such paintings under threat of her family being sent to a labor camp. My mere knew she would pay a price for acquiescing, but she clearly had no choice. Of course, she agreed. However, members of the French Underground saw her as some sort of a traitor. One day, a group of them found her alone and carved the letter "T " for traitor on her left cheek. My mother was such a beautiful woman, Monsieur!" Jean-Paul wept openly. Steward was not far behind as his eyes glistened with emotions within. When Jean-Paul regained his composure, Steward continued.

"If she was not allowed to work as a nurse at the hospital, what exactly did your mother do at the hospital?"

Having cleared the tears from his cheeks with his handkerchief, Jean-Paul replied, "She taught the wounded American soldiers to paint. Willis, my father, was one of them. Most of the wounded Americans did not have the patience or desire to learn how to paint, but my father was different. My mother told me later that he was gifted in absorbing the concepts of color combinations and brush strokes to create a particular mood. As my mother told me later, he was like a child in a sweet store, discovering the marvelous taste of the chocolatier's creations. My father spent nearly a year at the Chateau. He and my mother met daily for lessons. How odd it must have been for a man of my father's background to be so taken with the beauty and complexities of painting. She learned of his background and the things he went through growing up in the south in the twenties and thirties. She taught him how to transfer those experiences onto canvas and turn his nightmares and dreams into something real. He made her feel wanted and beautiful no matter her disfigurement."

Jean-Paul leaned back, visibly fatigued in his chair. The telling of his story had left him emotionally drained. He looked at Steward with a tired smile, then shrugged his shoulders and sighed, "What is it you Americans say, the rest is history?"

Steward laughed at the Frenchman's most appropriate use of the idiom. He believed the brief humor had recharged Jean-Paul. He wanted to probe further. This was an excellent story.

"That certainly explains what happened then, but what happened between then and now?"

The energy returned to Jean-Paul's voice.

"That, my friend, is what we French call le miracle."

Steward's pen moved quickly. A letter from a woman named Sylvia Markham informed Anastasia Bouchet that Willis Carpenter was alive and living in Los Angeles, California. Anastasia wrote to him, and he wrote back. In time, the two realized there was an opportunity to make a dream come true, their dream, a dream long denied because of circumstances each thought they could not control. Even more important, Willis Carpenter had a son.

"My father spent a lifetime dreaming of returning to the place where he learned to paint and to the arms of the only woman he had ever loved. My mother inspired my father to follow his dream, which was to paint and create a vision of the past and the future that would live forever on every canvas he touched. But in her heart, she harbored another dream that someday he would return to her, and she was right. That phrase, Monsieur that you had so much trouble pronouncing, Mon Chercheur de Rêves, was a pet name my mother gave to my father. It translates into 'My Dream Seeker.' In fact, my father signed all his paintings with 'Le Chercheur de Rêves for 'The Dream Seeker.'"

Steward let his pen rest. He stared at Jean-Paul as if the phrase Dream Seeker was suspended in the air between them. At that moment, he realized how much the phrase epitomized the lives of Willis Carpenter and Anastasie Bouchet. Steward saw the beauty and wonder of the words Dream Seeker for the first time. Steward hated to ask the next question, but the story demanded it.

"Jean-Paul, did your mother and father have much time together before they passed away?"

Menuisier was at peace with himself and spoke with an unusual sense of contentment as he finished the love story of his mother and father.

"Nearly six months, but they were six months filled with the ecstasy of lost lovers reunited."

Steward listened. His pen hardly moved. There was no need to write it down. Steward would remember it forever.

LITTLE WAS SAID on the way back to the hostel. Renee asked Steward if he had found the person he was seeking. When Steward replied tersely, "Yes," no extra details, no explanation, Rene left his passenger to his own thoughts. Had he been able, Steward would have heard the voice of his boss echoing in his mind. "Connect the dots, kid!"

Sitting at the window of his small room back at the Boudreaux Ville, Steward watched those walking the narrow streets below. Conversations filled with laughter and talk of the excitement that tomorrow brings echoed up to his open window from the youthful passersby. Steward thought of Willis and Anastasie. How powerful their dreams must have been to have survived over thirty years despite their differences. How wonderful to have even shared those dreams. How would their lives have been had they not sought to make their dreams come true? Steward mused about his past, a past that started with eternal hope and optimism and yet ended in horrible tragedy. What was his future to be? Dare he have the courage of Willis and Anastasia and even dream of one, or live a life avoiding what might be? Steward thought of his wife and how she embraced life. He closed the window and went to bed. For the first time in months, Dylan Steward slept in peace.

GABRIELLA WAS gracious enough to have her nephew take Steward to the train station the following morning. Steward thanked her for her generosity and promised to speak highly of the Bordeaux Ville when he returned home. The five-hour train ride from Bordeaux to Paris on the Renault motor coach afforded Steward ample time to review his notes and begin a draft of his article. The Renault carried some forty passengers in bench seats facing each other. Selecting a place near the rear of the coach, Steward took his notepad from his bag and began reviewing his notes. As a reporter, he had developed his own unique form of note-taking—half sentences, abbreviated adjectives, catchphrases, and arrows indicating more emphasis or direction. He began scripting the story into a spiral binder. He wrote slowly and deliberately, frequently glancing back and forth between notepad and binder. He found himself in awe of Willis and Anastasie. They had dreamed the improbable, if not the impossible. What "powers that be "had determined their dreams would come true, escaped Steward. What he was beginning to understand was at least they dared to dream. Steward had a habit of making side notes in margins to remind him to emphasize this point or that point. This made the process even more concentrated, so much so that Steward had completely ignored the young woman who had taken a seat across from him on the train when the train had stopped at Bayeux. She had watched him for some time before asking, "Excuse me, but are you some sort of a writer?"

Steward was typically somewhat aloof when approached by strangers, but the sweet shyness in the woman's voice caused him to look up. Thinking she meant something along the lines of an author or a scripter of literature, he nodded politely and responded, "No, I work for a newspaper. I'm a reporter."

Steward turned his attention back to his notepad, hoping not to be interrupted again.

"Well, that makes you a writer, doesn't it?"

Hating that he was being interrupted, Steward replied rather tersely, "If you say so, yes," without even giving his new traveling companion the courtesy of looking up. The woman grinned smugly at having her suspicion confirmed. Oblivious to his lack of interest in having a conversation, the young woman announced, "I've dreamed of being an artist all my life, and I will, at least I will when I finish art school."

Like a parent faced with a persistent talkative child, Steward was prepared to give the young woman an "I'm not interested in talking" look. Closing his notepad, he looked at the woman. What he saw changed his mind. She appeared to be of average height, with curly brown hair extending to the middle of her back. She had stretched out, taking almost all of the bench to herself. Turning sideways on the bench seat to face the window, she brought her knees up and braced her feet on the bench's armrest. The light of the midmorning sun shone through the window, highlighting the bluest eyes Steward had ever seen. Dark eyelashes blinked in reaction to the sun's rays. She had taken a sketch pad and a small bag with pencils and charcoal sticks from a large satchel that she had placed under the bench on the floor. If the young woman's natural beauty weren't enough of a distraction, the scent of an intoxicating vanilla perfume she was wearing alone would have caused him to notice. Now, completely distracted from his original task, Steward was amused by the impish behavior of the woman. With a childlike smile on her face, she stared at the window as if it were a mirror where she could see her thoughts. In rapid motions, she moved a pencil across the page of the sketch pad, occasionally smudging whatever lines she had drawn. Then she would replace that pencil with one of several she held between her teeth and continue drawing.

Ignorant of artistic endeavors and feeling the need to question the young woman further, Steward said, "Don't artists use paints?"

"Yes, some do. I happen to prefer to work with pencils or frescos."

His curiosity now piqued; Steward strained his neck to see what creation the woman was putting on paper. Even with a profile view, Steward could see a smile forming on the girl's face as she coyly shifted her sketch pad to shield it from Steward's view. Steward refused to be dismissed so quickly.

"You said you were in art school?"

"Yes, in La Rochelle. I saved for nearly three years to go here."

"Art school in France must be expensive?"

The young woman had heard that before. She turned to face Steward to give him the same response she had given those back home who questioned the wisdom of her decision considering there were less expensive art schools in the states. The conviction in her voice put Steward on the defensive.

"Yes, but studying in France gives you a perspective on the history of art you could never get in the US. It's a place where art lovers dream of going, and after all, what price do you put on your dreams?"

God, how idealistic! Steward thought as he turned his attention back to his notes.

For the next hour or so, Steward focused on organizing his draft, paying little attention to the woman sitting opposite him, though the scent of her perfume definitely had a calming effect on him. As the train rolled to a stop, the woman hurriedly stood up and placed her sketchpad and pencils back in her satchel.

She looked thoughtfully down on Steward, indicating it was her stop. "Good luck with your writing. I hope it's everything you want it to be."

Before Steward could answer, the young woman was gone. As she passed by the window to the car on the train platform, she gave Steward a casual wave then disappeared into the crowd of those departing and those boarding the train. He managed a small smile, finally able to stretch out his long legs. That's when he noticed a folded sheet of paper on the seat where the young girl had been. He took the paper and opened it. He was shocked by what he saw. In near-perfect detail, the young girl had drawn a virtually faultless sketch of himself, his hair, beard, even down to the few remaining facial blemishes from a case of severe acne he endured as a teenager. Above his head, she had drawn several shapes resembling clouds. With her gone, he had no one to ask what, if anything, they represented. Were they ideas? Were they omens? What? It would be up to him to decipher. There in the lower left-hand corner of the sketch, she had written the letters 'KT'. Steward never believed in the adage that things happen for a reason. Inexplicably, he folded the drawing and put it in his shoulder bag. The scent of that vanilla perfume lingered as if the woman had sketched it into the very air he breathed.

CHAPTER 37

For an assignment that he had grudgingly accepted, Steward now found himself captivated by the story of Willis Carpenter and Anastasie Bouchet. He stared out the airplane window into the starlit heavens over the Atlantic Ocean and thought of a quote by Jimi Hendrix: "May the dreams of your past be the reality of your future."

Willis Carpenter had a dream, a dream that he kept alive through painting his love for Anastasie Bouchet. Her hair, the color of her skin, the scent of her perfume lived within him with every brushstroke on every canvas he ever completed. Anastasie Bouchet had an interlude with a man different from her in many ways, yet they shared the same dream. After they separated, the life that grew within her would sustain her for decades until that dream became a reality.

As he gazed into the midnight heavens, Steward thought of dreams from the past, mainly his wife, Willow, and her dreams of conceiving a child, their child. The wondrous feeling of anticipation in that dream had caused Willow to ignore serious health risks. She also had a dream for her husband, but that was in his past, or so he thought. Steward lowered the window covering and propped the small pillow, provided by the flight attendant, against it. He closed his eyes and thought of what had been. Somewhere in the night, Steward's mind turned to Willis Carpenter and Anastasie Bouchet. Each had endured horrific tragedies and survived by the sheer power of a dream. Could Steward also survive?

TRY AS HE MIGHT, neither the five-hour train ride from Bordeaux to Paris nor the fifteen-hour flight home to Los Angeles afforded a suitable environment to transcribe his notes into text or his memories into words. The rumbling of the train over aging tracks made legible handwriting impossible. The cramped coach seat on the airplane had the same effect. The story of Willis and Anastasie had Steward's mind asea with the power of their dreams, even dreams in general. Can they actually be that enduring? Does it take a lifetime for them to come true? Willis and Anastasie had dreams for a lifetime but had only a few months together before both of them passed away. How fair was that? How do aspirations today make life more bearable tomorrow?

With a small carry-on suitcase and his shoulder bag, Steward could again avoid the confusion at the luggage pickup carousels. Between the fifteen-hour flight and the nine-hour time difference between Paris and Los Angeles, Steward's body clock needed a period of adjustment before reporting to work. One of the many taxis outside the arrival terminal would be his conveyance home and salvation.

THE ANNOYING CAWS of blue jays involved in some territorial feud in his backyard brought Steward out of a restful sleep and into the reality of morning. He was about to give the nagging avians a piece of his mind when he remembered what Willow would have said. "They're only trying to get food for their babies. Don't get so upset." He smiled to himself and let the disdain ebb from his body.

The silence in a house occupied by one person was soon broken as the first of several long-playing albums dropped onto the turntable of his retro record player. Something was soothing about the soft jazz riffs of Kenny Burrell matched with a warm shower and shave that set Steward's mind on an even keel. Sadly this sense of equilibrium would soon be shaken.

Once dressed, he proceeded to the kitchen for the requisite morning cup of coffee. Necessity had taught him how to operate the GE electric coffee pot they had received as a housewarming gift from Willow's boss, Joe Skaff. With the water added to the max level and four scoops of Folgers Coffee measured into the top, Steward plugged in the device. He had about a ten-minute wait for that first jolt of caffeine. He took a seat on the couch and opened his bag, which he had carelessly dropped there upon arriving home. He took out his notepad, laying it on the coffee table in front of him. He failed to notice the folded piece of paper that had fallen from his bag in the process. He started rereading his notes, including the scribbled asides he had noted in the margins. His brain began organizing his ideas into a coherent flow of ideas. He imagined the formatted articles before him. To his amazement, there was a real sense of excitement, something he had not felt in a long time. He leaned his head back against the headrest and visualized the introductory paragraph.

Then, looking past his mental imagery, Steward noticed the painting on the wall. It was one that Willow had brought home. He remembered her chiding him for not grasping the imagery of the artist. In that moment of sentimentality, he stood up and approached the painting. There it was before his eyes. All he had learned from Jean-Paul about his mother and father suddenly made sense to Steward. In the painting, a young black woman, pregnant, sat amidst the racial animus both the past and present but still dreamed of a future yet to be. The enormous power of dreams can transcend the present and take one to a different reality. Granted, the future may be uncertain, but without a dream, the only certainty is an endless series of yesterdays. Feeling somewhat smug with his newfound understanding of the artist's interpretation, Steward saw the writing in the lower right corner, smoothly integrated into the brush strokes was the name Le Chercheur de Rêves. He stared at it briefly before he realized what it meant. Steward hurried back to the coffee table and grabbed his notepad. Flipping through the pages rapidly, he found the page he was looking for. There it was. According to Jean-Paul, Willis Carpenter signed all his paintings, Le Chercheur de Rêves. HIs mouth agape, Steward stood there, unable to move. How? When would his wife have ever met Willis Carpenter? Was this some bizarre coincidence? He had just been to France, where he had interviewed Willis Carpenter's son only to return home and find a painting by Carpenter in his living room. He worked at the *L.A. Times*, and Carpenter had operated the newsstand in the lobby of the *L.A. Times*. Had he ever mentioned Carpenter's name to his wife? Had Willow ever mentioned talking to Carpenter? Nothing made sense to Steward.

He could see the GE Percolator on the edge of the kitchen counter from where he stood. Its red light indicated the brewing period was complete. He laid his notepad down on the coffee table and went to the kitchen. He took a mug from the kitchen cabinet and poured himself a full measure. He brought the steaming brew up to his nose, inhaling the aroma of the fresh-roasted Colombian coffee beans—if you were to believe the advertisement on the side of the Folgers can. Careful not to spill any, Steward returned to the couch and sat down. Cupping his mug with both hands, he took several slow sips. Another album dropped. Between the melodic sounds of Charlie Parker's alto sax and the java blend from Folger's, Steward's mind settled into a state of contented amazement. The digits of his right hand began to emulate the finger positioning in an imaginary accompaniment to Parker on the side of Steward's coffee cup. Steward closed his eyes and envisioned being on stage with Parker. He had just finished a great improvisation when Parker smiled at him and said, "Man, you're in the groove!" With his eyes still closed, Steward enjoyed the applause from the imaginary crowd of jazz lovers. He smiled at them and then nodded his appreciation to Parker.

When he opened his eyes, Steward would discover another piece of enlightenment. There, on the floor directly under the painting Willow had brought home, was a package, wrapped in white butcher paper and secured with brown twine. Donahue had given it to him the day he sprung the trip to France surprise on him. No explanation as to what it was, just a gift from a friend, Donahue told him. *No time like the present*, he thought. *Let's see what it is.*

He set his coffee cup down, walked over to the package, and picked it up. The twine was loosely tightened, so slipping it off the paper was simple. Taking hold of one edge, Steward carefully removed its contents. It was a painting. When he held it up to look at it, his hands began to twitch, followed by tremors so severe he could barely hold on to the painting. His eyes blinked spasmodically as if his brain was refusing to process the image before him. His breathing began to race along with his heartbeat. No coincidence could explain it.

Steward returned to the couch, carrying the painting as if he were holding a fragile piece of crystal. Settling onto the sofa, Steward's eyes remained fixed on the painting. He gently laid it on the coffee table. Staring at it as if it were some sort of miracle on canvas, Steward saw a small stage against a black backdrop. On the stage was a painter's easel. On one edge of the easel was a small can containing brushes next to a palette with smeared blotches of various colors. A guitar leaned against the other side of the easel. Not just any guitar, but a Gibson SG, and not just any Gibson SG, but a left-handed Gibson SG, identical to the one he played, even down to the mother of pearl pickguard he had specially ordered with the guitar. It was as if he were engulfed in some vortex of paranormal current swirling around him. His brain fought for control, much like someone caught in the turbulence of a raging river. He could not take his eyes off that painting. Then he noticed it. There, in the lower right-hand corner of the canvas, as clear and detailed as the body of the guitar, was written Le Chercheur de Rêve. At that moment, the transformation of Dylan Steward began to take place. Think your dreams, and they stay dreams; pursue your dreams, and they become reality.

Like the Dylan of old, Steward was in his cubicle twenty minutes before anyone else arrived. He was proofing his assignment, probably the most expensive human interest story in the *L.A. Times* history, he thought. He sipped on a hot coffee and munched on a warm croissant that he had purchased in the lobby while doing a line-by-line read. Satisfied with its format and content, Steward stretched back in his chair and glanced over at the closed door to Donahue's office. He couldn't help but wonder if there was more to Donahue giving him this assignment than just another human interest story. His thoughtful questioning of his bosses' motive was interrupted by the arrival of Roberts and Alunda.

"Well, look who's back. Welcome home, stranger!" chuckled Roberts, who had genuinely missed his cubicle partner. "How was Paris?"

"There's a lot of French people there, G.O.," replied Steward, making a nonsensical reference to the obvious. His facetious remark clearly demonstrated that the trip had done him benefit.

"Uh?" answered a completely confused Roberts.

Before Steward could explain his obtuse remark, Alunda interrupted. "He's being a smartass, G.O.! Come on, Dylan, I want to know about the food. Did you try escargot, truffles, maybe duck confit or coq au vin?" Alunda put her lips together. "Mumm, I can just imagine!" she said, as her eyes rolled upward.

"I'm afraid nothing that exotic, Liz. I didn't really have much time to try out local restaurants. I was pretty limited to some French cheeses, which were absolutely delicious, and a couple of glasses of Bordeaux at the hostel where I stayed. Donahue had me on a shoestring budget."

"Well, I would have made time," smiled a defiant Alunda. "A trip to Paris is a once-in-a-lifetime opportunity. It would be a dream come true for me."

Alunda's response triggered something in Steward. "What would be a dream come true for you, Liz? A trip to Paris, dinner in a fine restaurant on the banks of the Seine, a walk down the Champs Elysees?"

"Seriously?" Alunda asked.

"Yeah, seriously. What would be that once-in-a-lifetime dream for you? A once-in-a-lifetime dream is pretty limiting."

"Well, I don't have to think at all," interrupted Roberts. "I'd have my own ranch in the Owens Valley. My grandfather still has property there, and I'd raise prize Arabian horses. If you've never been on the back of a purebred Arabian, there's nothing like it in the world!"

"Damn, G.O.! I've never thought of you as a cowboy," Steward said, smiling at his friend's revelation.

Roberts blushed a bit at his acknowledgment. "Well, you said a once-in-a-lifetime dream, didn't you?" The smile of enthusiasm on Roberts' face faded as the thought of a dream come true faded into space.

Steward felt instantly sorry for his friend.

"Okay, Mr. Soothsayer, here's my once-in-a-lifetime dream,"

said Alunda, whose moment of contemplation was over. "I'd be a lawyer for the Southern Poverty Law Office and work for Morris Dees. Writing about social injustice is one thing; doing something about it is another matter altogether."

There was a sense of real pride and accomplishment in the tone of her voice, which was quickly squelched by the caveat, "But that means the expense of law school, much less getting into a good law school, and fighting the good ole boy admission system."

Steward's empathy grew for her, another dream destined to remain just a dream, no doubt.

A seed had been planted in Steward, and it was starting to germinate. To dismiss an aspiration for any reason, to forsake a goal because of its potential hardships, no longer seemed tenable. Life should be more than living a day-to-day existence, with no expectation that tomorrow would be any different than yesterday; that would be a living death.

CHAPTER 38

In the past, Steward's writings had been generated in equal parts by a passionate desire to right wrongs and expose injustice. That passion brought a forceful touch of his fingers to the keys of his Olivetti, a hard, determined force intended to drive home his point to his readers like a knife through their hearts. His language was confrontative, like a prosecuting attorney questioning a serial killer. He typed with a sense of urgency reflected by his furrowed brow, a clenched jaw, and eyes focused on the keys to the point of straining them. The Steward, who had returned from his trip to France, wrote with a completely different mindset. He had handwritten his first draft slowly and thoughtfully, at times rephrasing key passages while searching for that perfect combination of words, adjectives, and verbs. All this to properly convey the emotions of the story of Willis Carpenter and Anastasie Bouchet. When it was ready for typing, his fingers flowed with a soft, tender touch to the keys, very much like an improvised run-up and down the pentatonic scale on his Gibson. Like the painter who employs colors and brush strokes, shadows and light for perspective, Steward employed an easy reading narrative style with gentle language intent on bringing the reader to an unavoidable conclusion; the power of dreams can overcome impossible obstacles until they become, at last, reality.

Steward removed the last sheet of paper from his Olivetti. He gently shuffled it along with the other pages, aligning the edges. He placed a paperclip at the upper left-hand corner and took the finished document to Martha Irons' office. This time Steward thought he'd get the boss's secretary to give his article the 'once over' before handing it to Donahue. Iron's door was ajar, but Steward knocked anyway.

"Come in, Dylan." Her voice resounded firmly.

Steward made his entry with a surprised look on his face. Martha recognized it immediately as that "How did she know it was me" look.

"The convex mirror in the corner," she chuckled. "What can I do for you?"

"So, it wasn't mental telepathy after all," replied Steward.

"Let's keep that a secret between you and me," said Irons, as she rose from her desk to close the door behind Steward.

Steward held up his multipage article. "I was wondering if you wouldn't mind going over this. I'd like it to be as perfect as possible before I give it to Jimmy."

Irons face lit up with a most gracious smile. "Well, that's a first around here, Dylan. Most of the egos out in the city room think a mere secretary has no business critiquing their work." She was clearly pleased.

"Then they don't know who's the real power behind the throne, do they?"

Compliments like that were few and far between for the fiftyish woman, and she basked in the flattery.

"Well, that might be a bit of an overstatement, but I appreciate the kind words. Is this from your trip to France?"

"Yeah," Steward responded, handing the work to Irons. "I can't say, in all honesty, that I was that excited about this assignment at first. All that changed when I found out one of the principals was

Willis Carpenter, who used to run the newsstand in the lobby. You know, Martha, a reporter, wants his articles to have an impact on the readers. Sometimes the impact is even greater on the reporter."

Taking the document from Steward, Irons said, "Let me go over this. Jimmy got a call to report to Willard's office as soon as he got in this morning. I'll try to have this ready when he gets back."

"Thanks, Martha. I've got to turn in my travel claims to the business department. I picked up the forms before I left. They look like they need to be filled out by a CPA."

Irons laughed. "Nothing's ever simple, is it?"

Steward nodded then said, "I'll be back when I'm finished with the bean counters."

"Dylan, could you shut the door behind you? I don't want to be interrupted once I start."

"Thanks again, Martha," Steward replied as he shut the door behind him.

Irons took a seat behind her desk. She spun her chair toward the window to face the rising sun. She smiled to herself as she twirled a red pencil between her fingers; how thoughtful, he double spaced, anticipating room for corrections. By the time she got to the bottom of the first page, her eyes had welled up with tears. Halfway done with the second page, tears streamed down her face. She put the red pencil down, never to pick it up again, replacing it with a small box of tissue which she turned to repeatedly through the entire length of the article.

To be summoned to the editor-in-chief's office with a phone call from his secretary that said, "Mr. Willard wants you in his office immediately" was a bit authoritative and over the top as far as Jimmy Donahue was concerned. He had suffered the bombastic Willard's infuriating sense of self-importance for too many years. Donahue's ire only grew as the secretary forced him to wait outside Willard's office like some petulant junior high schooler sent to the principal's office. Harriet Southard had been Otis Chandler's secretary and every editor-in-chief after him. She sorely missed Chandler's genteel southern manner in dealing with staff as opposed to Damon Willard and his imperialistic edicts. When Donahue reported as ordered, Southard rolled her eyes upward as an omen of what to expect. When the clock indicated that Donahue had spent over ten minutes cooling his heels, he stood and said, "Harriet, tell Damon I'll be in my office if he wants to see me!" There was no mistaking the intent of the stubborn Irishman. Donahue would await Willard's arrival at his office. Donahue had barely taken two steps when Southard's desk phone rang. She picked up.

"Yes, he is. Yes, I will."

Southard set the telephone back on its cradle as if she was holding a piece of fecal matter.

"He'll see you now, Jimmy."

Donahue shook his head as he turned to enter Willard's office. He found Willard standing at his window, staring out at the expanse of interweaving Southern California freeways.

"You wanted to see me?" Donahue said. His irritation was evident in his tone.

"Have a seat, Donahue."

"I'll stand, just the same."

Still facing the view of the freeway system, Willard said, "Care to explain why you needed to use the balance of this year's discretionary account and all of the next years as well?"

"Not that it matters, but I sent one of my reporters, Dylan Steward, on assignment to look into a story about a man named Willis Carpenter and a woman named Anastasie Bouchet from a human interest angle."

"It matters because I'm the managing editor, Donahue. Who the hell are Willis Carpenter and Anastasie Bouchet?" The names meant nothing to Damon Willard, and he demanded more explanation.

Donahue was outraged at having to speak to Willard's back about the picayune accountability suddenly demanded of him.

He was a man, dammit! Look me in the eye if you've got a problem with me!

He found himself clenching his fists and barely about to contain the string of profanities he wanted to spew. His patience with Willard's regal perception of himself and his insulting treatment of those who worked under him had been strained for years. This latest inquiry into Donahue's spending brought forth an unexpected and noncompliant pushback.

"For one, Willis Carpenter spent thirty years at the *Times* running the newsstand in the lobby and harbored a dream about a lost love, Anastasie Bouchet, a woman he met in France during WWII. Remember him, Damon, the old black man with one leg, who greeted you every day with a smile when you came through the lobby, or was he just another person to use and forget about during the course of your day? And for another, my account is called a discretionary account for a reason, Damon, which by definition means I don't have to explain how I use those funds!" The combative tone in his voice rose as he drew a line in the sand.

Damon Willard spun around to face his defiant city desk editor. No one ever talked to him that way and expected to stay at the *Times*. He fumed at the impudence of Donahue. The blood vessels in his temple began to bulge. An irate redness spread over his face.

"Who in the hell do you think you're talking to! You've got the breeding of an alley cat and are hardly deserving of your position at the *Times*. You're dreaming if you think you can talk to me in that tone of voice. Your tenure at the *Times* is on the thinnest of ice, Donahue, and by the way, the term discretionary is no longer applicable! Do I make myself clear!" screamed Willard, on the verge of losing total control of his emotions.

Donahue lunged forward then stopped suddenly. He stood there, visibly shaking. How he was able to control his temper, he had no idea. Every fiber in his body wanted to grab Willard by the neck and choke him until the capillaries in his eyes burst. Willard crossed the line when he added with equal venom and volume, "You're finished here if you think for one moment I'll approve expenditures to interview some Sambo who peddled newspapers in the lobby!"

Something snapped inside Donahue. Whatever element of self-control he clung to was gone. Consequences be damned, Donahue screamed back, "You son-of-bitch, I'm gonna give you the ass beating of your life!" He tossed a chair aside to get at Willard. At that moment, Southard pushed the office door open. She made no effort to contain her displeasure with what she had heard nor convey the necessity for the bickering to stop.

"You two need to stop this now! There are people outside who have heard everything!"

Like raging bulls in a standoff, Donahue and Willard stood staring at each other, neither willing to give an inch. Donahue found some measure of self-control within himself, though hardly ending the confrontation.

"If you want to finish this discussion, let me know where and when!" With that, Donahue turned, slammed the door shut, and left the office.

Southard stood there in disbelief at what she had heard from her boss. She had covered for Willard's behavior for years, but she could not unhear the racial slur, nor was she willing to smooth over the outburst to those in the outer office who had heard it as well. The disgust in her eyes said everything. She slowly turned and shut the door leaving Willard alone to contemplate Donahue's invitation and the necessity for damage control by those who heard everything.

CHAPTER 39

His rapid pace and the iron look on his face told everyone in the city desk room that this was not the time to approach the assignment editor. Donahue emphasized the point by slamming the door to his office behind him. Donahue wanted nothing more than to pummel his boss with both hands, to feel that adrenaline rush when his fist broke Damon's nose and he crumbled to the ground, weeping like a baby. He paced back and forth in his office, even slamming his fists on his desktop until his rage began to subside, and his heartbeat slowed to something less than stroke level. He took several slow breaths before answering the ringing phone on his desk.

"Donahue."

"Is it safe to come in?" the female voice asked.

Recognizing his secretary's voice, he replied tersely, "Yes."

Irons did not completely trust her boss, so when she got to his door, she knocked before entering.

"Martha, I said Yes! Didn't I!?" traces of his rage remained.

Irons opened the door, then shut it behind her.

"Harriet called. Apparently, your meeting with the big boss didn't go well."

"That's an understatement," Donahue replied, with a bit of a growl still in his voice. "You'll never understand how much I wanted to rip him apart."

Irons smiled. "Oh, yes, I can. But this will help calm you down. It's Steward's article on his interview. He asked me to look it over before sending it to you." Irons handed him the article she had proofed.

Somewhat incredulous that Steward would ask his secretary to review his article, he asked, "What did you think of it?" as he set the folder with Steward's article inside on his desk.

There was a sad, almost puppy-like look in her eyes. "Jimmy, I think you're going to be looking for a new reporter."

Her remark caught Donahue completely off guard. He cocked his head at an angle and said, "You're kidding?"

Irons shook her head. "No, I'm not. What he wrote would cause any reader to ask themselves, 'what if?', and then do something about it."

Donahue took off his coat and placed it on the back of his chair. He sat down, loosened his tie, and picked up his red pencil before opening the folder Irons had given him.

"You won't need that," Irons said, referring to the red pencil, as she turned to leave. "I will call Harriet and see what kind of damage control she's got in mind."

Donahue nodded. His mindset was hardly prepared for sentimentality as Donahue was not one to forgive and forget quickly, if at all. Ignoring Irons' advice, he held on to his red pencil as he opened the folder. The kid had been reluctant to take the assignment when Donahue first proposed it to him. What reporter in their right mind wouldn't jump at the chance to fly to France on assignment? But then Steward was hardly in his right mind considering the circumstances of the last few months, and Donahue knew it. The sudden death of his wife, torturous nightmares followed by bouts of depression, and turning to alcohol for relief was a recipe for suicide, and any hope of saving his young reporter lay in Steward taking this assignment. As his eyes began to read, Donahue hoped he had not made a mistake. By the time he had finished reading the article, not once but twice, he knew he had succeeded. He knew the kid understood what power had reunited Willis Carpenter and Anastasie Bouchet and the course to being truly happy. He would soon realize the portent in his secretary's words.

Le Chercheur de Rêve
The Dream Seeker
By Dylan Steward

There was an eerie feeling that day as I entered the lobby of the Los Angeles Times Building. The customary greeting that so many employees had heard for nearly thirty years, and one I had come to look forward to, was not there. The smile and the hand giving you your favorite read was gone. There was no one to ask about your favorite sports team. The purveyor of such niceties had retired to follow a dream. This is his story, the story of Willis Carpenter.

He came to Europe in late 1944 as a twenty-year-old soldier in George Patton's Eighth Army, intent on ending the horror of Hitler's Nazi Germany. He would suffer terrible burns to his back and the loss of his left leg from a run-in with a 37mm cannon on a German Panzer tank during the Battle of the Bulge. The US Army hospital in Bordeaux, France, known as the Chateau Rêves, became his home for almost a year. His nights were filled with the cries of agony from the never-ending pain. In the light of day, he dared not dream of what his life would be like back home with only one leg. During these most discouraging and seemingly hopeless times, he met a young woman who gave the scarred and wounded GI something he would cherish forever; one, a passion for painting and the other, forbidden love.

Her name was Anastasie Bouchet. She was in her early twenties and a woman of unusual beauty and talent but for one thing. French Resistance had carved a T into her left cheek with a razor blade. The stigma was the price she had paid for cooperation with a Nazi colonel who had threatened her family with being sent to a labor camp in Poland if the young woman did not assist him in stealing priceless works of art from a museum. Shunned by her own countrymen, Anastasie found purpose and acceptance in helping at the US hospital. A talented artist in her own right, she began teaching anyone who was interested in the art of painting. No one absorbed her efforts more than the young black GI.

Indeed, they were an odd couple. She was well educated, spoke three languages, and had worked at the Musee des Beaux Arts in Bordeaux. He had not finished high school, had no discernible skills, and had little prospects of earning a decent living. Oh, and did I mention that she was white, and he was black? Every day, young Anastasie would bring a collection of brushes, oils, a sketch pad, and an easel to the hospital at Chateau Rêves. Every day, the young GI, Willis Carpenter, would wheel himself outside to the patio area on the side of the hospital and meet his instructor. There, with a sweeping view of the French countryside to their back and the beautiful Garonne River to the front, the teacher worked with her student. Raw at first, the young GI was fascinated by the process of transforming imagery to canvas. Whatever he might dream of, whatever he may imagine, could come to life on a simple piece of canvas. A whole new world opened up to the wounded GI by the stroke of a brush, by some mystical combination of colors. Constantly questioning, constantly seeking more information, he soaked up every bit of knowledge available. Anastasie obliged, ever so grateful that someone would look at her without disdain and see her as a person of value. Their laughter and often intimate conversations brought disparaging stares from some. The two did not care. Being looked at as different, even out of place, was nothing new to the young black man whose own country was steeped in discrimination and segregation. Thanks to her facial marking, Anastasie knew precisely where she stood with many of her own countrymen.

The chemistry between the two was unmistakable as their sessions grew longer and longer. "Think of the brush as holding the stem of a fragile flower in your hand. The brush must respond to your mind's direction, not the grip of the hand that holds it," she would say, laying her hand on his. The simple physical contact stirred the imagination of the student. Once in a particularly private moment, she placed her hand over his heart and said, "The canvas is like a mirror. It reflects what is in your heart. Whatever you can dream of, you can put on a canvas."

Willis thought of Anastasie as a dream that became alive before his very eyes. She inspired him and encouraged him in ways he never thought possible. The teacher was fascinated by how quickly her student absorbed what seemed like complex techniques for some students, using contrasting colors to create a three-dimensional feeling and using different size brushes to define and differentiate planes, masses, and areas of the painting.

In time, Anastasie got permission from the hospital administration to take her student to the local museum on the pretext of viewing great works of art, or at least that is what she told them. By this time, Willis was able to walk using a cane despite his locked knee prosthetic leg. In fact, she took Willis to her family cottage a few miles away in La Reole. In the privacy of her home, Anastasie shared more than her knowledge of painting with her student. In walking through the idyllic setting of her father's small Bordeaux vineyard, she shared with Willis her deep anguish for the disgrace she had brought upon her family. There, in between vines full of ripened Merlot grapes, her fingers traced the jagged scar on her cheek as she said, "They made me ugly to shame him."

Willis's heart cried out, "No, No. Y'all ain't ugly!"

His hands shook as he took her hand in his. Tears welled up in his eyes. He gasped as he struggled with words he had never said to any woman, much less a white woman. "No, you ain't. I'd love you forever if I could."

Emotionally broken, Anastasie fell into Willis' arms. That afternoon Anastasie was loved without any thought of her disfigurement. Willis Carpenter was held in the arms of a woman who saw him not as a black man or a cripple but as the reflection of the goodness and caring in his heart.

With the passing months, Willis and Anastasie became one, not just when stolen moments would allow, but one in spirit and heart. Anastasie honed her domestic skills by doting on her lover. She prepared meals at her home for Willis whenever he could get a pass from the hospital. She took to washing and ironing his uniforms. Even an occasional hot soak in the claw foot bathtub became a sacred and much-anticipated ritual. Willis, somewhat of a natural handyman, made himself as useful as he could with one leg, helping out repairing broken machinery used in the small vineyard. His carpentry skills were put to good use in helping Anastasie's father repair damaged storage structures. In every way possible, Willis and Anastasie were a couple.

When Willis Carpenter got the word that he was being sent back to Americato, a VA hospital in Los Angeles, California, he had never felt more alone and abandoned. All that he had come to care about was here, in France, in that small town near the Garonne River outside Bordeaux. The thought of life without his Anastasie was unbearable. Artistry would become the only way to keep her by his side. Unable to find the words to tell her, Willis kept the news to himself. But the despair in his eyes and the struggling, fading voice when he spoke made it all too apparent to Anastasie that he was leaving. One day the two were standing on the lawn overlooking the Garonne River, "They are sending you back to the states, aren't they, Willis?" He could only nod.

With stoic fatalism, Anastasie said, "Oui, I knew this time would come someday."

Holding her in his arms, Willis's heart broke. He could say nothing, even as his lungs filled with the air necessary to tell her how much he loved her. His arms tightened around her, and Willis sobbed uncontrollably.

"Qui sait ce que la vie apportera, mon amour. You must always seek your dreams mon Chercheur de Reve, never stop."

You may ask yourself, where is Willis Carpenter now? Whatever happened to him? Willis Carpenter spent nearly thirty years operating a newspaper and magazine stand in the lobby of the L.A. Times Building in Los Angeles. He never married. He lived alone in a small house he rented in south-central Los Angeles. He filled his spare time with his paintbrushes and an easel that never left his side. Willis Carpenter pursued what Anastasie Bouchet had taught him with a passion. Dreams of the past and dreams of the future found themselves on pieces of canvas. The teaching genius of Anastasie Bouchet found fertile ground in the heart and soul of Willis Carpenter, who produced hundreds of works of art representative of his past, and always with the theme of the power of dreams. In a stroke of irony, Willis signed his paintings not with his name but with the letters LdR, French for The Dream Seeker. Willis Carpenter painted his dreams, but there was one dream he wanted to live, not paint. A dream that he had lived every night for the past thirty years. On that fateful day, Willis left his job at the *L.A. Times,* sold all his belongings, and traveled to Bordeaux, France.

For six brief months, he was happier than he had ever been in his life. He and his wife, Anastasie, lived in her family's home in La Reole, France, a small town outside Bordeaux. Willis spent his days painting. Anastasie volunteered at the local museum giving guides to tourists and conducting art classes for children. Willis lived out his dream of painting with his beautiful Annie by his side. Anastasie thought no more of being branded and ugly.

One day Anastasie came home from the museum to find Willis dozing in his chair next to his easel. She called out his name but got no response. Let him sleep, she thought. Anastasie returned to the house to prepare Willis's favorite dinner, fried chicken with white gravy. Standing at the kitchen sink, she cranked open the kitchen window and called out, "Mon Ami, would you care for a glass of wine?" A chilling sadness filled her heart when he failed to answer a second time. Anastasie exited the side kitchen door leading to the patio. She walked slowly to his side, her cane struggling to support her. As she looked upon his ashen face, Annie knew the love of her life had left her once again. She pulled a nearby chair to sit next to him. There were no tears, no crying, only the joy of having loved and been loved filled her heart. She had taught him to pursue his dreams, and he did. She placed her hand on his and rested her head on his shoulder. That is how their son, Jean-Paul Menuisier, found them the next day. To the readers of this column, let me say there is one simple lesson to be gained from this story: pursue your dreams or be prepared to live every tomorrow as if it were a repeat of yesterday.

―――

IRONS HELD her phone to her ear with one hand and shut the door to her office with the other.

"You're kidding!" Irons said into the receiver as she collapsed back in her chair.

"Did he have any idea who was waiting to see him?"

Grinning from ear to ear, Southard said, "Oh heavens no. He told me not to interrupt him when Mr. Donahue arrived, so I didn't. I can tell you this, Martha," now cupping her hand over the receiver to conceal her delight, "the look on Mayor Bradley's campaign manager's face when she heard Mr. Willard call Mr. Carpenter a crippled old Sambo, was priceless! Ms. Savitch told me the mayor had sent her to speak with Mr. Willard about a series on the rising racial tension in south-central Los Angeles. After Mr. Willard's outburst, she told me it was no longer necessary to speak with Mr. Willard. I can only imagine the call from the mayor's office to the Chandler family."

"One can only hope," replied Irons. "I'll talk to you later, Harriet."

CHAPTER 40

Sitting at his desk, Steward felt a strange but certain feeling of purpose come over him. There was no angst about the next assignment and what it would entail, no foreboding sadness about returning to an empty house. Facing the future with a sense of calmness and clarity of purpose was something entirely new for Dylan Steward, and he liked that feeling. He took his wallet from his back pocket and skimmed through several small pieces of paper until he found what he was looking for. He unfolded the small handwritten note that read Eddy Isles 310-499-3827. Steward reached for his telephone and punched in the number. It rang several times before Steward heard, "Isles residence."

"May I speak with Eddy Isles, please."

"Speaking."

"Eddy, this is Dylan Steward. It's been quite a while."

There was genuine excitement in Isles' voice. "Damn Dylan, it's great to hear your voice."

Steward was prepared for the inevitable.

"You know, Dylan, we were all shocked when we heard about

Willow's passing. I can't imagine what you've been through. You were never out of our thoughts and prayers, man!"

The mere mention of her name caused that familiar contraction of his heart. But this time, it did not cripple him. It hurt, painfully so, to be reminded, but at least he could respond without becoming a complete emotional wreck.

"Thanks, Eddy. I appreciate that. I really do. I'm not sure how. I've managed. Probably prayers and well wishes of people like you."

"Never discount the power of prayer, Dylan," came the reassuring voice of Isles.

"I suppose," replied Steward, who at least now believed in the inexplicable power of dreams, if not in a higher power. "Eddy, are you and the guys still playing at Pogo's?"

"Yeah, buddy. Business really started to pick up after that entertainment writer for the *Times*, Feldman, did an article on Lenny's place. Agents from RCA and William Morris drop in now and then to scope out new talent. Why? Are you thinking about coming back to jam a little?"

With more conviction than he had been able to muster for some time, Steward exclaimed, "If you've got the room, yeah."

Obviously delighted, Eddy said, "Dylan, I'll make room! It will be great to have you there."

After hanging up the phone, the sweet anticipation of playing again, experiencing the acknowledgment of other musicians and hearing the applause of an appreciative audience brought a sense of serenity as sweet as any piece Steward had ever played. He leaned back in his chair. His fingers began the rhythmic beating of his favorite riff. He closed his eyes. His head rocked side to side to the imaginary sound of snare drums. He was 'in the pocket,' as musicians say.

THE MINUTE he stepped inside the doors at Pogo's, Steward felt a sense of exhilaration come over him. Lenny had crammed more than two dozen small tables into every conceivable nook and cranny in the place. There appeared to be a string of bar lights over the stage. A Pulser M-56 electric piano had replaced the bulky old upright. A row of Peavey monitors lined the stage's front-facing the musicians for feedback. *Very professional*, Steward thought as he surveyed the scene before him. The excited voice of Eddy Isles rang out.

"Hi Dylan, you made it! I'll be right there!"

Isles was talking with a young woman at the back of the room. He continued his conversation for a few minutes, directing the woman to some highchairs against the back wall. She appeared to nod, then headed in that direction. Isles hurried forward to Steward. He brought his clenched fists up in excitement. His smile was equally as emphatic.

"Man, I can't tell you how excited I was when you called. The other guys too."

"Me too, Eddy," echoed Steward, as the two men shook hands enthusiastically. "Do the same guys still play?"

A slight frown appeared on Isles' face. "I lost Flint. He couldn't get used to the electric key. Said the sound just wasn't authentic enough for him. I met a guy through Buddy Feldman, the music scene guy at the *Times* , named Ivan Clay. Buddy has a soft spot for those needing a second chance. It seems this Clay guy spent some time in prison, but he plays the piano like another Earl Hines. That brother makes the sweetest sounds on that Pulser. Phil is still on the sax, and Bobby Evans gave up that old-fashioned upright bass for a Harmony. He finally gets to sit down. You make five, a real quintet!"'

Steward was suddenly filled with self-doubt. "I haven't played in a while. I've sort of been out of touch with things since..."

Before Steward could say more, the young woman who had

been talking with Isles when he arrived approached them. Her attention was focused on Isles.

"Uncle Eddy, do you have a moment?"

He gave but the briefest of introductions. "Dylan, my niece, Kathleen, this is Dylan Steward. Give us just a minute, will ya, kid?"

He was annoyed by the interruption.

"Dylan, we were all crushed when we heard about your wife. She was the sweetest, you know." His sincerity in this remark was genuine.

"Yeah, I do. Thanks, Eddy." Steward hoped there would be no more mention of his deceased wife. He wasn't so lucky.

"Uncle Eddy, do you want the sketches in color or shaded pencil? I can do either."

Eddy thought for a moment, then said, "Honey, you're the one who went to art school. What would look best in the magazine?"

She paused for a moment to consider the options. "Color will give everyone more individuality, but shaded pencil will add to the ambiance. If I were you, I'd go with shaded pencils."

"Then I defer to you, honey." His favorite niece smiled at his confidence in her.

Isles turned his attention back to Steward, who had completely ignored the young woman, as he focused on the stage, envisioning the positioning of the musicians.

"I've got to talk with Lenny. Why don't you get set up? We'll catch up more when the guys arrive."

"Sure, I'll be fine," replied Steward, still grappling with his lack of confidence.

"You don't remember me, do you?" said the niece.

Turning to face her, Steward felt slightly embarrassed at his memory lapse. He studied the young woman a moment longer before meekly uttering, "No, I'm sorry, but I don't."

She gave Steward that cute "I remember you" look.

"You were on the train from Bordeaux to Paris. You said you

were a reporter, but now it looks like music is more your thing." She gave a laugh at the last remark.

Steward gave her a more studied gaze. Then it came to him, that annoying girl with her snippy remarks regarding his being a reporter or a writer. He gave her a polite, if guarded, smile.

"Yes, I was. And If I recall, you were going to be an artist, right?"

She smiled at Steward, and for the first time, he realized how white her teeth were and, awkwardly, how beautiful her smile was.

"Well, aspirations have a way of taking you down different paths. It took a couple of months beating the bushes before my uncle introduced me to Buddy Feldman from the *Times*. He recommended me to Music Weekly, and I became their illustrator."

Remembering their brief repartee, Steward chuckled and said, "Artist, illustrator, does it really matter?"

Again, the radiant smile, "No, I suppose not. My uncle said something about being sorry about your wife. Do you mind if I ask what happened?"

Well, you already did, didn't you? He thought.

Why he felt compelled to say anything, he couldn't understand. There was a genuine sincerity in her voice. He forced the urge for a sarcastic response from his mind the way Willow would have.

"She was pregnant with our first child. It was supposed to be a routine medical examination. Something went wrong. She died in the emergency room. It was her dream…"

Steward stopped himself before he went any further. He didn't need to relive the past, certainly not with a perfect stranger. The woman placed her hand on his shoulder. Her touch brought an unexpected sensation to Steward. It was somewhat chilling but ultimately satisfying and transforming. Her subsequent response was thoughtful and guarded. She looked down at the floor and then met Steward's gaze. Slowly she uttered, "Dreams sometimes have a way of turning into nightmares in an instant."

He didn't need to ask anything more. He could have let the subject drop, and each would move on to the tasks at hand. More self-revelations were really not necessary, but Steward felt a strange desire to know more.

"How so?" he asked, feeling totally at ease in the presence of a stranger who suddenly didn't feel like a stranger.

A somber look came over the woman.

"Oh, five years ago, I was this happy-go-lucky creature with not a care in the world, living life in the moment. Then without warning, I began to experience health problems. I was diagnosed with kidney failure. My dreams became nightmares. I spent a year on dialysis three times a week before a suitable donor was found. It turned out my Uncle Eddy was a perfect match. Everything came out better than expected, but it taught me a few times about nightmares."

Her radiant smile returned. Almost reflexively, Steward smiled back. "Do you mind if I ask you something else?"

"Sure, but then I've got to get to work."

"Eddy called you 'KT.' What kind of a name is that?"

"Oh God, you know musicians, everyone's got a nickname of some sort. K stands for Kathleen. The T is for Thomas, my last name. He gave me that tag when I was a kid, and it stuck."

Steward nodded with a smile. "Okay, then KT. I'll let you get to work."

As she turned away, Steward caught a subtle whiff of her perfume. He never thought vanilla would smell that good. For the first time in a very long time, he was captivated by a woman's aroma. He hoped it would not be the last.

———

IT DIDN'T TAKE three days for the fallout from Damon Willard's racial epitaph to take effect. Speculation at the *L.A. Times* was that once Tom Bradly, the black mayor of Los Angeles, heard that the

Times managing editor referred to a disabled black veteran of WWII who operated the onsite the newspaper stand, as a "crippled old Sambo," a call was made to Otis Chandler's family. The next day word spread in the Times Building, faster than a tornado through Oklahoma that Otis Chandler himself was in the building. Accompanied by an entourage of three men dressed in black suits and all carrying leather briefcases, they made their way through the lobby and up the elevators to the fourth floor and the office of Damon Willard. Chandler had purposely made his arrival public for a reason. It surprised no one when a brief memo from the Chandler family was published thanking Damon Willard for his service to the *Times* and wishing him well in his pursuit of other professional opportunities. What did surprise those working at the *Times* was his successor.

CHAPTER 41

He stood behind the ornate desk of the former managing editor. This thing has got to go! He thought. Its only purpose had been to create a barrier between the person who sat behind it and those who reported to him. All he needed was a working desk, not a monument to the Danish designer Kaare Klint. To appreciate the size of his new office, he walked from wall to wall. Easily four times bigger than his previous one, smiling to himself. The empty spaces on the walls where the accolades of the former managing editor were hung for all to see would soon be replaced with portraits of "Man of the Year" and "Woman of the Year" awarded annually by the L.A. Times board of directors. After all, the L.A. Times was a paper of the people. Who better to be recognized on the walls of the office of the managing editor?

After ten seconds of sitting in the oversized Italian leather chair, he knew he wanted his old chair back. An intercom had replaced his more comfortable telephone. It contained three rows of three-digit extensions to departments he had never called in the past. He called names, not extensions. Small changes at first, he thought. Let him become acquainted with the staff as the new boss, not the other way around. He walked to the large double doors made of dark mahogany and opened one. He addressed his remark to the woman sitting behind a desk to the right.

"Excuse me, but do you prefer Harriet or Mrs. Southard?"

"Please, Harriet, if that's not too familiar for you? And do you prefer Mr. Donahue or Jimmy?"

"Jimmy will be just fine with me," he replied with a broad Irish smile. He was already beginning to loosen up in his new role.

"In that case, Jimmy, this letter was delivered to you earlier today. It appears to be from one of your reporters," holding up the envelope, "a Dylan Steward, I believe," she stated.

A premonition of its content chilled Donahue as he took the envelope from Southard. His instincts told him, "Don't bother opening it; you know what it will say."

"Do you mind if I sit out here to read this? His office is still a bit awkward for me."

"Please do," replied Southard, who immediately took a liking to the affable Donahue.

Donahue slid into one of several cushioned high back chairs Willard had specially ordered for visitors next to Southard's desk.

These uncomfortable sons-of-bitches are out of here, Donahue thought to himself as he adjusted his arms awkwardly on the chair's narrow wooden armrests.

He took a folded letter from the unsealed envelope and opened it. It was handwritten. He liked that, more of a personal touch than something typed. He reached inside his coat pocket for his reading glasses. Once opened, he placed them on the bridge of his nose, just far enough down so he could look up over the rim if necessary and still look down without adjusting them. He hadn't noticed it before, but the kid had nearly perfect penmanship, more like a woman than a man. Making himself as comfortable as possible, Donahue began to read the letter.

Dear Jimmy,

Forgive the handwritten letter, Jimmy, but I write better than I speak. Getting this job at the *Times* was a fantasy come true, and I will be eternally grateful to you for that. In the darkest hours of my life, you were there for me. When I failed you, you gave me a second chance. Because of that second chance, I was led to Jean-Paul Menuisier and the story of his father and mother, Willis and Anastasie. By the way, Jimmy, Menuisier is French for carpenter. In many ways, they were like my Willow, determined to pursue their dreams. In the pursuit of their dreams, they found each other a second time. Jimmy, for years I've had my own fantasy, one that Willow always said I should go after. But like most people, things come along, circumstances change, and fantasies remain just that. It's my time, Jimmy, to go after mine. I will never forget you made it all possible. I will always be in debt to you for your kindness and mentorship.

Thank you,
Dylan Steward

A CRACK of a smile began to form on Donahue's face. He felt a bit like a father watching his only son about to set out in the world to seek his desires. Like any father, unashamed tears of pride slowly flowed from the corner of his eyes. The sentimental Irishman cleared his throat, which had constricted with the emotions one would expect from such feelings. The tears of pride flowed freely.

CHAPTER 42

THREE YEARS LATER

One of the perks for being the managing editor of the *Los Angeles Times* that flattered Jimmy Donahue's ego was the chauffeur service available to him for work and social events. If only the boys from his old neighborhood could see him now! This thought floated through his mind as he slid into the backseat of the luxurious Bentley T-series sedan. Heated seats made of rich Moroccan leather gave the passenger a sense of unbridled luxury.

"You look quite charming tonight, James," remarked Markham, who looked stunning in an off-the-shoulder black lace cocktail dress. As she crossed her legs in the extra roomy backseat of the sedan, Donahue caught a glimpse of her Betty Grable-like legs. He was truly inspired.

"You got great gams, Syl!" said Donahue, giving her a comical but lecherous smile.

Markham let out a tired sigh.

"Oh James, you're not Bogart, and I'm not Bacall, but thank you anyway."

The driver, appropriately adorned in a black blazer with a matching captain's hat, turned his head to the backseat and asked, "Your destination tonight, Mr. Donahue?"

It was a habit Donahue had tried desperately to break the driver of—without success. But he would try again.

"2301 North Highlands Ave, just west of the French Village, the Hollywood Bowl, and for the umpteenth time, Frankie, it's Jimmy, not Mr. Donahue."

"Sorry, Mr. Donahue, I mean, Jimmy, but it's company policy."

"I don't give a damn about company policy, Frankie. When we're together, you're Frankie, and I'm Jimmy, not Franklin and Mr. Donahue. By the way, I've got an extra ticket for you, so there'll be no sitting in the car for you tonight, pal!"

The driver smiled. Of all his clients, Donahue was the only one who didn't treat the sixty-year-old black man like he wasn't some kind of subhuman automaton whose sole purpose in life was to follow their instructions. Franklin Carter, Frankie to Donahue, had been his regular driver for three years. Carter was nearing thirty years with Celebrity Escort Services and looking forward to retiring to his home state of Louisiana. He had worked hard to lose his Cajun accent, which had proven difficult for his high-end clients to understand. His attire consisted of a black suit, crisp white shirt, and pale blue tie. With his muscular frame and close-cropped hair with a trace of gray at the temples, he might well have passed for someone in the Secret Service and not a mere chauffeur.

"May I inquire about the evening's event?" asked Carter.

"The West Coast Jazz Festival, Frankie. You'll be sitting with us," answered Donahue.

"Maybe even hear a little Dixieland?" mused Carter out loud.

"Without a doubt, Frankie. It'll be like being back home."

"You ain't just a kiddin' Jimmy," Carter gloated as adherence to company policy quickly disappeared.

The rest of the forty-five-minute ride was one of sheer anticipation for Carter to hear the music of his roots. For Jimmy Donahue, the evening would bring together two old friends.

"That certainly was an extremely gracious letter he wrote to you, Jimmy. I certainly did not expect him to include tickets to tonight's event, as well," remarked Markham.

Donahue rested his head against the plush black Moroccan leather visualizing the letter and remembering how he felt when he read it.

"You know, Syl, I always hoped for the best for that kid. I never thought sending him on that assignment to France would have the consequences it did."

"The girl or the music?" replied Markham, who had read the letter as well.

"Oh, I guess the music not so much. That was always his destiny. He just needed an opportunity to realize it, and I thought the story of Willis and Anastasie was the perfect venue for that. Now the girl, that was something else altogether. I had nothing to do with that. Apparently, he met her on the train coming back from Bordeaux to Paris. 'Met' is probably not the accurate word. They barely spoke to each other. According to Dylan, some banter back and forth about writer-reporter, painter-artist, was the extent of any conversation. Anyway, she left a sketch she had drawn on her seat. It turns out she had drawn a picture of him. He never even got her name, just the letters 'KT' at the bottom of the sketching. When he left the *Times* , he reunited with the guys he used to jam with at Pogos. They formed a quintet and started playing again. His career took off. The real irony, Syl, was that the niece of one of the quintet members turns out to be the girl he met on the train. She worked as an illustrator for Music Weekly, and they wound up spending time together. It certainly wasn't anything he expected, but in time, they became an item and eventually got married. Go figure?"

"It's called the hand of God, James," responded Markham to the rhetorical question.

"Is this where you tell me God works in mysterious ways?" He was amused and attempting to amuse with this remark.

Markham leaned over and gave Donahue a gentle kiss on the cheek. "Darling, look at the two of us and ask that question." Her smile could not have been broader.

ORIGINALLY BUILT IN 1922, the iconic amphitheater known as the Hollywood Bowl with its concentric arches had a seating capacity of nearly eighteen thousand. The Hollywood Bowl rests in the backdrop of the Hollywood Hills, a genius location as it shielded its guests from the brilliant glare of the setting Pacific sun. Tonight's performance drew a near-capacity crowd. Carter edged the Bentley slowly into the VIP parking area. He soon saw the designated slot that read, "Editor, *L.A. Times*." Bringing the Bentley to a gentle stop, Carter exited the luxury sedan and opened the right passenger door. Donahue got out first, adjusting the front of his tuxedo.

Carter extended his left arm to take the hand of Donahue's wife, Sylvia Markham Donahue. As they headed toward the golden turn style, Donahue put the tickets in Carter's hand and whispered to him, "Walk in front of us and say, Security, if asked, and hand him the tickets."

Approaching the turnstile, an elderly man with silver hair and dressed in a double-breasted crimson red coat trimmed with brass buttons and gold epaulets on his shoulders reached for the end of a golden rope barrier, then paused. Taking his cue, Carter announced rather firmly as his eyes scanned the area for imaginary threats, "Security, the *L.A. Times*, Mr. James Donahue," and handed the usher the tickets. Reacting as if the president of the United States was in front of him, the usher immediately removed the barrier and said most graciously, "Sir, the VIP entrance is directly ahead to your right." Carter, who was beginning to enjoy his role as a quasi-Secret Service Agent, took great delight in announcing "Security" whenever they neared groups of attendees in idle chit chat blocking their path. Donahue could hardly keep a straight face. They came upon the last usher, a near-perfect image of the first usher, glasses included, who inquired, "Good evening, may I show you to your seats?" Carter dutifully handed the man their tickets. The bespectacled man looked at them and then stated formally, "Please, this way." He led them to their front row center seats off the main aisle. To remove the doubtful look on the usher's face as Carter entered the row first, Donahue interjected, "My security man will be staying with us."

"Of course," replied the obedient guide. The nearby conversations hid Carter's audible laugh. The three settled into their cushioned chairs, complete with retractable drink trays soon to be filled by a bevy of young waitresses attending to the tastes of the elite. To Markham's surprise, they had a high-end red Bordeaux on the wine list their waitress gave them. She leaned to her left and whispered to Carter, "Franklin, would you care for a beverage?"

Fully into his role, Carter replied smugly, "Tonic with a lemon twist, Mrs. Donahue. I'm on duty."

Markham looked up at the waitress and said, "One Tonic with a lemon twist for our security, a glass of the Chateau Bordeaux for me, and whatever my husband wants. James?"

"I'll have Hiram Walker, neat." Donahue smiled at his wife, "Willis would like that."

The lights dimmed, and the conversations of nearly 15,000 jazz enthusiasts hushed. Still inspired by the evening, Markham asked him, "Did you ever in your wildest imagination think this would happen?"

"You mean Steward playing at the Hollywood Bowl?" Donahue was not tracking with his inspired wife.

"No, James, this," said Markham, as she held out her right hand displaying a two-carat diamond ring.

Donahue smiled at his wife. "Oh, that. No, I would have to say you were more a fantasy than a dream. You were so far out of my league, honey. I never thought it possible!" he said with the satisfaction of one who had accomplished that impossibility.

"James, a fantasy or dream? You know what they say, a rose by any other name is…."

"I know, I know," smiled Donahue."

That night under the starlit heavens over the Hollywood Bowl, a star was born, and a dream came true. The announcer's voice boomed out over the Hollywood Bowl's unique structure to the near-capacity audience.

"Ladies and gentlemen, the West Coast Jazz Festival proudly presents this year's Artist of the Year, Dylan Steward, performing from his album of the year, Jazz Billboard's number one song for the last sixteen weeks in a row of the same name, "The Dream Seeker."

―――

THE EXCITEMENT of dreams coming true is beyond the description of words.

LAILAH GIFTY AKITA

ACKNOWLEDGMENTS

I truly appreciate the editing assistance from my friend of forty years, Rob Gordon. He continually strives to make me a better writer.

To Frank Eastland, Raeghan Rebstock, and the staff at Publish Authority, my deepest thanks for your continued support.

ABOUT THE AUTHOR

Michael J Sullivan, a native Californian and U.S. Army veteran, began his career in teaching, served in the U.S. Marine Corps Reserves, and retired as an associate warden with the California Department of Correction. He is the author of several books, including the popular Forgotten Flowers trilogy, and resides in Sonora, California, with his wife, Virginia,

FIND OUT MORE about the author at MichaelJSullivanBooks.com.

facebook.com/Michael.J.Sullivan.Author
twitter.com/MichaelJSulliv8

THANK YOU FOR READING

If you enjoyed *The Dream Seeker,* we invite you to share your thoughts and reactions online and with family and friends.

Publish Authority